I0715526

THE
LAST BRIDGE
ACROSS
MOSTAR

JEANA KENDRICK

Also By Jeana Kendrick

Conspiracy Series
St. Abient Run
The Paris Conspiracy

The Last Bridge Across Mostar

Memoirs of a Bible Smuggler

THE
LAST BRIDGE
ACROSS
MOSTAR

JEANA KENDRICK

NORTHRIDGE PRESS

USA

Library of Congress cataloging in publication data
Library of Congress Control Number: 2023900816

Kendrick, Jeana

The Last Bridge Across Mostar / Jeana Kendrick—First Edition
pages; cm

Cover Design: Tim Barber—Dissect Designs
ISBN: 978-1-952406-10-2 (trade paperback)
ISBN: 978-1-952406-11-9 (e-book)

Northridge Press
PO Box 2561
Conroe, TX 77305

Printed in the United States of America

To my husband Jeff, my sister
Kathryn, my brother-in-law Evan,
and nieces and nephews Rachel, Shelly,
Andrea, Caleb, Andrew, and Seth

Map of Bosnia-Herzegovina and Surrounding Countries

CHARACTERS IN CONSTANTINOPLE

Captain Antonio: Christian captain.

Antonio's mother and brother.

Antonio's fiancée.

Christian women, children, and men.

Greek and Roman Christian soldiers.

Giustiniani: The Christians' greatest warrior.

Giustiniani's captains.

Christian Emperor.

Ottoman Turks, Anatolian Turks, Turkish irregulars, elite Janissaries.

Turkish officers.

Mehmed II: Sultan of the Ottoman Empire.

Moslem holy man.

CHARACTERS IN BOSNIA (Children's ages at the novel's start.)

Katrina Winslow: An American professor who teaches orphans at the Mostar Mission.

Dr. Winslow and his wife: Katrina's parents. Americans who started the Mostar Mission.

Giles Winslow: Katrina's brother who worked with her at the Mostar Mission.

John and Ellen Harrington and daughters Rachel (15), Shelly (13), and Andi (11): An American family who helped the Winslows establish the Mostar Mission.

Captain Lucien Brezak: An Austrian Croatian in the Croatian Army stationed in Bosnia.

Sara: An Austrian Croatian married to Martin. She's the mother of a toddler and Lucien's sister.

Martin: A Bosnian Muslim Christian. Sara's husband.

Martin's parents: Bosnian Muslims.

Vita: A Bosnian Muslim Romany who oversees the Mostar jail.

Lucien's Croatian commander.

Ratko: A Croatian soldier.

Kiro: A Bosnian Muslim Romany who is a gunrunner.

Cosic: A major in the Serbian Army stationed in Bosnia.

Alija Izetbegovic: Bosnian President.

Izzy: A Bosnian Muslim who works at the Mostar jail. UN Peacekeeping troop captain.

Croatian commander: Befriends John and Ellen.

Milo: (6) A Bosnian Serbian orphan.

Caleb: (7) A Bosnian Serbian orphan.

Samuel: (8) A Bosnian Serbian orphan.

Tanya: (10) A Bosnian Serbian orphan.

Drew: (1) A Bosnian Croatian orphan.

Robbie: (5) A Bosnian Croatian orphan.

Rena: (6) A Bosnian Croatian orphan.

Ana and Dinko: (7) Bosnian Croatian twins and orphans.

Baby: (6 months) A Bosnian Muslim orphan.

Tito: (2) A Bosnian Muslim orphan.

Ismael: (14) A Bosnian Muslim orphan.

Kovačević: Vice president of Prijedor Crisis Staff.

CHARACTERS IN SERBIA

Stefan Jovanovic: A general with the Serbian Army.

Dianne Jovanovic: Croatian wife of Stefan. Mimi's mother, Lucien's aunt, and Creto's daughter.

Mimi Jovanovic: Daughter of Stefan and Dianne. Lucien's cousin and Creto's granddaughter.

Lieutenant Alex Nikolic: A pilot in the Serbian Army, married to Ennis with a son.

Ennis Nikolic: She is Alex's wife, also a mother, and General Stefan Jovanovic's secretary.

Slobodan Milosevic: Serbian President.

Željko Ražnatović: Nationalist Serbian Military Leader.

Peter Ražnatović: A rebel student leader and nephew to Željko Ražnatović.

Michael Venac: The archrival of General Stefan Jovanovic.

Chauffeur to General Stefan Jovanovic.

Police chief in Belgrade.

Stambolic: Former Serbian president.

CHARACTERS IN CROATIA

Creto Brezak: Lucien and Mimi's grandfather, and Dianne, Josef, Ivan, and Feodor's father.

Ivan Brezak, his wife, Marie, and children: Creto's son and family who are Croatian.

Feodor Brezac, his wife, and children: Creto's son and family who are Croatian.

Tony and his wife Natalia: Lucien's Croatian friends.

Babic: Croatia resident of Serbian lineage and an anti-Croatian politician.

Raskovic: Croatia resident of Serbian lineage and an anti-Croatian politician.

Franjo Tudman: Croatian President.

Serb policeman.

CHARACTERS IN AUSTRIA

Josef Brezak: CEO who is Lucien's Croatian father, Creto's son, and Dianne's brother.

Anita Brezak: Lucien's Austrian mother and wife of Josef.

CHARACTERS IN HOUSTON

Aunt Jeanine: Katrina's aunt.

Uncle York: Katrina's uncle.

Doctor Bill Hyatt: Katrina's friend, an expert authority on medieval Christian antiquities.

The University of Houston Dean: A friend of Katrina's family.

Houston Police Department (HPD) policeman.

Preface

The closest I came to the Bosnian War was in 1993 when my husband and I were almost stranded about fifty kilometers from the fighting front. Our vehicle's fuel tank was nearly empty, and due to the war embargo, there was no gas to buy. Thankfully, we made it safely out of the country.

My interest in the Balkan region had developed earlier in the thirteen-year period when my work with Door of Hope International took me repeatedly through the former Yugoslavia and much of Eastern Europe. When war broke out, the firsthand reports I read moved me deeply, partly inspiring this novel.

My job was to report the horrendous events occurring in Bosnia, and they occupied my mind and prayers greatly. One morning, I awoke and heard my protagonist, Katrina, speaking so clearly that I grabbed a pen and began writing *The Last Bridge Across Mostar.*

Although the 1992-1995 Bosnian War between Croatians, Muslims, and Serbians is historical, I have changed some dates for plot continuity and dramatic effect. Mostar's bridge, Stari Most, was destroyed on November 9, 1993, rather than in the winter of '92. War broke out between Bosnia's Croatians and Muslims early in 1993 instead of 1992. Serbian President Milosevic orchestrated Serbia's war of maps to gain control of most of the former Yugoslavia and Kosovo. But his conversations with the fictitious General Stefan Jovanovic did not take place.

Bosnian President Izetbegovic and Croatian President Tudman served during the Bosnian War, but their conversations and interactions with fictional characters such as Katrina Winslow, Serbian Major Cosic, and the fictitious Rogue Muslim Army and their imagined plot to destroy Mostar did not occur. During the war, Serbia controlled the Yugoslav People's Army (JNA). The acronym is JNA because Yugoslavians spell it *Jugoslavia,* and their word for people is *Narod.*

It would have been challenging to write *The Last Bridge Across Mostar* without the support and encouragement of my dear friends and fellow authors in our critique group, Jacqueline Pelham, Beverly Butt, and Joy Zeigler, who have inspired me, while generously sharing their editorial skills and insights. I want to thank our mentor, Guida Jackson, who gave us a safe place to grow in our craft. She and Jackie helped chronicle my opening. My gratitude goes to my sister, Kathryn Kendrick, who has cheerfully read all my books repeatedly, and to my brilliant editor Beverly Butt.

Special appreciation to critique friends and fellow authors Ann Anderson, David Bumgardner, Joyce Harlow, Wanda Dionne, and the late Jack Crumpler, Pasty Burk, and Bob Quinn. Thanks to Barbara Sissel and the late Ruby Tolliver, Betty Jeffrion, and Ellie Milon for an afternoon of brainstorming that led to my protagonist being an American schoolteacher.

I am indebted to: my late mother and aunt, Dean Griffin and Rebecca Rodenbaugh, for reading my books and saying lovely, constructive things about them; my nieces and nephews, Rachel, Shelly, Andi, Caleb, and Andrew, who in part inspired the children's characters; my late in-laws, Jim and Elaine Kendrick, for their support and suggestions; Marianne Herring, Anne Campbell, and Rhonda Mayfield, for their help and insights; and the late Dr. Paul Ruffin for his support and critiques.

My profound thanks go to Dr. Borislav Arapovic, the Bosnian Croatian poet who founded the Institute for Bible Translation in Stockholm, Sweden. His firsthand reports of his return to his native Mostar to aid family and friends during the Bosnian War, in part, inspired my novel. His descriptions and diary sincerely moved me.

My appreciation also goes to Door of Hope International President Paul H. Popov, who shared his longtime friend Borislav's letters and generously consulted with me as needed on cultural, social, and political issues.

I would also like to thank the late Dr. Davorin Peterlin, former director of Keston Institute, for his incredible encouragement, insights, letters, proofreading, and generous offer to help with a prequel set in Croatia. Sadly, the time for such a project eluded us.

I am immensely grateful for sources such as *The Balkan Express* by Slavenka Drakulić. Her experiences and poetic expression genuinely influenced me, providing insight and inspiration, particularly regarding Stari Most, as my characters Katrina and Lucien dealt with the bridge's destruction and the symbolic significance of this to them and Bosnia.

Basher Five-Two by Captain Scott O'Grady with Michael French was an enormous aid in writing the scenes in which Alex's plane was shot down in enemy territory. Donn Taylor, a former air force pilot, was most helpful, as was my husband, who accompanied me to air shows and museums.

Yugoslavia: Death of a Nation by Laura Silber and Allan Little and *The Fall of Yugoslavia: The Third Balkan War* by Misha Glenny were invaluable resources, as was the Discovery Channel Video Series *Yugoslavia: Death of a Nation*. My thanks also go to Lisa Bell, a dear friend who directed a center in Zagreb for refugees during the war, for recommending the video series and sharing her expertise.

I especially want to thank my husband, Jeff, for his support and faith in me.

Any mistakes in the content are entirely mine.

Jeana Kendrick
September 2023

BOOK I

Escape from Mostar

Prologue

Constantinople 1453

Determined to withstand the enemy one more day, Captain Antonio examined the breaches in the city's massive stone walls. The Ottoman Turks' cannons and bombarding artillery had blasted the Christians' defenses for seven weeks, testing their strength.

That night, it rained. The guns quieted as if by some miraculous decree, and silence filled the city. Frightened women and children streamed into Hagia Sophia, Europe's grandest cathedral, and prayed, kneeling shoulder to shoulder, for perhaps the last time. Antonio's jaw clenched, his nerves taut from the waiting. Despite the day's reprieve, he feared a Turkish invasion would end Christendom as he knew it.

For eight centuries, the Turks had been scheming to seize Constantinople. Control of the city meant a bridge to the West and access to the power and wealth Christians had enjoyed for more than a thousand years. At midnight, Constantinople was as hushed as it had been early that morning. An hour later, terrifying battle cries clamored from without. Warning bells clanged as men and women rushed to stop the attackers.

Thousands of Turkish irregulars, armed with swords, bows, and arrows, scaled the walls and pounded the gates. Antonio ran from one weak spot on the battlements to another, urging his men to fight valiantly. The irregulars withdrew, replaced by a barrage of Anatolian Turks.

The Christians repulsed the second wave of foes until a Turkish cannon ball struck a vulnerable place in the wall, and it collapsed. Three hundred Turks rushed through the gap. Greek and Roman Christian soldiers closed in to form a brigade, using their bodies to halt the Turks. From the enemy's ranks, the elite Janissaries advanced. Still, the Christians resisted, prayed, and held the infidels at bay.

Then Giustiniani, their greatest warrior, fell. "Leave his body lie. Keep fighting," the emperor urged. But Giustiniani's captains carried him off, and their men followed, leaving the inner gate open for attack. The Turks invaded. Christian soldiers stumbled across one another in their haste to escape.

Antonio's heart constricted as the Ottoman flag rose ominously above the towers. As the metal gates clattered open, he saw his mother on the church steps and ran toward her. He was scarcely a yard away—when the Turks stormed the sanctuary. "Mother," Antonio cried as a barbarian lodged a knife in her chest.

Rage such as he had never experienced filled him. He drew his sword and killed five Turks before the infidels seized him and forced him to watch as they butchered his neighbors: the innocent young, the old, and the disabled. He saw his brother's tongue cut out, then his eyes. Hate seethed in him, and he tasted bile as two Turkish officers argued over possession of his fiancée, tearing her dress and braiding it into a rope to tie her to the winner's side. Antonio stood rigid, venom coursing through his veins as the Turks ripped his garments and bound his wrists and ankles. They chained him to his fellow nobles to be auctioned as slaves.

Huddled in misery with the other captives, Antonio straightened in defiance as Mehmed II and his Moslem holy man passed near him and entered through the wide-open doors of the church. In vain, Antonio's hand clenched, reaching for his sword.

The two Moslem men knelt at the altar and proclaimed, "Only Allah is God! Mohammed, his most holy prophet."

Antonio refused to weep as he witnessed the grandest edifice in Christendom being turned into a mosque and his beloved Constantinople becoming Istanbul, the new Turkish capital.

He prayed instead that Christian hatred for the Moslems would never die—that the malice of Antonio and his people would reach down through time and avenge the Christians for this day.

Chapter 1

Mostar, Bosnia-Herzegovina, Spring 1992

The Kosovo soldier slipped through the American mission's side door and searched for a place to hide the relic. Despite the winter chill that lingered into spring, perspiration seeped down his back and under his arms. He suspected the Serbians had followed him from the cathedral in Pazaric. All morning, the small icon hanging from the ribbon around his neck seemed to burn a hole in his chest. Its sale meant everything to Kosovo's survival. If it were as valuable as he believed, its revenue would help purchase arms to defend his country and people. Without those funds, they wouldn't stand a chance against the Serbs.

His gaze roamed the whitewashed room furnished with several upholstered chairs, two worn sofas, a piano, and a dark pine desk in the corner. Envy coiled in him as he imagined the Reverend Winslow and his family relaxing there in the evenings. How different life was for these Americans, who came to teach others what they did not understand themselves.

The soldier mourned his family, once wealthy and respected. He'd seen the Serbs beat his father to death in the streets. His own life had often almost been forfeited. Death was a given, but his life must count for freedom. That meant war, an army, and the money to equip it.

Troubled, he hid the icon, which his contact would later retrieve and sell. He scanned the room to ensure it was as he'd found it. Relieved, he departed and then turned into a narrow, shadowed alley.

An unseen assailant's blade plunged into his back. He gasped and fell, one hand outstretched.

His love's sherry-brown eyes gazed at him, her oval face moving near to kiss his lips, silken black curls touching his brow. His beautiful young wife, a widow, just as he'd foretold. There was no comfort in the thought.

Captain Lucien Brezak had been standing in the doorway of the supply house diagonally across the street from the American mission when he saw a lean, dark man rush through the side entrance into the Winslow family's living quarters.

Lucien touched the pistol on his belt, thinking the man might be a thief. Since Lucien had left his comfortable home in Austria to take up the Croatian cause, he'd learned how base people could be. As a second man entered the mission, Lucien sank into a desk chair facing the window. The two must be carpenters. Dr. Winslow was continually ordering more rooms built for the growing number of orphans. How could a man with his intelligence dare to bring his wife, daughter, and son across the ocean to aid him during a bloody war?

For Lucien, there had been no choice. From his parents, he'd inherited the bittersweet privilege of being both Croatian and Austrian—forever torn between East and West. Sometimes, it was better not to reflect but to act like the animals Lucien and his men were becoming, the beasts the war was making of them. He shook off thoughts of loved ones, dead, wounded, or imprisoned. Losses he couldn't do anything about.

Across the street, the first man walked out of the mission's side entry, and the second one followed, both men disappearing into the alley.

Lucien stood to investigate as Katrina Winslow hurried out the mission front door, a shopping basket on one arm and the other wrapped around a child. Months ago, when Lucien had been shot, Katrina rescued him and enlisted her father and brother to carry him to their home, where he'd recovered. He'd never forget her courage and kindness.

He watched her leave, admiring the graceful sway of her figure in the pink cotton dress, the pastel soft against the grayness of life in Bosnia. One seldom saw color these days. Katrina was asking for trouble, naïvely drawing attention to herself. What might pass as innocent in the West was an open invitation here. She and the child rounded the corner, moving out of sight. Lucien sighed and gathered his supplies. All appeared well at the Winslows' mission.

Fifteen-year-old Rachel Harrington entered the mission family room and crossed to the piano. She missed America and her friends. Her parents, John and Ellen, were wonderful, but Rachel wished they weren't missionaries, that she and her sisters, Shelly and Andi, could have stayed home in the States.

Rachel felt sorry for the orphans in Mostar and didn't mind helping them. Still, she didn't understand why the locals didn't care for their own children. Bosnia comprised three main groups who seemed to hate each other. Rachel had gotten pretty good at telling them apart. Croatians were mainly Roman Catholics who made the sign of the cross once when they prayed. Serbians were chiefly Eastern Orthodox. They crossed themselves three times when they prayed. The Muslims prayed to Allah. They said his name a lot and gave alms religiously. Most of them were of European descent and looked much like other Europeans.

Her dad said Serbia had started the war because it wanted more land and control. Now, all three ethnic groups were fighting. Everyone hurting each other. Yesterday, Rachel had seen a man shot in the street. It terrified her.

What if they killed her mom and dad? Then, she and her sisters would be orphans. They would be stuck in Bosnia. What would happen to Andi, Shelly, and her? It would be up to Rachel to protect her sisters. How could she count on the Winslows, whom her family was here helping, when they might also be murdered?

She rummaged through the piano bench for her music, then glanced up, noticing a stone on the fireplace wall had come loose. Curious, she crossed to it, jiggling the stone from its resting place.

Andi dashed into the room. "You're supposed to be practicing."

"Shh. Come see what I found."

Andi wrinkled her nose. "It's an old picture of the Madonna. Those are for sale everywhere, even at the train stations."

"Look at the gold frame. It must be worth some money."

"Bet you it's fake. See that dirty old ribbon it's hanging on."

Undecided, Rachel stared at the tiny picture cupped in her palm. There was something exquisite about the painting of the Madonna that moved her, no matter what Andi said. Rachel dusted off the ribbon and slipped it around her neck, tucking the small memento inside her shirt. She'd ask her mother or Aunt Katrina about it later. Of course, Katrina wasn't really her aunt. She let Rachel and her sisters call her aunt because their families were such good friends.

Chapter 2

The next day, Katrina Winslow slid into a chair at the breakfast table, mumbling, "Good morning."

Her mother laughingly handed her a mug of coffee. "A rough night?"

"Maybe a late hot date," her brother Giles teased, "or am I venturing into the realm of the impossible in Bosnia?"

"Improbable will do," her dad said, his blue eyes, so like hers, gleaming at Giles's remark. "What say you, Katrina, on this fine day in May?"

She brushed a hand through her blonde curls. "I'm still half asleep. I stayed up too late reading." She peered at her mom. "A walk might revive me if you can spare me for a few hours." Katrina taught at the mission school and worked in the orphanage her parents had started for children who'd lost their families in the Bosnian War. Thirty-seven orphans lived there now, though the number seemed to keep multiplying. Somehow, her family always squeezed in one more child.

Her mother said, "John and Ellen are taking some of the kids to town to buy shoes, so there won't be as many in school today. Enjoy your walk and the fresh air, but be careful."

"I'll stick to the woods where it's safer." The town streets had become dangerous with the influx of Serbian snipers in January, and the situation had worsened. The war and infighting in Mostar had everyone on edge.

Katrina's mood brightened when Lucien, a captain in the Croatian Army and a family friend, stepped into the room and greeted everyone. His gaze softened as it fell on her. From their first meeting, she'd secretly crushed on him.

Some months ago, she'd found Lucien with a gunshot wound to his leg. Katrina bandaged his thigh, draped branches over his body to hide him, and then summoned help to carry him to her home. There, she nursed him to a full recovery, and ever since, he'd stirred her protective instincts despite his being a capable soldier.

Her mother invited, "Please join us for breakfast. As you can see, we have plenty."

"Thank you. I've already eaten, but I won't say no to coffee." He sank into a chair beside Katrina's dad. She passed Lucien a mug of the steaming brew. He smiled his appreciation and took a long sip. "I don't want to alarm anyone, but there are rumors of Serbian forces planning to attack the mission."

Her dad rubbed the back of his neck. "I'm grateful for the warning and will keep a close watch. Being prepared gives us a chance to get everyone to safety."

"We could practice escape drills," Giles said with a sideways glance at his dad.

"A good idea, Son."

"What do you think, Mom?" Giles asked.

"Everything is moving too quickly to process. We're all in God's hands, whatever happens."

Lucien frowned. "It's important for you to be well-armed in case of trouble."

Katrina shivered, images of what could happen in an attack blazing through her mind. "I'm unsure about that with so many children around. Dad taught us how to shoot to protect ourselves. We have guns, but we keep them locked up for the young ones' safety."

"She's right," her father said. "In a surprise confrontation, we might not reach the weapons in time."

"I requested a protection detail for the mission, but the

commander said he can't spare even one man. The war has spread Croatian forces too thin."

His concern warmed her. "You did your best. I feel better knowing you're in the area."

Lucien waved off her compliment with a grin. He drained his cup and set it on the table. "The coffee was tasty, ladies, but I'd best go." Lucien stood, said a quick goodbye around the table, and departed.

Sometime later, Katrina left for her walk, feeling selfish but needing to escape for a while. She tramped through the woods, struggling with her biological fears: twenty-seven, unmarried, and not likely to meet anyone in Bosnia who could change that. Even her close friend Vita had Kiro to love. Katrina's parents seemed to have the perfect marriage. How she envied them. She wanted what they had. Someone who loved her—Katrina. A man who would take her in his arms and cherish her. Loneliness chipped at her contentment. As marvelous as her family was, she yearned for babies of her own.

In April, the Serbian Army had mounted guns on the hills surrounding Mostar. Katrina and her family had watched as the Croats forced the Serbs farther back into the hills. From the Serb's new vantage point, they blew up six of the city's seven bridges across the winding Neretva River and continued to bomb Mostar from above. When the Serbs withdrew, fighting broke out between the town's Muslims and Croats. Now, all three factions were at war.

How long, she worried, before Stari Most, the last bridge across Mostar, would be destroyed? The centuries-old bridge embodied Bosnia's confluence of cultures, peoples, and religions.

Katrina stopped in a clearing and stared at the darkening sky. Before leaving America, she'd taken a history course on the Balkans and its troubled past. In 1917, a Bosnian Serb assassinated Archduke Franz Ferdinand, the heir to the Austro-Hungarian empire, setting off World War I.

During World War II, Germany and its allies annexed regions of

Yugoslavia. Tito, formerly a wanted man because of his communist activities, formed the Communist Yugoslav Partisans to liberate his country and, after the war, became supreme commander and president of the Socialist Federal Republic of Yugoslavia. It comprised six republics: Slovenia, Croatia, Bosnia-Herzegovina, Serbia, Macedonia, and Montenegro. Also, Kosovo and Vojvodina were separate autonomous regions in Serbia.

Until recently, Croats, Muslims, and Serbs had lived in Bosnia-Herzegovina harmoniously. But President Tito's death in 1980 put Yugoslavia on the chopping block again as the republics and provinces formerly united under his leadership resisted Serbia's massive quest for power and territory and fought for independence.

Tragically, in 1989, Serbian President Slobodan Milosevic's plans for a Greater Serbia incited its mostly Eastern Orthodox population to war against the predominantly Roman Catholic Croats and Bosnian and Kosovar Muslims.

Her family was jubilant when Slovenia and Croatia were the first of the six republics to declare independence in '91. Slovenia's exit was fairly bloodless. Croatia had to contend with its minority Serbian population, supported by the Yugoslav People's Army (JNA) and Serbia, which had launched a violent campaign of ethnic cleansing against Croats. The atrocities cited in the news horrified her.

Then, in April of '92, Bosnia had declared its independence, and its Serbian population, backed by the Serbian-controlled JNA and the Serbian Army, waged a deadly and ongoing war against their countrymen. Now, Katrina's family and the mission were smack in the middle of it all, trying to maintain neutrality and care for the displaced children, who desperately needed to be loved and protected.

The dark clouds receded, and fog rolled into the surrounding woods and mountains where Katrina walked. The mist hung over Mostar like a veil of doom. It was time to return to her native Houston and rebuild her life. There, she'd have the chance to meet someone she could love. Sadly, her deepening feelings for Lucien forced her to realize there was no future for her in Bosnia.

War loomed too large and real. It tore at everyone. How could tender feelings grow amid such hate and animosity, where guilt and betrayal crushed love's innocence? Katrina yearned for security. She was ready to go home to Houston. Excited to share her decision and confident her parents would understand, she hastened back to the mission.

Her pace slowed as she approached the school. The place was unusually quiet, and there were no children in the yard playing and no noise coming from the classroom. A sense of unease filled her as she walked gingerly forward.

Katrina stepped inside the mission's schoolroom and staggered, stopping short at the sight of the horrible carnage. "No. No." She gagged on the smell of death. Blood coated the ground and splattered the walls. Children and staff murdered. Dear God, Giles's head lay severed and bloody on the floor. A spike pierced her father's right eye. Katrina choked and covered her mouth. Cold nausea swamped her swimming senses. Then she saw her mother lying in a pool of blood. Her chest rose and fell. She was breathing.

"Mother!" Katrina dropped to her knees beside her. Sobs overcame Katrina, but she shoved them aside. Her mother's anxious gaze held her together as Katrina started to ease the knife from her mom's stomach, then stopped. *To remove the blade could kill her.* "I'll get a doctor. I won't be long."

The school sat at the rear of the mission property. Katrina ran outside through the schoolyard toward the house until she reached the street and spotted Lucien at a nearby café. "Bring the doctor! Hurry, please." Lucien took off running.

She rushed back to her mother, jerked off her coat, and pressed the cloth around the wound to stanch the bleeding. Her mother's beloved face turned gray, and Katrina feared she'd killed her. The grayness faded to white. Katrina prayed it was a good sign. "What happened? Who did this?"

"A raid." Her beautiful hand clasped Katrina's. "Run . . . save the children."

"Shh, I'm going to take care of you."

"Prom . . . ise you'll protect . . . the children." Her hand fell away, and her eyes closed.

"Mom, I promise. Please don't give up. You're alive. Stay with me."

"The Serbs . . . think . . . we're spies." She shuddered, her efforts to speak exacting an enormous toll.

Katrina reeled, unable to understand how anyone could believe they were spies.

Her mother's lips barely moved as she struggled to speak.

Katrina leaned closer to hear the faint thread of words.

"God will . . . help you." She gasped, and then her head lolled to the side.

"No! Don't die. Please don't leave me." The mission's stillness closed in on Katrina as she clung to her mother, weeping and pleading for her to answer.

Chapter 3

Katrina looked up as Lucien entered the school with the doctor and his assistant. The three gaped at the devastation.

"Lord, have mercy." Lucien signed the cross with three fingers, touching his head, chest, left, and right shoulder. "Katrina, are you hurt?"

A whimper escaped her. "Mom just died, and the others are gone, too."

He helped her stand and held her while she sobbed out her loss. "Katrina, I would give anything for this not to have happened. Your family was kind and generous. They'll be missed."

The doctor's hand rested briefly on her shoulder. "I'm so sorry. Take comfort that they're at peace and out of this war." With a sigh, he bent to examine the bodies and to check for survivors.

"If only you'd been here, my family and the others might still be alive." Katrina was sure Lucien could have saved them.

He released her. "I'd barely arrived at the café with some of my men when you shouted for me. I guess no one else heard anything earlier because the school is so far from the road. It doesn't appear there were any gunshots, either."

She shuddered. "They used swords and machetes instead of guns."

"It's a miracle you weren't killed, too."

"I wasn't here. John, Ellen, and some of the kids went shopping. They must have taken their girls. Thank God, they were gone." Katrina told him about finding her mother alive, how the soldiers believed her family was spying, and her promise to protect the children.

Lucien pressed her hand. "We've got to get you somewhere secure, but let's bury your folks and these poor souls first." He rounded up about a dozen soldiers under his command and led them behind the school into the woods beyond. There, the soldiers dug graves for her parents, her brother, the sixteen orphans, and the three staff members murdered in the raid.

With a heavy heart, Katrina prepared the bodies, cleaning the faces and hands of dear ones, straightening their clothing, and combing their hair. She looked away, trembling as the doctor picked up Giles's head from the floor. He and his assistant pieced together the severed bodies as much as possible and then helped Katrina to lay out the others.

Lucien took several men and searched the woods for anyone who had escaped the raid. He came back with thirteen kids found hiding in trees. After Lucien had assured them they were not in danger and Katrina was alive, they'd run inside to her.

She hugged them all, especially glad to see John and Ellen's daughters had survived. Rachel, Shelly, and Andi were like nieces to her and, with their parents' permission, had long ago christened her Aunt Katrina. The two families had flown together from the States to Bosnia to set up the orphanage. Thank God that John, Ellen, and the orphans with them hadn't been there during the raid. They should have returned by now. If they didn't come soon, Katrina and the children would have no choice but to leave without them.

She and the girls prepared a bag for each of the kids. Katrina thrust a small plastic framed photo of her family and a change of clothes into her knapsack. She gathered supplies, and the boys loaded them into Lucien's van. He sent his men to the Croat base.

Finally, everyone congregated around the burial mounds marked with wooden crosses, aware that the enemy could attack at any moment and wouldn't hesitate to kill again. Lucien stood with his arms about the young boys. Katrina knelt by her family's graves and prayed over those who had died. She bowed her head and spoke aloud of their goodness and love for one another and the orphans. Tears slid down her cheeks.

Afterward, Katrina did a headcount of the thirteen children: Rachel, Shelly, Andi, Caleb, Drew, Baby, Ishmael, Robbie, Tanya, Rena, Milo, and the twins Ana and Dinko. Then they all climbed into the van Lucien had borrowed. He drove them into the hills outside Mostar. Katrina remembered how Giles had always wanted to explore the caverns surrounding the town but never had the opportunity. Now, she was fleeing to one. The cave Lucien chose for them was one of many in the Dinaric Alps, the heart of which lay in Bosnia. The mountain range stretched from northwest Italy to southeast Albania, separating the Balkan Peninsula from the Adriatic Sea. Dinaric Karst, the limestone where caves flourished, covered one-third of the country's landmass.

When Katrina entered the cave, she was relieved. The thick walls helped maintain a warm temperature, and the top layer of sandstone sealed out moisture, making it a relatively dry place for them to live. How long would they have to stay?

Frightened by the bleak interior, the little ones cried. Rachel, the eldest at fifteen, took charge, quieting the children and bolstering their courage. "Everything is going to be okay," she said. "We need to do our best and obey Aunt Katrina."

Their glum expressions lifted at Rachel's words.

Katrina surveyed the cave as Lucien carried in their supplies. Thankfully, on a clear day, the sun's rays would seep around the boulder that camouflaged the entrance, letting in enough sunshine to lighten the shadows in all but the deepest recesses. She was pleased to see Rachel assume the mantle of big sister to all the younger kids.

Thirteen-year-old Shelly pitched in. "Come on," she said. "We can't live in this dump. Let's clean it up."

The children set to work, and Katrina was kept busy directing them.

After a bit, Lucien said, "I hate to leave you alone like this, but I must rejoin my unit."

Still numb from losing her family and friends, Katrina said, "I understand. You're an officer in the army."

"I'll try to check on you soon and bring more supplies. Will you be all right?"

"I think so. We're not alone. God is with us in this place." But was He? Where had He been when her family died?

Chapter 4

Bosnia-Herzegovina, Summer 1992

The cave walls seemed to close in on Katrina. Last spring, the landscape of family and home, her finite universe, had fractured in a matter of hours. She squeezed her eyes shut at the memory. She would give her life to reverse events and save her loved ones, finding it hard to believe they were dead after giving so much of themselves. If only she'd treasured them as she should have.

Angry and grief stricken, Katrina wrestled with feeding and caring for the children while rationing their dwindling supplies. Despite Baby and little Drew's cries of hunger, she couldn't give them more food.

In the cave's pitch-black depths, the only plant life was the fungi that survived on animal remains and acted as prey for other animals. Occasionally, foot-long white salamanders crawled across the soft sand floor. The boys liked to capture them, then sneak up and wave the amphibians' blunt snouts and frog-like eyes at the girls, who then screamed and ran. Katrina worried they might grow desperate enough to eat the creatures.

Lucien had returned once, bringing a jeep load of provisions, and sadly, no news of John and Ellen. Lucien should have brought more supplies by now. Katrina dreaded leaving the cave, afraid of what marauding Serbian troops might do to the children and her.

Placing Rachel in charge, Katrina would take fourteen-year-old Ismael, the eldest boy, and fish in a nearby stream Lucien had shown her. Perch and trout supplemented their dreary diets, and nearby berry patches provided fresh fruit for everyone.

She appreciated Ismael's reflective nature and quick intelligence. His manners and speech showed his parents had raised him well. After enemy soldiers killed his family, he'd arrived at the Mostar Mission holding a six-month-old baby he found abandoned on his street. Katrina's mother had christened the babe Baby and, since Ishmael rescued him in a Muslim neighborhood, assigned him a Muslim heritage.

Concerned about eleven-year-old Andi, Katrina noticed she'd isolated herself, rarely speaking and doing her chores alone. Katrina felt the burden of the wounded confusion on their youthful faces.

Caleb, a seven-year-old Serbian with dark hair and expressive brown eyes, wiped off the large boulder they used for a table. "But why is there war? Why do we have to live in this cave?"

Katrina's explanations brought more questions. "Why do people hate me?" he asked. "What did I ever do to them?"

She knew no suitable answers. Perhaps her parents or Giles would have magically woven some reassuring tale. Katrina said, "I don't know, honey. It's hard for me to understand, too." She hugged him, and he rewarded her with a crooked grin.

The children's presence forced her from the cavity of grief that threatened to consume her. She feared John and Ellen were dead. With a troubled frown, she recalled Rachel's resentment of the present situation. "I want to go home to America," she said, tossing her head. "I hate this country."

"We can't leave your parents. They might still be in Bosnia with the orphans they took shopping for shoes."

Rachel cried, tears running down her face. "They're probably already dead. I won't lose Shelly and Andi, too. Help us escape."

She wrapped her arms around Rachel. "All right, but I can't do it alone. I'll need everyone's help."

The girl nodded and bit her lip. "You think our mom and dad are dead—don't you?"

Katrina's throat ached. Rachel struggled to be brave and realistic for her sisters, but her inner child yearned for reassurance. "I keep expecting them to walk in here any moment." She squeezed Rachel's shoulder. "And if they don't, there's the chance they've already left the country safely."

Fall 1992

Katrina peered outside the cave into the night, where armed soldiers were passing merely yards away. She was relieved that the children, except for Shelly, the quietest of the bunch, were sleeping, though they had all gone to bed hungry. The tiniest sound could draw the troop's attention, resulting in death. She whispered to Shelly. "Can you hear them? They're marching north." Katrina tugged Shelly against the wall, willing the troop not to come any closer.

Shelly brushed several strands of long blonde hair from her face with a hand that shook. "Aunt Katrina?" she asked, a hesitant quiver in her voice. "Will we see our parents again?"

The girl was already so brave. What could Katrina say to comfort her? Next, her sister Andi would be asking. Despite not knowing the answer, Katrina had to believe the girls would see their parents again. She forced a light tone. "God will protect them." But would He? How could any of them rely on Him after everything that had happened?

Sometimes at night, she longed to cry out for help, but this wasn't America, where police officers patrolled the streets and highways ready to offer assistance. No, this was Bosnia, where neighbors and police officers were prone to kill for no reason other than they suspected you might differ from them. Katrina had experience with being different.

Chapter 5

Winter 1992

When Vita stumbled into the cave looking half-frozen one morning, Katrina suppressed a cry of relief at seeing another adult. She hugged her. Vita had been Katrina's closest friend since her family started the mission. At their first meeting, they'd clicked—two women of the same age facing war and hostility. "How did you find us?"

Vita brushed the snow from her jacket with a grimace. "Praise be to Allah. I've been searching for days whenever I could get free."

"I've never been so happy to see anyone. Any news of John and Ellen and the other children?"

"No. I was hoping you'd heard something." She reached inside her coat, brought out a package, and handed it to Katrina. "It's for you. Open it."

Katrina untied the string and tore off the coarse brown wrapping to find a sweater and a pair of slacks. "They're so pretty. Thank you. You always find the best things even when there's so little available."

"I figured you'd need a change of clothes."

"You've been such a wonderful friend to me." Katrina thought bleakly of her family and then, chiding herself, refocused. "I'm glad it's snowing, or your footprints might have led the soldiers to us."

"I was careful. No one followed me. Let me feed the brats, and then we'll talk." Vita crossed to the kids, who sat huddled against the wall, took a seat, and greeted them. They barely acknowledged her.

Their unfriendliness embarrassed Katrina. They'd never taken to

Vita, not even Ismael and Baby, who were Muslims. And she had been so generous, often dropping off food packages at the mission. Vita shivered, and Katrina realized she must be cold and damp.

"I wish we had a warm drink to give you, but at least there's a blanket." Katrina shook out the cover before handing it to her.

Vita draped the wool around her shoulders and unbuttoned her jacket, tugging out a loaf of bread and a long sausage roll. "I thought you'd all be hungry."

The children's eyes widened, and Caleb licked his lips.

A smug smile lit Shelly's face. "I told you God would provide."

Andi frowned. "For now, maybe. But aren't evil men after us?"

Vita said, "I'm afraid so, and what's worse is the Muslims and Croats also believe Katrina's a spy."

At the children's frightened faces, Katrina hurried to interrupt, giving Vita a stern look. "I'm sure it's not as bad as that." She took the food and passed it to Rachel, pointing to the other side of the cave, which received more sunlight. "Take everyone over there to eat." Rachel led them away.

"How could you frighten them like that?" Katrina asked.

Vita shrugged. "It's better for them to know what they're up against." She stretched out her long legs, crossing them at the ankle. She wore army fatigues and thick, clumpy boots as usual, yet still appeared feminine.

Katrina, feeling short and dumpy in comparison, reproached herself for entertaining vain thoughts when their lives were in danger. Her appearance didn't matter. "Tell me what's been happening? Is Lucien well? He's only come once."

A commotion at the front of the cave drew everyone's attention as John, Ellen, and several orphans entered. Rachel ran and wrapped her arms around her mother and father as if she were afraid they would disappear. Shelly and Andi wiggled into the encirclement, and their parents hugged the girls close.

Amid many kisses and exclamations of joy, John and Ellen greeted everyone, including Vita, who quickly left, leaving them to enjoy their reunion. Katrina cried as she embraced John and Ellen, reminded of her mom and dad. John rested his hand on her shoulder. "Ellen and I are grief stricken about your parents, Giles, and the others. If we hadn't taken these young ones to town shopping for shoes . . ." his voice trailed off, leaving the horror unsaid.

Ellen pressed Katrina's hand in sympathy. "John and I can never repay you for saving our girls. After days of futile searching, we feared the worst." She gulped in silent relief.

"You're alive. That's all the thanks I need. Besides, it was Lucien who found the children hiding in the woods outside the mission and brought us here. I've been so frightened. How could people believe we're spies?"

"I don't understand it either," John said.

Katrina sighed. "I was hoping you could explain the false accusations against us."

"Like you, we've been in hiding and without communication."

"We waited for you that day as long as we could," Katrina said. "What happened to you?"

"The car broke down, and it took hours to fix," Ellen said. "By then, it was so late we spent the night with friends. John phoned the mission, but no one answered. We thought the line was out of order. We didn't hear about the raid until the next morning and rushed back immediately. You had already left, and no one seemed to know where you'd gone." She swallowed and teared up. "I won't talk about what we learned. You were there. Before leaving, we knelt and prayed over the graves, my dear." Ellen hugged her.

Katrina clung to her tightly for a moment, struggling to gather her composure to keep from falling apart. "How did you find us?"

"It was God's grace," John said. "We hoped that, like us, you all had found refuge in the caves. We've been searching systematically every day for hours, praying to find you."

"Thank God you did," Katrina said tearfully.

Ellen said, "John found several connecting caves with furniture and rations, and we've been staying there and conducting school lessons to keep the children occupied."

In Katrina's mind, a warning buzzed. The furniture and rations must belong to someone. She ignored the threat, glad to know there was food for them anywhere. To survive, they had to accept the risks. Everywhere in this wilderness of Bosnia was fraught with danger. She would remain vigilant.

Despite her initial misgivings, Katrina and the others grew to depend on John and Ellen's cave, hidden among the hundreds of caverns in the mountains surrounding Mostar.

John, Ellen, and Katrina organized a schoolroom with rough-hewn chairs and orange crates stacked and tied together for desks. The main den included an enormous fire pit, pots, pans, dried meats, and fish. They used the smaller connecting enclosures for sleeping quarters. Thankfully, she concluded they were in no danger because of the cave. Her mind must have been playing tricks on her.

A colony of bats lived in the cave's cold, dark inner recesses, which everyone avoided. Each evening at dusk, the small furry mammals flew out en masse in search of food. Their exodus was an eerie sight, as was their return shortly before dawn. The children soon became accustomed to the phenomenon and learned to keep out of the bats' path.

Vita came with more supplies, warning them to stay inside. Soldiers were in the area. A routine of schoolwork helped keep everyone sane. Before their reading assignments, Katrina led the kids in daily physical exercise sessions, hoping the jumping jacks and sit-ups would burn off some of their raw energy. The class used the back-ordered textbooks that Katrina had Vita pick up at the post office. She also brought paper and pencils.

One day, they were all in the main chamber drinking tea with Vita, who had brought supplies. While they were talking, Katrina said, "We haven't heard from Lucian for some time. I hope he's okay."

"He's a fine soldier. I wouldn't worry," John said. "Besides, Lucien doesn't know where we are."

"It's better he doesn't find you," Vita said. "Croats can't be trusted, especially him."

"What nonsense!" Ellen said. "Like you, he's always been willing to give us a helping hand."

"Well, I warned you."

John said, "You haven't given us any reason not to trust him."

Vita shook her head firmly and rose. "I better be going."

Katrina continued to worry about Lucien's failure to appear, but Vita insisted he could not be trusted. Tight-lipped, she refused to say why. Katrina tried not to imagine the worst.

One afternoon in the schoolroom, after the others had migrated to the main chamber, Andi's trusting gaze met hers. "Where do you think Lucien will take us when he comes?"

Katrina spoke impulsively, wanting to protect Andi from being hurt, forgetting how many hours the two had spent together while Lucien convalesced at the mission. "He's not coming." She strove to keep the bitterness out of her voice but failed.

"You blame him for everything that's happened. It's Vita's fault! You always listen to her, even though Lucien's our friend."

"Andi, I don't want you to depend too much on Lucien. It's not like we're his family, or even Croatian."

Andi retreated into rigid silence, her face an unreadable wall.

Katrina realized Lucien might have been captured, killed, or ordered to another province. Had she allowed Vita's distrust of him to sway her? She'd be more wary of her friend's influence in the future.

Yesterday, Rachel, Ellen and she had come upon Vita sifting through the children's meager belongings. "What are you doing?" Katrina asked.

Vita glanced up impatiently. "I need to know what these orphans have to determine their needs."

Rachel and Ellen appeared upset, but Katrina shrugged off the possibility of any calculated wrongdoing. Vita had been a good friend. They'd grown closer in the last year, but Vita should have asked for permission before shuffling through the youngsters' stuff. Maybe Andi had a point. Sometimes, children saw through people's facades when adults couldn't.

Rachel didn't trust Vita, especially after discovering her rifling through their things. The woman's presence left her uneasy. She fingered the ribbon around her neck. Nosy Vita would ask to see what was on it next. Rachel grinned, thrusting a fist in the air. She would hide the Madonna in one of Aunt Katrina's tennis shoes with the secret compartments built into the heels. Giles had given them to her on her last birthday, a special surprise he'd bought in the States. Aunt Katrina had laughed about them and probably forgotten the compartments existed. Those shoes were her favorites. She wore them every day. That night, while Katrina slept, Rachel tiptoed into her space, carrying the Madonna she'd sealed in a plastic bag. She grabbed a tennis shoe and slipped the tiny bag inside the compartment. Really, she was making this into one of those mysteries she loved to read. Still, it was nice to have a secret all her own.

Ellen and Katrina had organized game time for the afternoons. Despite the ongoing war and tension, today's game of charades should induce a few giggles and grins.

As the kids clamored into the room, several younger ones cried, "I have to go potty."

"John and I will take them," Ellen said. They took off down the corridor, leading the littlest ones toward the outside entrance.

Minutes later, gunshots rang out. Katrina's stomach churned. "Hush!" she said to the children. Above their terrified squeals, she motioned to the two eldest girls and instructed them. "Rachel, Shelly, keep everyone calm while I see what's happening."

Tanya, who was usually shy and quiet, dashed to her side. "No. I don't want you to get killed." The children's anxious gazes clung to Katrina. She squeezed the girl's shoulder and nodded for Rachel to take charge.

Katrina rushed to the cave entrance, peered out, then retreated in anguish. Soldiers filled the area, shooting at John and Ellen as they tried to get the kids to safety.

Katrina couldn't reach them without crossing directly into the path of fire, which would leave her dead and those in her care defenseless. She ran to the schoolroom and gathered her small band.

Dear God, where could they hide? Fear of what could happen spurred her into action. She led the kids farther and farther into the carved rock recesses, stumbling from one dark alcove into the next until Katrina worried they would never find their way out again. It seemed like hours had passed when suddenly the cave opened into the outdoors, and they were in the hills, the chilly wind against their faces, the crescent of a new moon blessedly hiding and guiding them through the night.

In the weeks following, Katrina and the children lived in the forested mountains, hunger driving them to approach local farmhouses for food. The farmers fed them a thin potato soup or potato bread, hard and white with mold. None of the people welcomed them. It was invariably the same.

One night, while the children slept in yet another cave, Katrina knelt on its rough floor. "Show me the way, Lord," she prayed, struggling to trust amid her disbelief.

The next morning, they moved on. Rain and melting snow drenched and soaked the earth, making travel dangerous and difficult in the mountains. Katrina and her band had no destination. Yet they pressed on, too frightened of what might happen if they dared to stop. Day followed day, each leaving them hungrier and wearier than the preceding one. The edge of her hatred and defiance wore thin as the overwhelming need for survival dominated her every sense. And always she was plagued by Lucien's failure to return, John and Ellen's disappearance, and her doubts about Vita.

Had Rachel, Shelly, and Andi's worst nightmare come true when their parents vanished in the raid? So far, Katrina had kept her band of thirteen together, but how long could they continue? Deep within, she knew it was almost over. They had nowhere to go. The horror of her parents' and Giles's deaths haunted her. When the kids slept, she stood guard, somehow grabbing an hour or two of sleep toward morning.

During those nights, silence filled the cracks of her life as she wallowed in self-pity and despair. Katrina couldn't elude the truth. She'd failed, lost. The realization was sometimes so intense that she trembled, fearing she would never recover.

The children never complained. They doggedly trooped on, trusting her to keep them safe. That evening, they'd been so spent. Katrina let them bed down in an open meadow that left them exposed. What if they were captured? She couldn't bear the thought of what might happen. *Dear Lord, these precious ones, please don't let them die—don't let those in my care die again.*

She studied the resting children. They were so thin, their faces gaunt and haunted. All but Baby, who was amazingly robust despite the deprivation the children suffered. She was worried about young Drew, who had grown unresponsive and wan. Worse, he could hardly tolerate food when they found any. He looked angelic as he slept. So like the twins, dead now because of her. No, she mustn't think of them. She needed rest—then she'd consider what to do tomorrow and where to go next.

Exhausted, she closed her eyes and fell into a deep and dreamless sleep.

Katrina jerked awake as someone shook her shoulder. She was in the mountain meadow where she and her small band had fallen asleep the night before, too tired to continue walking.

Vita stood over her. "Finally, I thought you were going to sleep all morning."

"Where did you come from?" Katrina sat up, and Vita handed her a bottle of water. Katrina drank thirstily.

Vita squatted beside her. "I was out for a walk and stumbled across you. I've been searching since you disappeared. It's good to see you."

Katrina rubbed her eyes sleepily. "Where are we? It was too dark to see when we got here."

"Mostar is down in the valley. I'm surprised you didn't notice the temperature change when you came from the mountains."

Katrina rose and saw the city spread out below. "Last night, I didn't notice much, but it is warmer and sunnier." She knew the nearby Adriatic Sea gave Mostar a more Mediterranean climate, while the snow-covered mountains above created an Alpine effect.

"Mostar gets the occasional winter snow, but it's usually light."

"I need to wake the children and get moving. It's dangerous for us to stay long."

Vita rose. "You realize the militia doesn't care about those orphans. It's you they want, and they're closing in. What will happen to the brats, then? You need to settle them while you can."

"How? We've nowhere to go." Katrina slumped, her arms crossed, clutching her body as if she could somehow hold it together. What if Vita was right?

Vita planted her feet in a wide stance. "I can place them in an orphanage where they'll receive care. A Swiss family has opened one since you left. It's even nicer than the one your family had."

"I promised Mother I'd keep the orphans safe." Her promise and the children were her reasons for getting up every day.

Relentless, Vita continued. "So keep your promise. They'll be safer in the Swiss orphanage than with you. You're a target and having the kids with you turns them into targets."

Feeling powerless over now and the future, Katrina realized keeping the children she'd grown to love was selfish and not in their best interests. If the enemy caught her, they would be guilty by association and risked execution. At an orphanage, they would have beds and plenty of food. Could strangers be trusted to love and protect these precious ones? *Did she have the right to reject their best opportunity to survive?* Vita had often brought food and provisions for them. If only Katrina wasn't so tired and hungry, it would be easier to think. Her brain was in a fog, and hunger gnawed at her stomach.

"If you really loved the orphans, you would want them protected. They aren't safe with you. Soldiers could arrest you today. Please let me help. I have the resources you lack. I can hide you in a secure place, too."

Katrina sensed nothing would ever be the same again. How had she failed so terribly? And how would she ever tell the children? It would be one of the hardest things she'd ever done. She looked across at them and saw they were waking up. She had no breakfast to give them or lunch or dinner—and no shelter, just her love.

Vita grinned. "You'll do it. I can see it in your face. Praise be to Allah!"

Katrina leaned in, her hand on one knee. "All right. If they're harmed in any way, I'll hold you responsible." Despite the sinking sensation within, she determined to make the separation as easy as possible for the children. They'd accept the change better if they believed it was necessary for her to leave them behind.

Vita was still talking and making plans when Katrina said, "It's time I spoke with the children."

"Wait." Vita handed her a hotel card and room key, then pulled a scarf out of her bag. "Cover your hair and face with this when necessary so no one recognizes you. Don't speak to anyone if you can avoid it. I will come to you after I take care of the orphans."

"Be gentle with them." Katrina crossed the meadow and gathered her small band. Agonizing over their separation and praying it wasn't a mistake, she adopted a languid pose and smiled. "I must go away for a while. The soldiers are closing in on me, and I can escape faster alone. The good news is the Swiss have opened a wonderful new orphanage. Vita will take you there."

Their frightened faces and silence hurt, but she must be strong, for their sakes. "I love each of you and will never forget you. When it's safe, I will find you again. Come hug me goodbye."

The children shuffled forward, sniffling and teary-eyed. Their young arms wrapped tightly around her, telling her how much they loved her.

"I'll miss you. Remember to say your prayers." Katrina kissed them and walked away so they wouldn't see her crying.

Vita said, "I've paid for your room for a month. You'll be safe there."

Katrina looked at the hotel card. On the back was the name and address of a hotel in Mostar.

Chapter 6

Streaks of fire lit Mostar's sky, and powerful explosions rocked the night. Katrina stared out her hotel window at the golden domes of the sole remaining cathedral in Mostar, listening to its bells toll a message of hope. Someone had rung them in defiance of the raging civil war and placed a flare near the top. In moments like these, she could almost believe and feel again.

A light knock signaling Vita's arrival broke into her reverie. Anxiety, sharp as a blade, sliced through Katrina as she hurried to open the door. "All is well?"

Vita nodded, removing her coat and gloves. "Praise Allah. The brats are fine, but the police are seeking the American spy. You realize you must leave."

Katrina pushed the blonde curls back from her face, raising her chin in what her mother would have called a stubborn tilt. Since Vita had encountered Katrina and her brood sleeping in the mountain meadow last week, she'd been pressing her to leave Bosnia, convincing her the Bosnian police were closing in. That it was Katrina they wanted, not the orphans. Reluctantly, she'd entrusted the youngsters to Vita's care and consented to hide in the hotel room Vita had arranged.

Now Katrina regretted letting Vita sway her. The kids were her responsibility. She owed it to her parents to care for the children and intended to rejoin them at all costs. Katrina had tried to find the Swiss orphanage where Vita had taken them, but no one seemed to have heard of it. Had Vita invented the place to set Katrina's mind at ease? Could the kids be back in the cave? She faced Vita, determined. "The children—"

"Should stay where they are. Your presence is a threat to the orphans your parents took in. Do you want the kids' massacre on your conscience as well?"

Katrina stiffened, hurt pride blanketing a deeper wound. Lord, please don't let me fail them. Already, she had watched Andi's once mysterious eyes turn listless, Rachel's dimples cease to smile, and Caleb's natural inquisitiveness falter. Tanya was quieter than ever, and even gentle Shelly occasionally snapped at the others in anger. The children had grown thin, especially the twins, their small ribs protruding against threadbare clothes. Katrina worried about Drew's illness, terrified he might die.

"Sorry," Vita said in an uncustomary apology. She dropped onto the bed, stretching her lithe limbs. A Romany Muslim who ran the Mostar jail, Vita was attractive despite her worn mud-splattered pants and heavy shirt. Her face pensive, she said, "It's getting to me, fighting, working, and scrounging for food so your sniveling brats can eat. The Muslim youth are all I care about."

Katrina tensed. If Vita didn't help, who would? "I don't believe that, not after all you've done."

"You are a fool, then. Your parents might be alive today if you weren't so trusting."

Katrina groped for the wall, guilt thrashing inward while she fought to remain upright. "You can't know that."

"Can't I? What if I said your brave captain is a mercenary? Lucien is manipulating the Croats and Muslims for the Serbs. He met with that pig of a Major Cosic shortly before the Serbians raided your home."

Katrina gaped at her in stunned disbelief.

Vita shrugged. "Don't stare at me like I'm crazy. Your brother

Giles overheard their conversation and told me about it. An hour later, he was dead, and so were your parents."

Katrina blinked back tears. Could it be true? She remembered seeing Giles and Vita talking before the raid that day. Her brother had appeared upset. Lucien had arrived earlier while her family was eating breakfast. He'd warned them of Serbian soldiers in the vicinity and soon left. Had he returned while she was out walking? Could Lucien have watched her family die and, afterward, fearful Katrina might identify him, pretended to help her? Had he led her and the children to the cave, knowing they would die without food or weapons?

Katrina knew of no reason for Vita to lie and yet couldn't imagine Lucien betraying them. She couldn't accept Vita's accusations against him without proof and should be wary of them both.

She crossed to the window and gazed out, wondering if she could trust Vita, who seemed to hate everyone and everything that wasn't Muslim. Katrina had believed she and her family were the exceptions, but no longer knew what to think. She had to move the children in the morning without Vita knowing.

Katrina shuddered, unable to forget—to stop visualizing the day her parents died and hell had torched its way into her existence. Thank God, John and Ellen had taken some of the orphans into town. Lucien had found Katrina clinging to her mother's lifeless body and comforted her. He'd rounded up the children who'd taken cover in the woods during the raid, then drove them all to the cave. No one had come in pursuit.

He warned, his gaze concerned, "Stay out of sight. I'll return as soon as I can." He'd driven away, knowing they had little food or protection.

For days, she'd anxiously awaited his return. Sometimes, she would stand outside the cave's rocky entrance, peering below, where snow cascaded across the mountain, winding down the icy trail.

When he'd finally arrived with a jeep full of provisions to sustain them, she'd been beside herself with joy and relief.

Lucien hadn't returned. Katrina remembered staring at the predawn light, wondering how they would manage. She'd found hope with John and Ellen's arrival. Now, she didn't know if they were alive. Were the girls strong enough to accept their parents' deaths if necessary? They had to be.

As wrenching as the possibility was, the three had known happiness and stability, something Caleb, Drew, Robbie, Tanya, and the rest of the orphans might never experience. The innocent trust of these young ones terrified her. If they guessed how unfit she was or of the disaster in her past—they'd run as far from her as possible. She pushed aside thoughts of those lost or dead, the pain pressing too deep.

Katrina peered at her watch, wishing Vita would leave. One hour remained until curfew. Lanterns flickered sporadically in deserted apartment buildings, but few ventured into the icy street. Fear of sniper fire or random explosions that had shattered or ended too many lives kept most people inside.

Vita spoke into the silence growing between them. "The war is getting worse. Srebrenica is under siege. The Serbs have surrounded the city, cutting off food and supplies. People are dying of hunger and bullets. Yesterday, they found fourteen bodies in the schoolyard, Muslim children murdered while clinging to the playground fence."

It pained Katrina to see anyone killed, but the murder of innocent youth appalled her. "I'm sorry. Not having seen a newspaper, I wasn't aware of the recent deaths. Do you have many friends there?"

"Enough. Please consider leaving. It's forty-eight kilometers to the coast and not much further to Dubrovnik, where you can get help."

If Katrina could reach Neum, the nearest coastal city, maybe she could pay someone to brave the Adriatic and smuggle her across to

Italy. Or, from Dubrovnik, she could journey through Macedonia to Greece. But then what?

Vita seemed desperate to see her gone. Katrina studied her friend, disliking herself for doubting Vita's motives. Everything was so gray, and nothing as it appeared. Katrina had no intention of letting anyone drive her away. "Sarajevo is as close, and UN troops are there."

"You might get airlifted from inside because you're an American. But how would you enter the city? Since February of last year, the Serb Army has had Sarajevo surrounded and cut off from power, water, and food supplies. No one can travel in or out. People are barely surviving. The UN has to fly in provisions."

"UN peacekeeping troops could get me in," Katrina said.

"There's a strong chance you'd be shot before you could ever fly out. Some days, the Serbs fire three to four thousand shells at Sarajevo's inhabitants. Bosnian troops inside have no ammunition to strike back. It's the last place you should go. Vedran Smailović has romanticized the situation there."

"Thank God for brilliant musicians like Smailović. He is an inspiration to the four hundred thousand people trapped there. In May last year, he risked his life, playing his cello for twenty-two days straight on the very spot where Serbs had killed twenty-two Bosnians and injured seventy more. They were all waiting in a bread line. Smailović continues to play on the streets and at funerals. He is brave."

Vita tapped her foot, fidgeting. "He's foolhardy. Sarajevo is bombarded with shells every day."

"At least he's focusing international attention on the situation. This month, Joan Baez flew in and sang. I cried when I read about her visit."

"You're becoming sentimental like the rest of them. It's too dangerous to exit the country through Sarajevo. There are workable routes to leave by. Let me arrange your trip," Vita said.

"Perhaps later." Katrina's satisfaction in quashing Vita's jubilation at seeing her gone was confusing.

Vita's dark eyes sparked. "Forget about the traitor who deceived you. I tell you, it's Lucien. Why does it matter who killed your family? Today, most people will sell their souls for a loaf of bread."

Something in Katrina locked and refused to give. "Those who committed the massacre at the mission will pay. My family, the staff, and the innocent children will be avenged."

Her friend's eyes widened in speculation, along with an emotion that vanished too swiftly to identify. "You are a bloody cool one. If I didn't know Americans were such a soft touch, I'd be shivering in my boots."

Lava-hot anger erupted in Katrina, fueling memories and an unfamiliar hatred. "Whatever happens, don't hurt my little band."

"You're impossible to reason with. It's late. I'll return in the morning and arrange your departure."

"I'll think about it," Katrina said as Vita left.

Screams and gunfire, too near to ignore, jolted Katrina from sleep. She heard Serb soldiers barking orders, ransacking hotel rooms, and shouting for the guests to go below. Katrina hastily slipped on a scarf and coat over the jeans and jacket she'd slept in and crossed to open her door.

A soldier blocked the entrance to her room. Without asking, she somehow knew they were hunting for her. She slammed the door and raced to the window.

At first, she saw nothing to fear. The cathedral's golden domes glowed in the morning sun, the freshly fallen snow glistening on its lofty crown. People scurried below, some carrying round loaves of bread or plastic bottles of water. Suddenly, furious commands shattered the calm as hotel guests were forced into the square with AK-47s at their backs. An officer spoke through a megaphone. "We want the *Amerikanka*. A reward for anyone who can lead us to her and death to all who help her."

A rifle butt hammered on her door. Terrified, Katrina turned from the window as the militia burst inside. She drew the head covering closer to her face and stumbled into the hall, urged by jabs from the men's rifles. Several of them stayed behind, searching.

Soldiers prodded her downstairs and outside to the square. She sought an avenue of escape, taking in the stone houses, the terra-cotta roofs piled lightly with snow. Katrina flinched as bullets struck two young Croatians. They crumpled to the pavement. More shots slammed into their backs and legs. Blood oozed from their wounds and trickled onto the bricks.

A blind fury shook Katrina. Was this how her family and those from the mission had died? She brushed aside tears as more soldiers toting rifles and submachine guns swarmed from the hotel into the area.

A crying girl knelt beside a wounded man, clinging to his hand. The soldiers opened fire, and the girl collapsed on the man. A second and third round of bullets hit those standing next to them. Katrina's resolve faltered as people fell with anguished cries.

Soldiers elbowed a path through the crowd, prodding the bodies with weapons. When outraged family or friends protested, the soldiers shoved them to the ground and fired.

Fearful, the people retreated and allowed themselves to be intimidated into a corner of the square. Katrina bit down on a whimper. An uncontrolled shiver ran through her. Peasants hurried by, averting their faces. Soldiers moved about, checking people's identification papers. An army truck arrived. The driver and his cohort climbed out and tossed the corpses into the truck bed. An old peasant woman hosed away the blood.

Stricken, Katrina stumbled over a rock. Her scarf dropped back, revealing her face and hair. Startled, she stared at an officer who had known her family.

"It's the *Amerikanka,*" he shouted.

Others picked up the cry, pointing, "There she is! Over there!"

Katrina bolted, dodging from side to side, trying to elude her pursuers. "Run, Katrina," someone yelled. A gun popped. She turned to see Lucien stumble, but she raced on, dashing from the square into a side street. Bullets whizzed by, missing her ear. A round of machine gun fire shredded a nearby bush.

Then, the old bridge, Stari Most, from which the town derived its name, exploded. She could see Croatian forces by the riverbank, pushing back Muslim troops. During the diversion, Katrina darted down the street, running to the edge of town and into the hills.

She slowed, her breath coming in huge gasps and her shoulders shaking with terror. Frosted mountains and forests known to be riddled with land mines surrounded her. To escape seemed impossible until Katrina remembered the children and her mother's dying plea. "Care for them, darling. They're innocent. Try not to be bitter . . . and remember, God will see you through." She kept walking, needing to devise a way to reach the children.

Out of nowhere, gunshots cracked again and echoed around Katrina as she hurtled to the ground. A soldier bellowed into the wind. She scrambled to her feet to escape a Serbian battalion's fire. She tripped, fell downhill, smashed into a rock, and continued rolling. Katrina felt a piercing pain—and then peace. Her one regret was the children. What would become of them?

Chapter 7

Katrina opened her eyes to a pounding, blinding headache. The swirling snow and cold made her dizzy. She tried to clear her head, to understand what had happened.

She lay in a mountain meadow. The evergreens' low-lying branches that camouflaged her had saved her life. With a groan, she sat up, touching the lump on her head, relieved to find that a bullet had not struck her.

Her limbs tingled, and her feet ached from the frost. In the distance, she could hear the rattle of machine gun fire. Katrina forced herself to stand. She surveilled the surrounding terrain for enemy soldiers and, seeing none, started walking. The meadow heaved and tilted with her first few steps.

Somehow, she'd escaped the soldiers. Enemy fire might have drawn them aside, or another prey could have lured them on. Katrina didn't intend to linger and give her enemies a second chance.

Halfway up the icy white hillside, she heard gunfire again and ran. Not too far off, soldiers advanced, tromping through the encrusted snow and brush.

Lucien's voice rang out, "Katrina. Katrina!" The sound rumbled, gaining in volume and intensity as he and his men drew closer. "Wait. Stop!"

She stumbled on, panting, head throbbing, legs aching, grappling with the reality that Lucien had found her. She couldn't trust him. After witnessing the senseless slaughter that morning, she hesitated to trust anyone. What if Vita had spoken the truth about him?

She was lost in the battle of nerves and will. The steel of Russian

Kalashnikovs glistened in the surrounding countryside. The threatening silence circled her like a vulture. Finally, she dropped to her knees and huddled beneath a bush.

What was one American woman amid the war and hatred consuming generations of Bosnian Serbs, Croats, and Muslims? Her family had tried to befriend all three sides, but tragically, each faction suspected the Winslows of betrayal. Suspicions that the American missionaries were spies had mushroomed. None of it made any sense. Earlier, the Serb Army had flushed her out of the hotel. Then, the Bosnian Muslim Army crossed her path and chased her. Now, it was the Croats led by Lucien, a man she'd once trusted and liked.

She caught a glimpse of him. No. She didn't want to think about the past—to consider how he might have betrayed and killed her parents and brother. Whatever his reasons, he'd deserted her when she needed him.

Vita's story of events created a limbo of sorts for Katrina. Who was she to believe? Lucien had neglected to send a message or arrange supplies, while Vita had often trekked through the mountains to bring them provisions and news. Yet Vita lived and worked in Mostar, while Lucian had to obey orders and go wherever the army sent him. *But why chase her if not to capture her?*

"I know you're there," Lucien called. "Katrina! You'll die out here alone."

Better alone than with a traitor . . . traitor . . . traitor. The words barreled through her mind as she rushed down the hillside, the echoing refrain squeezing out everything but fear. Her family had taken these people in, cared for the wounded, and nourished them to health—and this was the Winslows' reward. Their home ransacked, ravaged, destroyed. Katrina's family was dead, with no one and everyone to blame. Where was justice?

Where was the God her parents had loved, and she once trusted? Was He watching, or didn't He care? Warmth enveloped her, and she could almost hear her mother's low, gentle voice. "God will always be there for you, dear. Open your heart to Him. Let Him in." But was He there? How could He be in the middle of this horror?

Her conscience pricked. Wasn't it herself she really doubted and blamed? Katrina tried to ignore the inner voice while she waited, fortified in the depths of her aloneness, too frightened to move.

"Katrina."

Lucien's voice coming from behind her kindled terror. She burrowed deeper into the snow. She couldn't stay like this much longer, or she'd freeze.

Dear Lord, why was it so cold? She blinked at the tears. How could she have ever trusted Lucien?

A firm hand yanked her to her feet. "Fool, you're half-frozen. Do you want to die?"

"Yes." She wrenched away, nearly knocking them over, feeling as if the veneer of civility she'd worn most of her life had been buried with her family. "I prefer death over the company of a murderer."

Lucien didn't deny it. He fetched a small rope from his pocket and tied her wrists together. "This will keep you from escaping. If I leave you here alone, you won't survive."

She wanted to believe he cared, but the butt of his rifle urged her forward. Lucien called to his men, and they fell in line. She marched with the soldiers to a fate that filled her with trepidation for herself and the children.

Where was he taking her? The Lucien she'd known would never harm her. Katrina had heard stories of rapes and firing squads. *How much courage did she need?* She shuddered and stumbled. Lucien barked an order, and the men formed a semicircle about her, prodding her onward.

Tears threatened anew at the thought of journeying from the home her family had shared, one her parents and Giles would never leave. Mostar's Muslims controlled the east and west banks of the

Neretva River, while the Croats commanded the city's western sector. Before being forced into hiding, Katrina had lived on the Croat side with her parents, where she first met Lucien. She sniffed, feeling both vulnerable and defiant. How long would he and his men keep her, and for what purpose?

She stared at the ragged soldiers' worn and lean faces. It was hate that kept them going. Hate that waged wars. And hate that had destroyed her home.

Mostar. The name moved her like a sad refrain. The city's beauty demolished. Its glory no more. A song based on Psalm 137, her mother had taught her about the Jews' captivity in Babylon, sprang to her lips. She sang, every word a weight pressing against her spirit. Though Lucien and his men stared, she sang on.

'By the rivers of Babylon, we wept.
When we remembered Zion, our home.
Our captors required a song, saying,
Sing us a song of Zion.
We hung our harps on the willows,
By the riverbanks and sang.
How could we sing a song in a strange land?
If I forget thee, O Jerusalem. . . .'

Chapter 8

Silence framed the night. The stars hung in clusters, the moon waxing gibbous. Lucien paced outside the tent to keep warm, struggling to reconcile matters with his conscience. It had been a gruesome day. His mind wouldn't stop replaying the morning's nightmare, Katrina in the square surrounded by machine gun fire.

His jaw tightened, thinking about it. He kicked the frozen ground in frustration. What was he supposed to do with Katrina?

He opened the pages of the worn diary he kept hidden under his shirt to record war events and track family, friends, and fellow soldiers. The pages were divided into four sections with the headings: Dead; Wounded; Imprisoned; Disappeared. He entered his brother-in-law Martin's name under the last. He was married to Lucien's sister, Sara.

Martin and Sara's Mostar apartment stood near the boundary between the Croat and Muslim sectors. For weeks, as the constant battle of machine guns blasted the area, Lucien had begged them to leave. Then, one afternoon, Martin went to buy bread and never returned home. Sara, frantic and inconsolable, sought Lucien. Despite the pain and awkwardness of wanting to help, words failed him. Actions were more his thing.

Before the war, Mostar was a growing metropolis with one hundred twenty thousand residents. Forty thousand remained, and a scant five thousand lived in the Croat sector, where Lucien stayed. Each side had dug trenches, built fortifications, and barricaded streets to defend their territory while they fought for more. He was sick of war and the dying, of seeing men go berserk and kill and kill and kill.

Death notices were posted everywhere in the city, on the trees, walls, and windows. Too often, those he cared about were among them. Amid the smoldering ashes and sand, Bosnians survived in bullet-riddled concrete apartment flats, which were barely habitable. People often moved from one building to another to escape the gunfire.

Though raised a Muslim, Martin had converted to Christianity in his late teens. Unlike Lucien and Sara, he was from Mostar and refused to leave. While stationed nearby, Lucien endeavored to help the sister he'd never felt close to and Katrina's family, the Winslows, who had saved his life. Now Sara and the baby were alone and unprotected in their apartment. She refused to believe Martin might be dead or that he might not return. Lucien feared her innocence and blind faith would lead to hurt and pain.

Didn't she see the black posters everywhere announcing the dead? Burials were the sole purpose behind public gatherings. The city parks had become graveyards, headstones crowning the former playgrounds. The journey up and down hillsides to bury their dead at traditional cemeteries was too dangerous. Besides, the park grounds were softer to dig up than the rocky hillsides.

How could his sister hold to her faith? Where did she get the strength? He didn't understand her, or women like her.

His thoughts went to Katrina, a problem as explosive and nearer at hand. She believed he'd abandoned her and the kids in the caves, leaving them to die. If she had asked, Lucien would have told her the army sent him on a reconnaissance mission that prevented his returning to help. He owed her his life. How could she think he wanted to hurt her? Her best chance of survival was to leave the country. He regretted her family's death even more since she had become his responsibility. She wasn't safe in Bosnia. The Serbs, Muslims, and Croats suspected her of spying, each for the other. Lucien considered it a ploy orchestrated by Serbian Major Cosic and the Roma Vita to divert attention from their covert operations in the area. He didn't know what Cosic and Vita were up to, but he bet they were behind Katrina's plight and the mission raid that destroyed her family. Had they also set in motion today's pursuit of her?

Lucien flipped his diary to the heading: Dead. He entered the names of the three men killed today. There were twenty-two of his original ninety-five men left. Next, he turned to the heading: Wounded. Mihail took a slug in the shoulder, and Lucien received a light nick in the thigh. The bullet only grazed him, but it was his bad leg. The third section was marked: Imprisoned. He studied the list. No new names, but the ones there tore at him. His uncle, two cousins, and eight of his soldiers. He shut the notebook, glanced at the moon, and entered the tent.

He spread a blanket before the small opening that served as a door. Katrina slept in the corner in his sleeping bag. He was used to the cold. The frost was inside and out, his sole defense from the urge to escape from himself and the man he'd become. He knew nowhere to turn but to the vast wasteland of numbness, where day after day and horror following horror, he placed one foot before the other and forced himself and his men to keep moving. The goal? He had long ago lost sight of it. To pause was to die.

He closed his eyes and slept.

When he awoke, sunlight poured through the canvas roof, leaving splotches of frond-like leaf shapes on the tent ceiling. Lucien studied the woman sleeping across from him, her vulnerability bared. The stubborn tilt of Katrina's chin hinted at her persistence even in sleep.

War was a hard thing. It ate away at a person or a nation until it destroyed all trust. What future was there for the two of them in a divided land?

Across the tent, Katrina stirred. She sat up with a start. "Get out."

Lucien sighed. "Not a nice way to say thank you. Still, it's what I've learned to expect."

She shot him an unhappy look. "I don't recall asking for your help yesterday."

Without comment, Lucien knelt beside the small opening and slipped through it, holding the cloth back for one long moment, making sure she saw the soldiers outside. "Don't get any foolish ideas. We break camp in half an hour."

He headed for the creek to wash up. Sparkling evergreens dressed in icicles glittered beneath the sun's rays. He'd first met Katrina on a cloudless morning like this. The same crisp chill hung in the air, and the winter's snow still held the earth captive in frozen abeyance.

Lucien had been hunting for meat to take to the barracks when he'd spotted the Serb patrol. He quickly reversed and ran toward the forest. A few steps from the woods, he stumbled over a large rotten log, and his leg gave. Lucien collapsed, stifling a grunt of pain as his leg landed at an awkward angle.

The alerted patrol fired into the surrounding brush.

"Only a deer," one said.

"It is nothing," another agreed.

"Still," a third voice said, "it never hurts to be sure." Another round of fire split the air. Lucien bit down to keep from screaming as a bullet tore into his hurt leg. Minutes later, he heard the patrol leaving, calling jovially to one another through the woods.

He strained to get up. Impossible. The slightest movement brought excruciating pain. On his next attempt, he blacked out. When he regained consciousness, he was staring into eyes as blue as the Adriatic Sea near his grandfather's summer home.

As the woman's concerned and wary gaze fell on the bloody mess that was his leg, he forced a smile. The effort to mask the pain was too much. Lucien passed out again.

He came to hours later in the white stucco house belonging to Katrina's parents, who he learned were American missionaries. Lucien stayed with them for a month while his broken leg and the complications from the bullet wound healed enough for him to return to the army barracks. During his visit, he grew fond of the Winslows. He shuddered to think what would have become of him without their help. He might have died if he'd been left wounded in the forest.

Shouts from the camp broke into Lucien's reverie, jolting him to his surroundings. In the privacy of the small mountain meadow, he knelt beside the creek and splashed cold water on his face, then rose to prepare himself for the day.

At the camp, a strained silence met him. Ratko, his sergeant, held Katrina in an armlock, a gun to her head. Her face white with anger and fear, she struggled to maintain a posture of proud defiance.

Lucien frowned. "What's going on here?"

The scruffy sergeant gave her a shake as he spoke. "We caught her sneaking out of camp with your pistol. She hit Darco over the head."

Lucien considered the teenage soldier, rubbing his head in embarrassment. The boy should be home carrying water for his mother and playing soccer in the yard with his brothers and sisters. But Bosnia's playgrounds had become burial grounds, and most boys were in the army or under the earth.

"I'll teach her a lesson." Ratko's hold on Katrina tightened, his elbow digging into her chest, suggestive of the treatment she would receive.

"Let her go," Lucien said.

Katrina's lower lip quivered, and her hands made tight, pale fists.

He would never allow his men to have their way with her. Yet, in his frustration, the temptation to let her escape was real. The return of her pistol would help guard against rape by marauding troops until she ran out of bullets. What was one more casualty, another statistic for Western analysts? Katrina deserved better.

Lucian admired her courage and loyalty to the orphans. In the past, he'd experienced her kindness. She was beautiful, sweet, and trouble.

If he returned to the army base with her as a prisoner, she might face rape and the firing squad. The Croats wouldn't welcome her.

Decide he must. The soldiers stood at attention, waiting for his command. "Tie the prisoner's wrists in front of her," he ordered and left to collect his belongings. There had been no dinner the night before. Lucien realized they would have to leave without breakfast. If she stayed, his hungry men would soon wonder why they were traveling so far from the barracks. And if they guessed who Katrina was, they'd question why he hadn't locked her in jail.

Chapter 9

Katrina winced as a soldier bound her wrists, the skin already angry red from yesterday. She wanted to spit in his face like some wild creature who'd lost all dignity but didn't dare with the sergeant's gun trained on her. She realized her rage and confusion were a coping mechanism for grief. What right did she have to judge Lucian on Vita's say-so? Katrina hated feeling scared and at his mercy. Resented his power to keep her prisoner and decide whether she lived or died. Repressed tears threatened. Why must he draw this out? He treated her like the enemy. Why the pretense of protecting her when his men weren't present?

She fought to tamp down her emotions as Lucien strode forward. "Surround the prisoner and see she doesn't escape."

"Yes, sir," barked Sergeant Ratko. "All right, men, you heard the captain." The soldiers encircled her as they had the day before. Lucien tossed her knapsack in the air.

With her hands tied, Katrina leaped to catch it. That knapsack held all she owned. Humiliated and embarrassed, she stumbled, praying her passport and purse were still wrapped inside, layered between the attire she'd shed in favor of jeans and a pullover. A rifle poke prodded her forward.

The sun dried the dew as they marched on and on through the forest. Shards of ice fell from the trees and melted in the noon heat. Katrina didn't know where she was. Beneath the blue skies, never-ending valleys dipped, and mountains marched before her.

When night came, she collapsed on Lucien's sleeping bag in the small tent. Even overwhelming hunger couldn't keep her awake. With sleep came bad dreams, dredging up the past, the fragments swirling in the riptide, waking her with a start.

She saw the rowboat in her nightmares, heard the twins' cries and shrill, panicked pleas. Katrina couldn't reach them then and was powerless now to vanquish the recollection of that ill-fated day. She'd been twelve years old, a child in everything but conscience.

Resignation slumped her shoulders, curling down her spine. A lump of fear settled in her stomach, and against her will, as if motivated by some inner destructive force, her mind conjured the turbulent aqua waters, tossing the pristine white rowboat with the twins in it. She saw it carry them farther and farther from shore.

Katrina and Giles had been playing with a litter of kittens sheltered under the deck of their summer bay home. A chance glance out to sea, and she'd seen her four-year-old brother and sister giggling in the boat as their antics rocked it, tumbling them about. They weren't supposed to be outside without her parents. How could they have untied the boat?

"Giles! Go, call Mom and Dad! Hurry!" Katrina kicked off her thongs and ran to the water.

As she dove into the bay, the twins' laughter changed to screams. They'd drifted too far, too quickly. The choppy bay waters fought her every movement. Katrina swam until her lungs seemed about to burst. Her arms and legs burned painfully with every stroke and kick. Yet she couldn't reach the wooden boat with navy stripes painted along its top. Frantically, she prayed she wouldn't be too late.

A glance back showed the shore far in the distance. Where were her parents? Why weren't they coming in the speedboat? She surged onward.

But it hadn't been enough. She wondered if it would ever be. Katrina didn't remember losing consciousness or giving up, but she must have.

The twins' deaths marked the end of existence as she'd known it. Familiar foes, guilt, and bitterness to this day warred in her as fiercely as the hatred consuming Bosnia. She refused to yield, then and now, to admit her life was broken, the future hollow.

Her enemies mustn't triumph. If they won, it wouldn't be because she was too cowardly to fight. She needed to save the mission children. Besides, Winslows always kept their promises.

Despite all the bravado she could muster, Katrina realized she'd failed twice. Who could say it wouldn't happen again? The book of Ecclesiastes taught that time and chance affected everyone. Sometimes, it seemed unfair.

If only she could find the children. Katrina didn't know where they were. And there was nothing she could do about it while she was Lucien's prisoner.

As Lucien's troop continued north, days merged into nights. Katrina lost track of time, her sole reality war. It was everywhere. She survived on the occasional rabbit the soldiers snared, or the treat of fish caught with her bare hands and smoked in a contrived earth pit.

The soldiers rarely spoke to her. Katrina could hear the men's restive murmurs when they were forced to share their meager resources. Lucien's silence was the most daunting. Her life was in his power, her every move dependent on his whim. How much longer before his men demanded a reckoning?

One evening, when food was handed out, she noticed Ratko staring at her. He'd had it in for Katrina since her failed escape attempt. Ratko's boot stomped on her foot as she passed, and he caught her arm. "If we killed her," he said to his comrades, "there would be one less mouth to feed." He tore the fish from her hand and dropped it into his pouch.

When she pulled away, his arm snaked around her waist. He yanked her to him.

Katrina's fists pushed helplessly against him as his mouth bruised hers. Finally, Ratko released her, and she saw Lucien approaching from the forest. Ratko walked out to join him as if nothing had happened. She sensed bitterness, changing her into someone masquerading as Katrina, a person she no longer knew or understood.

That evening, she huddled in Lucien's warm sleeping bag, thinking of how to escape and find the children. God, please let them be alive and well.

Katrina reached into her knapsack pocket and brought out the small but well-made plastic framed photo of her family. It was the sole memento she'd taken when she fled the mission. There was a secret hinged hollow in its back in which to hide cash. When the war began, her father had ordered one for each of them in case of trouble. Only hers remained.

Through the worn canvas walls, the soldiers' angry voices penetrated. "We will die out here like cowards with empty bellies while our wives, mothers, and sisters are murdered. And for what?" one of them asked. Grumbles of agreement rose.

"Our captain protects the foreigner like a lover. We haven't fought the enemy since we captured the *Amerikanka*."

Katrina shivered as she recognized Ratko's voice. She strained in vain to hear Lucien's response above the disgruntled mutters. The soldiers broke into peals of laughter amid noisily slapping sounds. Lucien must have defused their hostility.

The men were hungry, tired, and ready to fight. They didn't understand their captain's reasons for moving undetected through the countryside, farther and farther from their army base. Katrina didn't understand either. She saw how it grated on the men to stay low, traveling back routes rather than meeting the opposition head-on. Open clashes and confrontations were ever the Yugoslav way. Exhaustion finally overcame her, and she fell into a troubled sleep.

Chapter 10

Lucien hunkered outside his tent, warming his hands on the mug of hot water he held, glad the grueling day was finished. His stomach grumbled with hunger. Katrina didn't know he'd given his portion of tonight's fish to her and that he'd been sharing his meager food rations with her for days.

Tension among the soldiers kept mounting. It was crazy to have a woman traveling with them, especially a troublemaker like Katrina, whom Lucien felt compelled to protect. He couldn't restrain his men much longer. Besides, it was wrong to wear them out walking in circles when they had a duty to fulfill, a duty to kill the enemy to protect Croats.

Six months ago, Lucien's commission had been clear: undermine Serbian forces. His orders were to keep the enemy occupied away from Croatia's interests and gather intelligence on enemy operations. Then Lucien had been wounded and taken in by Katrina's family. How could she believe he'd reciprocate by murdering them? What were his moral obligations? To sacrifice his command and ask his men to protect her? His shoulders drooped as he considered doing exactly that. Where did his loyalty lie?

His parents, Josef and Anita Brezak, had argued against Lucien entering the war. They lived in Klagenfurt, Austria, a universe away from the brutality in Bosnia. His mother was born and grew up in Villach, Austria. His parents still lived near there, less than an hour from the Slovenian border. By birth a Croatian, Josef had staunchly resisted Yugoslavia's communist leanings despite his father's influence. As a young man, Josef realized he had no future in Croatia. He began crossing into Austria to sell Yugo-vacuum cleaners. Lower manufacturing costs in the East netted him a nice profit across the border. From a storefront in Graz, the business grew into an international concern. Many of his Yugo-vacuum factories were in the former Yugoslavia, though increasingly more were being built in the West.

Once, Lucien might have considered sharing his background with Katrina, but not anymore, not when she believed he'd murdered her family. His Aunt Dianne was married to a Serbian general in Belgrade. His cousin Mimi wanted to fight for Croatia too.

In part, guilt had driven Lucien into the war. His family had so much compared to his Croat relatives. He'd seen their cities burned on TV. Lucien mourned his cousins who had been killed in the war. When his uncle disappeared, Lucien felt he had to strike back as if, in doing so, he could counterbalance the raw injustice of Croat losses.

That was more than a year ago. Since then, right and wrong had lost meaning. Justice had faded into a bitter afterthought, left in the hands of war crime tribunals, far removed from the horrors of battle.

The worst had been when his battalion unwittingly foraged for food near a Serbian prison camp, detaining Bosnian Muslims. Trapped by Serbian troops, he and his men hid in the area. Lucien's stomach curdled at the awful screams, and he crept close enough to peer over the barbed wire, seeing the emaciated bodies, skeletal humans.

"How do you stand it?" he'd asked a prison field hand whom Lucien had bribed to help them.

"I feel sick eating the vegetables we grow, but a body's got to stay alive. The human remains enrich the soil. I try to forget about the people buried in it."

Lucien loathed the notion of concentration camps. If he'd listened to his parents, he'd be safe in Vienna, an executive in his father's firm.

Lucien worried about his Grandpa Creto, whom he hadn't seen since Serbia declared war on Croatia. His grandfather lived in Knin, which had been hard hit as Serbia funneled soldiers and weapons into the region. Croatia's Serbian population was only 4 percent. Unfortunately, most of those Serbs lived around his grandfather, uncles, and their families.

His thoughts bent to Katrina, and he remembered a different woman, a spirited, generous soul who worked long hours caring for orphans. A woman who'd reached out to help others, losing all she held dear, and was now stranded in a foreign land. He sympathized with her resentment and hatred. He had plenty of his own and disliked having her animosity directed at him. To watch those melting blue eyes that had once shone with concern and a secret joy become cold and defiant was tough.

Lucien dropped onto his stomach, lifting the tent flap slightly off the ground. He could make out Katrina crying in the dark. He steeled himself against the sight.

Her hands wrapped around a picture of her family, she sobbed. "I'll find the children, Mom. Winslows always keep their word." Katrina's shoulders shook. "Dad, you promised to travel home for a break. If you had, you'd be here." She buried her face in her palms, stifling the sound of her weeping.

It tore Lucien up to hear her crying. He wanted to hold her, stop her misery, and give her back her parents and brother. All he could give Katrina was her freedom.

Chapter 11

Two Years Earlier, Croatia 1991

The sizzling summer sun beat against Creto Brezak as he propelled his bicycle down Knin's main street, his frail, aged body bowed with effort.

"Go home, *Ustashas!*" A Serb policeman threw an empty Pepsi bottle at Creto.

He pedaled harder, wheezing as the bike climbed the hill and eventually coasted out of the Serb's view. Fifty years before, Creto had held that same Serb on his knee, crooning silly songs to hear him laugh. Creto peered cautiously over his shoulder before turning off the nearly deserted street onto his lane.

Croatians weren't safe on the street since Babic had seized power in Krajina, spinning his tale of discrimination. He'd ousted Raskovic from the Serbian Democratic Party leadership. Croatia's 4 percent Serb population, backed by Serbia's army and power, declared Krajina a Serbian proto state in Croatia.

Rural Serbs feared a revival of the fascism of World War II. Milosevic, Serbia's president, greedy for more territory and power, fed their fear, grasping any excuse to plunder and seize control.

Creto stopped in his drive and caught his breath. He should have known better than to go out alone so late in the day. He could have been killed. The Serbian goal was genocide for all Croatians. His son Ivan would be sure to scold him.

From where Creto stood, the city's enormous hill gave the illusion it was part of the scattered, jagged peaks majestically silhouetting the distant sky. At first glance, it made Knin appear more breathtaking than it was.

He swelled with pride that didn't flicker when his gaze moved to the Tvik screw factory, its smoking chimney stacks pumping the foul black exhaust the people breathed.

Yugoslavia's Communist Party had promised progress, and there it stood, the largest employer in the city of ten thousand. It didn't matter that it was failing or that there was no longer a market for the shoddy nuts, bolts, and screws produced. What counted was the party had kept faith with the people and delivered. It was up to the young to modernize and build new dreams. If only the world could hold together long enough for them to do it.

He loved this city his family had lived in and fought in for generations. He leaned his bike against the side of his modest stucco home and entered through the back door, clutching the milk he'd foolishly ventured out to buy.

Creto sank onto a hard pine kitchen chair, his bent back molding to its curve as his knees folded beneath the table. He poured himself a glass of milk and reached a trembling hand for his daughter's letter, which had come yesterday from Serbia, where she, her husband, and daughter lived. The envelope lay beside it. Creto shook his head at her married name in the corner, Dianne Jovanovic. What worry that name had brought them. Almost reluctantly, he reread the letter.

June 12, 1991

Dear Papa,

Stefan has changed so much. Sometimes, I feel he is
a stranger. Our Croatian heritage is never to be aired.
He works tirelessly to support Milosevic's efforts to
ignite the fervor of nationalism sweeping the country.

Stefan says it is for our good. He doesn't see that, in the end, it will destroy our daughter and me. Mimi is confused and daily grows more rebellious. She is eager to do anything her father says not to do.

I would send her to you, except Stefan insists it is politically unwise. I'm concerned, knowing you are there in the house alone. Perhaps you should leave and visit Josef in Austria until this foolishness of the Serbs dies down. I will write Josef and suggest it. No, I will call instead so you can be safe sooner. Papa, please go. There is trouble coming.

Any sensible person can see it. Since Milosevic ousted Stambolic and took the Serbian presidency from him, Milosevic has been like a madman with one purpose. Stambolic's wife is a dear friend of mine. She says her husband is crushed and disillusioned. He trusted Milosevic and, for twenty-five years, had carted him up the ladder behind him. The two men were best friends in law school.

Stambolic should never have sent Milosevic to handle Kosovo. The man realized the power he stood to gain and, on national TV, gave his outrageous speech to the Serbs, 'No One Should Dare to Beat You,' and set Yugoslavia on this slippery slope to war. The irony is that the Albanians never dared to beat the Serbs any more than the Croats. But to hear Serbian media, genocide of the Serbs rather than the Croats is widespread throughout Croatia.

I am especially concerned about the Serbs' uprisings
in Knin and throughout the Krajina where you are.
I'm frightened, Papa. The wheels are in motion for an
all-out war against Croatia.

Well, enough of war and politics. Besides these problems, we are fine, and Mimi's university grades are
good. I suppose it is a mother's job to fret. What else
would we do? Take care of yourself, Father mine.

Much love from your daughter,
Dianne

Creto dropped the letter with a shaky hand, knowing his daughter
was right. He gripped the table's edge at a loud pounding against the
door before his son opened it.

"Ivan, Ivan," Creto admonished, "why would you frighten an old
man into a heart attack?"

Ivan's scowl eased, and he grinned. "No, Father, it is not possible.
You'll outlive the rest of us."

Creto shook his head sadly. "Your sister has written. I fear we are
in for a spate of unrest." He handed him Dianne's letter.

Ivan grunted and skimmed it, a frown marring his handsome
face. "What did you expect? The noose has been tightening for days.
Tudman is a fool who cannot see what is right in front of him. He'll
get us all killed. Babic and Raskovic are deceiving him."

"Son, in my home, I will have respect for Croatia's president.
Tudman has been trying to instill a balance among the working class
and make the Croats equal with the Serbs."

"He doesn't understand the Serbs or try to reassure them when he
gives us their jobs," Ivan said. "Tudman's plan might have worked if
Milosevic and his followers weren't spreading their Serbian mythology

everywhere. But they are, and Tudman blindly refuses to see." He paced, more agitated than Creto had ever seen him. "Dianne is right. You should stay with Josef."

"No." Something deep inside Creto refused to budge. "This is my home. It was my father's home. Through every war, we've stayed. Vienna, the Germans, Tito. I'll go nowhere." His words were a battle cry.

"Just for a visit. Besides, you didn't stay. You went to war, and Mother hid us children, or we'd be dead. It's the truth. You can't deny it."

"Sometimes the truth has many levels. My spirit is at peace. If I must die, I would that it be near your mother. I want to be buried beside her in the churchyard. My place is here in Knin."

"Think," Ivan said. "Who will bury you with Mama if you are murdered? We should camouflage her tombstone so our enemies won't desecrate her grave. I've been to the meetings. I've heard things, horrible things, too terrible to share. Take Marie and the children out of the country. Feodor's wife and kids, too. We would be fools not to be prepared."

Creto couldn't refuse to take his grandchildren and their mothers to safety, but he would return. Then there would be another confrontation with his nearby sons, Ivan and Feodor. They would both feel pressured to care for him. Well, Creto would deal with them then. He looked up. "So be it, but for your sake."

Ivan's face relaxed into a smile. "Thank you. Should we call Josef now and arrange it?"

He nodded. "It will be good to see Josef and Anita. Maybe Lucien can come down from Vienna to visit." Creto hadn't seen his grandson for some time.

Ivan cleared his throat. "I know we disagreed with Josef on politics. Still, his business sense has never been lacking, and Lucien takes after him. I want Vasslei and Timothy to train with him."

Creto studied his son sharply. "Who will handle the factories in Vukovar and Ljubljana?"

Ivan avoided his gaze. "Feodor's eldest two can. It's time they had more responsibility."

Creto's heart beat faster. "Has something happened you're not telling me?"

"I swear, everything is fine. Take the family to relieve my worry. That's all I'm asking."

A portent of disaster whipped through Creto. The air was thick with fear. Ivan's gaze silently pleaded for him to ask no more. "All right, son, it shall be as you say."

Chapter 12

Bosnia-Herzegovina, Spring 1993

Vita scowled at her reflection in the mirror, despising herself for what she was about to do. Her heart had belonged to Kiro since she was eight when he found her after a gang of Serbian thieves had raped her and raped and killed her mother. With gentle hands, Kiro had washed the blood away, muttering curses on every Serb ever born. He'd rummaged through the cupboards and fed her, helped her dress, and packed her stuff.

Afterward, Vita sat on the back porch and watched while he dug her mother's grave and then recited a solemn prayer, swearing retaliation. When she had flung herself at him, sobbing, he'd picked her up and sat with her on his lap, rocking her until she quieted. That afternoon, she moved in with his family next door. Vita was eight years old, and Kiro, at twelve, was already the head of his household.

They lived as close as any brother and sister until, at seventeen, she'd found him with a strange woman. Shocked and hurt, Vita took in his flushed face.

"Get out, you brat!" he said, angry at her intrusion.

Vita tore her gaze from him. "I hate you! I never want to see you again, you—you!" She ran from his room and out the front door, fleeing across the pavement, neither knowing nor caring where her feet would lead her. Her side aching, she stopped in a mosque doorway and leaned into the stone wall, wanting to hide from the burning knowledge of what she'd seen.

Why did it hurt so much? She knew how girls got pregnant.

Tears ran down her cheeks, and sobs shook her. Could it be she was reminded of her mother's death? Her own rape? She could never let anyone touch her like that. Could she? Kiro being with other girls bothered her. He was all she had. They loved each other. When his mother yelled at her, he took her side. Since the day he cleaned her up and brought her home, he'd taken care of her, and she had obeyed him.

Vita wandered through the streets until late. When she crept into the house, feeling ashamed and confused, she learned with relief Kiro was out. Vita was already in bed when he barged into her room, half drunk, and accused her of being jealous. "What if I am?" she screamed. "At least I'm loyal. I would never do that with another . . ." She stopped speaking, becoming self-conscious.

His eyes held a knowing gleam.

She felt naked and bewildered. She set her face toward the wall. "Please, Kiro, I'm sleepy."

"Liar." The bed creaked under his weight, and he soon convinced her she was meant for him. But that was then.

She forced the memory aside and came back to the present.

Vita was working for Kiro and her people. The Serbian Major Cosic liked her in black, and she wanted the guns and power he gave her in return for pleasing him. Vita half-twisted, angling her head for a rear view of her flimsy polyester dress, the best she owned. She sprayed a mist of the cheap cologne he'd given her, frowned, and sprayed twice as much.

Vita pasted on a seductive smile. She would do whatever it took for rogue Muslim forces to win this war and to earn her and Kiro a chance for a future together. They were through begging for dinars to buy a loaf of bread.

Major Boris Cosic waited in the half-lit room for Vita. Their affair was temporary. These Roma were all alike. They'd knife you in a moment. Thieves, every one of them. They'd steal your clothes and money while rousing your passion to a point past bearing. Vita kept him at arm's length, playing him for every dinar and privilege she could get.

She'd started pumping him about military maneuvers, thinking he was too enamored with her to notice. He might sink to using women like her, but he'd never trust them. She was friends with the Winslow girl, and he suspected the stolen Madonna icon from the cathedral in Pazaric had inadvertently fallen into Katrina's hands.

He'd need Vita's help to retrieve it if he was right. Meanwhile, he was doing some digging on his own. He wanted a backup in case the affair became known and threatened his career. When word got out about his liaison with Vita, and it always did with these kinds of relationships, Cosic had the perfect cover-up in place.

From the start, he'd had her followed and had proved she was actively aiding rogue Muslim forces with illegal arms shipments. No one would believe he'd provided them and had a profitable side business, selling the weapons and stealing them back. General Jovanovic certainly didn't know. Ultimately, Cosic expected to be rewarded for protecting Serbian interests from Bosnian militant advancement, rogue or not. And the arms deal Cosic had helped the general pull off with the Russians should bring an even bigger prize.

Chapter 13

Belgrade, Serbia 1993

General Stefan Jovanovic read Cosic's letter and thrust it aside with a curse. In a situation where failure was unacceptable, Cosic had dared to write, "I have been unable to discover Bosnia's weapons depots but am investigating other leads."

Serbia couldn't plan a war on supposition. Its military needed concrete details of arms supplies and troop movements. They'd stationed Cosic in Bosnia to gather the intel. Stefan scowled at the letter again and dictated a scorching reply.

Afterward, he phoned home, but Dianne didn't answer. Stefan stared moodily at the large silver-framed photo of his stunning wife and daughter on his desk. They'd endured so much in the past year. He scraped his hand over his face as if to wipe away the turmoil. Every decision he'd made had been for his family. Yet each rise in his career laid another brick on the wall that had sprung up between them.

Stefan buried himself in paperwork the rest of the morning and then, with a start, realized he was running late. He walked from his office into the reception area where his secretary, Ennis Nikolic, sat. "I need those reports." He glanced at his gold wristwatch, a standard gift presented to Milosevic's generals. "Hurry, would you? It's an hour's drive from Belgrade to Nis."

"Almost done." Her green eyes were like the forest in the spring, and her auburn hair glinted like the autumn leaves in the afternoon sun, reminding him of his mother when she was younger. Ennis held the documents for his meeting in one hand and an envelope in the other. "Sir, about this brief from Russia—"

"Sorry, Ennis. It will have to wait." He took the papers and placed them inside his briefcase. "You're sure everything's here? The graphs for our strategic defense?"

"Yes, sir." Her gaze fluttered from his and strayed to the window. "It's a nice day for the trip."

"Would you like to come along for the drive?"

She gave him a speculative look. "Thank you, sir. I'd better get this work finished. Besides, Alex may come in."

Stefan nodded, snapped the case shut, and left. His mind was already on the strategy he would present that afternoon to protect Serbian arms from Bosnian rebels. His plan required a steady flow of intel on Bosnian activities. Tips from sources like Cosic were vital. In light of his failure, it was fortunate Stefan had other sources in his arsenal. Meanwhile, the enormous arms loan he had arranged from Russia should at the least bring him into Milosevic's cabinet.

He greeted his driver and climbed into the Mercedes with a sigh. On the journey, Stefan gazed at the wintry landscape, searching for some sign of a thaw. How had Serbia gotten to the place where his wife and daughter were the enemy? He considered his country's history as the kilometers sped past.

After World War II, with President Tito at the helm, Yugoslavia comprised the six republics of Serbia, Slovenia, Croatia, Bosnia-Herzegovina, Macedonia, and Montenegro, along with Kosovo and Vojvodina, two autonomous provinces in Serbia. Tito's death in 1980, followed by communism's collapse and the resurgence of nationalism throughout Eastern Europe in the late '80s and early '90s, affected all of them.

Yugoslavia's intense political and economic crisis had disturbed Stefan. He'd watched the central government weaken and militant nationalism strengthen, never imagining the changes would alienate his family. Slovenia and Croatia, his wife's homeland, supported outright independence for the republics, while Serbia, where Stefan's loyalty remained, wanted to increase its territory and power by absorbing them all.

At that time, Ivan Stambolic served as Serbia's prime minister. He became president in '86 and helped his friend Slobodan Milosevic become the Serbian Regional Communist Party president. Then, in April '87, Stambolic made the mistake of sending him to Kosovo to settle the ongoing dispute between its Albanian majority and Serb minority.

In Kosovo, Milosevic felt the energy of the masses and seized his chance, fanning the wave of Serb nationalism to enormous proportions to gain political power. Back in Belgrade, he purged Serbia's Communist Party and the media of his opponents. His party wing ousted Stambolic from the party presidency in December 1987. Not much of a return for Stambolic's twenty-five years of loyal friendship, Stefan reflected.

When it came to borders, Serbia possessed the memory of an elephant. Like every school child, Stefan had been taught of the reign that began with King Nemanja and reached its zenith under Emperor Dušan. Unfortunately, Serbia's powerful reign had faltered in 1389 when the Turks defeated Serbia, forcing them to surrender Kosovo and parts of Croatia and Bosnia, ending nearly a century of Balkan power. Stefan wasn't interested in restoring ancient boundaries, but Milosevic was obsessed with the idea.

Thus, on the 600th anniversary of Serbia's ancient defeat, Milosevic addressed 1,000,000 Serbs at the Kosovo Polje battlefield in June '89. In the ultimate coup, he authored the first television-generated war and had it broadcast live by local and Belgrade TV to all the republics.

He'd bused in about 300,000 Serbs to Kosovo. A truckload

of stones was parked nearby. In a staged attack, Serbs dressed as Albanians threw stones at Kosovo's minority Serbs. The fake assault happened during Milosevic's speech on national TV, "No one should dare to beat you." He spoke those exact words in his speech when it looked as if the Serbs were being beaten. His deception prompted the revoking of Kosovo's autonomy and spurred Serbian national pride, rousing Serbia's chiefly Eastern Orthodox to fight Croatian Catholics and Bosnian and Kosovar Muslims.

Milosevic rode the wave of Serb nationalism to the presidency on December 9, 1990, in Serbia's first multi-party election since WWII.

Then, in March of '91, he declared:

> We must secure unity in Serbia if we wish, as the larg-
> est and most populous republic, to dictate the further
> course of events. These are the questions of borders,
> essential state questions. The borders, as you know, are
> always dictated by the strong, never by weak ones. If
> we must fight, then my God, we will fight, and I hope
> they will not be so crazy as to fight against us. Because
> if we don't know how to work well or to do business,
> at least we know how to fight well.

Thundering applause had greeted the president's speech. But Stefan was troubled. His wife was Croatian, and a war with Croatia, where her family lived, would be disastrous.

Soon after, Milosevic met with his generals on the battlefield of Kosovo Polje, where the long-ago Serbian defeat had occurred. Drinking heavily, Stefan and the other generals pored over maps detailing Serbia's ancient boundaries, which Milosevic meant to restore. That night, they laid their battle plans to claim most of the former Yugoslavia and Kosovo.

The following day, Stefan awakened with a hangover. His heart constricted over his role in Serbia's war plans and the hurt his wife and daughter would have to endure.

Stefan continued to wrestle with his conscience as Milosevic stoked the fires of propaganda and orchestrated demonstrations and military interventions, pressuring allies and enemies alike to engage in battle.

Despite Stefan's concern for his family, he was forced to endorse nationalist rhetoric and policies that eroded Yugoslavia's shared identity and fueled fear and mistrust among the various ethnic groups. His apprehension mounted as the republics and provinces, once united under Tito, now fought for independence, resisting Serbia's massive quest for power and territory. By '91, the federation's breakup loomed, with Slovenia and Croatia blaming Serbia for unjustly dominating Yugoslavia's government, military, and finances. Serbia accused the two republics of separatism.

In June of '91, Slovenia and Croatia declared independence. Croatia's minority Serb population, backed by the Yugoslav People's Army (JNA) and Serbian Army, instigated a campaign of ethnic cleansing against the Croatians. Stefan's indignant wife and daughter clung furiously to their Croatian heritage while Stefan walked a tightrope between their wishes and the president's orders to destroy Croatia.

Bosnia declared its independence in the spring of '92. Its Serbian population, also supported by the JNA and Serbian Army, waged an ongoing deadly war against Bosnian Muslims and Croatians. Stefan's wife blamed him for not intervening and speaking up for her people. But to have done so, he would have signed his family's death warrant.

Tyranny wasn't new to the Balkans. President Tito had been an authoritarian communist dictator. During the first fifteen years of his rule, between 1945 and 1960, mass shootings, death marches, and concentration camps claimed almost a quarter of a million Yugoslav lives. Tito's secret police had terrorized those who refused to align with his brand of communism.

Was it so different in present-day 1993? Wasn't Stefan forced to accept President Slobodan Milosevic's sham of restoring ancient boundaries? From the beginning, Stefan had acted to secure his family's future. They saw him as a selfish bigot. His wife didn't have to say she was ashamed of him. Stefan could read it in her eyes, register the strain when she spoke. They had taken to avoiding one another. Hence this awkward attraction to his secretary.

Last week, he'd bailed his daughter, a university senior, out of jail for distributing anti-Milosevic tracts. He'd also bribed the magistrate, but one could never be too sure who could be trusted. Despite Stefan's wife's and daughter's opposition, he couldn't disregard the president's plans without enormous cost to himself and his family.

Meanwhile, Stefan was determined to edge into the president's inner circle. Unfortunately, Stefan had been on holiday with his family in June of '91 when Serbian television falsely reported Croatia's killing of Serbs who lived there. Serbian national pride blazed as expected, yielding the excuse to invade Croatia. The opposite was true. Serbia was intent on Croatia's genocide. Again, Milosevic had carefully set the stage, dividing the former Yugoslavia into rival ethnic groups, while he moved to seize control. War was declared.

In northern Bosnia in early '92, Serb leaders alarmed that Yugoslavia's breakup might leave them a minority, fought to unite the territories where they lived. This meant pushing out or eliminating Muslims and Croats. The Serbs, under the SDS (Serb Democratic Party), began creating parallel governing structures. The Serb Army and local paramilitaries surrounded cities and set up checkpoints. In each town, the SDS established a crisis staff of local party leaders, army commanders, and police officials.

In January '92, Milan Kovačević founded the SDS in Prijedor, establishing a shadow city government, police force, and security unit. Kovačević was vice president of the Prijedor Crisis Staff, which staged a coup in April, replacing the Muslim-led elected government. Serbs herded Muslims and Croats into Keraterm and Omarska concentration camps a few miles away, where guards often brutally beat and tortured inmates to death.

That summer, Stefan had sensed a presence of evil as he stood at attention, for the first time seeing and hearing Milan Kovačević address the top military.

Kovačević's glance feverishly swept the crowd.

> Comrades, today I call upon every Serb to create a
> homogeneous Serbia, one which encompasses every
> region where Serbians live. It is our duty to organize
> and do everything possible to ensure strategic lines
> remain open and in Serbian control. Only then can
> we guarantee a free economic, political, and cultural
> life for Serbia forever.

Fists in the air, the crowd roared with applause, shouting the Serbian word for people. "Narods, narods, narods!" Thus, the war of the people began, otherwise known to the military elite as the war of maps.

Remorse filled Stefan at the death trap they'd created. One-third of Croatia had already been burned and destroyed, and now Bosnia faced the same fate. For weeks, he couldn't meet his wife's accusing eyes. When would she accept that her ties to Croatia belonged in the past?

His mind slammed to the present as his car halted before the white high-rise hotel adjoining Nis's most prominent recreational resort. He both dreaded and anticipated these councils. He drew a deep breath before stepping from the car. Stefan doubted his ability to oppose the violent storm of destiny thundering through his life. For now, Milosevic had to be faced in the upcoming meeting.

Chapter 14

Ennis stood by her office window and watched the general leave before wearily returning to the pile of letters and receipts demanding her attention. She hadn't slept well last night. The baby's teething had kept her awake for hours. At least, Ennis hoped that's all it was.

"Hi, beautiful."

She whirled to see her husband standing there, so cocky and handsome her breath caught. "When did you get in?"

With no apparent thought about who might be there, Alex pulled her against him. "A while ago, Mrs. Nikolic."

"You shouldn't." Ennis squirmed under the pressure of his lips.

He nuzzled her neck. "Mmm. I love you." He kissed her again, lingering over the act. "Did you miss me?"

"You know I did. Sometimes, I wish you weren't a pilot. Then there wouldn't be a need to take these trips."

He cupped her face. "Listen, love. It's safer flying the brass to meetings than beating the bushes with a machine gun."

She hugged him. "I'm scared when I think about what the baby and I would do if we lost you."

"Keep that in mind." His hands molded her to him and he leered comically. "I like my woman crazy about me."

That evening at home, half-listening to the radio, Ennis stared at Alex across the small, crowded living room. She'd been wild about him since the moment they met. Yet their daily reality was so different now. Ennis couldn't shake the sense that the war was wrong and was destroying the Yugoslavia she'd loved.

As always, it had begun with the Albanian population of the Kosovo region. Tito had granted Kosovo autonomy, relinquishing to the Albanians the region Serbian nationalists held sacred and believed they'd rightfully won in World War II. One of Milosevic's first acts to gain Serbian support had been to retract Kosovo's autonomy. The Serbians believed he'd corrected a wrong, which Tito, who was half-Croatian and half-Serbian, had failed to grasp. But with Tito dead, Milosevic fought to win control and enlarge Serbia's borders.

Then, in '91, he bombed Slovenia and Croatia, and then later Bosnia as the republics struggled for independence. Serbian news reported the Slovenians, Croatians, and Bosnians had attacked Serbia first by targeting Serbs in those territories. Ennis suspected it was all a lie. It wouldn't be Milosevic's first. He controlled the television and news media.

Her right hand worried at a frayed cigarette burn hole on the edge of the sofa cushion where she sat. "Alex, do you think what we're doing is right? I mean this war."

He peered up from playing with the baby on the floor, and his understanding expression changed to hardness. "It's better not to think about morality and ethics."

"Our country is being ravaged."

"Ennis, the Croats were committing genocide. No one's safe. We've got to believe Serbia's right." Alex sounded angry. "What good does it do to discuss scruples?"

Pressure within Ennis drove her to voice her fear of their world being out of control with a madman at the helm. "I wish there were some way we could stop this war and rewind time."

"Well, there's not," Alex said. "You've got to accept that it is kill or be killed."

Ennis knelt, hugging him. She sat beside him. "I'm sorry. I get so frightened sometimes." She could feel Alex's pulse beating as his lips sought hers. Anxiety flared into passion.

"Put the baby to bed," he said, his voice ragged. "You're the single good thing that's happened to me, ever."

Ennis rose shakily to her feet and carried the baby, already half asleep, to the oversized crib in the room's corner while Alex pulled down the Murphy bed set into the opposite wall. She went to him and forgot the war and hate surrounding them.

Afterward, he held her close, and as they talked, he confided, "Something's cooking up north. The Muslims are getting arms from the Iranians."

"Don't." She placed a finger to his lips. "Don't ruin tonight."

"Honey, you started this talk earlier, and you're right. We have to face the truth. The war is going to get a lot worse. I want you and our son out of here, somewhere secure."

A stone, broken and cold, lodged within, almost choking her. "Is there such a place?"

"Austria or America."

She gave a small cry. "Not without you." Suddenly, her world caved in. Sobs shook her.

Alex stroked her hair. "I hate when you cry, Ennis. Okay, we'll wait. Don't be upset." He lifted her chin, and she gave him a watery smile, trying to blink away the tears and pretend everything was okay.

Chapter 15

Bosnia-Herzegovina, Summer 1993

They came upon the clapboard house in the late afternoon. John could almost imagine himself in New England but for the muddy roads and sparse facilities. He shifted Tito, the three-year-old Muslim orphan he held, and met Ellen's wistful gaze. "We don't know who's in there."

"Maybe it's empty." Her innate optimism rushed to the forefront, and she moved toward the house.

"Maybe." He reached out to stop her. Shadows lay beneath her eyes, and her once full cheeks were hollow. John hoped they'd find food in the house. He ignored the inner burning ache of loss, his arms tightening around Tito. Were their daughters, Rachel, Andi, and Shelly, okay? Were they alive? Had he come to save others only to lose his family?

Lord, let this be a place for Ellen and Tito to recuperate. Please have mercy on our girls. He swallowed past the enormous lump in his throat.

John wanted to fall on his knees in the mud and plead with God to deliver them from this nightmare. Instead, he transferred the boy to his wife's arms. "Wait for me on the field. Keep low while I check out the area. I won't be long."

Ellen's excitement appeared to have fled, fear taking over as she realized the house could be a trap. "Be careful."

He hugged her and then hurried down the path to the rear of the dwelling. Even this close, it appeared deserted. He glanced back to see if Ellen and Tito were hidden. Careless of them to have stood there gawking at the place. John blamed their recklessness on hunger and weariness.

He crept near enough to peer through the windows. The kitchen looked as if the inhabitants had disappeared while preparing dinner. The dust-laden table was set with thick ceramic plates, bowls, and cheap stainless-steel cutlery. A sprinkling of flour overlaid the dried mud on the floor.

John crossed to rattle the door. It swung open with a creak. On the worn counters, a mound of dough sat shriveled and hard. Gnats swarmed around the rancid pot of cabbage soup on the stove. A scrutiny of the rooms revealed no hint of occupancy.

He shut his mind to what might have driven the former inhabitants to abandon the house in such haste. A broken porcelain doll and an upside-down wagon in the room meant there had been children. He stared at the blue-wooden wagon with the ghost of a smile, remembering their girls' first shiny red wagon. They'd clambered inside and entreated, "Please, Daddy," confident he'd pull them around the yard while they giggled and held on, squealing in glee.

He went outside to get Ellen and young Tito. When they entered the house, Ellen saw the broken doll and bent low, scooping it up. "Oh, John." Her words held a wealth of meaning and a heartfelt cry. She clasped the doll close as if, in doing so, she could somehow gather their girls in her arms. Then she set the doll down and went to him, showing him he could count on her to be strong.

"We'll find them," she said, bending to lift Tito into the wagon. She ruffled his hair before turning to John. "They're alive." She bit her lower lip and touched her heart. "Or I'd know, and so would you."

Then she smiled, and he felt as if the sun had come out, wrapping him in a sensation of rightness, thrusting aside the doubts. He loved her. Her smile imbued him with the strength that left him ready to believe in and tackle anything.

He grasped her fingers and squeezed. "I sense it, too."

As if to confirm their burst of faith, a shaft of sunlight filtered through the front window as the clouds receded. Tito grinned, raised his hands in play, and let them fall against the wagon. "Dada." He reached out with his arms to John.

John lifted him and cuddled his wiggly little body, wondering if Dada was one of those words that were the same in every language. So innocent and happy, the child radiated a naïve faith in humanity and them. Over Tito's head, John's gaze met his wife's, and they wordlessly renewed their pact to find their daughters.

John's strength and courage inspired Ellen to believe in good. He strove to put on a brave front for her sake, but she doubted whether he realized how much of an actress she'd become. She sat on the floor by Tito. Escaping with a toddler hadn't been easy, but Ellen felt as if a part of her would have died if they'd lost Tito, too.

Her girls. She could picture Rachel, lost in a book, masses of wavy chestnut hair haphazardly pulled back with a clip; Shelly, in the kitchen helping with the cooking, pausing to bandage a child's hurt knee; and Andi, her intrepid, talented youngest, playing the piano, her green eyes alive with curiosity.

Ellen tried to hold on to the images, but her psyche jetted back to when she'd lost her daughters. There wasn't a word or nuance about that day she'd forgotten.

Bullets had ripped across the cave, striking children as they fled. "God, please no. They're babies." Ellen shielded those closest to her while searching for John and the girls.

From behind, John pulled her to him, his eyes filled with anguish. "I've looked everywhere. Our girls aren't here. We've got to escape with the children in our care."

"No." The word was a wrenching cry. "What about those injured?"

"We can't reach them without risking these kids' lives."

"John, we can't leave without our daughters."

"Ellen." He shook her. "They may be out there searching for us. We have no choice. We've got to escape now," he repeated.

She realized he was right and followed him, helping as he herded the children from the cave through a hidden exit, and they continued into the mountains. After seeing them safely away, John hugged her close. "You'll be okay," he said. "Keep them quiet and pray I can find the others before it's too late."

She clung to him for a moment, unable to let go. "Our girls are out there somewhere, needing us now more than ever." Finally, she pushed him from her. "Don't worry about me. I can manage here with the children. Find our daughters."

Though John hadn't found them then, they never stopped searching. Mercifully, they'd been able to place the orphans in trucks with UN workers headed to the West, except for Tito, who'd been too young to travel without a relative to care for him. Ellen rebelled at the thought she might never see her girls again. She pushed the idea aside.

"I'll go clean a room for us to sleep in tonight." John took Tito and walked toward the bedrooms.

Ellen went to check on what they could do about dinner. The kitchen was a mess and smelled rank. She grabbed the pot of rotten soup, marched some distance from the house, and dumped the brew. After an hour of scrubbing the room, some order prevailed.

She found a sack of flour, salt, and potatoes in a bottom drawer and several onions in the cupboard. Ellen washed and peeled the vegetables, then boiled them in an aluminum pot on top of the older model butane stove. She hummed, savoring being in the kitchen, preparing a meal as if it were an ordinary affair. She reflected on the things she once took for granted. If they were all together, none of the rest would matter.

She mixed the flour, salt, and water into a tortilla-type dough and decided to cook extra, stirring in more ingredients before shaping the dough into small rounds. Anything could happen between now and tomorrow. She flattened the circles with her palm, setting the rounds one by one to bake on the hot iron skillet on the stovetop.

Soon, dinner was ready, and she called John and Tito to the table. John surveyed the cleaned kitchen, the table laden with the first hot food they'd had in days, and hugged her. "I don't deserve you."

She laughed and sat in a wobbly wooden chair, holding her arms out for Tito. "Quit your foolishness. I'm starving."

John settled Tito into the chair between them. After saying grace, they forced themselves to eat slowly, conversing normally. Such rare occasions ensured their survival and sanity. After eating, they sat at the table, savoring the moments like misers, afraid their time would run out.

When soldiers flung open the kitchen door, it seemed like the planets were conspiring against her family. John jumped to his feet. Ellen pulled Tito into her arms and drew back in fright. "Please, we're Americans," she said. "We have nothing to do with this war. Can't you leave us alone?"

John tried to reach her as Tito was torn from her, but the gun barrel leveled at her husband's upper body stopped him.

He strained toward her, but the soldiers held him. "Ellen, are you okay?"

She nodded, struggling to compose herself. The men shoved her outside before she could grasp what was happening. Rifles urged John and her into the back of a waiting military van filled with more soldiers. At the last moment, a man shoved Tito into her willing arms. Doors slammed, and the engine revved as the vehicle moved forward. She huddled next to John. "Who are they?"

"Renegade soldiers?" he murmured.

What did that mean for them—help because she and John were innocent or hatred because they were considered American capitalists? She shivered, in no hurry to learn the answer.

Chapter 16

Distant machine gun fire woke Katrina. Lucien's calloused palm covered her mouth. "Shh," he said. "This is your chance to escape."

Dazed and half asleep, she tried to pull away and, when she couldn't, instinctively bit his hand.

"Ouch." He clutched his palm. "I ought to leave you here to fend for yourself." Lucien grabbed for her, and she ducked. "I could throttle you," he said, pinning her down with his arms. "I've had about all I can take. Listen. The enemy patrols are getting closer."

The battle was growing louder. Her mind raced at the roar of the approaching planes, probably supporting Serbian ground troops. Croatian and Bosnian forces could not compete with Serbian air power.

"Katrina, I can't protect you here any longer. Run for it. No one will notice until after the skirmish."

The realization that he sought to save her washed over Katrina. She wanted to see his expression but couldn't do so in the dark. "Why would you help me?"

"Because I've never hurt a woman. Katrina, trust me. What choice do you have? It's me, the enemy, or my men." He gave her a pistol and her knapsack. Katrina secured the knapsack on her back and concealed the weapon in her jacket. She didn't like guns, but she was grateful her father had taught her how to use one.

Katrina tugged on her shoes and the extra pair of socks Lucien provided.

"There is a deer trail due north in the forest." He pressed a compass into her hand. "Follow it until you reach the creek. Wait for me there."

"What are you going to do?"

"I'll fight beside my men. Afterward, they'll return to the base." Lucien lifted the back side of the tent and helped her crawl out. "Run."

Terrified, she sprinted through the woods, a sliver of moon lighting the path. Gunfire cracked all around her. Panting, she reached the creek and hid in the cluster of dense shrubbery along its bank, her dark clothes blending into the night.

The opportunity to escape she'd yearned for had arrived. Yet leaving Lucien behind seemed dangerously foolish. With enemy troops in pursuit, she wouldn't go far alone. How ironic her sole protector was the man Vita claimed had killed her family. Like it or not, she needed his help. Her resentment flared, and for the second time since her parents' deaths, her conscience was ill at ease with its weight.

What if she was wrong about Lucien's duplicity? Was Vita's word that he'd betrayed them enough? Her dislike of the Serbs and Croats was well known. Unsure what to believe, Katrina prayed Lucien would survive the attack. He and his men had rifles and pistols but needed missile launchers to shoot down planes. If enemy jets overhead spotted them, his men stood scant chance of survival.

She waited for some time and was about to give up and head out alone when she heard Lucien call in a low voice, "Katrina, come."

Relieved, she followed him through the woods, wary because of what Vita had said he'd done. The hours stretched unrelentingly before her until dawn etched a gray-yellow shroud across the horizon.

It seemed as if she had been running and hiding forever. Would it never cease? She fell, exhausted, fearing Lucien wouldn't stop to help her. He'd grown more remote with every kilometer that separated him from his men.

Lucien drew her to her feet and handed her his canteen. "Drink this."

She took a sip, wishing it were warm.

He retrieved the canteen. "We've got to keep moving."

"Your men . . . are they okay?"

"What do you care? More than half of them are dead." He forged ahead, leaving her to follow.

She hadn't asked him to take her prisoner. He claimed it was to protect her. Katrina longed to think Lucien was the generous, witty man she'd first glimpsed beneath the war-weary soldier's uniform. She wanted to believe Vita was wrong about him. Still, Katrina's suspicions persisted.

Her step faltered, and she slid to the ground. When Lucien returned to check on her, she said, "I can get to the children from here. You go on."

Lucien dropped beside her. "You're a liability to them. You don't belong here."

She raised her gaze to meet his. "My family's blood is in this ground. Can you say the same?"

He shook his head, as if refusing to be drawn by her words. "You're grieving, Katrina. Normally, you'd have the time to mourn those you've lost, but we're engaged in a bloody war." He grasped her hand. "It will take every ounce of ingenuity to get you out of the war zone." His grip tightened. "Be reasonable. If I could secure your passage to Italy, it would be better for everyone."

She dragged her hand from his. "You mean better for you?"

"You'd be safe."

Didn't he realize she'd never feel safe again, that the memories and nightmares kept her awake nights? Besides, she'd promised her dying mother. "No. I can't—the children. You don't understand. They're my responsibility."

"You're an American outcast here."

"My parents—"

"Your parents are gone. Most of the orphans they cared for are, too." His voice gentled, "I'll arrange for a boat to ferry you across to Italy. Tell me where the children are. I'll see they're taken care of."

She shook her head.

Lucien said, his face drawn and sad, "I can't help if you won't trust me. I had nothing to do with your parents' deaths."

"Murders. They were murdered, and Vita can prove—"

"Nothing," he interrupted. "You're blind to your real enemies. Vita is sleeping with a Serbian major. How do you think she came by the supplies she gave you?"

"I don't believe you." Still, doubt took root as she recalled her friend's avowed hatred of everything but her people. Had Katrina misjudged Lucien? Sick with fear and confusion, her thoughts flew to the children. She had to get back to them. The truth could wait until later. Her heart wanted to believe him.

Chapter 17

Bosnia-Herzegovina, Summer 1993

Katrina and Lucien marched toward Konjic, the nearest town. Refugees trudged alongside them in search of safety anywhere they could find it. Sunshine warmed the breeze and brightened the tree-lined road. Birds chirped, their songs buoying Katrina's spirit. She smiled at Lucien. For the first time since he had left his men, he'd agreed to risk entering a city for food, a bath, and a bed to sleep in that night.

A traveler called out the Yugoslav greeting for good morning. "*Dobro juto.* Have you heard the news?" another said. "They destroyed Stari Most, the old bridge in Mostar."

Katrina and Lucien exchanged stricken glances. She'd been in Mostar escaping Serbian soldiers when the bridge exploded, and afterward, Lucien and his men had captured her.

Lucien sighed. "News travels slow these days."

A young man beside him said, "Most of these people are refugees fleeing enemy troops. They've been on the road for some time and have heard little news."

"Where will they go?" Lucian asked.

The young man shrugged and turned onto a side road.

They caught up to an older couple and walked alongside them. The man stumbled and bumped into Lucien. "Are you all right?" Lucien asked, reaching out to steady him.

The man nodded, his faded black eyes awash with feeling.

"Fifty-three years ago, my wife and I walked across that bridge on our honeymoon, and now my granddaughter will never see it."

His wife's jaw trembled. "In the good days," she said, "before there was war and hatred and killing, we would vacation in Mostar. Our two sons would stand on Stari Most with the other boys and leap into the Neretva to show their fearlessness." Tears fell down her cheeks. "It is more than a bridge that's gone. It's our heritage, our future, vanished in a puff of smoke." She wiped her eyes with a grubby handkerchief. "Only savages could destroy such beauty."

Lucien touched the woman's shoulder in understanding, his gaze sympathetic. "As a boy, I also jumped from Stari Most. There was nothing like it to make me feel I was part boy and part man."

As they continued into the town, all the talk was of Stari Most, the marble bridge that legend claimed was held together by egg whites and horsehair, erected in 1526 by the ruling Turkish sultan. People spoke as if Stari Most were almost human, capable of wrapping the hearts of those who had passed over it inside its exquisite marble anatomy. It was as if the bridge, an inanimate object, had held the essence of Bosnia's culture and art and borne the people's burdens and joys, unmindful of nationality or creed. Now Stari Most was no more.

Katrina sighed. She and her family had often walked across it to enter the Muslim sector of the city. In her mind, she saw Mostar as it was before the war. The stone houses washed white in the old town, the sun sparkling off terra-cotta rooftops, her father making calls in the city, her mother waving from their doorway.

In the summer, she and Giles would swim across the sea-green waters of the Neretva River. They'd float on their backs and stare up at the elongated stone arch . . . and then Katrina's memories rushed forward to the moment when she saw it exploding, heaving debris like an erupting volcano as the river engulfed it. No longer uniting two sides of an ancient city, it was gone. The bridge. Her family. The children.

Inside Konjic, she yearned to join those lamenting the bridge's destruction. People wept, who had faced ethnic cleansing, rape, concentration camps, and piles of countrymen buried in mass graves. Katrina's heart ached that Stari Most was no more.

She struggled with her pain and Bosnia's. "Is the death of a bridge more important than those who died defending it or the massive daily loss of human life?"

For once, Lucien didn't snap at her. Instead, he gave her a wary look, but answered patiently. "We all assume people will die from sickness or accidents or any number of causes. Stari Most was a tribute to a civilization's enlightenment. People wanted to believe the bridge was ageless and would prevail no matter what."

Moved by his words, she almost forgot her animosity. They were two hurting individuals, part of a whole that made up the sorrowful heartbeat of the former Yugoslavia. They mourned the lost future of a nation, its people, and its symbols, which had become as transient as the masses of humanity who gorged its highways. Katrina's joy at entering the city faded.

They booked into a hotel, and she enjoyed the luxury of a bath. The warm water washed over her, rejuvenating her spirit. She would never take a hot bath again without giving thanks for the privilege.

Invariably, as her mind wandered, it stopped at Lucien, both nemesis and protector. Better not to dwell on the incongruity but to think of the children. She must return to them, which meant separating from Lucien.

Her decision reached, Katrina slept deeply that night.

Chapter 18

At dawn, Katrina gathered her knapsack and crept from the hotel. She had enough money from her hidden stash to buy a train ticket to Mostar, about forty-five minutes away. Inside the crowded station, the dirt and stench gagged her. Babushkas and gaunt older men leaned against the walls, staying out of the militia's path. Several soldiers had cornered three young women who shrank from the men's rough advances.

"Please, let me go," the youngest girl said. The soldier smacked her and tore at her blouse, pushing her into a dark corner.

Nauseated and shamed, Katrina hurried past. Any interference by her might worsen their plight.

She boarded the almost empty train, relieved when it heaved out of the station. The war had driven many people north. A survival instinct almost compelled her to turn around and rejoin Lucien. If her mother were alive, they would have cared for the children together and confronted the enemy as a family. Winslows always kept their word unless it became impossible, like when her dad had died. Before his death, he'd promised to return to Houston that summer for a rest. Grief choked her.

She conceded her father had his reasons and accepted that her parents had willingly given their lives for a cause they believed in. Could their daughter do any less? Katrina wasn't sure.

The train arrived in Mostar. She left the station with her head bent low to avoid recognition. Katrina headed to where she'd last seen the children. *Lord, help me find them and bring them to safety.* In her mind, a plan had been forming for days. She and her little band would escape to the West. Her aunt and uncle would gladly purchase plane tickets to fly them home.

She peered at the darkening sky, worried a storm was coming. Katrina walked from the city to the surrounding hillside. What if soldiers stopped her and demanded to see her papers? Vulnerable, she climbed upward past grimy armed men who hopefully took her for a native. One slip could end her life.

The six-mile hike was charged with tension. Midway, her anxiety eased at seeing no militia ahead. She pressed on, reaching a valley, and her breath caught at the beauty of a cluster of pink and lacey-white wildflowers.

The sky blackened as a storm blew in, the wind and rain beating against the flowers. Matted and torn, the struggling blossoms flattened into the mud. Katrina saw herself in those wildflowers, matted with resentment and torn by adversity.

She heard the cry of a raven as it swooped down, dropping a crust of bread on the ground before opening its wings and flying south. God's care for her warmed Katrina. Hungry, she reached for the bread and bit into the crust.

As she did so, she envisioned a whirlwind soughing and swirling, enveloping her. The words from Isaiah 43:2 embraced her. "When you pass through the waters, I will be with you; and when you pass through the rivers, they will not sweep over you. When you walk through the fire, you will not be burned; the flames will not set you ablaze." Reassured by God's promise, she stood as if in a revealing mist on the edge of a precipice and surrendered her anger and resentment.

Hatred had led her to despair. The bitter burden of guilt she'd been shouldering lifted. Freed from the weight, Katrina sank to her knees in gratitude. God's love brought true happiness.

Still on a spiritual high and feeling invincible, Katrina hiked on until she came to a cave surrounded by soldiers. She drew back with a gasp.

They'd spotted her. Too late to run. The press of machine guns held her immobile. A soldier pinned Katrina against a large boulder. Another tore off her head covering and threw it down. The first man struck her cheek and tugged at her blonde locks. "You are no peasant. You are an impostor."

She spoke in Slovene, thinking it was her best chance of fooling them. Her voice quivered, and the words tumbled out badly.

He released his hold on her, grabbed her pack, and dug through it until he found her passport.

She ran, but the man caught her. The other opened her passport and then spat on the ground. "She's the American spy."

Half-dazed, Katrina heard the soldiers muttering as if from a distance. She should have buried her passport in a secure place, but had feared she might not be able to retrieve it.

The tinkling sound of a woman's laughter caused her to lift her gaze to the cave entrance. Vita strolled out, arm in arm, with one of the Muslim rebels. He rattled off several questions, leading Katrina to conclude he was in charge.

She took in the scene with immense relief, then broke loose and ran to them. "Thank God, Vita. Tell them this is a mistake."

Vita ignored Katrina and congratulated the men. "Good work. You've caught the American spy. Take her away. No. Wait." She peered at the man at her side. "What do you think, Kiro? Is it better to kill her now?"

Katrina fell back a step. Her thoughts spun in shocked disbelief, struggling to understand how she'd been so misled. Self-recrimination poured over her. The insidious idea crept in that she deserved to suffer for mistreating Lucien. Why had she failed to trust him?

Vita and the men spoke in muted tones, determining her fate.

Her naïve belief in Vita sickened her. Katrina regretted her harshness toward Lucien, to whom it appeared she'd owed her life.

"Why? What did we ever do to you? You killed my parents, didn't you?" she asked, wanting to hear it wasn't true.

Vita's eyes glittered with scorn. "Grow up. People die in wars. Your family members were enemies of the Muslim faith, teaching our children heresy. The Winslows were spies, working with the Croats and Serbs to undermine us. Can you deny your parents' mission wanted our people to forsake their Muslim faith?"

How clever Vita was, twisting everything to suit her.

As if she could read Katrina's thoughts, Vita said, "Hate me, and know what it is to hate as we do, to see blood spilled and children die."

Katrina didn't hate her. Yesterday, she might have, but today, her grief mingled with a stabbing pain that she'd been so wrong. She had trusted Vita and brought her home to her family. "What I feel for you is pity. Not purely for you, but the whole of Yugoslavia, consumed with its perpetuating hate." At Vita's angry glance, Katrina asked, "What has become of the children? Where are they?"

Vita's expression hardened. She slapped Katrina. "Filthy American pig! You have no right to question me. A girl who grew up with everything and crossed an ocean to tell us what to do and how to live and worship. I warned you to leave, but you refused."

"Did you warn my parents, too?"

"Shut up!" She gestured to the soldiers to take Katrina.

Katrina dodged the men and ran past Vita into the cave to see if the children were inside and if they were alive. Footsteps hammered behind her. She rushed into a room, colliding with stacks of long wooden crates, then losing her balance, toppled across them.

Seconds later, the soldiers grabbed her and pushed her from the room, but not before she glimpsed the opened crates of machine guns and recognized the Iranian markings on the cases. The soldiers dragged her outside.

She confronted Vita. "You were using us all along, weren't you?"

Vita sneered. "How wise you've grown. Maybe when we

next meet, you'll learn what has become of those sniveling brats. Meanwhile, I want you to picture your loved ones' deaths, and when you do, remember who is in control." She signaled again for the men to remove the prisoner.

Katrina shuddered and lowered her head. The soldiers led her down the mountain into the city. Who could she turn to? Not even Lucien could help her now. And she had no one to blame but herself. She thought of the children and how she'd let them down. Another Winslow and another broken promise.

Chapter 19

Several days had passed since Lucien stormed into Mostar, pursuing a delinquent Katrina, worried she might have been captured. He searched the town without a glimpse of her and finally conceded defeat. He couldn't continue to ignore his orders.

Lucien reported to the temporary base he and his men had helped build into the side of the mountain. Wary of his reception, he opened the rough-cut office door and stepped inside.

To his surprise, the commander leaned across the makeshift desk and shook Lucien's hand in a genial greeting. "We feared the Serbs had killed you. Your men have been at each other's throats, blaming themselves for your death." He paused. "Somehow, they got the idea they're responsible for their captain in battle."

Lucien shifted under his superior's piercing gaze, bracing himself for the severe reprimand sure to follow.

With a grunt of exasperation, the older man pushed a hand through his coarse, graying hair. "I realize your circumstances are unusual, but desertion is the same in every army. There's no special dispensation for Westerners."

Lucien's jaw set. "How long have you known?"

"Zagreb sent your papers when they posted you here. Besides, it was obvious the West had tainted you."

Lucien supposed it was bound to come out at some point. "Does anyone else know?"

"That you're an executive in a successful Western firm? Hardly. I burned the papers after I read them."

Relief swept through Lucien. If knowledge of his background got around, his life wouldn't be worth much except for ransom. "Thank you, sir."

The commander handed Lucien his mail and surveyed him curiously, a grudging respect in his craggy face. "What made you risk everything to fight here?"

He bit back the word guilt. "I'm half-Croatian. My relatives were dying. What else could I do?"

"Wage a publicity campaign in our favor. You have connections and wealth. It would do Croatia a lot more good than you marching about, waving guns you've no taste for using." He settled deeper into the chair behind his desk as if allowing Lucien time to reconsider his involvement in the war.

The idea wasn't new to Lucien. His doubts, however, were more recent. He deplored Croatia's war against Bosnia's Muslims. Croats and Muslims were fighting each other when they should unite and defeat the Serbs.

Lucien admired the efforts of the UN peacekeeping troops, however short they may have fallen. Though he served in the Croatian Army, Lucien recalled his satisfaction when he'd saved a young boy from enemy fire or returned a grubby toddler to his distraught mother following an attack on their village. Once, he'd wrapped a little girl's wound, saving her leg.

Lucien never minded sharing his army rations with the starving older men, women, and children he encountered. He and his men frequently guarded Red Cross food and medical shipments through dangerous terrain. Yet, too often, the supplies never reached those for whom they were intended.

As a volunteer captain in the Croatian Army, he'd seen the same poisonous hate and malice on every side. Lucien considered the truth that he'd buried beneath torn loyalties. His army service was of nominal value. He met the commander's steady gaze. "I'm willing to do whatever I can to help bring peace to Croatia."

A discussion of viable options ensued, which ended with Lucien securing a week's leave to ponder the matter.

When he rose to depart, his superior motioned him to stay seated. "Do I have to drag it out of you? Or will you fill me in on the woman you arrested whom the men have been arguing about?"

Lucien contrived to steer the conversation from any mention of Katrina or her movements. He explained about being separated from his men.

The commander threw him a knowing glance. "She must have been some woman to cause you to forget your duty."

Lucien longed to be at his desk in Vienna, where he was in charge. Instead, he forced a grin. "That she was." He shrugged as if to say he was flesh and blood. The commander was free to think whatever he wanted.

Lucien stuck as close to the facts as possible. "She attempted to escape as the enemy engaged us. I followed her for some distance but failed to recapture her. Somehow, I lost her and my way as well. On foot, it was slow traveling," Lucien finished lamely. Heat flooded his face. How inept could an officer pretend to be?

"And the prisoner's identity?"

Lucien hunched his shoulders. "Her name was immaterial. We caught her escaping from enemy soldiers. I have a sister, sir. The best way to ensure the woman's well-being was to arrest her."

"What exactly were you doing out there, miles from headquarters?"

"I was on a reconnaissance mission that took us farther than expected."

The commander dismissed him, but not without a parting shot. "Next time your hormones act up, don't involve my men."

Lucien left and found a quiet corner to read his mail. There was a letter from his mother.

Dear Lucien,

It has been too long since you've come home. We miss you terribly. I am sorry to write that your Grandfather Creto has died. Your father has taken it hard. Serbian soldiers were harassing Creto at his home in Knin, telling him he had to leave, and his heart gave out. The doctor said it was a heart attack. He died in his home, and they buried him next to your grandmother as he wanted. He is at peace now with his beloved wife.

Lucien gulped back sobs, pressing a fist against his chest.

Chapter 20

Mostar, Bosnia-Herzegovina, Summer 1993

Rogue soldiers dragged Katrina to a jail on the north side of Mostar. She regretted how her foolish defiance had blinded her to Vita's duplicity. She cringed, recalling the accusations she'd hurled at Lucien. Katrina couldn't bear to think her family might be alive if she hadn't trusted Vita. What would become of the children?

Her cell was bathed in blackness. She heard machine gun fire and explosions in the distance as the war seethed between the city's Croats and Muslims. The two should have united to fight the Serbians instead of turning against one another. How had they gone so far astray? Hours passed with her huddled on the ground, her jacket wrapped around her for warmth. She awoke with a start, realizing she'd fallen asleep. Her parched throat ached. She wasn't sure when she had last eaten.

Katrina struggled to hang on to the renewed faith that had enveloped her earlier in the valley, faith in God, her mission, and herself. She could hear rodents rustling nearby, closing in on her. She stifled a cry as fur brushed against her leg.

The night dragged on. Katrina alternately kicked at the rats and paced. At some point, she sank to the floor, exhausted, and hid her face in her arms.

Katrina must have dozed off. She awakened as dawn filtered dimly through the cell. Thankfully, the rats seemed to have skittered into the shadows. In the silent recesses of her mind, she prayed for strength and forgiveness. And the Lord sustained her.

Soon, two guards entered and grabbed her roughly. "Get up," the taller one snarled in a Bosnian dialect, difficult for her to understand. They led her deeper into the prison, down the stairs. A woman screamed, and her cries grew louder as they got closer.

The guards pushed Katrina into a dingy basement. Horrified at the sight of a shrieking woman strapped to a torture rack, Katrina shut her eyes.

A club whacked her from behind. "Watch!"

She stared in revulsion and pity. The woman's hands and legs were fastened to a movable bar at either end of an oblong wooden frame. Her shrieks increased as the men ratcheted the tension higher.

Katrina felt faint as the seconds stretched into minutes. She vomited at the sound of snapping cartilage. Finally, the guards shoved her from the torture chamber and returned her to her cell.

After they left her, an officer entered. "Miss Winslow, I'm here to consider your case for appeal." He sounded Serbian. His hair was as black as coal and his eyes cold and dark.

"Exactly what are the charges against me?"

He eased himself onto a bolted-down wooden keg that passed for a stool. "In Bosnia, the law is relative, if you get my meaning."

She opened her mouth to speak, but he raised his hand. "Let me finish. Think back to before the raid. There have been allegations that you seized stolen government property. We'll deal with those charges first."

"I had no involvement with any government goods. What's this about?" In her experience, Serbian officers seldom cooperated with Muslims. Unless Vita was playing both sides against each other. What was she after?

"A Kosovo soldier stole an icon from the cathedral in Pazaric and hid it inside your family's mission." He studied her reactions carefully.

Katrina frowned. "Pazaric is in Serbia. How would I have ever gotten there or met any soldiers from Kosovo?"

"The icon might have been hidden at your home without your knowledge and later discovered by a family member."

"I suppose it's possible, but my father would have reported it. What does it look like?"

"It's a tiny, exquisite painting of the Madonna set in a valuable antique gold frame strung on a ribbon. Someone could easily wear it around their neck."

"I'm sorry, but I haven't seen any miniature paintings."

He handed her paper and a pen. "List everything you took when you left the mission."

Confused, Katrina said, "I took food supplies, blankets, clothing, and the children." All her focus had been on escaping while they could.

The officer said with a trace of impatience, "You expect us to believe you left with nothing else?"

"Soldiers had just killed my family and friends. I was frightened. Those men could have returned at any moment. We were desperate to find the children and go."

"We?"

She'd caused Lucien enough problems. "A few of the older children helped."

He studied her in patent disbelief. "You didn't stop to gather provisions or a keepsake to remember your family by?"

"My parents and brother had been brutally murdered. I was in shock." Her voice trembled at the memory. "We took the food and clothing we could carry."

He gave her a sharp glance. "Think back to any unusual discoveries in the days before your departure. A valuable icon is missing that we believe is in your possession."

Katrina didn't know what he was talking about. "A guard has already searched me. I have nothing."

He grunted. "Hmm. We shall soon know." He stood and called to the guards that he was ready to leave.

Could Vita have stolen the items, traded them for Bosnian arms, and then thrown the blame on Katrina?

After a week of interrogations and torture, Katrina felt light-headed and feverish. The soldiers fed her a cup of murky water and a crust of bread twice daily. If only she could quench the thirst blazing in her throat and cool her body.

Vita entered her cell and appeared shocked at the sight of her. "How are you?" she asked, a flicker of emotion veiled behind the tight words.

Katrina might have laughed at the irony of the question, but the effort would have been too painful.

Vita continued. "You've had time to think, which is good. I want to offer you a deal."

Katrina gazed at her blankly. This was it, a deal, the reason for the long days and nights. The meager rations and the afternoon interrogations on the torture rack, where questions followed questions. Her body strapped to that wooden contraption, the ratchet pulling tauter and tauter until her pleading sobs ended in unconsciousness. A deal? How strange, when once Katrina would have done anything for her, believing Vita was her dearest friend, someone she could always trust.

Vita's words penetrated the fog of Katrina's thoughts. "Your confession in exchange for the children, or they'll be shot like other enemy agents."

"They're children—orphans."

"Your life for theirs. You'll sign a confession to spying and running guns."

The familiar adrenaline rose in Katrina, fueling her temper, strength replacing weakness. "As if I could trust you."

Vita's green eyes radiated menace, the effect mesmerizing. "You'll die, anyway. Why not let it count for something? You've always been fond of duty. Here's a chance to atone for every mistake you've ever made—to your parents, Giles, Lucien."

She sidled closer and held out a paper and pen. "I've had a statement drawn up. You merely have to sign." Her voice softened, its cadence as potent and seductive as a cobra before it struck. "Come, Katrina. Then you can join your family. Think how happy you'll be."

"Get out."

"You'll regret this."

Her cell door slammed, and after the thud of Vita's army boots faded, Katrina covered her face, then stooped down, snatched the paper, and ripped it to pieces.

Chapter 21

Vita stomped from the cell to her office at the front of the jail. Katrina's thin, drawn face haunted her. She had once envied her full, rosy cheeks and smiling dimples, a reflection of a happiness Vita had never known. In frustration, she kicked at the floor, stubbing the toe of her boot. Best to remember the misery these Christians wreaked on her people. Neither the Croats, who were primarily Catholic nor the predominantly Orthodox Serbians, had shown the Muslims any kindness in this war.

No, these Christians sought to destroy Bosnia. The Serbs had already bombed more than three hundred Bosnian mosques, destroying even the parking lots. Weren't they supposed to practice the Christian love Katrina's parents had babbled about?

She sank into a chair behind her desk and lowered her head against its scarred, brittle veneer. Perhaps Katrina and her family had been different. Maybe they'd helped a few people. Still, they perpetuated the myth of a messiah bringing deliverance.

There was no rescue from the bitter malice roiling across the land. Without it, they'd die. She'd learned that lesson as a young girl at her mother's knees. Vita withdrew the small rabbit's foot she always carried, which her mother had given her. The good luck charm was her sole memento of her mama.

Without conscious thought, Vita lifted the soft fur across her cheek in a caressing motion that drew her into the past. Unlocked memories tumbled forward, freezing Vita in the nightmare. She saw her beautiful mother beckoning, her delicate features terror-stricken as a blue-red haze separated them.

Vita's small girl voice said, "Don't kill her. Leave my mama alone!"

The men turned and swarmed toward Vita. "Please, Allah! Don't let them touch me. No! Don't." Pain exploded through her as they bore her to the floor, one after the other, throwing themselves on her.

When she heard the last one leave, Vita tried to stop crying at the sight of blood oozing from her body, scaring her even more. "Mama," she called across the room, seeing her mother asleep on the floor.

Vita crawled across the chipped linoleum, trembling and afraid the men would return, the trail of blood swelling her terror. She shook her mother's arm. "Wake up. Please, I hurt," she whimpered. Thick tears slid down her face, dripping past her nose as she stared down at her pretty mama. Frightened, Vita shook her harder, refusing to believe she was broken and dead.

Vita's small body convulsed with sobs. After a while, she stumbled into the bedroom to get a blanket, then crept to the front room and lay beside her mother. She spread the cover over them and clung to her, listening through the night, waiting for the rhythm of her mother's even breathing, desperately wanting to hear her snoring softly.

Gradually, Vita returned to the present. Shamed and shaken, she rubbed her clammy hands together in search of warmth where there was none. She hated remembering, but needed this reminder of what the war was about and all that the Serbians had done to them. Vita shivered and strode out of her office, colliding with a soldier.

"Are you okay?" Martin asked.

She forced a nod and left, but he stopped her.

"Can we talk?"

"Later. It's been a long day." She wanted to leave before someone else remarked she wasn't herself.

"I heard you caught the traitor," he said.

"You and everyone else." He seemed to sway toward her. Or was she the one moving? Vita straightened. "So, what do you want?"

"What's going to happen to those orphans?"

She studied him, her mind clearing as suspicion gripped her. "Is there a reason for this inquisition?" Vita registered the concern in Martin's dark eyes. Hadn't she heard a rumor he was a Christian? She splayed an upraised hand against her aching head and wished simply to escape.

"I heard they were going to be shot. You wouldn't murder a bunch of helpless orphans?" He gave her a strange look, as if he'd been repeating the question to get her attention.

"They're not orphans. They're the enemy. Hasn't this war taught you anything? Then you married a Croatian, didn't you? Go home, Martin, before I ask her name and order her arrested."

He paled. "You're no different from the Serbs. You don't care who you kill." He left.

Power and survival were all that mattered—and Kiro. She flinched, recalling her date with the Serbian major that evening. She loathed his touch. Initially, she'd enjoyed her power over him, knowing she was defrauding him, never believing she'd have to follow through with the act. Now, she detested herself and him. Vita slammed out of the jailhouse, realizing there wasn't much she didn't hate these days.

Chapter 22

Martin walked away from the jail. He'd been a fool to leave Sara and cross to the Muslim side. What else could he have done? Marriage to a Westerner who was part Croatian was hard. For him to live in the Croat sector was suicide. Guilt ate at him, knowing Croats were murdering his people and Muslims were killing Sara's people. He'd left without telling her. Swimming across the Neretva River to the Muslim side at night was easy.

He found the same bitterness and hatred there. War forced everyone to take sides. When he married Sara, their nationalities didn't matter. These days, the Croats wanted to murder him for what other Muslims were doing, and the Muslims resented and distrusted him because of his Croatian wife. Emotionally, there was no shelter zone.

The past was choking them. This hate shouldn't have anything to do with their lives. It belonged to his grandfather's era. It wasn't supposed to touch him and Sara, kill his friends, or rip apart his marriage.

How could malice take on a life of its own, spiraling into a never-ending abyss of retaliation? It swallowed the innocent whole, regurgitated the injured and dead, and reduced their cities to burning embers and black smoke.

He loved Sara. They were Christians, separate from this evil. Still, how had the enmity crept inward, insidiously shadowing their lives and marriage? Day by week by month, long before 1989, the past stalked Bosnians as Milosevic stirred the Serbian nationalists' hatred, first toward the Albanians in Kosovo, then non-Serbians throughout Yugoslavia.

Martin wanted to deny the coming danger, to view it from a distance. His generation wore Nike tennis shoes and Levi's, watched Sony TVs, and carried Walkmans. They attended university.

He had believed he and Sara were immune, and the discrimination and greed could be contained. Ethnic prejudice was a trend in modern politics that would fade. What could Milosevic's relentless drive to possess more land have to do with them?

Serbians had long resented Tito's granting Kosovo autonomy. When Milosevic revoked it, Martin had assumed the Serbs would calm down. With Milosevic driving them on to larger conquests, they'd only grown more bloodthirsty, raiding and burning first Croatia, then Bosnia.

Now, worried and unsure of what to do, Martin stomped through the city, kicking at the torn-up road, wanting to see Sara. He couldn't continue like this.

After sunset, he swam across the river to the Croat side and walked to their apartment. The closer he came, the more apprehension churned in his gut. Let Sara be there, he prayed. Let her and their baby be safe.

Chapter 23

In Mostar's Croatian sector, Martin and Sara's apartment was three hundred meters from the line that divided the Croatians from the Muslim districts. Martin slipped inside the bullet-ridden stucco building and took the stairs two at a time. Out of breath, he thrust his key into the lock, entered, and secured the door behind him. The silence was deafening. Panicked, he ran through the sparsely furnished three rooms, searching for some sign that his wife and child remained.

He collapsed onto the mat used for a bed in the corner of the empty bedroom and stared at the wall, memories of Sara and their son all around. Where were they? Her brother Lucien might know, but Martin didn't dare show up at Croatian headquarters. Lucien had gotten them a pass, allowing them to stay in the Croat region. He would have checked on his sister and nephew. Martin had to believe they were safe. His sanity rested on his relationships with Sara and God.

He waited in their dismal apartment for days, alternately fearful and hopeful for his wife's and son's return. He even risked calling on neighbors to ask after her. On the third night, he'd drifted off to sleep when the noise of the front door opening and heavy, booted footsteps awakened him. His senses on alert, he drew a pistol and moved to a position behind the bedroom door. It creaked open.

"Sara?"

Martin recognized his brother-in-law's voice and shoved the gun into his jacket. He let out a pent-up breath as he realized Lucien hadn't seen her either. He stepped out from his hiding place. "She's not here."

Lucien's gaze swept the empty room. "Where is she?"

"I was hoping you could tell me."

Lucien sank to the floor, a pained expression on his face. "She was grieving for our grandfather and searching for you when I left town."

"Lucien, I'm so sorry. Was it your Grandfather Creto?"

Lucien nodded, but glanced away. "When did you see Sara last?"

"Weeks ago. Poor Sara. I did not know, or I would have stayed. I left to cross over to our side."

"You're married with a son. There aren't supposed to be any sides."

Martin paced. "What do you call the battle lines drawn right outside this building? You ought to understand. I couldn't sit back and do nothing."

Lucien looked as if he wanted to slug him. "I'm not married. It's different when you are."

"Is it?" Martin taunted. "You think it's easier to see your people raped and murdered?"

"You have a responsibility to Sara."

"I'm a Muslim first. It's who I am."

"And I thought you were a husband and father. Long before you married, you converted and became a Christian. What happened? You couldn't stick it?"

Martin swung at Lucien's jaw, then grunted, his fist striking the door as Lucien ducked and swore. Martin hung his head. "You're right. I deserted Sara. I've got to find her."

"Was there someplace she might have left a message? Someone you both trusted?"

"You mean besides you?" Martin shook his head in denial. "I wish there were. Wait—" He clapped his hands to his head. Why hadn't he remembered? Hope burrowed through him. "Maybe? We haven't used it in years. When we first married . . ." He ran to the kitchen, rummaged in the cupboards, and brought out the sugar bowl. In the absence of flour and sugar, she'd filled it with coarse salt. His spirits soared as he reached the bottom and drew out a note, realizing the salt was Sara's way of disguising it from prying eyes.

> Dear Martin,
>
> I can't stay. It's not safe without you or Lucien. With the soldiers pounding on the door and the bombs and sniper fire—I'm so scared for us all. I'm going to take our son to your parents' farm. Please hurry to us.
>
> All my love,
> Sara

His eyes moist, Martin handed the note to Lucien. "I'll go tonight."

"And then what?" Lucien asked. "The war hasn't stopped. How long before you decide to choose sides and leave again?"

"I've been to the other side and seen the enemies on all sides. Muslims, Croats, Serbs—all Bosnians. And they are you and me, and all of us. I don't know, but if I can find a way, we'll emigrate." He realized Sara and his son meant everything to him. If there was no life for them together here, they'd travel to some place where there was.

"West, you mean?"

Martin nodded. "Where else could we go?"

Chapter 24

Bosnia-Herzegovina, Summer 1993

An eerie stillness marked the route Lucien drove to Martin's parents' farm, where they hoped to find Sara. The borrowed jeep bounced along the torn-up abandoned roads, the foggy night creating the illusion of driving through a vaporous valley. The absence of rapid staccato machine gun fire and intermittent explosions sounded strange, the quiet unfamiliar. Almost a portent, but of what Lucien didn't know. Was Sara in trouble? Like him, she was grieving Grandfather Creto's death. His uneasiness grew and centered on Katrina and the missing children.

Martin broke the silence that stretched between them, speaking of Sara. He poured out the difficulties of their marriage and the confused loyalties, ripping them and the country apart as if searching for a means to absolve himself.

Lucien was sympathetic, offering a comment now and then until Martin finally fell mute.

After a while, Martin asked, "Did you hear soldiers captured Katrina Winslow? She's in the Mostar jail, the same place as the children. I am afraid it will not end well for any of them."

Lucien gripped the steering wheel as it spun to the left. Fear rattled through him. He swore under his breath, bringing the jeep under control. "Why didn't you tell me sooner?"

"I'm sorry. Finding Sara gone wiped everything else from my mind. I know how much Katrina's family helped you. I should have remembered."

Lucien reined in his anger and drew a calming breath. "It's not your fault. Sorry, I blew up. Tell me what happened."

Martin hesitated, clearly wary of revealing too much. "There's not much I can say. I signed on as a soldier. I—" His voice broke.

Lucien steered the car into a small gully on the roadside and stopped. "Don't clam up all moral and patriotic. Katrina's a person, not some war casualty, whatever your convictions." Martin looked hurt. Lucien slumped, leaning his head against the steering wheel.

For days, ever since he'd awakened to find Katrina gone, Lucien had carried this sense of impending doom. He'd searched for her in Mostar and found nothing, not a trace. She'd vanished, leaving her spirit to unsettle him, he reflected in frustration.

She was a Westerner. Despite what Katrina thought, she couldn't pass as a native for long. One misplaced word or look could get her killed. There were countless clues besides the obvious. How far could a blue-eyed blonde with an engaging Texas drawl travel unnoticed? He remembered the spring in her step, the proud lift of her shoulders, how her chin stuck out in stubborn determination. Eastern Europeans had never learned the knack of optimism. They walked more often with their shoulders bent and heads down. But not Katrina.

Martin broke into his reverie. "You think you owe the Winslows your life? I'll admit they never seemed like spies to me, and those children don't deserve to be executed."

"Vita set Katrina up," Lucien said. "Vita's having an affair with Major Cosic. He's in the Serbian Army. In exchange, he's supplying her with arms for the Rogue Muslim Army. The two ordered the Winslow slaughter after discovering Giles had overheard Cosic and Vita discussing their plans to destroy Mostar's Croat sector."

At his brother-in-law's mien of skepticism, Lucien explained. "Vita became a person of interest. We were tailing her. Two of my soldiers were there, listening to the same conversation as Giles, except no one spotted them."

Martin said, "It doesn't follow that she ordered the raid on the Winslow mission."

"She'd already arranged it and had rogue Muslim combatants in place. My men heard her give the go-ahead over the telephone after Giles left. Before they could warn the Winslows or contact HQ to send more men, it was over. What a difference a working cell phone would have made that day. My two men considered confronting Vita right then, but they were hopelessly outnumbered. Tragically, I didn't learn about it until later, when Katrina found the bodies and shouted for help."

"I shouldn't be too surprised at what Vita's capable of doing. Why haven't you warned Katrina about Vita? She has a right to know who killed her family."

"She was dealing with so much already. They'd murdered her parents and Giles. I didn't want to add to her grief then. I was sure Vita wouldn't find Katrina before I told her the truth. But military duties interfered, sending me off on a mission. When I next saw her, Vita had already spread her poison. Katrina believed I was a murderer."

"That's too bad." Martin shared what he knew about the current situation.

Lucien listened with growing dread. To penetrate Muslim territory was challenging, but for him to break into their jail would be suicidal. He wouldn't help Katrina or anyone else by attempting it, though she had saved his life. "I warned her Vita was poison, but not soon enough."

Martin frowned. "Kiro and Vita are tight, and both are heavily involved in the Iranian arms shipments. Katrina stumbled across some crates of weapons in the caves. That's one reason Vita is coercing her to confess. Katrina's a liability to them. If she refuses, Vita will order the orphans shot."

"You're sure of this?"

"I heard it straight from the jailer holding the children."

"Martin, can you think of any way to get those kids out?"

"Sadly, it's impossible to free them or Katrina. It would take a miracle."

"Pray harder than you ever have because I'm going to try. Can you draw me a map of the jail layout?"

Martin smiled. "I'll do better than that. I'll help."

"What about Sara?"

Worry and fear clouded his eyes. "Sara will wait for me. A couple more days won't matter."

Though his offer was tempting, Lucien refused it. Martin's first responsibility must be to Sara and their son. He resigned himself to the return trip alone, thanked Martin, and pointed the jeep toward the nearest town, where he planned to leave his brother-in-law.

Meanwhile, Martin drew a map of the jail's layout and gave Lucien the name of a man on the inside who might help.

"I'll meet you at your parents' farm afterward, and hopefully, I'll have Katrina and the orphans with me." He dropped Martin at the train station, and Lucien headed back to Mostar.

Chapter 25

Rather than continuing to the Croat barracks in Mostar, Lucien spent the few hours until dawn at Martin and Sara's lonely apartment, alternately resting and prowling its three small rooms. He was grateful for the extended leave. He'd need it to liberate Katrina and the children.

Lucien stumbled as an explosion shook the building. He hadn't told the commander who Katrina was, but Lucien wished he had. If she were in Croat custody, rescuing her would have been easier. He glanced across at his sister's picture on the wall. Lucien knew one way to free Katrina but wasn't sure he could pull it off.

His stomach growled. It had been hours since he last ate. He rummaged through Sara and Martin's tiny kitchen and came up with a half loaf of molded bread. He sliced off the green and ate, washing the bread down with a glass of water that Sara must have drawn before leaving. Without electricity, they had to carry the water in.

Lucien wandered to the bedroom window, standing to its side to avoid being seen. Not much had changed in Bosnia. Explosions still blasted the buildings with punishing cruelty, and bursts of fire lit the night sky. Lucien realized how much he'd changed. He couldn't stay, couldn't continue in the hell surrounding him. Why couldn't humans get it right and stop repeating the same mistakes? All the senseless killing and destruction? Why—why?

He dropped onto the mat in the corner and tried to sleep, but worry kept him awake. The situation in Bosnia continually grew worse. Last week in Sarajevo, bakeries announced there was no flour to bake bread. Sadly, the Serbian military frequently intercepted UN relief supplies scheduled to arrive.

Lucien rolled onto his side. Despite negotiations by interested parties, he saw no signs of a cease-fire. Yesterday, he'd read the latest briefing from the United Nations High Commission, reporting that the war had created more than four million refugees, with over 3.5 million displaced internally.

Lucien couldn't sleep. He sat cross-legged and drew his diary from his back pocket. He entered his sister's name under possibly missing and Katrina's under imprisoned. In the line below, he wrote, "The children." Katrina would know their names and how many.

He closed the book with a heavy spirit. If there was a God, where was He? Lucien's parents had raised him Catholic. His family attended mass on Christmas, Easter, and Ash Wednesday. He seldom asked God for anything. Lucien's father often said of World War II, "There were no atheists in the battle trenches."

He tried not to think about his growing feelings for Katrina and wondered if her faith comforted her in jail. She was at risk of rape and the firing squad. He felt sick. She and her family had saved his life, and he owed it to their memory to help Katrina. And what about Sara? He closed his eyes and leaned against the wall until dawn, listening and waiting.

Chapter 26

Mostar, Bosnia-Herzegovina, Summer 1993

Golden rays lit the gray morning mist as Lucien climbed into the mud-encrusted jeep parked outside his sister's apartment. Rain had left a mess of the roads into Mostar, as he'd discovered the night before on his return to town. The mud, at least, provided good camouflage.

With a shrug, he turned the key in the ignition and expelled an exasperated breath on seeing the empty gas gauge.

Lucien climbed out of the jeep and picked up the hacked-off fuel cap lying on the ground with its lock intact for all the good it had done.

His commander hadn't wanted to loan him the jeep. The half tank of fuel Lucien kept in reserve for the drive to headquarters was gone. It would be useless to try the gas stations. Those that hadn't been bombed had been out of fuel since the war began. Ration coupons were almost impossible to get.

To buy fuel on the black market was risky. Soldiers had been found beaten or murdered at the city's former garbage dump, where such exchanges routinely took place. Fuel in Bosnia belonged to the government except for what runners smuggled in from neighboring countries. Black marketeers, who were often disillusioned soldiers, were on the lookout for lost army planes, trucks, and tanks. The mercenaries sold the equipment and any remaining fuel to civilians and troops.

Lucien ran up the cracked cement stairs to Sara's apartment, grabbed the bicycle from the front closet, and tucked it under his arm. He darted back down the steps and swung onto the bike. He took off, zigzagging through the city with a bravado he was far from feeling. A bullet whizzed past his shoulder. Lucien lowered his head and pedaled faster, pushing past the occasional sniper and artillery fire to the outlying Croat barracks hidden in the surrounding hills.

He cautiously approached the Croat's temporary earthen barracks and identified himself before entering. Inside, Lucien went straight to the canteen, where the men kept a bucket of cool water drawn for officers. He filled a tin cup and drank deeply, the cool liquid quenching his thirst. He dipped a second scoop, dribbled the water over his hair and down his face, and then mopped up the excess moisture with his handkerchief. Lucien finger-combed his hair and braced himself for the coming confrontation.

He marched into the chief's cramped, shadowy quarters. "Good morning, sir."

The commander jerked around in surprise, sloshing coffee from his cup. A trail of brown liquid stained the papers and maps thickly scattered across his desk. He let loose a string of expletives in a loud voice. "Next time, knock if you don't want a bullet through the heart. Where's my jeep?" He set the mug down and stretched his legs under the desk, allowing the papers to soak up the spill.

"About that, sir." Unease spiraled in Lucien's gut as he met his superior's irritated gaze across the rough desk built from emptied rifle crates. Lucien sank into a nearby metal chair and told him what had happened.

"I should have never let you borrow it." The commander phoned an order to have it collected and brought to the base. The older man looked tired, his eyes bloodshot, as if he'd been working most of the night at his desk.

"Are you expecting trouble?" Lucien asked.

"The Serbs have identified our location and are planning a bombing raid to drive us out."

Yet another obstacle that would endanger Lucien's men and his plans to rescue Katrina. "How soon can you mobilize and evacuate?"

"Zagreb's orders are to remain here," the chief said in a careful, emotionless voice.

"It's a death sentence."

He raised a hand as if to deny it, then let it fall to his side, his face a cradle of despair. "It'll be an excellent test of the bunkers."

"With no one left to see the results?" Unbidden, Lucien's mind conjured up images of past massacres. He'd warn his men to clear out before the raid.

Zagreb's tactics wouldn't win the war in Bosnia. A vast chasm existed between the policy created in Croatia's capital and the reality in Bosnia. Bosnia's conflict shouldn't be handled like the ongoing war in Croatia. But it was almost impossible to convince a Croat who'd fought to protect Vukovar of this. Hate and suspicion blinded most of them. People couldn't forget the 1991 siege.

Civilians had come from across Croatia to defend the town. They fought three long months against 40,000 Serbian soldiers bent on Croatian genocide. The Serbs were heavily armed and had 110 tanks. The siege had ended with thousands dead and a Serbian victory.

Still, Croatians continued the fight against Serbian aggression in Croatia and Bosnia and, sadly, were at war with the Bosnian Muslims, too.

The commander lit a Marlboro and said with false bravado, "We'll survive or take an army of Serbs and Muslims down with us. I'm here to ensure that."

"What about the men? Don't they have any say?" In disgust, Lucien drew a piece of paper from his pocket and hurriedly scribbled out his resignation. During his stint in the army, he'd often withheld his opinion in the face of ignorance and prejudice. Today, he felt no such restraints. Lucien hadn't enjoyed working under this commander and was relieved to end his enlistment. In the early dawn, before leaving Martin and Sara's apartment, he'd worked out a plan for Katrina's escape.

He handed the chief his resignation. "Now it's official, one less person for you to worry about."

The commander scanned it with no outward show of emotion and tossed it onto the desk. "Can't say I'm surprised."

"I'm concerned about the men."

The older man squirmed beneath Lucien's accusing gaze and admitted, "I've sent most of them out on reconnaissance missions. The steel bomb shelter below will do for those who remain."

"That's good news." Lucien hesitated, unsure how to phrase his subsequent request. So much depended on this man's help. Perhaps he should have waited to hand in his resignation.

His superior glanced at the papers and maps as if eager to resume work. "Well, if that's all."

"Sir, about that prisoner?"

"You mean the woman?"

Lucien nodded. "She's in jail with several of the orphans her family took in. Soldiers arrested them in the hills outside the city." Lucien explained how Katrina and her family were innocent missionaries framed by rogue arms dealers who were acting in a defensive effort to throw suspicion off themselves.

"This is interesting," the commander said. "But we're in the middle of hostilities, and I've got problems enough without you dropping the American's escapades in my lap. Notify the American embassy and have done with it." He held up a hand to stop Lucien from speaking. "My orders are to shoot her on sight. Chances are the enemy has saved the rest of us the trouble. Now get out and let me be before we all get blown up."

Lucien hadn't served as the executive of an international

corporation without learning how to stand his ground. Nor could he have survived the war without knowing how to fight and when, despite the odds lining up against him. He leaned back in his chair in a gesture of defiance. "If the girl gets killed, it will be an international incident. The US is more likely to respond favorably to those who helped her. You have a grasp of how these under-the-table trades go. At the very least, the Americans would be obligated to offer some aid. The US might even help push the Serbian Army out of Croatia." Lucien paused, then added the final bait. "Think about the promotions in line for the man who could pull it off."

The commander shifted his bulk in the chair, his face a study of indecision. "All right, you've reeled me in. Let's hear your plan."

"For starters, we'll need a forged order requesting Katrina's transfer to Sarajevo, which will appear to be issued by Alija Izetbegovic. He's so high ranking that no one would dare to question his directives."

"Are you sure the name of the president of Bosnia-Herzegovina is enough?" the commander asked. "Why not use Boutros Boutros Ghali's name as well?"

Lucien said, "We'll leave the UN secretary-general out of this for now. While the rogue army are transferring Katrina from the Mostar jail to Sarajevo, we'll attack and take her hostage. The other option is to break her out, which would be near impossible in Muslim territory."

He appeared affronted. "Hardly that, but we would be bound to lose more men than we can afford. The plan is ludicrous. How do we come up with a transfer order that will fool their intelligence?"

Lucien forced a show of confidence he was far from feeling. "I've got an inside contact who can handle that."

"And what about your resignation?"

"I'll be helping unofficially."

The commander reluctantly said, "I'll do it—but I won't accept your resignation. I can hold you personally responsible if anything goes wrong."

One hour later, they'd arranged everything. The commander didn't like it, but in the end, Lucien convinced him Katrina's freedom would bring the Croat cause favor with the Americans.

Once again, Lucien was risking his men to ensure her safety. And he still had to figure out how to free the children. Katrina would never leave without them.

Chapter 27

Katrina sat in the cramped cell. It had been a week since Vita had demanded Katrina sign the confession. Her nemesis's failure to return left Katrina both worried and relieved. Were Vita and her comrades through with her and the children? Or were they busy tightening the web that held them?

Tap—tap—tap. The sound was soft and brisk. Katrina glanced at the door and then, with a shudder, slid down onto her stomach. The hard, damp ground was peppered with crawling vermin. She grasped her metal drinking cup and tapped three long taps against the thick stone wall.

A cracked seam in the lowest back corner between the floor and the adjoining cubicle allowed her to communicate with a young Muslim incarcerated for marrying a Serbian. His uncle, a religious man, was the night jailer. Katrina thanked God the jailer's sympathy for his nephew extended to the children and her. He was her primary source of news. Learning thirteen of her small band were in cells down the hall had unnerved her. She'd begged the jailer, "Please, sneak me in to see them."

"Never." He drew a finger across his throat, signaling his fate if caught. Now, when he came to empty her chamber pot or bring her a daily ration of water and bread, he maintained a reproachful silence.

Surrounded by stone walls, literally and figuratively, Katrina tried to devise a plan to break out.

Jeana Kendrick

Belgrade, Serbia

Lieutenant Alex Nikolic awakened before dawn. A fighter pilot with *Republika Srpska* (Serbian Air Force), he had early duty. He leaned across to kiss his wife and son. During the night, they'd placed the baby between them to soothe him. Alex slid one finger tenderly down his son's cheek, then climbed from the bed, helpless to protect those he loved from the ugliness erupting in Serbia, igniting people to do evil deeds no God could view kindly.

He dressed and ate in the kitchen, sipping tea with his bread and jam. He hadn't missed Ennis's boss, General Jovanovic, eyeing her for the past few months. It was common knowledge the general's marriage had hit a political stalemate, and his Croatian wife was persona non grata. Who did Jovanovic think he was fooling?

Alex rose and crossed himself three times, repeating, "*In the name of the Father and the Son and the Holy Spirit. In the name of the Father and the Son and the Holy Spirit. In the name of the Father and the Son and the Holy Spirit, please keep my family safe.*"

On the way out, he zipped his bomber jacket. Its brown leather was a reminder of happier times: Italian markets, cappuccino in the plaza, the days when Yugoslavia's currency, the dinar, had value, and they could still travel.

He climbed into the jeep parked on the street and headed for the base. When Alex picked up his roster for the day, his resentment flared. His scheduled bomb targets were a Muslim jail in Mostar, known as an enclave of sedition, and a Croatian base spotted on an earlier mission in the hills beyond the city.

His hand closed over the gold cross beneath his shirt, a gift from his grandmother to keep him safe. "Bring me luck," he murmured before checking his plane.

⚜ ⚜ ⚜

Bosnia, Herzegovina

Katrina stirred in the night, shoving aside the rough hands that shook her awake. She sat up, realizing something was wrong. The jailer's worn, craggy face bent over her, the lantern he held casting an eerie glow in the rat-infested cell. He looked pale and shaken. She braced herself for whatever was to come. Had they killed the children? "What is it?"

His gaze shifted, avoiding hers. "They're planning an execution in twenty-three hours."

"Is it the children?" she asked. At his nod, her breath hitched. Dear God, what was she going to do? "You've got to let them go."

He trod to the door, shaking his head. "Not just the children—you too."

The room spun for a moment. Hot and cold flashes, with lightning intensity, whipped through Katrina. After everything, they'd escaped to fail now.

The jailer moved to leave, but she tugged at his sleeve. "Wait. You're our only hope."

He shrugged regretfully. "Allah is pleased that I warned you. For this, I could be killed."

Not sure what to say, Katrina's words tumbled over one another in her haste. "Allah is not happy. You've done nothing. What good are your words when we're locked in these cells, and you have the key? Will your warning save the children or me?" She caught his sleeve. "What if it were your children needing help?"

He swatted her hand away and turned to leave. "I must think of my family."

Katrina resisted the encroaching haze of hysteria. She had to think of a way to convince him.

Alex grimaced and lowered the plane over the targeted Bosnian area. He had lied to Ennis last night when he kissed her goodbye, letting her believe all he did was fly the brass to conferences. Most of the time, it was true.

More often lately, he was sent on bombing missions. Alex suspected it might be Jovanovic's method of getting rid of him. The military usually stationed bomber pilots closer to enemy lines. Jovanovic had initialed today's flight plan.

Alex's first target, the Mostar jail, was in sight. He moved to push the bomb-release button, then paused. He was ten minutes early. Yet, he couldn't afford to delay and risk running out of fuel or drawing enemy fire. Not that there was much chance of the latter. Croatians and Muslims couldn't compete with Serbian air power. Alex hesitated, his hand on the release button.

Exhausted, Katrina fell asleep until roused by the jailer bursting into her cell. He gave her the knapsack she'd thought never to see again after the soldiers had confiscated it.

His shirttail hung haphazardly over his army fatigues. "I dreamed they executed you and the little ones. Then the heavens opened, and Allah pointed his finger at me and said, 'You must prevent My children's murders.'" The jailer bowed his head as if to compose himself. "I am a religious man. Some might say superstitious. I make you a gift of your belongings."

Katrina took her knapsack and clasped his hands, her relief clouded by the danger to him. "You'll help us escape?"

He rapidly concealed the gleam of avarice in his eyes. "No. I shall pray that Allah is your eyes and feet."

Katrina realized he wanted a bribe. What made him think she possessed anything of value? She supposed he figured it never hurt to ask. But she had nothing. Unless . . . She forced herself to respond calmly. "Give me a moment to think."

He nodded his acquiescence and left.

She searched through her bag and drew out the framed photo of her family. Then, with her back to the cell door, she slipped off the backing and removed a crisp US one-hundred-dollar bill, hoping it would be enough to buy the jailer's help.

When he returned, she paid him. They worked out the details for her and the children to escape before he went off duty. Their executions were set for dawn. That would give them about four hours to get as far as possible from the city before they were discovered missing.

Katrina paced in the tiny cell. Everything hinged on the next few hours: the orphans' welfare and hers. If they failed—the firing squad waited.

Her stomach flip-flopped, her forehead beading in a sweat of fear. She willed the jailer to hurry. Her mother's dying plea echoed in her mind, "Promise you'll protect the children."

"I'm trying, Mom." Katrina's voice broke as she knelt on the hard floor and poured out her feelings, praying for strength and protection. There was so much against them.

Any minute, the jailer would unlock their cell doors. Katrina would lead the children to the city's outskirts. From there, a friend of the jailer, who worked with humane organizations to save Bosnian children, would guide them to the sea.

Katrina started at the soft clang of the door unlocking, then waited for the jailer's retreating footsteps to fade before wrenching it open and stepping out. She ran down the gloomy corridor to the children's cell. Her hands shook as she pushed the rusty metal door wide and cautiously entered. The children's faces lifted in fearful expectation. "Shh," she said, unsure if they could see her.

They hung back, but then the older ones, with muffled cries of recognition, ran and embraced her. Soon, the younger ones came to her. Katrina opened her arms in a big group hug.

She related the escape plan. "Follow me, but we must be fast and quiet." She motioned to the eldest. "Rachel, you take the two seven-year-olds, Ana and Dinko." The Croatian twins clasped Rachel's hands, excitedly tugging her along.

Katrina beckoned to Shelly next. "Can you hang on to Rena and Milo?" Shelly nodded and took hold of their hands.

Katrina turned to Andi. Solemn green eyes stared back, unblinking as if she had already worked out what was next. "I'll take care of Drew." Andi grasped the three-year-old's hand with ladylike dignity. "He's used to me," she said, as if that settled the matter.

Tanya said, "I will watch Robbie."

"I can help someone," Caleb said.

"Good, you help, Shelly." Katrina resisted the urge to hug again. They would have to hurry to meet the guide in time. The sound of an airplane engine loomed overhead. "Hurry." She placed a warning finger to her lips, signaling everyone to be quiet. Katrina hoisted Baby onto her hip and told Ishmael, "I need you to be our lookout guard. Let me know if you see trouble coming or if anyone falls behind. Can you do that?"

"I'll do my best, but what if I miss something?"

"It's okay. We're all going to help each other. Let's go." Katrina led her little band through the jail and outside.

Alex crossed himself three times in an unspoken plea. He lowered the plane in a predawn swoop over the area, a fading crescent moon his guiding light as the jail loomed into sight. One minute left. Thirty seconds—he spotted movement near a military jeep parked down the street from the jail. Twenty seconds—a person stepped from the darkness toward the jeep. Ten seconds—Alex slowed the aircraft.

Eight—seven—six—five—the jail door opened, and several shadowy people slipped out. Alex pushed the release button, then steered the plane onto an upward track. Air raid signals sounded below as a round of explosives charged skyward in a fool's race to destroy him.

Katrina glanced up at the roar of a plane overhead and saw the falling bomb. She and the children ran until the explosion rocked them to the ground. The girls screamed in panic as broken stones flew overhead.

"Keep your heads down!" Katrina draped herself over the child in her arms. Pebbles bit into her cheeks, and she tasted dirt and grit. The children squeezed against her, with the older ones wrapped around the younger to shield them.

Katrina stifled a cry as a stone gouged her leg. Would she ever become used to this war? The rising sounds of terror sweeping the area gave its own answer. The earth settled with a heave and groan. Katrina gathered the stricken children. They stumbled from the scene. Fear pounded in her heart, and she kept a tight rein on her little band lest they draw unwanted attention. Katrina prayed desperately for safe passage for them all. Their path through Mostar was dangerous as they wove their way to the city's edge. What would she do if the guide failed to meet them? *Please, God, let him be there. Help us.*

An older man dressed as a peasant approached her. "My friend said you needed a guide."

"Yes. Thank you. Truer words were never spoken. Let me introduce us all to you."

"It is better not to speak any names. I will be your guide. If anyone asks, you are lost and choose to follow me until you find your friends. Let us leave now while we still can."

Katrina yielded control to the guide with relief. They matched their steps with his, following a few steps behind him. "Thank you, Lord," she whispered, glad to be out of jail and leaving Mostar behind.

Chapter 28

Earlier

Dressed in nondescript garb, Lucien knelt in the bushes about 150 meters from the Mostar jail, where Katrina was a prisoner. He'd completed his plans for the escape. The forged papers he'd arranged, requesting Katrina's transfer to Sarajevo with Alija Izetbegovic's signature, had been delivered. At dawn, she was scheduled to be transferred to Sarajevo, and his men were outside the city waiting to rescue her as the convoy passed.

Meanwhile, he'd been working to free the children. Martin's friend proved sympathetic and, for a price, agreed to smuggle the orphans out to Lucien. Lucien had arranged temporary shelter in Sarajevo, which for the present was a UN safe zone.

He cast an anxious glance at his watch. What could be keeping Katrina and the little ones? It was four a.m. Hour after hour, he'd invented excuses and continued to wait. Finally, he realized they weren't coming. More likely, the jailer had pocketed the bribe with no intention of aiding them.

Lucien pondered how to free the children without inside help. The danger remained that the jailer may have alerted Muslim intelligence of Lucien's plan. He supposed he would have been arrested upon arrival if not for the man wanting to keep his blood money secret.

Lucien stepped from the bushes and headed toward the jeep he'd borrowed from the meager supply at the Croatian base. A plane whined overhead. His instincts rammed into high alert. But before he could react, the street shook beneath him as an explosion knocked him to his knees. The jail had been hit. He struggled to his feet and ran there as fast as he could. Inside the jail, he tore through the rubble and burning ruins. "Katrina! Where are you?"

"Watch out!" someone yelled.

Lucien peered up as a beam crashed onto his back, pitching him to the floor.

Chapter 29

Vita was at a hotel with Cosic when Kiro burst into their room. "The Mostar jail has been bombed! I came from there. It's awful," Kiro said.

She sat up and yanked on her clothes. "Were any of our people hurt?"

"Yes. Some wounded and some dead."

The two men eyed each other warily. Cosic looked absurd standing in his trousers, his stomach flab protruding where muscles should have been. Vita brushed past him to get her shoes.

He grabbed her elbow, towing her in front of him. His outflung hand pointed at Kiro. "How did he learn we were here?"

"If you don't mind." Vita tugged to break free. When he held firm, she shot Kiro a warning glance not to interfere. Then, to appease the major, she said, "I always tell Kiro where I'm going."

Cosic's hand dropped from her elbow, and he gripped her shoulder, shaking her. "Not when it involves me. Got that?"

Vita lowered her gaze and nodded. Somehow, she straightened and faked a contrite expression. One day, she'd kill Cosic for this and every other occasion when he'd humiliated her, but not today. She still needed him.

Vita drew a calming breath and leaned into him. "He didn't know I was meeting you. I meant nothing by it. I'm in charge of the jail. If there's trouble, they've got to reach me."

She watched the expected gleam of interest light his face. She had let the bit about her job fall to distract him. He'd thought she worked in a menial position there. Her arms slipped around his thick waist. "You understand, don't you?"

Certain his senses were reeling, she stepped into her shoes and gathered her purse. "I've got to hurry. Sorry to rush off like this."

Vita knew she'd overplayed the scene when Cosic dragged her into his arms and kissed her hard. "Be here tonight."

Vita repressed a shudder. There were other arms dealers besides him. "I can't. I have to work."

His hold on her tightened. "You'll show, or the Muslim command will learn about the under-the-table deals you've been running." He shoved her aside and slipped on a shirt.

She hated him. Cosic seemed pleased by the contempt she couldn't hide. He thrived on tormenting her.

"I'll send her home with a tip on some more arms shipments for you," he said to Kiro.

Angry and humiliated, Vita stomped from the room, leaving Kiro to follow. They got into his beige Lada and drove off in silence toward Mostar. Halfway there, Kiro drove a few feet off the highway onto a dirt road and stopped the car. He reached across the seat and drew her gently to him. She pushed him away, and he let her.

Kiro said, "I'm sorry this is difficult for you. What do you think it does to me, letting him touch you? I wanted to gut him."

Vita didn't respond. She stared ahead, trying to keep from crying and wanting to believe Kiro wasn't using her. Unfortunately, she didn't have time to think about it with the jail torn apart. They'd wasted too many hours on Cosic.

Kiro shifted beside her. "Vita, speak to me."

After a long pause, she finally said, "Later. Drive to the jail and fill me in on the attack."

Kiro started the car and roared onto the highway at a recklessly high speed, winding through densely forested mountains.

"Slow down. You know I hate going fast on curves."

Kiro gave her a repentant grin. "All right. Sorry." He cleared his throat, and she watched his expression grow bitter. "A Serbian aircraft attacked. The cells and prisoners were practically wiped out."

"What about Katrina and the children?"

"They're probably dead, buried in the rubble."

"Cosic's going to give us trouble over this. He believes Katrina hid the icon he wants. If she's dead, how will he ever find the Madonna? Maybe we can discover where it's hidden. It has to be valuable, or he wouldn't bother."

"Nothing can be done about it in the wake of this disaster. The offices near the front are intact but severely damaged. Two officers who were down in the Croat woman's cell died."

Vita spat. "Serves them right, the swine."

"They were rightly avenging the rapes of so many of our own. 'An eye for an eye and a tooth for a tooth.' You, of all people, should understand that."

"No. A pig is a pig in any country." She clenched her fists as the thought struck her. "Kiro, you wouldn't ever, would you?"

His laugh was brittle. "What? Be an animal? Is that how you feel when I touch you?"

She shivered as his hand slid up her arm. "How I feel about you is no secret. You're different from all the others."

"Because I saved you?"

She held her open palm against his cheek, gazing at the passing highway. "Because you cared. No one else ever did. We want the same things—to watch those Serbian pigs roast."

His long, strong fingers dug into her shoulder. "No, we want more than that. We want power and wealth, too." His hand gentled. "For our children, yours and mine. One day, we'll start our own family, and everything will be different. We'll take the money and go somewhere else if it doesn't work here. Revenge will not fill our bellies or warm our beds."

His words left a bitter taste in her mouth. How could she ever forget? If he loved her, how could he bear for her to be with Cosic? Though she wanted to trust Kiro, doubts plagued her. She pushed them aside. It had only ever been Kiro. No matter the cost, she'd never let him go.

They drove without speaking for the rest of the journey. When Kiro halted in front of the jail, Vita could see that the north side of the building had been destroyed. Other parts were severely damaged but standing. She sprang from the Lada. The explosion had blown a hole where the jail door once stood. Vita rushed through it and was sickened at the sight of the wounded, bleeding people scattered about.

Medics had arrived and were doing their best to treat the worst cases. Her stomach churned. A young soldier was lying there with no arms and legs, still breathing, blood everywhere.

Chapter 30

Lucien groaned and struggled to open his eyes, but the effort was too great. His entire body ached. He heard men's voices, speaking as if from a distance.

He fought the swirling darkness closing in. Danger signals prickled up and down his spine. He strained to hang onto consciousness with every fiber of will he possessed. Finally, the room stopped spinning, and his vision slowly cleared. Lucien forced himself to relax, to remember.

Gradually, it came back. The bomb—his searching for Katrina and not finding her and the beam falling on him. Now he lay in the jail's reception area with other wounded men, the debris of shattered stucco walls thick around them. He wiggled his toes and flexed his legs, then expelled the breath he'd been holding. He was not paralyzed.

Lucien scanned the room anxiously, assessing his chances of escape. Once the soldiers realized he was Croatian, his life would be worthless. He needed to move before they had time to organize.

He started to rise and fell back in shock as Vita and Kiro entered. Tension gripped him. His mind screamed, *run for it!* His stiff and sore body refused to obey.

Half-dazed and confused, Lucien hid his face. He caught a whiff of cheap perfume as Vita brushed past, snapping out questions.

Lucien opened one eye, and the room spun sideways. He saw Vita and the officers drifting about.

He pried his eyes open as Vita followed the men into the next room. *Did he have the strength to walk?* From where he lay, he pushed himself to his hands and knees and crawled toward the door, the pain in his shoulder intense. Lucien fought the urge to black out. He had a few more feet to go. He couldn't quit.

Lucien reached the blown door opening and rested against it, taking in the chaos. His eyes closed, and he sagged forward, the swinging motion rocking him to his senses.

He gripped the ruined wall, heaved himself to his feet, and stumbled through the door and down the street. In the bombing's aftermath, no one paid him any attention.

His one thought was to reach the Croatian base. There was nothing he could do for Katrina or the children. He was sure they'd been killed. Lucien would face that later. For now, it would take a miracle for him to bolt from the Muslim sector in the daylight. He should lie low until nightfall. But where?

He'd parked his jeep nearby. Maybe miracles still happened, and it was still there. Fifty meters from the jail, Lucien paused in a recessed entry. The way would be shorter if he could cut through the house and across the back alley to his jeep.

Lucien braced himself against the frame, grasped the knob, and slid inside. A young woman sat in the corner. Her vacant blue stare registered no reaction to his presence.

His gaze on her, he walked backward to the opposite door and ran outside. He half-dragged himself to the jeep. The woman might come to her senses and send the authorities after him. He climbed into the vehicle and was closing the door when it was wrenched from his hand. Lucien turned and almost cursed aloud to see an armed Muslim soldier speaking to him as if they were comrades. Lucien motioned the man closer while resting one hand on the butt of the weapon tucked into his waistband. The soldier lowered his head to hear what Lucien had to say. He grabbed his gun and struck the soldier, who fell to the ground. Lucien sped away.

⚜ ⚜ ⚜

Alex lowered the jet and searched the hills for his second target, a Croatian base hidden in the brush. The poor, unsuspecting idiots would be annihilated.

He spotted military activity on the ridge. Alex tracked the ragged soldiers below as he zeroed in on the base's location. He positioned the plane and verified the instrument panel readings. His radar did a broad sweep, scanning for enemy aircraft. A green light on the panel beeped the go-ahead. Alex counted slowly to ten. One thousand—two thousand—five—seven—ten thousand.

He pushed the release button, then accelerated in an upward streak, steering due south. His conversation with Ennis the night before plagued him. Had he murdered innocent people? Alex shrugged, aware he had no choice.

He wished he could take an hour to scout the route to Italy. A glance at the land to the south was all he could risk. In the back of his mind, a plan had formed. If he could smuggle Ennis and his son to the coast, it would give them a fighting chance to survive.

He could hire a boat to take them across the Adriatic to Italy. They could start a new life in the West. Maybe he was naïve to believe in dreams, but what was life without hope and love? Weary of wanton destruction, he hated what he was doing and who he was becoming. The war made little sense. It was immoral. If he continued, it would destroy him and his family.

Chapter 31

Bosnia-Herzegovina, Summer 1993

The plane on autopilot, Alex drank in the beauty of the distant coast, half lost in a dream of freedom for himself, Ennis, and the baby.

He pictured the three of them picnicking on a sunny Italian beach, a large umbrella overhead to protect the baby, not from bombs but from sunburn. He could almost see the warm sands covered with people like ants, everyone bowing to the god of commercialism, freedom confidently in their grasp.

Before the war, he and Ennis had worked for Yugoslav Air, he as a pilot, she as a flight attendant. They met while vacationing in Brisbane. It seemed natural to become a twosome, strolling hand in hand, their bare feet digging into the honey-colored beach. The wind blew auburn curls across her face and sand into their eyes as they basked in the sun and later watched the sky fade into evening. They enjoyed the quiet, moonlit nights.

He pictured Ennis lying on the sandy shoreline, the sun's warmth kissing her delicate nose as he splashed through the cresting waves. A white-capped breaker threw him to his knees, and he came up gasping. Brisbane's turbulent surf mirrored his inner turmoil at falling in love, feeling knocked off his feet while heady and alive.

Later, along the wharf, they ate frozen yogurt swirled in cones with icy chips of banana and pineapple, titillating Alex's taste buds. For dinner, they visited a quaint Mexican restaurant and ate enchiladas Aussie style by candlelight. Then they took a ridiculous bus ride, seventeen hours across the plains of Australia to Sidney, and finally, a bumpy flight to the coast. They had fallen in love, never imagining the evil lurking at home ready to destroy them.

Alex realized the beckoning coast had lured him into traveling farther south than he intended. As if his very thought conjured up evil, at precisely four p.m. Belgrade time, a bright blip appeared on the console of Alex's aircraft, a signal from the threat warning system. Adrenaline raced through his veins, and his chest constricted. He had been spotted by ground radar.

Bosnian SAM rings, otherwise known as surface-to-air-missiles, were an ever-present threat. Alex switched on the radio, reconnecting with his base. Earlier, he'd cut communications so Belgrade would not track him flying farther south than ordered. He felt disgusted at his recklessness. Desperation bred fools. More than anything, he wanted to get Ennis and his son across to Italy.

As his thumb moved to the bomb-release button in readiness, Alex flinched at the uselessness of the gesture. The plane's weapon arsenal was empty.

A steady voice came over the radio, "S Core One, your dirt five communication remains unconfirmed."

Sweat beaded on Alex's forehead as a warning screeched over his headset, alerting him to a radar threat. A tremor shot through him as he spoke into the radio. "S Core One, dirt five bearing one-eight-zero."

The voice from Belgrade called out. "S Core One, do you read me? Over—S Core One." Static dominated the airwaves, then a muffled curse. "We've lost contact. S Core One, confirm." Another expletive rang out. "S Core One awaiting your signal, answer. Repeat. Unable to track."

Alex flipped the radio buttons furiously to reestablish contact. A second alarm screamed through his headset. Three enemy aircraft appeared out of nowhere. Overhead, the jets circled like vultures.

A programmed voice dictated through his headset. "Counter. Counter."

The enemy aircraft were on him before he could counter their moves.

Everything happened in a split second. A picture of Ennis and his son streaked through his mind. One hand brushed the Saint Christopher medal his grandmother had given him, and he crossed himself three times, praying. Without weapons to counter an air-to-air or surface-to-air strike, all he could do was strive to evade a direct hit from either. He searched the sky for a furrow of white smoke, his one chance to get a visual identification before the rocket took off at a deadly speed twice that of an F-16.

Alex headed the plane into a string of radical climbs and dives. The odds stunk—a gang war, and he had to be the solitary pilot on the block. Where was Belgrade when you needed them?

A direct hit clipped his right wing, which shattered, sending his plane into a spin. Alex reeled as a brilliant flame of fire lit the sky.

Wham! A deafening roar hammered at his eardrums. His body jerked at the impact as the plane was struck. Alex pitched wildly about as flames leaped through the cockpit, the plane on a downward plunge, out of control.

He grasped the seat eject handle and wrenched it hard. The bubble canopy burst off the cockpit and tumbled backward.

Microseconds later, attached to the ejection seat, he rocketed out of the cockpit into space. The next few minutes seemed like an eternity. In an upside-down plunge, he barreled through stinging chilly winds, counting, unsure if his parachute would work.

At what he calculated to be about fourteen thousand feet, Alex pulled the handle on the side of his seat and heard a reassuring pop as the drogue chute opened and he decelerated. A second pop followed, and his parachute billowed out. Still strapped to his chair, he found himself upright. A jet roared above, increasing his sense of vulnerability. But a glance around revealed a cloud cover too thick to expose him. He tore off his oxygen mask, tossing it.

His drop rate of forty feet per second left him five and one-half minutes in the air, valuable time needed to set his rescue in motion. Alex flicked the radio beacon on his seat frame, sending a distress call across the emergency guard channel. Soon, Belgrade would realize he had survived, as would every radio dispatcher in Bosnia.

The altitude sensor kicked in, and a motor fired, detaching Alex from the seat. He seized the handheld radio attached to his belt and tried to contact his Serbian base to give his location. All he got was static. Enemy Bosnian units would soon be combing the area for him. He clung to the memory of his last evening with Ennis and his son, detesting his fear. He knuckled the Saint Christopher medal around his neck and prepared for landing. "Don't worry, babe," he said, bracing himself. "This can't be the end."

Alex ran through a mental list of his gear: flashlight, radio, survival sack, weapons kit, and life raft. He drew a deep breath and murmured a prayer to his grandmother's God in case He was real. His head up, legs together, Alex prepared to drop into a sideways curl that would end with him rocking onto the balls of his feet.

He could see green hills now. A gust of wind blew him sideways, and he saw the forest divided from the meadows by a highway. Alex sailed closer to the ground, and it seemed to rise, smashing into him like a mountain boulder.

He landed on his left side and rolled to a stop in the grassy meadow. In a rush to escape, Alex freed his parachute harness, gathered his equipment, and ran for the cover of the nearby woods.

Flames shot up, and smoke furled into the distant sky. His plane. Of every foolish thing he had ever done, none could have matched this. His right hand slid over where the medal lay, and then he crossed himself three times. "I'm not saying I believe, God, but just in case, thanks for the landing. And if there's a way out of here, I could use some more help."

Sheepishly, he gazed skyward, wondering what had come over him. His comrades would laugh if they knew his thoughts had turned to prayer at the first sign of trouble. Prayer was for the elderly and people too weak to use the sense they were given. No, the thing that would save him was his own two feet.

He drew out a compass and began the long hike before him. Almost unconsciously, his fingertips skimmed the spot where the cross lay as he marched away from the burning plane. He hoped to stumble upon one of the Serb camps rumored to be hidden in the region. Of course, explaining what he was doing this far south wouldn't be easy.

He stepped through a clump of trees, brushing aside its limbs.

"You there, don't move. Hands up."

As Alex raised his arms, he felt a searing pain in the back of his head. With a moan, he fell, his last thought of Ennis and his son.

It was late evening before Vita and Kiro returned to her apartment after viewing the destruction at the Mostar jail. For once, she couldn't wait for Kiro to leave. She was so tired and dirty. She felt numb as his arms slid around her.

He hugged her tight. "Are you okay?"

"I will be after a bath and bed." She drew back, but he tugged her closer.

"Mmm." His kiss was heavy and demanding, taking more than giving. He broke off and swatted her bottom, propelling her toward the bathroom. "Hurry. I'll be waiting."

She didn't want him to touch her, not tonight. She turned on the shower and washed the grime and blood down the drain, wanting to scrub every trace of the wounded, dying, and Cosic from her life. The hot water and soap revived her. Kiro was right. Tonight, they needed each other and needed to reaffirm their commitment.

A terrycloth bathrobe over her gown, she entered the bedroom and sat in the chair across the room from where Kiro lay. "I want to talk."

He quirked one eyebrow and patted the bed. "Come here."

She shook her head. "Kiro, I can't do this with Cosic anymore, not even for you. I admit it was my idea to begin with, but he repulses me." Maybe Kiro had initially objected, but after he'd seen the gained arms shipments, his reservations had disappeared.

He crossed to her chair and drew her close, his thumbs wiping at the tears that slid down her cheeks. "It's destroying us both. I've been half out of my mind knowing you were with him." He kissed her cheek and her forehead. "It's finished, Vita. Don't cry. I won't ask you to see him again. You mean too much to me."

"Truly?" she asked through her sobs.

"Shush. We've enough money between us to escape now if we have to, to start a new life."

A rejuvenating release filled her as he plucked her into his arms. Kiro wasn't using her. He cared. Strange how she could be so cold with others and feel so soft and yielding to him, as if she were finally coming home.

Kiro took her tenderly, vanquishing her fears and filling her with mindless pleasure and passion.

"Tell me you love only me," he begged.

"Just you, Kiro. Nobody else."

"Promise me you'll do anything to help us escape from here. No matter what."

"Anything. There's nothing I wouldn't do for you."

Chapter 32

Bosnia-Herzegovina, Summer 1993

Katrina prayed her enemies would assume she and the children had died during the jail bombing. She shuddered, unable to forget her fear as they had escaped execution amid the chaos and destruction. She trailed several yards behind the guide with the kids grouped between them. Patches of light flickered through the heavy foliage, marking the rugged path. Her little band had been traveling in a constant state of alert, with scarcely any food or rest. Baby squirmed in her arms, and Katrina's grip faltered. She tightened her hold on the toddler and murmured a ragged endearment to comfort him. Not long ago, he was a small baby. All the kids were growing up despite the war.

Everyone was anxious and tired, but no one complained. They'd spent the first week after their escape hidden in the wet basement of a country cottage. The seven-year-old Croatian twins Ana and Dinko had found a permanent home there with the kind and childless couple who'd taken them in.

Katrina thought of the orphans who'd died with her family. She tripped on a rock, almost falling. She needed to concentrate on survival and quit rehashing the past. Regret couldn't bring her or Bosnia the peace she craved. Had God used adversity to shake up her life? To whittle at its narrow confines—the boundaries she'd drawn, aided by her disposition and circumstances? To ensure she saw the mountains and sky rather than the boulders obscuring her path? So she'd learn to trust both Him and herself?

Late afternoon, Katrina and her small band moved into a sparsely forested region, and the guide called a halt. "There's a farmhouse a few kilometers ahead where we can camp, but we'll want to approach it by the cover of night."

Katrina sat down beneath a beech tree, Baby on her lap. The children sank to the ground wearily. The sight of their bodies, thinner now, was wrenching.

She heard a commotion, the result of the guide throwing a rock into the nearby bushes.

"Ouch. Leave me alone!" A young boy burst into the camp, glaring at them. "I didn't hurt anyone."

The guide studied him. "Serbian, aren't you? You hanging around here planning on stealing something?"

A frightened expression appeared on his face as the boy scrambled behind Milo and Caleb.

Katrina swallowed her anger. "He's a child like the others."

"You don't know what he's been trained to do."

She held the guide's gaze and motioned the boy to her side. "No one here will hurt you. Tell me your name."

"Samuel." He shuffled his feet and looked down.

"How old are you, Samuel?"

"Nine."

Katrina studied his jacket thoughtfully, noting its quality. "And your family?"

A sob broke from him at the question.

She asked, "Do you know what happened to them?"

His lower lip trembled, and she strained to hear his crushed whisper. "They were murdered in the pit."

Mass graves where hundreds and thousands were shot and buried were referred to as the pit. Katrina inhaled sharply, struggling for words that didn't have the power to heal the hurt or return his lost loved ones. She touched his face, raising his chin. "I'm sorry, Samuel. My family was murdered, too."

She gestured toward the children. "Many of their folks as well." She gave Rachel, Shelly, and Andi a reassuring smile. "We're trying to find the girls' parents. Like you, we've been hiding. Will you join us? Another male to help would be a great blessing."

He nodded uncertainly, his face a mixture of hope and fear.

Katrina hugged him close, feeling his small frame quiver against hers.

How could people destroy these children? Their plight was one of the most heinous crimes in this war. Sixty thousand orphans had been left homeless, fighting for survival because their parents had died or disappeared in battle. Where were the grown-ups who should have been nurturing this new generation? The atrocities committed in the name of religion and nationalism were heartbreaking.

The guide grunted. Katrina studied him, curious to see how her acceptance of Samuel agreed with him. He nodded, visibly moved. The man wasn't as hard as he pretended to be. How could he be and risk his life to get them out of the country?

He patted the boy's shoulder. "My son was about your age when I lost him. Maybe we can help each other." The guide and Samuel talked. After a while, the guide asked, "What is your nationality?"

"My mother was Muslim, and my father Serbian." Samuel glared. "They never hurt anyone."

"I'm sure they were fine folks. I was asking for your own protection. So we'll know what we're up against."

Katrina squeezed his hand. "You're safe now. We're all mixed here." She pointed to the others. "The girls are American, except for Rena. She and Drew are Croatian. Milo and Caleb are Serbian, while Baby and Ishmael are Muslim. Your nationality doesn't matter to us."

The guide said, "Now that's settled, boy, can you tell us how close we are to the Serbs?"

Sniffing, he wiped his nose. "They're all around. The soldiers force people to dig huge graves and crawl inside, hundreds at a time. Then the Serbs shoot them."

The sound of enemy fire overhead and several warring aircraft drew Katrina's attention. They dove for cover. Katrina glanced up and saw a plane hurtling toward them.

Chapter 33

"Down, everybody," Katrina yelled as the plane smashed into the ground and burst into flames. She hid her face in a tall clump of grass. Scraps of sheet metal and paper rained on them. With a shaky breath, she tightened her arms around the children huddled against her.

In the background, a frightened donkey brayed as the guide's harsh voice burst through the turmoil, urging them to flee. "Hurry. There's no time to lose. Run before the fire draws the enemies' attention."

She stumbled to her feet with a gasp. "The pilot? There could be passengers in there." She raced toward the plane.

The guide wrenched her arm, hauling her back. "It's too late. Forget them!"

Katrina winced and half-turned, frantic at the delay.

The kind guide of the last few days had vanished, and in his place was an animal at war. "If you go there," he said, pointing to the burning wreck, "you go alone. I'm not waiting around here to die."

"We can't leave them."

He shrugged, his face set. "No one could have survived that explosion." As if to prove his conviction, he strode in the opposite direction.

"But the children . . ."

He halted. "Make up your mind. Is it the orphans or the plane you're interested in saving? You can't do both. That plane's Serbian. If there are survivors, all the more reason to get going. We're at war, and it's an enemy aircraft."

The kids were listening with scared, wide-eyed looks. Her first duty was to them. Torn and sick with self-loathing, she moved forward, then stopped. She couldn't do it. Not even for these little ones. She couldn't trade one life for another.

With a strangled bid to them for understanding, she said, "Go with the guide. I won't be long." Katrina turned and ran as fast as she could. Adrenaline pumped through her veins as she headed for the burning plane. Lord, she prayed, please, please—no more deaths.

When she reached the plane, she saw rescue was impossible. Flames were everywhere. The jet was an indistinguishable sculpture of melting metal and fire. She coughed, shielding her eyes from the roaring glare and smoke, and fell back. Most of the children waited alone, a few hundred feet downwind. They hadn't left. How foolish of her to have risked their lives. The guide had disappeared beyond the hill and into the dense forest. What had she done?

Dizzy and lethargic, Katrina collapsed and rested her head in her hands. She should go to the children. Yet she couldn't seem to move. A feeling of weightlessness overtook her. She coughed, trying to breathe, hindered by the smoke, the wind was blowing her way. Her vision swirled and dissolved into an obscure haze. She was so tired and weak from scarce food and the torture she'd endured in jail. Thoughts of the kids spurred her onward. If she were gone, who would care for them?

Katrina had enough strength to crawl away from the plane and then collapsed. She strained to move again but couldn't. She should be up and moving. Her body seemed so strange and heavy. What was happening to her? Why did she feel so weary?

Her eyes closed, and her thoughts drifted. She was going home at last. Giles and her mother and father hovered above her in the clouds, beckoning for her to join them. "Mother, I'm so sorry I couldn't help the orphans. I tried, Mother. Tried so hard . . ."

Her father's arms closed around her. "Shh, you're with us. No need to cry anymore."

"I've missed you so much, Daddy."

"Shh," he murmured. "No more worrying. You're safe now."

Chapter 34

Earlier

After leaving the site of the Mostar jail bombing, Lucien had checked in at nearby Croatian headquarters, apprehensive the facility had also been attacked. But as he drove into the compound, he was relieved to find it unharmed. He parked and went inside to his commander's office. "It looks like everything is still standing," Lucien said.

"Come in and have a seat. The Serbian air strike barely missed us," the commander said, appearing worn but jubilant.

"Glad to hear it, sir." Lucien sat on a reinforced gun crate and told him about his experiences in the Mostar jail bombing and asked if he'd heard any news about Katrina or the children.

He shook his head. "I'm sorry. You did what you could."

Lucien stood. "I'll leave you to your work, sir."

"Where are you off to?"

"I plan on staying on base long enough to recover and to scout about for any news of them or a jailbreak."

Lucien headed over to the barracks and sank onto a cot. His body ached all over, but mostly, he was heartsore about Katrina and the kids. The uncertainty left him in a purgatory of guilt. He alternately blamed himself, God, if He existed, and the war. For his sanity, he chose to believe Katrina and her charges were alive and had escaped before the Mostar jail bombing.

Several days later, feeling more himself, he drove out of the army base, determined to find her. He wound the jeep down Highway 17 through dense mountain terrain to the coast and navigated toward Split, moving on instinct. As a boy, he'd enjoyed holidays at Grandfather Creto's summer place in nearby Trogir. Lucien kept in touch with buddies there from his youth, a time of boating, fishing, and swimming. Innocence had marked those days when right and wrong were clearly defined, and trust was woven into their daily lives.

The jeep hit a rut, and Lucien grimaced as his head bounced against the metal roof. Besides his family, he trusted few people, but he hoped he could rely on his longtime friend Tony to sail Katrina and the kids across to Italy.

Around the next bend, his grandfather's house loomed. Lucien parked in the steep drive and walked to the back, overcome with memories of the man he'd loved. He reached under the geranium planter on the patio for the key and brushed aside the moist dirt clinging to it. He hadn't been certain it would be there. It was a mark of the villagers' respect that, with his grandfather's death, the house hadn't been looted.

Lucien trekked through the grass to the boathouse. He stood gazing at the sandy beach and the waves beating against the shore. On his last visit, he and his grandfather had spent hours talking and reminiscing. He'd taught Lucien to swim when he was five, fish at seven, and boat at ten. It wasn't hard to imagine him standing there now, white-haired and proud, his shoulders stooped with age, keen intelligence in his brown eyes.

Memories of him were all Lucien had. Mental images that faded and blurred with time couldn't speak or stretch out a comforting hand. He drew his diary from its hiding place inside his shirt and flipped to the entry under the heading: Dead. Creto Brezak's name, inscribed in cold black ink, stared at him.

Lucien broke down, and big heaving sobs shook him. He wept because Gramps was no more, and the war was unbearably abhorrent. He'd never be the man his grandfather had been. At thirty-four,

Lucien's existence seemed desolate and overwhelmingly useless. He had come, in his arrogance, to save a country torn by war and lost himself.

Eventually, his emotions spent, he rose and trudged to the house. He phoned Tony, keeping the conversation short. "Can you meet me here in an hour?"

Tony agreed, and Lucien rang off.

A massive stone fireplace dominated the den where the family had often gathered. Brown clay tiles covered the floor, and the picture window at the front looked out on spruce and fir trees. With a sigh, he sank into Gramps's worn leather chair. His journal lay on the pine table beside it. Half-fearful of what he'd find, Lucien flipped to the entry marking the start of the Croatian War and read until there was a knock at the door.

"Lucien, are you in there?" Tony called.

With care, Lucien set the journal aside and rose with renewed purpose. Though he missed his grandfather, a part of the man he loved would always live inside him.

He unlocked the front door, and a warm welcome stretched across his face as he embraced Tony's wiry frame.

Tony cuffed Lucien on the shoulder. "It took you forever to answer. I thought something had happened."

"Sorry," Lucien said as they sank into the chairs on either side of the fireplace. "Let's say I had some catching up to do."

His friend lowered his gaze, studying the octagonal-shaped tiles. "Yeah, sorry about your grandfather's passing. There was nothing we could have done."

"Thanks." Warmth spiraled through him at his friend's concern. "You haven't heard from my uncles, have you?"

Tony waved a calloused hand. "This was the first place the Serbs looked for them. Before the soldiers finished, they'd searched the entire village."

Lucien stared at the empty fire grate, remembering past visits. Tony was expecting him to ask who else had been hurt or murdered. Lucien determinedly shook off the past, not wanting to hear. He would concentrate on Katrina and the orphans. He hesitated to reveal so much, but he owed it to Tony to be completely honest.

Quickly, he filled him in on the situation and concluded, "I need your help, but I want you to understand the risks. Katrina attracts trouble. She's an American who has some formidable enemies. Though all she's done is to care for the children." He glanced at Tony expectantly. "What do you say?"

Tony's dark gaze held steady. "I owe you, big time. We'll never forget how you saved Natalia's life."

Lucien had paid for the hospital care when Tony's wife experienced a tubal pregnancy that ruptured, almost killing her. When his friend called on him, desperate for help, Lucien willingly did whatever he could. He spoke over the lump in his throat. "Don't agree out of a sense of gratitude. There's too much at stake. Think of Natalia and the kids."

Tony adjusted the worn blue cap on his head. "I'm already in deeper than you imagine. I couldn't back out if I wanted to. This war is larger than Natalia, the kids, and me."

"You're sure?" Lucien questioned him until he was confident Tony's agreement wasn't based on obligation. As he half suspected, Tony routinely ferried people across to Italy. Lucien didn't delve too far into the matter. Everyone had secrets, and the fewer who knew, the safer it was.

Tony said, "Don't worry. We'll sail her and the orphans to Italy."

They exchanged cash, shook hands on the deal, and then Tony left.

Lucien's plans had changed. If Katrina was with Martin's folks, they would protect her. And if she wasn't, he would find her soon enough. While he was in the area, Lucien needed to check on his family. He would never forgive himself if they were hiding nearby and needed help that he'd failed to give them. After a week of revisiting memories and searching for his uncles and cousins, Lucien gave up. He'd done all he could.

He locked the house and climbed into the jeep. His gut said he would find Katrina near Martin's parents' farm. He didn't understand the hunch, but Lucien had learned to follow his instincts.

Chapter 35

Bosnia-Herzegovina, Summer 1993

Anxiety for Katrina tugged at Lucien as he drove down the highway toward Martin's folks' farm. He heard an explosion and stopped the car on the side of the road. Lucien stuck his head out the window and watched as a Serb jet, hit by a retreating Croatian aircraft, plummeted to the ground. From the corner of his eye, Lucien caught sight of a woman with children in the distance. Terrified, he watched Katrina dart toward the plane and disappear on the other side of it. His heart slammed against his chest, and he forced himself to breathe.

Lucien sprinted across the road and around the burning wreck to where she lay unconscious. He gathered her in his arms and hugged her close as he plodded through a field of waist-high grass to where the children waited. Lucien inhaled the scent of her singed hair and clothes, wanting never to experience such dread again. Perhaps he'd overreacted, propelled by his fear of losing her.

He shifted her closer and stared at Katrina's precious face. How could he not have realized how deep his feelings went? He needed to get her out of Bosnia to somewhere safe, like his home in Austria. The orphans who had disappeared during the mission raid and those she'd told him about who'd fled with John and Ellen during the cave attack might have already escaped and been transported to Austrian refugee camps. Or they could be dead. He didn't know, but Lucien couldn't bear for Katrina to be in continual danger.

She remained unconscious as he bundled her and the kids into the jeep. "Everyone here?" he asked.

Caleb said, "There's just us now."

"Where are the others?"

"Tanya, Rena, Robbie, Milo, Ismael, and that new boy Samuel left with the guide," Rachel said. "Aunt Katrina told them to follow him."

"She told us to go to," Shelly said.

Andi chimed in, "We didn't want to leave her."

Lucien did a quick head count: Rachel, Shelly, Andi, Baby, Drew, and Caleb. There were six of the thirteen that he remembered left. "Where are the twins?"

"Ana and Dinko got a mommy and daddy," Drew said.

Lucien drove fast, wincing at every bump for Katrina's sake. The girls holding her in the back of the jeep were quiet, and Lucien, intent on reaching Martin's parents' farm, didn't talk. The boys had squeezed into the front seat beside him. Soon, they were talking and asking questions he didn't know the answers to.

They arrived at the farm about an hour later, and Lucien parked. He carried Katrina, the children trailing alongside. They should be secure here, and Katrina could recuperate.

His sister and Martin rushed out to greet them. Sara gasped at seeing Katrina's limp form. "What's happened to her?"

Martin's mother, close behind, said, "Tsk, tsk, this is no time for questions. Follow me." She picked up the two little tykes and urged the others inside. She settled Katrina and soon had everyone else fed and in bed.

Lucien bunked down on the living room couch. Unable to sleep, he stared out at the night. Apprehension spiraled through his gut and held him captive to his worst imaginings. Helpless to shake his anxiety, he checked on Katrina.

She lay asleep on her side with one hand curled under her cheek.

He brushed his hand against her forehead, worried she hadn't regained consciousness. Martin's mother had insisted her sleep was a natural result of hunger and exhaustion. His lips grazed the top of her hair, the brief touch bittersweet.

Chapter 36

Katrina awoke to strange surroundings.

Lucien rose from the chair by her bed. "Katrina?"

She closed her eyes and opened them again to find Lucien bent over her in concern. "Am I dreaming?"

His warm hands clasped hers. "How do you feel?"

"Where am I?" she rasped, a burning pain in her throat.

"We're at Martin's parents' farm." His thumb moved across her lips, silencing her. "Save your strength. I'll do the talking. Okay?"

Katrina nodded.

Martin's mom entered the room carrying a tray she set on the nightstand by the bed. "*Dragi,* you need some of my broth to regain your strength."

Katrina sniffed. No one had called her dear since her parents' deaths until now.

Martin's mom settled the pillows behind Katrina's head and helped her sit up in bed before placing the tray on her lap. She handed her some water. "Drink this first." She stayed until Katrina finished the water and soup, then kissed her cheeks and left.

Katrina started to speak, but Lucien stopped her.

"Do you remember the plane crash?"

In her mind, she saw the burning plane as she'd fainted. Yet how had she come to be here and with Lucien? His kindness and presence were unexpected. Surely, he despised her after the false accusations she'd hurled at him.

He squeezed her hand. "You're probably wondering why I'm here. I was driving to meet Sara and Martin, hoping you might be with them. I heard the planes firing overhead and stopped on the side of the road seconds before the crash." His pressure on her fingers increased until it hurt. "When I saw you disappear near those flames . . . What were you trying to do? Couldn't you see it was hopeless?"

"What if I could have saved them?"

He grasped her chin, tilting her face. "What is this? You're not blaming yourself? There was nothing you could have done." Lucien broke off as she gulped back a sob. "Katrina, I'm sorry. I've made it worse." He hugged her and tried to soothe her.

Her tears, silent for so long, spilled out. She wanted to explain but couldn't stop weeping. "It's all my fault."

"Nonsense. You've had a horrendous experience."

She touched his cheek. "After the awful things I've said to you, how can you forgive me?"

"It's not hard. I understood you were hurting." He kissed her, his lips conveying the depth of his feelings.

Katrina shivered as his lips left her breathless, the heat of his closeness awakening her.

Lucien let go of her, and she relaxed against the pillows. Her gaze sought his for an explanation. He ran his hands through his hair in frustration. "Get some rest. I'll be in the living room if you need me."

He kissed her again and then left before she could speak. Too tired to figure it out, Katrina slept.

Chapter 37

Katrina awoke from the nightmare with a start. The war was resurrecting memories she'd buried in Texas. She shuddered, recalling the turbulent waves carrying the rowboat with the twins out into the bay. The shock of seeing her young siblings playfully rocking the boat and laughing as they tumbled about.

"Giles, call Mom and Dad. Hurry!" Katrina kicked off her flip-flops and ran.

She dove into the water as the twins' giggles turned to shrill cries. If only they weren't so far out. Katrina swam, struggling against the choppy bay waters, to reach the rowboat, praying she wouldn't be too late.

She peered over her shoulder at the distant shore and saw no help. Why weren't her parents out there in the motorboat? She surged onward but failed to save them.

Katrina had been twelve when she was hauled to shore with the twins' dead bodies. No one had blamed her. Family and friends fussed over her, declaring her a heroine for trying to save her siblings. But they spoke with sad regrets. "If you had come for us," her parents lamented, unthinking in their sorrow.

Giles had flushed with shame, his eyes pleading. She should have realized that the shock would have left him too frightened to move when she'd sent him to get their parents. A nearby boat had found the twins and her and radioed ahead to notify her parents so they'd know what to expect.

The worst part of the afternoon was listening to the neighbors talk. Katrina had been so cold and scared. She overheard one say,

"Those poor babies." Another sad shake of the head. "The twins might be alive if Katrina had run for her parents instead of venturing out alone."

Tears fiercely held back burned her eyes. She wanted to shake the neighbors and tell them to shut up. They hadn't loved the twins as she did. Katrina clenched her fists, cleaving to the core of inner defiance, which refused to buckle in her grief. Nauseated, she'd stood by her parents and Giles, too terrified to let them out of her sight. In the end, she hadn't been able to save them either.

Whispers in the silence reached out, the long tendrils of sound suffocating her. Would she always shirk from the inevitable? Was there no end? No reckoning? No help or answer to her cry?

Her faith cracked like the snap of a willow branch. What crooked paths her doubts and fears had traveled. Not that she doubted God. Yet, to understand His will seemed beyond her. How could she know what horrific events might occur next? Hadn't she lost the twins, her parents, and Giles? Didn't scripture teach that everything worked toward the good of those who served God? Who else but the Lord appointed unto each a time to live and die?

Chapter 38

Belgrade, Serbia, Summer 1993

In her pale cream Belgrade living room, Dianne Jovanovic dropped the telephone receiver into its cradle, then stifled the sobs that racked her insides and drew several deep breaths. "Dear God," she prayed. "Take care of my baby. She's only nineteen."

Dianne swiped strands of mink brown hair from her eyes. It seemed like yesterday Mimi was a toddler, and her husband Stefan was a mere captain. *Oh, for the simplicity of those days before the war and Stefan's promotion to general in the Serbian Army.* Dianne wished she could rescue her daughter, and Mimi could travel to her grandfather's house in Croatia, where everything would be fine. But Dianne's family home had been destroyed, and her father with it. Her mother had died some years ago. Her brothers, except for Josef, lived there still and were all in the Croatian Army, fighting for their land and lives.

Mimi's Grandfather Creto's death had flamed her rebellion. Dianne stared at the phone, aware she'd have to tell Stefan and dreading it. She mentally rehearsed the conversation, inserting the warning the police chief, an old friend, had given her minutes before. "Your daughter's anti-Serbian pranks must stop, or she will be brought before the committee."

He had spoken to her as if she were a stranger. He'd always had a soft spot for Mimi, bringing her candy as a baby and concert tickets as she grew older. But her anti-nationalist activities were straining the relationship. Everyone's favorite pet was on the chopping block.

When Dianne had let a broken sob escape, the police chief's sternness turned to exasperation. "I found Mimi picketing with a group of university students in front of Milosevic's house. Stefan's career is on the line. If Mimi doesn't stop, Slobodan and his wife are bound to find out. Then, nobody will be able to save her. Get her out of the country if you must."

Dianne's hatred for what was happening went deeper than her daughter's. Dianne grew up in Croatia. Her homeland and people were being destroyed. There were far more effective methods of resistance than demonstrations, but the less her daughter knew, the better it would be for them all.

It wouldn't hurt Mimi to sit at the station for a while. Maybe she would learn to consider the consequences before taking foolish risks again. Unfortunately, the country and the president were too entangled in war to reverse the process because of the disgruntled students' protests.

Dianne was too often the buffer between her strong-minded husband and daughter, who was so like him. They were fighting a war neither could win, and Dianne was weary of being the battered wall protecting them from each other.

She gazed pensively around the room, taking in the lush Italian leather sofas and chairs, the antique Austrian tables artfully arranged on the marble floor, and accenting Turkish tapestries. In the beginning, Stefan had loved her. Maybe he still did, but his desire to give them the best had twisted and tainted their relationship until it seemed as if it would shatter. She composed herself to call him. Her hand trembled slightly at the thought of his anger.

Mimi Jovanovic stared resentfully at the police chief, an adopted uncle she'd known her entire life, but he wasn't acting like a relative today. He was almost shouting and probably would have been, except he didn't want anyone at the station to overhear their conversation.

His frown grew sterner when she didn't respond. "This has to stop. You're endangering your whole family and me with these scrapes. What if the president or his wife had driven up and recognized you picketing? You're not in this alone, Mimi. Think of your mother and father. These are hard days. No one's position is secure, not even your father's." He paused, his eyes troubled.

Mimi hated the fear she read in people's gazes more than anything else about this war. She'd seen it change them from friendly to ugly and hateful. Sometimes, it was as if the fear were choking her. She had to struggle against it, or it would strangle her, and all the lights would go out. If that happened, she'd die like her grandfather or, worse, change like her father. How could he threaten people he'd known for years and then order them killed or arrested? It was wrong!

It was drizzling and almost dark when Mimi's father picked her up from the police station. Her insides knotted as the chief walked her out to meet him. As she paused on the sidewalk, the letter in Mimi's pocket gave her courage. She wasn't in this alone. Her cousin Lucien was fighting with the Croatian Army. Her father and his henchmen couldn't stop her from attending tomorrow's rally. She wouldn't let them.

Her father sat behind the steering wheel, talking for several minutes with the chief before his penetrating glance fell on her. "Get in." He leaned across the car to open the passenger door.

She slid into the Mercedes, sinking into its leather upholstery, and hunched forward, rubbing her hands along the sides of her blue jeans.

Her father shoved a large manila envelope at her. "Mimi, I could throttle you for this. It will be virtually impossible to keep Milosevic from learning you were picketing on his lawn today." He steered the car from the curb into traffic.

Shakily, she opened the package, shocked at the rainbow of nine-by-ten glossies that slid out. Her nerves tightened until her stomach cramped, and her anger sought release. "You've been spying on me and my friends. I'll never forgive you if you've hurt any of them."

In response, his foot pressed harder on the gas pedal. "That's rich coming from you. You've done everything you can to undermine this family. It wouldn't hurt you to align with the current policies and follow Marko's and Marija's examples."

"The president's fairytale Serbian family with the perfect son and daughter! No, thank you."

"Whatever you may think, he loves his family dearly. And hear this: your revolutionary chums are history, and your protest days are finished."

She tried to control the tremor in her voice as images of her friends in jail lanced her. "What do you mean? What have you done?"

Her father shifted one hand from the steering wheel and stabbed it through his silvered black hair impatiently. "We'll talk when we get home."

She shivered at the expression of contempt on his face. Mimi stared out at the worn concrete complexes, yet another legacy of the Communists monopolizing the city.

A pallid gray hovered over Belgrade as her father sped along the damp, cobbled, smutty streets. Crowds filled the sidewalks, people hurrying to the shops or home after a long day's work. How could they be so taken in by Milosevic's propaganda?

Once, she had worshiped her father, imagining him to be the kindest man in the world. Deep down, a part of her still believed it, kept waiting for him to stand up for decency. Her hands formed into tight fists. She wouldn't argue, but Mimi wouldn't let him stop her this time. She was going to attend the rally tomorrow. In the past, he'd used her concern for her mother to rein Mimi in, but that wouldn't work anymore.

He maintained a grim silence for the rest of the trip home but broke it as he steered the automobile into the drive. "Pack your bags. You and your mother are leaving for Vienna tonight."

Her jaw dropped in surprise as she turned to him. "Why?"

"I think you know the answer to that. We're not stupid, Mimi. At least give us some credit."

"What are you talking about?" Her alarm at his reaction to the day's protest and the photographs of her secret meetings were nothing compared to the panic swirling through her now.

"You tell me. I'm your father, or doesn't that mean anything?"

Her pulse beat wildly, fearing he'd somehow learned of tomorrow's rally. "I won't go to Vienna." Her voice rose shrilly. "You can't force me."

"Do you think I want to fight with you over every decision?"

She could see he was trying not to blow up at her. Mimi was also trying not to let this evolve into the screaming match that ended most of their conversations these days. She choked back the accusations that usually wound so glibly around her tongue and forced herself to listen.

He stretched his arm along the seat, resting his hand on her shoulder. "You're my daughter, Mimi. What have I ever denied you?"

She winced. He couldn't understand her and her mother's pain. "You can ask that after—" Her stomach burned from the effort of holding in the hurt.

"Can't you forget what's happened for a few months until this blows over?" he asked, something her father, the general, rarely did.

She faced him. "Is that what you want? For me to forget, I'm half-Croatian. To pretend Mom doesn't have any brothers and my cousins don't exist. What kind of monster are you?"

He slapped her across the face. "All I've done has been for you and your mother, you ungrateful brat. Get out of my sight before I beat you."

Mimi clutched her cheek, reeling from the sharp sting of his hand. "You're a murderer, a traitor. You don't care about me. It's just an excuse for your conscience. It's your career that's important. Not me and Mother, or you'd have saved Grandfather."

Her tears fell, and her shoulders shook from the turmoil. He had never struck her like this. He reached out as if wanting to undo what he'd done, but she shrank from his touch. "I hate you!"

She jumped from the car and ran into the house to find her mother waiting in the foyer.

"Mimi, are you all right?"

"Leave me alone. If you care so much, why didn't you pick me up instead of sending Dad?"

Her mother paled. "You can't keep acting up like this."

"Is that what you call it? It's sickening how you cave to him, the same way he does to Milosevic. Grandfather might be alive today if you'd stood up to Father."

Her mother flinched. Mimi thought her mom might faint, then she straightened. "Go to your room and stay there until we leave. Pack enough clothes for a lengthy visit."

Mimi stared at her, wanting to unsay the words, but she'd be lying if she did. Then she'd be like them. She couldn't let it happen. Someone had to fight back, or evil would consume them.

In her room upstairs, Mimi closed the door and packed a small bag. She refused to miss the big student rally tomorrow. She snapped the suitcase shut and carried it across to the window. If she needed more, she'd borrow from friends.

Mimi swept the drapes aside, stopping as she spotted her father's bodyguard below. Her breath hitched. How dare her family treat her like a common prisoner?

More determined than ever, she rushed to the door, which refused to yield, and she kicked it in frustration. Another first. She had never been locked in her room. Furious, she paced, refusing to give voice to the storm within.

Several minutes later, Mimi collapsed on the bed, blinking back angry tears. Peter depended on her. She had to attend the rally. When they first met, he'd taunted her, labeling her the general's daughter. She'd worked so hard to prove herself, to overcome the evil her father endorsed. She must at least warn the group the authorities were suspicious. No, the group had their methods of learning, like her father had his.

Mimi shut off the lights and sat by the window, willing the guard to go to the bathroom so she could have the chance to escape without her parents finding out. They were arguing loudly downstairs, which they seldom did. To Mimi, it appeared they rarely spoke.

She heard the front door open, saw the bodyguard glance across, and then walk toward it. Her father had probably called him in to get her mother's luggage. Any minute, he would be in for her bags. Quickly, Mimi threw her case out the window and edged herself over the sill and out to the drainpipe. Determined, she wrapped her arms and legs around the narrow pipe and slithered down as fast as she could.

She was halfway there when the bodyguard returned, shouting curses as he spotted her. Her father, hearing the commotion, ran out as well. The noise caused Mimi to lose her grip, and she fell with a thud, her last thought that now she'd never get to the rally.

Chapter 39

It was midnight before Stefan got the family settled. He lay beside Dianne, aching at the empty mockery their relationship had become, detesting the walls that had hardened into icy contempt, separating them with a finality impossible to breach. His plans to send his wife and daughter to Vienna would have to wait. The doctor said it might be weeks before Mimi could travel. Besides a concussion, she had dislocated her shoulder, broken her left arm, and sprained her right foot.

Her fall from the upstairs window could have been fatal. With a frown, he squelched the idea the accident was his fault for having driven her to take such desperate measures. Mimi's earlier accusation as she reeled from the sharp sting of his hand was harder to silence.

"You're a murderer, a traitor. You don't care about me. It's just an excuse for your conscience. It's your career that's important. Not me and Mother, or you'd have saved Grandfather."

Stefan tossed restlessly, refusing to concede there was any truth to her charge. His thoughts spun to his wife, and as they did, he felt lost and hurt, as if the marrow of his life were dissolving. He wanted her despite their estrangement, wanted to wrap himself in her perfume, draw from the fountain of her virtue, and reaffirm he was the man she'd chosen to obey and love.

Obedience, he realized bitterly, was where she had failed him. The war had obliterated that part of their marriage vows. No longer did she depend on him, trusting his lead. Maybe it was time he showed her that, like him, she didn't have any choice. His patience had been in vain. He'd force her to see she had to obey.

Moonlight filtered through the window, and he saw she wore the lavender silk gown he'd bought for her in Paris before the war. He slid an arm around her waist and held her close, his anger fueling as she stiffened. "Dianne, you're my wife."

Elbows dug into him as she fought to break free. "In name only," she snapped, tossing her elegant head with disdain. Mink brown curls feathered across his chest, teasing his senses.

He swore as she struggled, wriggling against him. "Stop it. I'm a man, not some puppet to be tormented."

"And what about me? Don't I have rights anymore?"

His lips covered hers in a searing kiss. "I want you."

"It's no good, Stefan. It's always what you want." She drew back and touched his face as if to make a child understand he couldn't continue to behave as he had. Tears rolled down her cheeks.

They stared into each other's eyes for a pain-filled moment. He looked away, unable to hold her gaze. It didn't have to be like this. She chose to separate herself from him, walling him in the bitter place he now lived.

Her rejection filled him with wrath. His fingers bit into her arms. "How long do you think it'll be before I turn somewhere else?"

Her shoulders shook with sobs. "I don't care. The day you denied my family, you lost the right. Sleep where you will but leave me alone."

Stefan rose from the bed and dressed, slamming drawers and doors in his fury. How much more of this could he take? Dianne would never forgive him.

He drove to the office and sat at his desk, scowling at Dianne's picture and the one of their family beside it. He cursed under his breath, muttering. "Can't she see my hands are strapped?" No, not Dianne. She would never accept the situation, and Milosevic wouldn't stand for any deviations. He rested his head against his hands in despair. What had Serbia come to? His wife and daughter were deviations. In Serbia, anyone Croatian was.

Was his ambition so terrible? It had bought them the house and provisions his family took for granted and seemed eager to cast aside. Neither his wife nor his daughter appeared to care about his feelings. It was always grandfather or their cousin Lucien and uncle so and so. He was sick of the whole loathsome scenario.

So far, he'd protected them. But he had to get them out of Serbia for both their sakes. Mimi's injuries could be accommodated. She could rest in the backseat of the car. He picked up the phone and arranged for his chauffeur to drive them to Vienna. It was finished. His chest heaved with a suppressed sob. They'd be gone in an hour. He might never see them again. His marriage and his relationship with his daughter might never have existed. They didn't want or need him. Both had willingly rejected his every overture, choosing Dianne's homeland and family above his.

He slammed the pictures to the floor and rose to stomp on them, pausing in midair, the heel of his shoe inches from the framed protective glass. Stefan knelt instead and gathered the portraits. He carried them to his desk and placed them in the bottom drawer, unable to destroy the remains of such an integral part of himself. He turned the key, feeling as if a block of his heart had been ripped out and buried in the locked recesses of the wooden drawer.

Stefan poured himself a stiff drink and set to work. With his family gone, there would be no one to keep him from succeeding except his archrival, Michael Venac, who, like himself, was jockeying for a position in Milosevic's inner circle.

Thanks to Cosic, Stefan's plans were already in motion to bust the Iranian arms ring supplying Bosnian Muslims. To date, Stefan had some impressive hauls to his credit. Besides the large covert arms deal he'd brokered with their allies, he was negotiating weapon shipments and distribution arrangements through the black market.

He worked through the night almost feverishly. When Ennis arrived for the day's work, he had thrust his family from the forefront of his mind and was headed out the door for an appointment with Milosevic. He chose not to speculate on what Serbia's president wanted. His personal call had incited in Stefan a much-needed burst of optimism.

Ennis's hand clutched at his sleeve as he passed through the door. "Sir, may I speak with you for a moment?"

He took in her red eyes and glanced at his watch. "This isn't a good time."

"Alex never returned from his last flight. It's been three days, and Alex wasn't scheduled for an overnight stay."

He curbed his satisfaction at the news. His face suitably grave, he cupped her chin. "Don't worry. I'll see what I can uncover." His palm dropped to her shoulder comfortingly. "Unfortunately, I will be out of the office for the day. Meet me at Dušan's Café tonight at seven, and I'll have some news, good or bad. Dinner will be my treat." He squeezed her hand and left before she could protest.

He slid into the back seat of the Mercedes and waited until the driver put the car into gear before dialing Alex's immediate superior. Stefan had nothing against Alex besides a growing yen for his wife.

Mere sex had never been enough for Stefan. There had to be some sense of familiarity and continuity wrapped in the act, or it left him cold. Ennis was one of the few women who could entice him to overcome a lifetime of married fidelity.

With Alex gone, her vulnerability increased his chance of success. He was pleased she had a son. Perhaps it wasn't too late for him to start over and father a son—a pure Serb who would appreciate Stefan's work. One who, rather than criticize, would choose to follow in his father's footsteps. A bitter smile twisted his lips as he pushed aside the pain of Dianne's and Mimi's intrusive images. There was nothing he would have denied them, but what they'd asked was not his to give.

Stefan's meeting took place at the grandiose Palace of the Federation. An aide ushered him inside Milosevic's sizable ornate office.

In his customary dark suit and starched white shirt, the president invited Stefan to sit. Milosevic's ruddy face was fleshy around the edges with a jutting square jaw. He cleared his throat. "General Jovanovic, an unpleasant situation has arisen. A personal matter of the gravest national interest. Should you succeed in this task, it would certainly advance your career."

"I'm honored to be of service, Mr. President."

"Well, it's sensitive," Milosevic said with a curse. "It involves Željko Ražnatović's nephew, Peter, who, as you know, is a leader among the student revolutionaries and a close friend of your daughter."

"Sir, I'd like to say how sorry I am for Mimi's outrageous behavior. It will not be repeated."

"I am glad to hear that, General."

Željko was one of the president's closest advisers, although recently, Stefan had heard rumors of a rift. As the nationalist Serb military leader, Željko wielded enormous power.

The president continued. "It has been brought to my attention that Željko's nephew is running drugs."

"Sir, this sounds like a problem for the local authorities."

Milosevic's face became grim. "His substantial profits are invested in arms, which are then resold to the Albanians in Kosovo. I want you to investigate and then take action. Arrest Željko and his nephew Ražnatović for sedition, then order them killed."

Stefan inhaled sharply, wondering if it was true or merely a way to eliminate Željko.

As if sensing his uncertainty, the president reminded him, "War is more than bombs and bullets. Behind the scenes, diplomacy and intrigues are every bit as important." His gaze approving, he said, "Why else did you get rid of your wife and daughter so quickly?" He looked pleased at Stefan's slight flicker of surprise.

"There's little I don't know. My spies are everywhere. You would do well to remember no one crosses me and survives."

The meeting ended as abruptly as it had started, leaving Stefan more troubled. The president's request was any diplomat's worst nightmare. And while Stefan's success might bring promotion and power, failure would mean death.

Chapter 40

Mostar, Bosnia-Herzegovina, Summer 1993

Vita glanced around her living room despairingly. What was her home without Kiro? True to his promise, he hadn't asked her to be with Cosic again. But Kiro appeared to have vanished.

She knew she shouldn't worry. There was every reason to trust him. He might have left unexpectedly on a gun run. When Kiro returned, he would explain away her doubts, and they'd laugh at her foolish fears together. Soon, there would be enough money for them to leave.

Of late, Vita had accepted she couldn't live solely for revenge without losing Kiro. He wanted more from life, and so did she. She wanted a home and family, an end to hate and war. Surprised at her change of feelings, Vita imagined sharing them with Kiro. He'd worked for years to get her to recognize this. Those who didn't know him might mistakenly believe he was a mere gun runner seeking to gain from the fortunes of war. But Kiro hated war. Still, he fought for their people and country. There was nothing he wanted more than to settle down, marry, and raise children. Growing up, she'd watched him take care of his mother and her.

She jerked as the ever-present background cannon and gunfire grew louder, sounding uncomfortably close. Planes roared overhead, and bombs exploded nearby, sending tremors throughout the room. The bookshelf tilted to the floor, scattering books and shattering the porcelain tea set Kiro had bought her. Fists pounded against the door. She whirled in surprise as it was flung open. Three Serbian soldiers confronted her with machine guns poised to fire.

"Well, well," one of them said. "What have we here?"

Vita dove for the pistol hidden under the sofa cushions and pointed it at the nearest man's head. "One step closer, and I will shoot." She focused her attention on him, meaning every word.

Arms grabbed her from behind, toppling her. She squeezed the trigger, but her shot went wild.

She panicked as their lustful gazes roved over her. One man held her down.

"Looks like we got us a woman."

A soldier cruelly pushed his boot into her stomach, then leaned down and sliced her khaki blouse down the center, exposing her skin beneath. The point of the knife drew light patterns of blood across her flesh. The men watched in fascination as the red liquid beaded up here and there. Stinging pain coursed through her. She didn't dare breathe or move lest the blade dig deeper. Finally, he thrust the knife to the side and rose, unfastening his pants.

The next moment, an explosion occurred, and the lights went out. Vita groped for the knife the soldier had dropped and then rolled silently away from the men.

"Whore. Where are you?" The soldiers stumbled laboriously about, but Vita had the advantage in the dark. She crawled from the room and ran through the backdoor into the street.

Fear paralyzed her, and she crouched, hiding in the alley, remembering the night the Serbs had burst into her childhood home, raping her and her mother. Sweat dampened her forehead, hatred filling her as she recalled the shame and pain of the soldiers falling on her one by one. Afterward, she'd pleaded with Allah to save her mother, but Allah never listened to her. He was a man; she was sure of it.

Vita drew a shuddered breath, clutching her bloodied shirt about her. She had been fooling herself. She could never forget, never forgive, never again be at these infidels' mercy. Kiro would have to understand and take her as she was.

Somehow, Vita got to a neighbor's phone and called for a backup unit to her apartment to arrest the Serbian pigs who had threatened her.

It wasn't until the next day that Vita's ultimate plans for revenge fell into place. General Baharm wanted to meet with her. She was admittedly uneasy, worrying if she had inadvertently displeased the rogue army hierarchy. Had he learned of her part in getting arms for the troops? Would he regard her as only a common whore?

Soon enough, the opposite became clear to her great satisfaction. Baharm had nothing but praise for her bold and frequent initiatives on behalf of her country and its people.

One of Baharm's adjuncts escorted her to his office, unobtrusively built into the rugged hilly terrain on the Muslim side of Mostar. The general rose from behind a sturdy maple desk to grasp her hand. "I'm charmed to know the Bosnian Rose, whose praises the area troops sing."

Vita arched a brow, his obvious delight throwing her off balance. He was younger than she expected, but she found much to approve of. His gaze was intelligent and assured, inspiring confidence in his abilities. She understood why the troops under his command respected him.

"Sit, please." He waved her to a chair. "We have much to discuss." He studied her intently. "To begin with, I am aware of the gun runs. Kiro operates under my command."

Angst tore through her as she lowered her gaze. Had they both been using her, making her the army whore and the Bosnian Rose to the troops? In her youth, enemy soldiers had stolen the innermost intimate part of womanhood from her. Were all men barbarians?

Yet Kiro was gentle and must care to have protected and supported her throughout her childhood. She thought bitterly of her affair with

Cosic but refused to cower in disgrace. If it would help defeat the Serbs, she would sleep with the entire Serbian Army, no matter what her compatriots believed of her. She dared any of them to judge her.

Vita's shoulders straightened, and she aimed a defiant stare at the general, disconcerted by the kindly compassion she read in his eyes. Or was it merely an act to get whatever he wanted? Men—had they no mercy?

As if the man had read her thoughts, he said, "Whatever your doubts, remember our goals coincide. We must defeat the Serbs and Croats. Failure would mean national genocide. There's every reason to expect, no to demand, Bosnian Muslims unite to fight the infidels who are destroying and raping our land, women, and children."

His rhetoric was not new to Vita. She had heard it repeatedly and used similar words to incite those who worked under her, imploring them to rise to greater heights of dedication in their service to Allah to defend the Muslim cause.

She masked her impatience at his use of such tactics. "I am sure there is a point to this. Some particular problem in which you need my help?"

A gleam of respect lit his gaze. "You are quick as well as valiant."

"And quite immune to flattery, General. So, if we could get on with it."

He rose from behind his desk. "A woman after Allah's own heart." He gestured toward a map on the wall. "I'm sure a history lesson would insult one so clever. Instead, let me point out the practicality of annihilating the Croatian sector, or shall we say, rendering its present population extinct."

Vita stifled a surprised laugh. "Daring, but improbable. Even if you achieved the impossible, the Serbs would simply replace the Croats who live there now. To allow the Yugoslav People's Army to get so close again would be suicide. Think of their weaponry. There is no advantage in such foolishness."

His face turned hateful, and he strode toward her. "You forget yourself. Apologize at once." Steel-like hands bent her fingers backward.

Vita gasped, almost fainting from the pain. "Forgive me, sir. I didn't mean it."

He released her fingers.

"In the future, remember you are an officer, commanded to respect those in authority over you. Is that understood?"

"Yes, sir."

He shoved a list of explosives at her. "You are to arrange the purchase of these materials through Cosic. How soon can you meet him?"

"Friday night."

"No. Too hurried. Cosic might become suspicious. You know he has you followed?"

Vita contained her fury and kept silent. She hadn't expected Baharm to insist she continue her relationship with Cosic.

She left the general's office with a headache. Too many of the arms they'd bought through Cosic had disappeared. How could she ensure this shipment wouldn't go the same route? And what would the consequences be should she fail?

Vita returned to work in a rare state of indecision. She was curt and impatient with prisoners and officers alike. With relief, she finally drove home, steering her Lada through the bombed-out streets and buildings. Her irritation spilled over to the workers, who never seemed to finish repairing the road damage. She knew no one could control the artillery continually tearing up the streets, and that left her even more frustrated.

It wasn't until she entered her apartment and kicked off her shoes that the memory of the attempted rape the evening before overwhelmed her. She hesitated in the small entry hall, her senses intuitively springing into high alert, straining for any suspect sound or movement. There was no reason for this cloying fear. The Serbian soldiers who assaulted her were in jail. They were being tortured and would be killed once her people learned everything possible from them.

She quivered in alarm at the sounds drifting in from the bathroom. Vita stifled a scream and forced her muscles to stillness, listening. There. She heard it again. Drip, drip. Splash, swish. The harsh squeal of rust in the pipes and a running faucet. Vita drew an uneven breath, took the Beretta from the holster under her jacket, and crept through the living room. She paused outside the bathroom. With the gun in her outstretched arm, she kicked the door open.

Vita exhaled slowly. Her trembling arms slid to her sides. Anger and relief coursed through her. "Kiro, what are you doing here, scaring me like this?" She set the gun down, her hands forming fists to steady herself.

Kiro turned from the sink, appearing impossibly handsome and seductive. He laughed. "You frightened? I don't believe it."

They moved into the living room. "I thought you'd never get home."

Her hurt feelings fought for dominance and then faded as she rushed into his embrace, cherishing the touch and feel of him. It didn't matter whether his face was damp or if he was dirty and needed a shave. It only mattered that they were together.

"I've been so worried about you." Her words trailed off as he kissed her until she was dizzy, and she realized her devotion to this one man remained the anchor and compass of her existence.

Later in the kitchen, as Vita heated a tin of tomato soup and sliced bread for dinner, she realized they hadn't talked. She couldn't think of how to ask questions without sounding accusing.

She ladled the thin steaming soup into bowls and set them on the table with thick wedges of bread. Before she could frame the words, Kiro began telling her about his journey.

He ate, talking between spoonfuls. "Wait until you hear how much we brought in this trip." He laughed and reached for her hand. "Someday, I'll buy you a diamond big enough to make every woman in sight jealous, and when our daughter marries, we'll give it to her."

"Are you sure there will be a daughter? That we'll ever leave here? I hate being powerless. I want to hurt someone." The growing ache to strike back was as fundamental as the breath she drew.

Kiro's laughter faded. "I told you to forget about revenge. We have the brains to go places, to escape this war."

His spirit called to hers, reaching for what no other man ever had. His plea touched her. If anyone could heal her. . . . No, she shouldn't think of such things. It was too late for her and probably for Kiro, too, except he didn't know it.

She spoke hesitantly of her near escape from the soldiers the night before. The memory reinforced her hatred and anger. The conditioned emotional responses she depended on kicked in, reminding her love had never brought her anything but pain.

"You're doing it again," Kiro accused. "Hiding behind another injustice." He stared at her bleakly. "It's a war we're fighting. So the enemy hurt you. What else can you expect? It's not as if our side has behaved any differently." He rose and came around the table, hauling her to her feet. "Admit it. Our officers are banging Croatian and Serbian women, killing their children. Doesn't the enemy have as much right to hate us?"

"It's not the same. Serbia started this."

He shook her. "What about your American girlfriend? Who started that? It suited our purpose to have her family murdered—to have her tracked like an animal. What did she ever do to you?" Kiro asked. "Nothing but fatten our purses, because she was a distraction that took the heat off our actions. You saw to that."

"Stop it." Jealousy coiled itself around her. Why was he speaking up for Katrina? "She was the enemy." Vita slapped his face. "She pitied me. I saw it in her eyes every time we met. No one patronizes me and gets away with it."

He grabbed her, forcing her backward while his lips crushed hers in a punishing kiss. Then Kiro freed her and said, "Don't ever strike me again. The difference between you and me is I can kill with my eyes open. I don't need to hide behind glib lies. And I make sure I've gained something in exchange."

His rancor seemed to dissipate. He drew her to him. "Perhaps you're merely a woman, and I expect too much."

She pressed against him. "No, I can be whatever you want. Love me, now. We can talk later."

She saw the struggle in his eyes as he led her into the living room instead. Kiro slumped on the cracked vinyl couch, and she sat beside him.

"Okay. Tell me what's bothering you." He silenced her denials. "Something's happened. Your sensitivities are pouring through the calloused shell you project like a sieve."

Vita swallowed. "While you were out of town, I met with General Baharm."

Kiro's face shuttered. "I should have expected he'd move on you with me gone."

"Baharm knew about Cosic. You promised. It was supposed to be our secret. How could you have told him? He expects me to come up with enough explosives to blow up the Croatian side of Mostar. Think what that means."

Kiro spoke with reckless defiance. "Baharm already knew. His business is to be mindful of every detail going on in Mostar. The man came to me, pushing for more arms, mad as hell when the shipments disappeared. I finally informed him we were finished. You couldn't stand the pressure. The general is the one who put me on to this last arms deal—a ploy to get me out of Mostar while he approached you."

Her hands felt warm and sticky as relief cannoned through her. Kiro hadn't betrayed her. Vita could stand anything but losing him. She kissed him gently, forgiving and absolving him the one way she knew how.

In return, he deepened the kiss. "Let me say thank you."

"Not now. You're right. We have to talk." She kissed his jaw and couldn't resist running her fingers through his wavy black hair. She slipped from his grasp with a sigh. "We've got to decide about Cosic and Baharm tonight."

"Come here."

Amused at how quickly they'd reversed roles, she said, "We must think clearly, find a plan . . ." Her voice trailed off into a girlish squeal as Kiro rose and lifted her into his arms. "Set me down."

"Does Cosic make you feel like this?"

"Never." Lost in his touch, Vita realized she would have to see Cosic again, for Kiro's sake. Even now, he was preparing her to accept it as no one else could. Yet, at this moment, there was only Kiro. Later, she would decide about Cosic. What else was there for women like her?

Vita let Kiro settle the arms negotiations to supply Baharm. Midweek, Kiro called Cosic and arranged for the trade. Cosic had grown more demanding. He insisted on Vita spending an entire weekend with him rather than the usual odd evening out. The explosives would be delivered after their rendezvous, not before.

She and Kiro worked frantically with a group of Bosnian military experts, devising a failsafe plan to ensure the arsenal of explosives reached its target. Vita fell into bed each evening, more exhausted than the previous one, to awaken a few hours later and begin anew.

They agreed Baharm's plan to eradicate the entire population of Mostar's Croat side would never work. Instead, they concentrated on the television and radio stations, the newspaper press, the airport, utility companies, the police station, city hall, and the mayor's office. It was an ambitious and massive plan guaranteed to bring the Croat side down. The difficulty was getting the explosives across the Neretva River into enemy territory.

Chapter 41

Bosnia-Herzegovina, Summer 1993

Ellen wasn't sure how much time had elapsed since John, three-year-old Tito, and she had been captured and driven to the Croatian base in northern Bosnia. The soldiers holding them hostage treated them well. Thankfully, from the start, Tito had captured their hearts. The men couldn't get enough of the toddler. They shared their rations and played with him. The boy was a symbol of innocence, a reminder of family and all it encompassed.

Ellen prayed for the well-being and protection of her daughters, Rachel, Shelly, and Andi. Ellen often despaired of seeing them again. If she and John were released, how would they find their girls? John would say, "Have faith, Ellen. Don't give up on our daughters or God." She smiled at the thought.

A soldier entered the room with Tito and handed him to her. "The commander requests your presence in his office. All of you. I think he has some good news."

"Thanks." John scooped up Tito and grabbed Ellen's hand. The three hurried to the commander's office. John knocked lightly on the makeshift door.

"Come in."

Ellen saw at once he wasn't alone.

The commander rose and introduced them to a captain with the UN peacekeeping forces. After the men and Ellen had exchanged greetings, the commander said, "Everyone, please sit." Once they were seated, he continued, "The captain and his men are traveling to Vienna, and he's willing to take you to the US embassy there."

John said, "Captain, we appreciate the offer. The problem is we have three daughters here, and we don't know where they are. We lost them in a raid near Mostar."

"Your daughters most likely would have contacted the US embassy if they survived. There's a chance the embassy might direct you to them."

"John, he's right," Ellen said. "They would have been with Katrina, and she would have known to contact the embassy."

"If she could," John said.

The captain frowned. "If you don't find them, you can always come back. A better solution would be to have the US intervene on your behalf. The US has a lot of influence with the Croatians and Bosnians."

John raised a quizzical eyebrow to see if Ellen agreed. She nodded. "All right," he said. "We'll go."

Then it occurred to her to ask, "What about Tito?"

"We can certainly bring him with us," the captain said. "If you are considering adopting him, Vienna is a good place to start the paperwork. We need to push on. Can you be ready to leave in an hour?"

John stood. "Sooner if you like."

"Good. Let's meet out front in a quarter of an hour," the captain said and left.

John turned to the commander. "We appreciate you and your men's kindness and protection. You've been more than fair."

The commander shook John's hand. "The Americans have never been our enemy, though sadly, some can't seem to remember that. Godspeed in finding your daughters. One of my men will load your bag into the captain's jeep."

The three departed, calling goodbye to the soldiers they passed on their way out.

Ellen and Tito settled into the rear of the jeep. John sat up front next to the captain, who waved his arm for the convoy behind them to follow as he drove off.

"Mind if I ask where we are?" John asked.

"The nearest city is Samac."

"And how do we get out of Bosnia?"

"There are two primary routes to the West. One goes through Croatia and the other through Hungary. Our goal is to arrive safely, which means avoiding the war zones as much as possible. To travel into Croatia, with Serbia striving to destroy it as we speak, is too dangerous."

"We'll convoy across Hungary." The captain thrust a map at John. "Your job is to navigate. We're traveling north to Osijek, then to Budapest, and from there to Vienna. It's about a six-hour trip."

"How close are we to Hungary now?" Ellen asked.

"About three hours."

"Will there be trouble crossing?" she asked.

The captain frowned. "Most likely, but nothing we can't handle. My men are armed."

Ellen prayed for God's protection for them and their girls.

Chapter 42

Bosnia-Herzegovina, Summer 1993

A black Mercedes whisked Mimi and her mother from their home in Belgrade. Mimi ached all over from her fall off the drainpipe. She lay in the back seat with her feet propped on her mom's lap for the long day's drive. The two dozed during most of the journey. Toward evening, her mother awakened agitated and demanded to know where they were.

Mimi sat up abruptly as the chauffeur drove them into a Serbian concentration camp. He'd brought them unsuspecting into a killing field of horrors. Her father had lied when he said he wanted them safe in Vienna. His betrayal hurt deep in the pit of her stomach.

She was torn from her mother and locked in a small cell. Frightened and sick with worry, Mimi sobbed in despair. Then she straightened, wiping her tears. They'd find a way to escape somehow.

Despite the squalid conditions, her body healed, and soldiers thrust her into a tiny basement cell. Mimi stared out a barred window the size of her diary. The Serbs entered her cell and beat her often. For days and nights, she peered into the camp yard, witnessing murders and skeletal-like humans dragging their bones to perform shouted commands. She felt herself shrinking, becoming part of the wall surrounding the window she faced. Mimi grew terrified of losing herself and afraid she and her mother might never be free.

At times, she curled up on the floor and slept until the soldiers poured icy water over her head, jerking her awake. Half out of her mind from focusing on the Lilliputian space, Mimi cringed at the bloodcurdling screams and the noise of brutal beatings rising from other parts of the camp.

Then, one day, the iron door grated open, and a guard thrust her outside. Mimi cowered, shielding her eyes from the light.

Soldiers pelted her with stones. "Go! Leave! Get out of here."

She limped away, too weak to run or escape. She plodded feverishly onward, panting for breath, without knowing where she was going or what she could expect to achieve before the Serbs found her.

The first night, she camped beneath trees and covered herself with fallen leaves. By the end of the next day, she realized nobody was searching for her. The Serbs expected her to die in this wilderness, a convenient means to avoid reporting her death, leaving no repercussions for her father, the general. She stopped and stood, gasping.

The knowledge crushed her. How could her father have done this? Mimi dropped onto the ground, feeling as if fragments of her heart were breaking. Part of her wanted to deny her father's culpability, to rest in his arms, safe and childlike, his little girl again. *Oh, Daddy!*

She sobbed, her anger ricocheting inside, searing the hurt. Mimi struggled upright, her pride refusing defeat. What must her poor mother be feeling? It was all his fault. His fault. His fault.

Mimi scrambled through the brush, panting and holding her side to curb the ache. Tears of despair streamed down her cheeks. Sheer force of will kept her moving. "I won't give up—won't give up." The simple refrain prevented her from falling into the dark abyss she held at bay.

She lost count of the days and miles, slogging through forests and climbing mountains, but thought a week had passed. At least, the approaching fall temperatures were moderate. She survived on wild dandelions, radishes, parsnips, nettles, and other plants. The best Mimi could hope for was to reach Split and find a boat to smuggle her across to Italy. Yet, how could she leave without knowing her mother's fate?

At Martin's parents' farmhouse, Katrina awakened to Lucien hovering over her. His hand pressed to her forehead in concern.

"How do you feel?" he asked.

"Better." She took in the bedroom, pleased to be inside a home again. Lace curtains framed the window as dawn sprawled across the horizon in a kaleidoscope of colors.

Her thoughts were on Lucien, the hero she had miscast as a villain. He'd rescued her as she knelt by her mother's corpse, then gathered the surviving children and led them all to a cave. He'd hidden them, promising to return.

Instead, Vita had arrived, treacherously dangling hints of Lucien's culpability. Soon, Katrina was primed to believe him a traitor. Yet, he'd continued to rescue her. He was easy on her eyes, too. She smiled faintly. "How are the children?"

"Sleeping soundly. Martin and Sara have grown attached to Baby and want to keep him and adopt him once the war is over. He's about their son's age."

"I'm delighted for Baby. If only I could settle the rest of them so well."

"You should also know that Robbie, Tanya, Rena, Milo, Ishmael, and the new boy, Samuel, left with the guide."

"They'll be safer with him. Besides, Samuel and the old guide are a match. He lost his son, and Samuel lost his parents."

Lucien clasped her fingers. "I hope you realize by now you can trust me."

"I'm sorry I ever doubted you. You've done so much for me and the children. We owe you an enormous debt." She sighed. "I've created such a mess, blaming you and losing most of the children. I have no idea if the girls' parents are even alive." She tilted her head, wondering how she could have so misjudged him. There had always been a warmth and connection between them, even when she'd tried to deny it.

"Forget it. Vita is insidious, and you were understandably emotionally distraught." His face tightened. "You can't continue to wander about with the children."

"I don't expect you to solve all our problems."

"Those kids are in danger as long as they're here. You need to get them across to Italy."

Frustrated, she ran a hand through her hair. "I've thought of little else, but it's impossible without money or contacts."

"I have the contact. A friend of mine routinely ferries people across on his boat. So, if you're willing, I've arranged passage to Italy for the lot of you."

"Of course, we'll go!" She blinked back tears of joy. "Thank you."

They discussed the trip details. It seemed unbelievable that she and the children would soon be free, and Lucien had arranged it. Eventually, it dawned on her she'd be leaving him behind. Katrina knew little about his life before they'd met and questioned him, wanting to store up memories in the event she might never see him again. "Tell me about your family."

"You already know Sara. We grew up in Klagenfurt, a city in southern Austria. Mother was from Villach, a small town nearby. Dad was raised in Croatia but had no future there. He traveled into Austria selling Yugo-vacuums, then opened a store in Graz and, in time, developed it into an international concern. He met my mom, married her, and soon Sara and I were born."

"You must be proud of him."

"I am."

"How did you come to be in the Croatian Army?"

His voice thickened with emotion. "I couldn't bear to watch the cities where my dad's family lived burned and my cousins killed. When my relatives started disappearing, I had to enlist."

She expressed her sympathy, but neither wanted to dwell on the war.

"What about you? What was it like growing up in Texas?"

"There was always so much love," Katrina said. "We had my parents to thank for it."

She talked of the compelling call to serve that had driven her to give up a secure professorship in Houston and join her family of educators in a mission to Bosnia. "Dad wasn't a minister in the formal sense. His doctorates were in philosophy and theology, Mother's in French and art."

"Were they school *Lieblings?* Or maybe you say, sweethearts."

"No, Mother was from Quebec, French Canadian. They met while teaching at Rice University. A whirlwind courtship followed. They married, and along came Giles and me. We both became teachers, continuing the family tradition."

"And what are your degrees in?"

"Mine are in English, and Giles's in science and history. We agreed to set aside one summer and help our parents organize a children's mission in Bosnia. The summer spun into an unforgettable period of laughter, challenging work, successes, and, lately, disasters."

She drew a deep breath, wanting Lucien to understand. "When friends said we should leave, I kept thinking, what if this were me, hungry and persecuted, without schools, books, or anyone to care? What if, by some quirk of fate, America were sacked, and I was behind bars? How could I ask for help, knowing I'd refused it to others?" She frowned. "I was incredibly naïve to think I could make a difference."

He brushed her cheek. "But you have to many of the orphans."

"But—"

He raised his palm. "Let me finish. When you first came here, you believed you could do everything, and now you imagine you've done nothing. The truth lies somewhere in the middle. We do what we can and what we must, no more, no less. Don't fear the worst in the same manner you envisioned the best. Take what you've been given, these remaining precious children, and leave. Save them. Help them make a success of their lives. Let your suffering count for something."

Her voice cracked with emotion. "If we leave, will I ever see you again?"

"Maybe not, but I hope so." His gaze locked with hers. "Whatever happens, I wish you well, my American flower. Stay bright. Such a gift as yours is needed in this world."

She wrapped her arms around his neck with a half sob. "I'm missing you already," she said with a shaky smile.

"I'll find you when this war ends." His lips caressed hers in promise. He held her a moment longer, then released her.

At the sound of approaching footsteps, they glanced up, breaking apart.

"How charming," Cosic said, aiming an AK-47 at them from the doorway. "I'm afraid your plans have changed. Get up. Both of you."

Chapter 43

Katrina struggled to her feet as Cosic stepped into the room, his submachine gun pointed to ensure their silence. "Who are you?" she croaked, shoving the words past her tongue.

The man's mocking glare seemed to undress her, threatening violence. Then it fastened on Lucien. "So, Captain, we meet at last. Unfortunately for you, this will be the last time."

Tight-lipped, Lucien asked, "What do you want, Cosic?"

"What I've always wanted," he sneered. "To see you six feet under."

Lucien reached for his sidearm and cursed as a barrage of bullets ripped a semicircle into the floor before them. Katrina screamed, stumbling as Lucien shielded her.

Cosic ordered, "Toss the gun on the bed, nice and easy, or neither of you will live."

Lucien obeyed, a slight twitch in his jaw. He took a protective stance close to Katrina, and she leaned against him, praying for rescue. She feared that the children, having heard the noise, might enter the room and be endangered.

Cosic grabbed the pistol, gloating, as he slipped it inside the waistband of his pants. "Both of you start walking. One wrong move, and you're dead."

With the assault rifle, Cosic prodded Katrina and Lucien into the living room, where Vita and Kiro held the others hostage. Katrina scooped up Drew to shush his crying. She didn't like how Cosic stared at the children or the pinched fear on their youthful faces.

Rachel's voice trembled shrilly. "He's going to kill us."

Andi bit her lip. "No, he's not," she said. "God won't let him."

Shelly faced her sisters confidently. "We're going to be all right. Aren't we, Aunt Katrina?" Her doe-like eyes sought reassurance.

Katrina gulped and feigned a smile that encompassed the children, but before she could speak, Martin's mother said, "We are in Allah's hands." Her arm sheltered her grandson.

Vita fired into the air. "Quiet." She strolled to where Lucien stood by Martin and leveled her Beretta at them. "Undress." Silence reigned as he stood unmoving. Vita shrugged. "Have it your way." She cocked the trigger. "I'd as soon kill you now."

As if he realized they had no choice, Lucien started unbuttoning his shirt.

"I can't imagine what you think we might have," Katrina said. "Regardless, there are children here. Have Kiro take the boys and men to another room, and the girls and I will go with you."

"Fine," Cosic said. "It will be faster that way."

Vita pressed the weapon to Lucien's belly, laughing as he lurched backward.

"We haven't got all day. Vita, take the ladies and search them thoroughly," Cosic said. He pointed the AK-47 at Martin. "You. Quickly now, undress."

Vita urged them into the next room. The young ones cried and tried to break free. One by one, they all undressed, were inspected thoroughly, given blankets to cover themselves, and then pressed back into the main area.

Cosic had finished checking the men and turned to examine Katrina's and the children's clothing. Afterward, he secured it in a sack, then questioned them intently about their belongings.

Kiro said, "We can search the house and other stuff later. Let's get them out of here before anyone comes."

Furious and humiliated, Katrina shuddered, unable to comprehend why their captors hated them so vehemently. Cosic believed they were hiding valuables and information. Could it be about the icon they'd asked her about when she was in jail?

Cosic, Kiro, and Vita herded them outside and into the back of a camouflage-green military van. Any refusals to obey their orders garnered swift punches or kicks that sent the protesters reeling. After they were seated, Kiro insisted on blindfolding the children, although his comrades complained he was wasting time. Kiro stood firm. "There's no reason for the children to see what's happening before time. It will only make them more uncooperative." He covered the children's eyes.

The van took off across a rough pasture, tumbling them about. Cosic must be afraid to use the road. Katrina struggled to comfort the frightened, sobbing children. She wrapped her blanket sarong style about her and then, in a similar fashion, secured the children's covers around them. She had an awful feeling about what was to occur next. Katrina noticed Cosic staring and realized her blanket was slipping. Her cheeks burning, she wrenched it up to her chin, wrapped it under her arms with a tuck, and scooted nearer to the window, embracing the lull before the storm.

The children must be wrestling with their fear of death, a reality they had dodged for months as it chased them, destroying much of what had gone before in their young lives.

She encouraged them. "Remember, no matter how monstrous circumstances appear, God is stronger than us and our enemies. It's going to be okay." *Please, Lord, let it be true.*

Late afternoon, they reached a grave site. Katrina had heard that the Serbians lined up their enemies and executed them in massive pits. According to the news, the Serbs had filled multiple grave sites with hundreds and thousands of dead. Katrina fought the urge to panic, the scene more horrifying than any she could have imagined. Mercifully, the children couldn't see the scattered skeletal remains that left her feeling ill.

"Aunt Katrina, where are we?" Shelly asked, a quiver in her voice.

"I'm not sure."

Rachel squirmed in a restless, panicky motion. "Have we stopped?"

"Yes, but don't talk. We can't risk making these people angrier."

Andi fumbled for Katrina's hand. "It's scary not being able to see."

"I know, honey. You and Shelly hang on to me when we get up. Lucien can lead Rachel and Caleb."

Caleb tugged at the edges of his blindfold. "What will they do if we take these off?"

"They might kill us," Rachel said.

Martin and Sara's son began to cry. Her face pale with fear, Sara picked him up and held him close, murmuring in his ear.

Lucien's face was stern and unreadable, but his eyes softened when he spoke to the children. "Whatever happens, we're together."

Cosic loomed over them with a submachine gun. "Quit stalling and move out."

Lucien, Katrina, and their charges stood. She hoisted Drew into her arms, exchanging a swift glance with Lucien. The keys were in the ignition. If they escaped, they would have transportation.

There must be some way to save the children. She struggled to compose herself, praying for strength. Shelly and Andi plastered themselves on either side of her, making moving difficult.

She forced one foot in front of the other. Caleb and Rachel clung to Lucien as they walked beside him. His presence was a balm to Katrina and the children pressing against her. Martin and Sara, carrying their son and Baby, lagged with his parents. Vita and Kiro followed at the rear, waving their guns threateningly to hurry the group.

When they reached the grave site, déjà vu gripped Katrina, though she knew she'd never been there. *Lord, is this You preparing me to meet fate?*

The sun slanted across the sky as Cosic's jeering laughter echoed across the isolated landscape. Skeletons of razed farmhouses in the distance formed a surreal setting for the hundreds of emaciated bodies tossed to rot in the deepest, darkest hole Joseph Conrad could have conjured. If Cosic remained in control, their bones would soon join the others.

Above the children's heads, her gaze met Lucien's. A mixture of love, regret, and fierce pride in each other's strength vibrated between them.

For the children's sake, she must try. Anything was better than this willing passivity to accept death. Katrina wanted to speak, but Lucien shook his head, warning her to silence. It didn't help to tell herself that neither she nor Lucien could have prevented this. Who was to blame no longer mattered unless the knowledge could save them.

At a nod from Cosic, Vita jerked the trembling girls from Katrina's grasp.

"No!" Andi clutched at Katrina. "I don't want to go."

Katrina hugged her. "Hush, it'll be okay. We have to be brave, remember?"

Andi refused to let go. "I don't want to be brave. I want to stay with you."

Katrina kissed Andi's cheek. "If you don't go, the soldiers will shoot you. Take Shelly's hand. God is watching over us. I promise."

Shelly slipped an arm around her sister, whispering as they walked away.

As Vita positioned the children along the edge of the massive grave and Kiro took aim, Katrina's composure shattered. They meant to kill the children right then. She and Lucien needed more time to figure out an escape plan.

Katrina said, "Can't you see history is repeating itself? The Serbs raped and killed your mother. Now you're helping them destroy us."

She pointed her Beretta at Katrina. "Shut up."

"Cosic has you duped. He's the enemy. We don't deserve to be executed in a mass grave. Not when it's his country, Serbian forces, bombing mosques and raping Muslim women."

Vita's face whitened. A thread of uncertainty seemed to pierce the veneer she wore like armor. "No. It isn't true. I'm doing this for my mother, our people."

Kiro broke in. "She's trying to turn us against each other. Cosic, let's kill them and quit drawing this out."

Lucien said hoarsely, "Do what you want with me, but let the others go."

Cosic cursed and struck Lucien's face with the butt of his AK-47, forcing him to his knees. "All right, you American swine, which of you has the Madonna?"

Kiro focused his gun on Cosic. "You said we were after weapons. Enough to blow up the Croat side of Mostar."

Cosic looked murderous. "We're after both. You know that. The Madonna is more valuable."

"Not to us. You agreed to restore the arms the Croats have been stealing."

"Wait a minute," Lucien said. "My men could never get close enough to your supplies to take them. Believe me, I wouldn't have hesitated if there had been the slightest chance of success."

"Either he's lying." Kiro frowned and squinted at Cosic, "or you've been double-dealing. No one besides the two of us knew where we kept the cache."

Cosic backed away, uncertain, leveling the AK-47 at Kiro. "You're forgetting the men who moved the shipments. One of them must have betrayed us and reported the location to the Croats."

Vita flushed. "When I think of what you put me through."

She spun to Katrina. "Cosic's responsible for your family's deaths. He had the mission raided, thinking to kill Lucien there as well. And

I helped, believing Lucien was robbing our artillery stash and you and your family were in on it. He played us all for fools."

Cosic broke into a peal of cynical laughter. "Don't forget you thought the raid a nice diversionary tactic to keep the Bosnian government from learning about your Rogue Muslim Army." He centered his assault rifle on Drew.

As if he sensed the danger, Drew cried. "No," Katrina screamed, shielding the boy with her body. Time crept forward in microseconds as tension tightened her muscles.

His weapon directed at Katrina, Cosic strode forward. Was there nothing she could say to reverse his plans? Drew clung to Shelly now. Regret for what might have been overwhelmed Katrina. The kids shouldn't see her cry. Then she realized they were blindfolded and couldn't see that Cosic was about to murder her.

Once again, Katrina could not save those left in her care. Today, though, she wouldn't be left behind. Strange how the urge to live pulsed within her. Why was Cosic waiting to squeeze the trigger?

"Remember," she said to the children, "be strong." As a last rite, she stared across at Lucien and clung to the tenderness in his gaze. Tears slid down her cheeks.

A spark of courage swirled with the desperation that gripped her as she turned to Vita. "Why won't you let us go?"

Lucien stepped toward Cosic. "She doesn't have the Madonna. I'll take you to it. That's why you orchestrated the attack on the mission. Not to kill me, I was nothing. You wanted the place cleared out to search for the Madonna."

"You don't know what you're talking about," Cosic said, clearly lying.

Katrina gasped as someone shot into the clearing from the nearby woods, and a chopper sounded overhead. Cosic fired at her as Lucien thrust her to the ground. On the other side of the pit, she saw two Croatian soldiers in uniform who must have been scouting the area dive into a clump of shrubs. Shots rang out from the nearby grove of bushes, and Katrina realized the soldiers must be trying to help them. "Why don't you call out to those soldiers to help?" she asked Lucien as Kiro and Cosic returned fire.

"They're already doing all they can." With a groan, Lucien said, "Run for it!" Martin, his parents, and Sara were already herding the kids to the van. "Get the children away. I'll cover you."

Katrina shook her head.

"Think of the little ones. They need you."

"No." She raced to catch him, shouting to Sara, "Go on. We'll come later."

Sara didn't pause to argue, but Martin grabbed several guns from the stash on the van's floorboard. He pitched the weapons outside on the ground and tossed out a blanket.

As Martin drove away, Katrina grabbed a pistol and used the blanket to hide the side arms and Kalashnikovs.

She whirled and saw Vita standing next to Kiro. He'd taken a hit in the shoulder. "It's a superficial wound," he said. Cosic had taken cover behind the piles of dirt along the rim of the pit, striving to evade the hovering helicopter.

Katrina started toward Lucien.

Kiro reached for his gun, pointed it at her, and squeezed the trigger.

A burning sensation stung her arm as she shot back, aiming straight for his heart.

Kiro fell as the bullet struck him.

Vita's eyes widened in horror, and she bent over him, searching for a pulse. "He's dead." Her gaze turned to Katrina. "You killed him!" She ran at Katrina, grabbing for the pistol, and Katrina slammed it into Vita's head. She collapsed.

Katrina darted to the stash and, gulping back hysteria, hauled a Kalashnikov to where Lucien lay semiconscious, blood oozing from his leg. "Not again," she cried and ripped the edges of her sarong and wrapped the cloth around the wound until satisfied Lucien wouldn't bleed to death.

She examined and bound her injury, relieved the slug had merely grazed her. Then, with her good arm and Lucien's help, she dragged him a few yards across behind some scraggly shrubs.

The helicopter receded. Terrified, Katrina peered around the scrub and saw Cosic crawling with an assault rifle toward the larger grove of bushes where the fighting had started. Katrina bit her lip and fired.

The chopper was overhead again, attacking. Desperate, she hid Lucien and herself beneath the brush and prayed.

Helicopter shells bombarded the clearing. Her chest pounded in fear. Thank God the children had escaped. Martin would keep them safe. Katrina lay pressed against Lucien's chest, his heartbeat reassuringly steady.

The charge halted as abruptly as it started. The chopper circled low, and the earth seemed to tremble in response. Then she heard blades beating as the thundering engine faded and the helicopter left.

Relieved, Katrina gave her attention to Lucien. They had to leave. She jiggled his shoulders until his eyelids fluttered.

He groaned, tried to sit up, then collapsed, grasping her hand for support. "How bad is the leg?"

"Bad enough."

His hold on her tightened. "The kids?"

"Martin got them out."

"Good." He released her and wriggled his limb experimentally, grunting at the pain.

"Careful," she said, wishing there was help nearby. Fresh blood oozed from Lucien's wound, and she tightened the bandage.

He flinched. Sweat beaded on his pale face. "It's not the first time a bullet has hit me. What's happening out there?"

"I might have killed them all. I don't know for sure, but I shot Kiro and Cosic and hit Vita over the head," she said. "The Croatian soldiers seemed to have vanished, and the chopper's gone, too."

Lucien hugged her. "They had to be stopped. I'm sorry that you had to be the one to do it." He released her. "Ready?"

Katrina viewed his bloodstained bandage and doubted he could go far. "Can you stand?"

He eased into a sitting position and braced himself against her, placing most of his weight on his good leg. He stumbled to his feet, the brunt of his body almost causing her knees to buckle.

"Give me one of those Kalashnikovs," he said, the thin lines around his mouth white and his jaw clenched.

She passed it to him, worried it was too heavy for him to carry in his weakened state. Lucien strapped it on with a resolved expression, and Katrina realized there was no sense in arguing.

They hobbled along in plain sight of any lurking adversary. At least Cosic and Kiro would no longer be trapshooting them.

She stared at the massive grave site as they passed it, saddened immeasurably by the evil it represented, humankind's nature at its cruelest and darkest.

As they limped on, she glanced down to where Vita lay, her head twisted awkwardly.

Sickened and dizzy, Katrina swayed.

"Don't look." Lucien tugged her forward. "Vita waged her battle for gain in this hell. Let's get out of here."

Katrina twisted from his grasp, almost knocking him down as he tried to hold on to her.

"Don't," he croaked again.

She bent to check Vita's pulse. Nothing. Katrina took in Vita's blood-matted hair and bruised head. Katrina had done this.

Then she saw Vita's chest was riddled with bullets. The helicopter fire must have peppered her. Katrina straightened, relieved she wasn't wholly responsible for Vita's death—then realized the head injury had left her unconscious and unable to move away from the chopper fire. Katrina was to blame, after all, though she'd had no choice but to strike the once friend who'd become a deadly enemy.

Lucien pressed her shoulder as if he understood. How could he not? How many men had Lucien killed? Were there women and children he'd executed in the line of duty? She hoped not. It was too much of a burden, too much for one lone man or woman.

As they struggled to the road, Lucien leaning heavily on her, she blinked, but her tears fell harder. Lucien rested against a tree for support and held her, stroking her hair while she sobbed.

"Shh. You're going to get through this."

"For so long, I believed she was my friend."

He touched her cheek. "She had you fooled. Vita didn't know how to be a friend to anyone, least of all herself."

"How could I have believed her lies about you? If I had known the truth, maybe I could have spared us this."

He cupped her chin. "Not a chance. She was a deceitful, cold witch. What could a woman like her know of friendship?"

"Vita was hurt. Maybe she didn't have any choice."

He pressed Katrina's shoulders. "We all have a choice, even in this godless war. Moral choices are thrown at us every moment."

Now she held him close. "I love you," she said. "I don't mind anything, as long as you're near me like this."

Lucien muttered and shoved Katrina down, falling beside her. Then he rolled, his submachine gun poised to fire, but no one was there. He said, "I thought I heard footsteps closing in on us. Did you hear them?" She shook her head, and they cautiously scanned the area, but nothing moved.

He shifted to assist Katrina to her feet. But she steadied him and helped him to rise. "Sorry about that. We have enough problems without me imagining them."

"Maybe you heard an animal rustling in the bush."

"Maybe," he said, sounding skeptical. "Let's go." He groaned.

"Lean on me more. I'm not as weak as you think." Still, she could tell he tried not to lean on her too much as they shuffled laboriously toward the road. He'd taken three bullets in the same leg in this war.

Cautiously, they moved forward, often stopping to rest. When Martin stopped the van alongside them and climbed out to help them inside, Lucien said, "Thanks. Is everyone okay?"

Martin nodded. "I dropped my family and the children off at the farm. I was anxious about you two. What happened to Cosic and his comrades?"

Katrina ran an unsteady hand through her tousled curls as she settled into the rear seat. "They might be dead."

Chapter 44

Bosnia-Herzegovina, Summer 1993

Alex blinked, a low moan escaping as his head shifted. Gingerly, he touched the bump on the back of his skull. "Ugh." Where was he?

He sat up, leaning the brunt of his weight against a tree trunk. His head spun. Images of the plane crash came rushing in. He'd parachuted out and landed in Bosnian enemy territory. Then, someone had struck him from behind, hard enough to knock him out. A furtive study of the area assured him he was alone. But for how long?

He peered at his watch, estimating he'd been unconscious for about twenty minutes. Time to get going. His grandmother's Saint Christopher medal pressed against his chest, warm and reassuring. Alex mentally shook himself for succumbing to superstition but crossed himself three times.

His thoughts went to his wife and son in Belgrade. Ennis would be concerned. He needed to reach her. Her boss, the general, would be eager to take advantage of Alex's absence. Not that Ennis would ever betray him. Still, she might believe he was dead and turn to Jovanovic for comfort in her sorrow.

Alex lunged to his feet unsteadily and saw his survival pack was missing. Feverishly, he searched for it in vain. Whoever knocked him out must have stolen it. The pistol inside Alex's boot and the knife and compass in his pocket were safe. It could have been much worse.

He set out, hiking through the forest. As the days passed, he carved notches on his belt to keep track of them. Mostly, he avoided people, though a chance encounter with two Turks had almost ended in his death. Thankfully, their languages were similar enough to converse. The submachine guns they'd aimed at him motivated Alex to claim allegiance to Allah and dream up a long-lost Turkish relative, spinning the situation to his advantage. Ultimately, he'd bartered his watch and rings for a pair of machine guns, a canteen, and army rations.

Alex was nearing the coast, where he hoped to contact a Serbian ship and catch a lift home to Belgrade. As he crept through the woods, raised voices in a clearing several yards ahead stopped him.

He peered through the greenery. His stomach lurched at seeing several children lined up with guns trained on them. His forehead beaded as indecision held him. He started to retrace his steps yet couldn't leave. They were so young. Ennis was right. He couldn't pretend anymore. He shot into the clearing as a helicopter lowered, shelling the area. Alex dove under a bush. What had he done now? He had foolishly exposed himself, thinking he could help those kids.

He drew in a quick breath. The kids were escaping. He gripped the Saint Christopher medal in unspoken prayer until they were out of sight. Then he inched into the woods.

Chapter 45

Martin drove Katrina and Lucien back to the farm. Katrina had never been so happy to be anywhere. The children, whom Martin had driven there earlier, rushed out to greet them, smelling of soap and fresh clothes. They clung to Katrina, and she was incredibly grateful to have them close and safe. She hoped none of them ever experienced a day like this again.

Finally, she left them long enough to bathe and dress herself. Katrina slid into blue jeans and a sweatshirt, then put on a full skirt and baggy shirt. They couldn't carry much. She needed to make certain that the kids wore enough layers to keep warm.

Katrina stared out the same bedroom window she'd awakened to earlier that day with a sense of well-being. The sunlight sparkled, oblivious to their near-death experience. One moment, they had been safe, and the next, trembling for their lives.

Lucien arranged passage on a small trawler to ferry them to Italy. Leaving Bosnia, and she knew she must, for the children's sake, would place more than an ocean between her and Lucien. She straightened with resolve and went to meet the others.

Lucien gave her a strained smile as she entered the living room. "Ready?"

She nodded, too choked to speak. The children looked subdued. The trip to Italy would grant them freedom, but it also brought uncertainty. They were leaving the only country they'd ever known. Katrina wanted to promise them everything would be fine from here on. She didn't say the words, having learned that the future kept its own counsel and fate consulted few men.

They hugged Sara and Martin and his parents goodbye. Katrina promised to write as the family walked them to the jeep. She and the children crowded into the vehicle with Lucien at the wheel, and off they went. The children chattered, excited.

The sun hung low in the west when the jeep stopped at the dock. "Are we really going to Italy?" Caleb asked.

"You should be there by morning," Lucien said as he helped Drew climb from the jeep and motioned everyone out.

Andi held back. "We have to wait."

Shelly placed her arm around Andi. "She's scared our parents will be left behind."

"If we leave, we may never see them again," Andi said.

Lucien stood on the sandy beach, his gaze meeting hers. "If they're here, I'll find them and tell them you're in Houston waiting for them."

She seemed satisfied.

Katrina wondered what her life would be like after Bosnia—after Lucien. She'd be living in Houston, meeting family and friends who'd been an integral part of her life with her parents and Giles.

They walked to the small wooden pier and onto the dock to wait. Lucien glanced around. "Tony should be here any minute."

"Are there many smuggling outposts hidden along the coast?" Katrina asked.

"Most likely," he said.

Soon, a modest boat scooted into the secluded cove. The children pressed against her as Lucien's friend, Tony, a large man, his shoulders bowed from work, spared them a smile, and gestured in the setting twilight for them to come aboard. Lucien introduced everyone and settled them on the bench seats.

Tony pointed to the life jackets. "Put those on."

Lucien and Katrina ensured the children wore the vests and fastened them securely.

Tony stationed himself behind the wheel and set the trawler in low gear to reduce the noise as he cast offshore. Breaking waves drowned the roar of the engine. About one hundred yards offshore, he moved the throttle up, and it shuddered into a louder gear. Another hundred yards out, and they were past the whitecaps, riding the quieter swells. Three miles from the coast, the fleet of patrol boats was thick, but Tony sped past it, blending with area fishing vessels. The wind in his face, he sailed deeper and deeper across the Adriatic until night fell heavy, its mantle a camouflage against detection.

Lucien and Tony took shifts at the wheel, their expressions grim as they scanned the ebony waters ahead. As the evening wore on, Katrina's muscles grew stiff and cramped, and she longed to stand and stretch. Thankfully, the kids were asleep.

So much depended on a safe crossing—the children's futures and her promise to her dying mother. Fear trickled down her spine. They had to reach Italy. There was no going back now.

"Dear Lord, create a way for these little ones. You parted the Red Sea for the Israelites. Like Miriam, let my soul sing when we reach the shores of freedom."

They journeyed on, the ocean surf breaking against the small craft. A sea of uncertainty swelled in her with each surge, cutting at her faith and resolve. She tried to ignore the doubts towing her under. In defiance, she tilted her chin, tasting the salty spray on her lips, and smiled into the night. At last, the sun emerged from the cloak of darkness.

The sky, awash in brilliant pinks and tangerines, signaled a new dawn as she stepped from the rear of the boat. The children scrambled onto shore behind her, excitement temporarily banishing their weariness. "Is this Italy?" Andi asked.

"Yes, it sure is," Tony said.

Caleb frowned in concentration. "Which part?"

Tony patted the boy's head. "We're in Pescara."

"Do you think our mom and dad will find us here?" Shelly asked.

"I sure hope so, honey." Katrina turned to Lucien as he hopped off the boat. Satisfaction lit his face, a responding surge of exuberance lifting her spirits. There were uncertainties and negatives ahead, but they'd escaped Bosnia. "We're in Italy!" she said. "We did it."

He pulled her to him in a quick hug, then set her aside, pressing a leather money pouch into her hand. "This should get you and the kids home."

She quaked at the thought of the danger he faced crossing the Adriatic in daylight. How she wished he could accompany them to the States.

Lucien handed her several passports. "All we could manage were these fake American passports for you and the girls. These will at least get you into a hotel, but they won't bear scrutiny. Do what it takes to lose them as soon as you can. You'll need to sneak the boys into the hotel until you can work something out with the Italian authorities."

Katrina and the children's passports had disappeared when Vita arrested them. Now Katrina realized why Vita had checked their meager belongings so thoroughly when they'd lived in the caves. She'd been searching for the Madonna for Cosic. But happily, that was the past. The future awaited them.

Their parting with Lucien drew near. He'd been so good to them. "How can we ever thank you for all you've done?"

Knuckles, rough and sure, caressed the line of her jaw. "By taking care of yourself. Promise?"

She blinked at the moisture in her eyes. "Yes, I promise. You too?"

"It's a deal." He moved to tell the children goodbye.

Rachel squinted up at him, shielding her eyes from the rising sun. "Remember, you promised to find our parents."

Lucien squeezed her shoulders, clasping her close. "I won't forget, Sunshine."

Drew squealed, his short legs taking off at a run as he jumped into Lucien's arms. "Can I go with you?"

Lucien caught him and swung him around. "Maybe next time, Little Buddy."

He hugged Andi next, taking in her serious face. "Be good, Princess."

"Couldn't you stay with us?"

"I wish I could."

Andi pulled away, her goodbye brusque as tears dampened her cheeks.

"You have everything you need, right?" Shelly asked, her gentle eyes filled with concern.

Lucien embraced her. "Yes, Miss Nightingale. You worry about yourself and the others. Okay?"

He ruffled Caleb's hair and gave him a bear hug.

"How long will it take you to get to Bosnia? Will you be safe?" Caleb asked.

Lucien winked. "I'll be fine." His gaze shifted to Katrina. "Sorry about the boys. I don't know how you'll get them into the hotel, but you'll find a way. I couldn't risk you being caught with fake passports for them and the Italian authorities detaining you."

"It's okay. We'll be fine." She understood the boys' nationalities were the problem. Italy already had more orphaned refugees than it wanted, and that's how the boys would be classified. She and the girls had homes to return to in America. Katrina would do everything possible to ensure the boys soon had one, too.

"I'll never forget you. Stay bright, my American flower."

"We'll meet again. Someday." She smiled tremulously. "Won't we?"

Lucien kissed her swift and hard, then stepped away.

She sensed he was saying goodbye forever. He believed it was better for her. "Lucien, I won't ever stop waiting—"

"No," he said. "Don't. We can't know what the future holds." Then he walked away as a man does when he must, without looking back.

His courage made her love him more. Yet, she knew time might lessen the strength of memories shared. Still, Katrina stood on the shore and watched him leave until the small craft faded into the seascape. Then, with a sigh, she counted heads. Five of the original thirteen kids who'd left with her following the mission raid remained: Rachel, Shelly, Andi, Caleb, and Drew. Ana and Dinko were the first to leave her, and she was happy for the twins who had been taken in by a caring, childless couple. Robbie, Tanya, Ismael, Milo, Rena, and Samuel, the boy who had joined the rest of them after their jailbreak, had left with the guide. Hopefully, they were already safe in the West. Martin and Sara, who were wonderful and loving parents, had assumed care of Baby and, in their hearts, adopted him. They would have to wait until after the war to make it legal. Katrina wished them all the happiest of futures as she and her little band of five trudged up the shoreline to face a new day and destiny.

BOOK II

Return to Mostar

Chapter 46

Pescara, Italy

The dawn melted into the sunlight as Katrina and the children walked toward the bustling city of Pescara. She fretted that the steep hill leading into town would be too much for the kids after a night at sea. But no one complained, and even Drew's short legs kept pace with the others.

A quiet group, they enjoyed the early morning sights of the harbor town. Most of the fishermen appeared to have already set out to sea for the day. Women hurried to the market to buy and sell. Taxis frequently sped past, but Katrina pressed on, wanting to get her bearings before plunging deeper into this new world.

Caleb tugged at her arm. "Aunt Katrina, what's supposed to happen now?"

"We're going to have breakfast and then sleep and sleep and sleep," she teased.

Rachel glanced down at her grimy clothes. "I need a bath."

Shelly stifled a yawn. "Will we stay in a hotel?"

Katrina reassured her they would. Drew's small hand slipped into hers. "Will the people that killed Mommy and Daddy be there?"

She paused on the walkway and knelt before him. "No, darling, you're safe here." She hugged him rather tightly, and he submitted for a moment before squirming free and running to stand by Shelly. A surge of maternal pride swelled in Katrina. The three-year-old had been one when he came to the mission after seeing his parents killed, and he'd been only two during the raid that killed her family. Yet Drew had survived and would have his chance at freedom. Then it hit her. "We're free," she shouted into the wind. The children quickly echoed her words and whirled joyfully at the miracle of their arrival in Italy.

"People are staring at us," Rachel said, embarrassed.

"At least no one's trying to kill us," Shelly said.

"We've celebrated our freedom. Let's move on," Katrina said. Grinning, despite their weariness, they trudged on. Soon, the group was some distance from the docks and almost downtown. They passed several hotels. Since the boys didn't have passports, Katrina left them in the city park for a brief interval, praying no harm would come to them. Then she chose a nondescript hotel and went inside while the girls waited out front.

Feeling uneasy, Katrina approached the clerk behind the marble reception counter. She handed him the four fake passports for the girls and her.

He flipped to their pictures, then closed the booklets and set them aside. "How many rooms, Miss Winslow?"

"One, with extra beds, please." Until she contacted her family for more funds, it was necessary to conserve what money she had.

His glance took in her figure, seeming to stop at her bust. "What part of America are you from?"

She fidgeted, aware that her top had worn thin and shrunk from repeated washings. "Texas."

"Ah. Do you ride the horses like in the movies?"

"Not really. Is our room ready?"

Lazy black eyes mocked her. "How about helping me with my English tonight?"

"I'm sorry. I can't leave the children alone."

"You are their sister?"

She nodded, in a hurry to register and leave.

His hand skimmed her fingers, his gaze caressing. "You would make a wonderful teacher."

She stiffened, pulling her hand free. "I am a teacher. Doctor Winslow, to my colleagues."

He pushed the register toward her, leaning a little too close. "Your signature, please."

She should be glad he was bent on flirting and not checking on the validity of their papers. Impatiently, she signed the register, accepted the key, and turned to leave.

"One moment, Miss."

Was there a problem? Could he have discovered their passports were fakes? Katrina forced herself to pivot and face him. "Yes?"

"The children, are they expected soon?"

Relieved, she said, "They're outside and should be right in."

As if on cue, the girls strolled in, appearing a ragtag lot in their worn, crumpled denim and faded cotton tops. Before the clerk could remark on their shabby knapsacks and lack of baggage, she herded them into the elevator and upstairs.

From there, they found a back staircase leading downstairs and outside. Rachel and Shelly went down it to collect Caleb and Drew from the park. Katrina and Andi settled into a pair of chairs in the corridor to await their arrival. Katrina dared not relax her guard. The passport dilemma wouldn't be over until she received them back in the morning after the local police had been advised of their stay. The routine process had never bothered her, but she hadn't tried to pass off forgeries before.

Soon, footsteps pounded up the stairs, and she wondered how to get the boys to settle down.

Drew rushed onto her lap, the others trailing behind. "Aunt Katrina, I didn't cry at all."

She kissed his cheek. "Good boy."

Rachel said in exasperation, "I told them to hush, but they wouldn't listen."

"Yeah," Shelly seconded. "They were tromping everywhere, making lots of noise."

Katrina frowned, wanting to hug them more than anything. "Boys, you promised to be quiet, didn't you?"

They nodded sheepishly.

"Let's go, and no more cutting up." When they reached the room, she couldn't quite believe their escape wasn't a dream she'd wake from at any moment. The third-rate dumpy hotel was a palace compared to the caves, jails, and rough terrain where they had slept.

Rachel sank onto the bed with a grin. "Wow. This is more like it. I can't wait to get home and sleep in my bed."

A silence followed, and the girls exchanged stricken glances as if reminded of their parents and the fear that their family would never be the same.

Caleb said, "Who cares, anyway? This place is like a castle."

Drew scrambled onto the mattress, giggling. "Look, Aunt Katrina." His little hands stroked the pillow, and he buried his face in its fluffiness before sitting up. "Soft. Can we stay here forever and ever?"

Everyone laughed. Andi ruffled Drew's hair. "Hotels are for visiting, not living in."

Caleb shot Katrina a troubled glance. "We don't have a home. What's going to happen to us?"

Her composure about as thin as an eggshell, she said, "I don't know, but I will do everything I can to keep us together."

"They'll never let us go to America. Nobody here will want us either. They'll send us back to Bosnia, and we'll die. Won't we?" Caleb's gaze pleaded with her to tell him he was wrong, and the horror of war finished.

She crossed the room, and her hand smoothed his coal-black hair. "Whatever happens, I love you. No matter where you are, I'll never give up trying to get you." She tilted his trembling chin until, through a film of tears, she could see his face. "Trust me?"

He gulped a sob and nodded. "If I pray, will you come for me faster?"

"I will come for you as fast as possible, and God will comfort you and me, too. Even if we're in different countries, he can hear us both at the same time. When we pray, it will be like being together. Okay?"

Caleb squared his shoulders. "All right. I'll teach Drew to pray, too, so the three of us can be together."

Andi inched nearer, the move expressing her solidarity. "I'll pray, too."

"Me too," Shelly and Rachel echoed as they all hugged each other.

The children remained somewhat somber for the rest of the day and evening. The present wonder of their newfound freedom couldn't erase the past or their worries about the future.

After they were asleep, Katrina phoned Aunt Janine and Uncle York. Her aunt's voice quivered. "Katie, is that you? We've been so frightened. Where are you?"

"In Italy—I'm okay. There's no need to worry."

A gruff voice broke in. "Honey, are you coming home?"

She blinked at the moisture in her eyes. "You sound so much like Daddy."

"I'm heartbroken about your parents and Giles. The embassy notified us of their deaths. You know how much we loved your mother and father and brother. Their loss is beyond words. We love you, Katie, and we're here for you. Let's see about getting you home safely. Take a deep breath and tell me what we can do."

Katrina didn't want to think about her parents. There was too much at stake for her to break down. Five children depended on her. Still, she hesitated, resisting asking for her uncle's support in sponsoring the boys. As a lawyer, he would easily see to all the practical details.

Her conscience stirred. She couldn't risk her aunt and uncle's retirement. They'd worked hard their entire lives and helped others as well. It seemed unfair to ask them to sacrifice their retirement income after they had already donated much of their nest egg to cover part of the setup cost for her folks' mission in Bosnia. Then, there was their aging health. Sponsorship would mean the boys would have to live with them. Her relatives might be physically unable to care for young children over an extended period. She refused to risk their health. Sponsoring the children would be an immense responsibility, even with her, to relieve much of the strain.

Katrina needed to return to the States, where she could earn enough money to support the children. She buried her pride and reservations and asked, "Can you wire me the money or, better yet, arrange airfare for four from there? John and Ellen have disappeared, and their girls are with me." Katrina held little hope of bringing the boys with her, but if a miracle occurred, she'd be thrilled to call her aunt and uncle and request two more tickets.

There was a brief silence as her uncle understood the ramifications of John and Ellen being missing. "So sorry to hear they're lost, dear. You leave it to your old Uncle York. I'll purchase four tickets for your flight to Houston. You can pick them up at the airport counter before you board."

Katrina gratefully gave him the hotel number in case they needed to reach her and enlightened him about the boys and their situation.

"The Lord will take care of it, Katrina. You're going to have to trust Him for the long haul."

She cradled the phone briefly after they'd said goodbye. Wasn't that what she'd been doing these past months? With a heavy spirit, she knelt and asked the Lord for a miracle to provide the boys' visas to America. Then, as her Uncle York had advised, she strove to trust Caleb's and Drew's care to God's more than capable hands and prepared herself for bed.

Chapter 47

Earlier

That morning, when Tony started the trawler's engine for the return trip to Bosnia, Lucien reluctantly tore his gaze from Pescara's shoreline. Katrina and the kids were gone now, lost to him in the early morning haze. He might never see them again. Katrina would ensure the girls survived. But he felt torn about his two young buddies. If he walked away from the Croatian cause, he could adopt Caleb and Drew. Maybe marry someday. His blood raced at the notion as he struggled to assess his turbulent feelings in light of the war and his responsibilities to Croatia and his family.

He'd been ready to relinquish his command and resettle in Austria, where sanity prevailed in a civilized society with law and order and the freedom to move about without fear of ambush. One glimpse of the mass grave site had thrown his conscience into overdrive. How could he ignore such blatant injustice? Perhaps the more important question was, how could he most successfully engage the enemy? He pictured his Grandfather Creto, cousins, and uncles who had fallen, their wives unfairly made grieving widows.

An immense weariness filled him, and his stomach growled, a reminder that he hadn't eaten since yesterday. His parents' faces swam before him, and he saw his mother bent over the stove, serving up a plate of sizzling *Weiner Schnitzel mit Kartoffel Petersile*. His mouth watering, he pushed aside thoughts of food.

He and Katrina knew little of each other's backgrounds. Lucien hadn't mentioned that he was an executive in his father's company before joining the army. Yet, in the things that mattered, they were well acquainted. He knew of her kindness, loyalty, the overwhelming guilt she hid, and how she continually underestimated herself, unaware of her beauty and worth. And he might never get to tell her. He sighed, breathing in the salt-drenched breeze.

Sometime later, Lucien noticed the wind speed increasing as the rolling sea turned choppy. Black, threatening clouds loomed overhead.

Tony called out over the roar of the motor, his words tossed into the ocean as waves surged against the hull, and he struggled to hold their course.

Lucien careened toward the wheel, bracing himself against the boat's lurching movements. "Will this gale last long?" he shouted.

Tony gripped the wheel, his knuckles white and strained from the effort. "Hope not," he yelled over the wind and surf. "We don't have any fuel to spare if we're knocked off course,"

"How close are we?" he hollered.

Tony shook his head. "Not near enough," he roared.

Chapter 48

Pescara, Italy

Katrina and the children went to the American embassy the following day to resolve the visa situation. The kids sat in the outer office while she spoke with the consul general.

Mr. Jones was sympathetic when she outlined the boys' dilemma. But he insisted, "It's impossible to issue them visas. However, there are refugee camps in the area."

Despite Katrina's warnings to the children and herself, the boys' impending separation left her distraught. "Please, there must be some way to keep them with me." She glanced toward the waiting room, hoping Caleb and Drew had not overheard their future so abruptly dealt with. Not after what they had been through. "I'd like to sponsor them myself and am ready to sign papers agreeing to provide for their care."

Mr. Jones studied her. "I don't mean to be discouraging, but Italian law presides here, and it does not allow single-parent adoption of children, except in rare cases when the parties involved are related."

Adoption was more difficult than she had imagined. Katrina realized she must appear practically impoverished with her worn clothing, ragged nails, and makeshift haircut. She smiled. "I know I must look destitute, but contrary to appearances, I'm an English Lit professor and have a nice inheritance waiting for me at home. I will have ample funds to care for the boys."

He skimmed the forms on his desk. "It says here you are currently unemployed and will be job hunting when you return to Houston."

"That's true. But my parents recently passed, and I stand to inherit whatever—"

"Miss Winslow," he interrupted, "settling their estate could take months. I wish I could help you, but even with sufficient resources, the Italian courts would frown on a single parent adopting the boys. Meanwhile, I am responsible for ensuring these orphans are provided for to the best of my ability."

Her stomach took a nauseous turn. "How can a refugee camp be better than a home where they are loved? There must be exceptions to the law. Won't you please give the boys and me a chance?" Katrina knew she was begging. Yet what else could she do given the circumstances?

"Regretfully, Miss Winslow, I have no influence on Italian law. However, I assure you the camps here differ vastly from those in Bosnia. The boys will be treated well."

Devastated, Katrina protested. She knew the man was merely doing his job.

She and the girls would depart for Houston the following day. The boys were to be placed in a refugee camp. The crushing part would be telling Caleb and Drew.

Back at the hotel, the girls made everyone sandwiches and passed out sodas. Katrina noticed Caleb looked upset. After lunch, she pulled Caleb and Drew close. "Darlings, remember we talked about how we might be separated."

"You're sending us away like that man said, aren't you?" Caleb asked.

She nodded, grasping for words to explain why she seemed to be deserting them, like most everyone else.

Caleb's lower lip quivered. "I heard you," he said accusingly. "You didn't even try very hard to keep us." His childish voice broke into a sob. "Why did you make us believe you wanted us? You lied. It's not fair!" Then he was crying, and his arms twined around Katrina as if he would never let her go. "I don't want to leave you. I don't want to pray. It doesn't do any good, ever. Everybody leaves me anyway."

Katrina sobbed with him, rocking him in her arms as if the motion could somehow ease his anguish. Though he was almost nine, he seemed to find comfort there.

Drew wrapped his small arms around her neck on top of Caleb's. "Don't cry, Aunt Katrina. We love you. I won't let nobody hurt you."

She held him close and prayed. How much more could they take? *How long, Lord? How long before the sun shines again? Before the pain no longer rips us apart?*

Caleb eventually quieted. Both boys bathed, and Katrina gathered their few belongings, regretting they owned so little. She could change that. Katrina grabbed her purse and said to the kids as she reached the door, "I'll be about fifteen minutes." She walked across the street to the gift shop, calculating how much she could spend. Paying soaring prices with her funds so low seemed like a terrible waste. Yet she needed to provide Caleb and Drew with the necessities.

She chose three outfits for each boy. Katrina also bought an underarm money pouch, a phone card, stationery, stamps, toiletries, and snacks. She paused before the toys and selected a yo-yo and puzzle for Caleb and a stuffed puppy for Drew.

Katrina paid for the items and rushed to the room, where she placed most of her remaining funds and a slip of paper inside the pouch. She gave it to Caleb. "Here's two hundred dollars and my address and phone number."

He frowned. "What if those people steal it from me?"

"Keep it hidden. But don't worry. If you must give up the pouch, I'll send another one."

His gaze dropped to his shoes. "Will you come see us?"

She grasped his hand. "I promise to find a way to adopt you and Drew, and when I do, I'll come for you both and bring you to live with me in America."

Thin arms slipped around her. "I love you, Aunt Katrina."

She ruffled his hair affectionately and showed him how to wear the money pouch beneath his shirt, wrapping it over his shoulder and under his armpit. "Write to me every week and if you can't, then phone me. I put stamped postcards, stationery, and a calling card in the pouch for you to use."

Caleb blinked back tears, and his hand clung to hers. His quiet courage and acceptance broke through her defenses. How would these precious sweet boys, who'd been downtrodden and left with nothing, survive on their own? It might be easier on them both if he cried. Then she could hold him and weep without his even knowing. Be brave; she ordered her breaking heart—for another day, night, week, or however long was necessary. She pushed against her fears of what could happen to Caleb and Drew in that wretched camp.

Katrina forced a smile, pretending there was nothing wrong. How could she do less with Caleb as her example? She showed him the clothing and toys she'd bought. They elicited a meager response from the wary, listless youth, who seemed to have given up.

Finally, she turned to Drew, handing him the stuffed puppy dog. "For me?" he asked, eyes wide with wonder.

"Yes. It's yours."

Andi said, "Drew, pull the string."

He jerked it, and the puppy barked. "Ruff, ruff."

Even Caleb laughed, regaining a spark of interest. "Wow, how does it do that?"

After a while, everyone, even the stuffed puppy snuggled under Drew's arm, settled down for the night and slept.

Chapter 49

Bosnia-Herzegovina, Summer 1993

Lucien stood on the boat deck. The surging waves bent on absorbing them into the sea's darkness had abated. Frothy whitecaps lapped gently against the hull.

"I'm glad the storm's over," Tony said.

"I imagine you've sailed through countless storms."

"There have been a few."

Lucien wondered how fishermen found the courage to brave the elements year after year. Was it the danger in part that drew them? The challenge of man against nature?

The important thing was Tony's boat was safe, and he'd continue to do whatever it took to protect and nurture his family. Smuggling paid more than soldiering, and the risks were no greater. But it was about more than the money for Tony. He acted out of compassion.

Lucien stared into the Adriatic's unfathomable depths. If there was a God who cared, why didn't He stop the carnage? Raised Catholic, Lucien grew up attending mass with his parents on Christmas, Easter, and Ash Wednesday. He'd never given God much thought. Still, deep inside, Lucien banked on Him. In his first few skirmishes with the enemy, he prayed desperately. Then, as family members and comrades were wounded or killed, his doubt grew.

Lucien had stopped praying the day his eight-year-old cousin Boban, his boyish face shattered by shrapnel, died in his arms. God no longer seemed real until he met the Winslows, whose faith had affected him. Not that he became a believer, but it left him with a sense of disquiet, uncomfortable in his disbelief. Wrestling over God's existence was useless. Either He was or He wasn't, and what Lucien believed had no effect.

The evening sun hung low in the sky as Tony steered the trawler into the Bosnian cove they'd departed from yesterday. Lucien dropped anchor, shocked as Serbs emerged from the surrounding shrubbery, their AK-47s ready.

"Don't move," a familiar hateful voice ordered.

Lucien froze at seeing Cosic, who he thought was dead, standing on the shoreline.

Seconds later, Cosic's men swarmed aboard the boat. Lucien took the first blow and felt the air whoosh from his lungs. He reached for his gun too late, and the enemy knocked it to the deck. Rifle butts slammed into his face and stomach until his ears rang. Reluctantly, he surrendered. Tony fared no better. The soldiers frisked them, bound their hands, and shoved them onto land.

Cosic gave a few curt directives to the soldiers, and they thrust Lucien and Tony into the rear of a military vehicle. Cosic and his men got in and drove off.

From the front passenger seat, Cosic swiveled around and aimed his gun at Lucien. "I want the Madonna. Now!"

"I don't have any idea what you're talking about." They were nothing but money-hungry scum bent on killing Lucien for something he'd never seen.

"Maybe your memory needs refreshing." Cosic nodded, and the nearest soldier pounded Lucien's body while the others held him.

He groaned, fighting the searing pain as blow after blow left him bruised, bloody, and near senseless.

He was close to fainting when Cosic snarled, "Where is it?"

Despair gripped Lucien. Their chances of survival were low. But he had to try. "All right. It's buried in the hills outside Mostar. In exchange for leading you to it, I want your word we'll be set free."

Cosic moved to the bench across from Lucien and Tony. He aimed and squeezed the trigger.

The bullet winged Lucien's shoulder and burned like fire. Beside him, Tony swayed as a shot hammered into his upper arm.

Cosic said, "Do we understand each other now?"

Lucien glanced at Tony, sorry to have involved him.

The single plan Lucien could think of was to lead Cosic and his men north toward Croatian headquarters, hoping to alert Croat troops of Lucien and Tony's whereabouts. The strategy held out the slim possibility of a rescue.

To his dismay, Lucien caught himself drifting in and out of consciousness as waves of pain hit him. From the front of the vehicle, laughter startled him awake. Cosic and two of his men were talking.

"Izetbegovic is going to roll some heads over General Baharm's latest maneuver," Cosic said.

A man guffawed. "I'd like to see his rogue army destroy all those Croat soldiers."

"That will do for starters," Cosic said. "Serbia won't stop until we've destroyed the entire Croatian sector."

Lucien's fists clenched in repudiation, desperate to retaliate. Instead, he surreptitiously nudged Tony, relieved at the returning prod from Tony's boot.

Five thousand people lived in Mostar's Croat sector. Some of them were Lucien's friends and relatives. He wanted to kill Cosic, and in doing so, he'd save thousands of innocent lives. It's what the army taught: kill or be killed, a philosophy bearing its own burden of guilt. Was Lucien becoming a statistic to be duly reported on the news as one more example of how the Serbs, Croatians, and Muslims couldn't stop murdering each other? Proof positive—they were doomed to remain uncivilized throughout their gory history.

His head ached, and his shoulder was on fire. He was hungry and thirsty. The fear of what he had become ate at him. He shied from the twisted complexity of his emotions. Was he, like Cosic, attempting to mete out his personal brand of justice?

Lucien needed to believe he was nothing like Cosic, to feel that he had retained some sense of decency. Feverishly, he considered the last two years. He had never willingly killed women and children. When he had inadvertently done so, grief rather than glee had filled him.

Lucien returned his attention to the men up front. Now was not the moment for absolution but to devise a plan to counteract Cosic's. It wasn't hard for Lucien to visualize the smirk that marred Cosic's face as he bragged to his men. "It's almost a joke how we've been running their rogue army in circles, selling them arms and then seizing them again in raids."

Another man said, "Yeah, and all along, you getting extra for the trouble."

A third crotchety voice added, "Anyone with eyes can see the Croatians and Bosnians can't even rule their women, much less a country."

The soldiers grunted in agreement. Silence prevailed for several moments, then Cosic said, "I'm going to miss bending that Roma Vita to my tune, hating herself and me, and locked in with no choice." He paused. "Contacts like her aren't easy to find. We need another link to Baharm. General Jovanovic keeps pressuring me for more intel."

The Serbs seemed to sober. One of them asked hesitantly, "Major, what are the chances of winning this?"

"The odds are better since we've got the Rogue Muslim Army concentrating on destroying the Croatian television and radio stations and public buildings." He laughed derisively. "Their idea would have never worked. The challenge was moving the explosives across the Neretva River into Croat territory. With that resolved, the operation should succeed."

Cosic's words beat home the reality that Croatian lives were at stake. Lucien would have to maneuver Cosic and his men into the patrolled area surrounding the Croatian Army barracks. It was a dangerous gamble that could backfire, costing his life and Tony's. He could think of no other means to defeat Cosic. Lucien had to risk it.

As they neared Mostar, a soldier untied Lucien's feet, leaving his hands bound. "All right, Croat, which direction?"

Lucien quelled his misgivings and led the enemy into the hills. The rugged terrain forced the Serbians to abandon the military vehicle and walk. A gun pressed to his back, Lucien stumbled ahead. Tony followed behind, hemmed in as well.

Lucien figured the barracks' sentry would spot them about midway up the pass. He inadvertently prayed, making God a myriad of promises if He brought Tony and him through this. He prayed for the entire city and that Sara, Martin, and his young nephew would stay at Martin's folks' farm away from the destruction.

When the attack came, there was no warning. Before the Serbians realized what was happening, a roving Croatian patrol ambushed Cosic and his men from behind. As shots rang out, Lucien and Tony dove for cover in the nearby shrubbery, bullets whizzing over their heads.

Artillery pounded Cosic's men, felling them in the first few minutes of battle. When Cosic ran out of ammunition, they captured him with two of his soldiers. Like Lucien, Cosic took a shot in the shoulder.

Lucien and Tony showed themselves, and thankfully, one of Lucien's men, who was part of the patrol, recognized him and helped them to the medic's station. Meanwhile, they locked Cosic and his officers in the stockade.

After the doctor patched up Lucien and Tony, the commander had a soldier drive Tony home. Then Lucien and the commander interrogated the Serbian prisoners. It took hours of forceful persuasion before Cosic talked. He admitted to ongoing operations to destroy the western sector of Mostar, but insisted the campaign was put on hold. "The plans were in the van your sister's family and the children fled in. I lost the plans with the van."

The commander said, "We're not stupid. You had studied the plans enough to carry them out. I want to know what was in them."

Despite the harsh methods used to compel the major to talk, he refused to reveal any specifics and was returned to his cell to reconsider.

Unfortunately, Cosic escaped in the night. On a routine check, a soldier discovered the guard unconscious and bound in the prisoner's cell. An immediate search of the area ensued, but Cosic eluded them. And Lucien's commander's curses failed to bring him back. They dispatched Sergeant Ratko to Martin's parents' farm on the off chance that they might have found the documents.

At headquarters, they wrestled with countering the expected attack, but they knew too little. Any moment, the enemy could strike the west side, killing innocent civilians. They were up against a time bomb of explosives delivered courtesy of the Bosnian Serb Army, which Serb Nationalists backed.

Chapter 50

Pescara, Italy

The next day arrived much too soon. At the knock on the door, Katrina clasped the boys close and then rose to answer it, wondering how she could bear parting from them.

Mr. Jones from the embassy stood there. "Good morning, Miss Winslow."

She stepped into the hall, closing the door behind her. "Sir, couldn't we apply for sponsorship now, and by the time it comes through, I'll have found a job to support them?"

"We've already been over this. Your single state makes an Italian adoption impossible. Your lack of employment is not the main impediment."

She couldn't suddenly change her single status or invent a fiancé. After hearing their history, how could any civilized court deny her and the boys? Katrina would fight to adopt Caleb and Drew just as she'd fought for their survival. She refused to give up. Her credentials were as good as ever, and with her PhD, she'd have no trouble securing a position.

"There may be nothing I can do now, but when I'm gainfully employed and my income is suitable to care for two children, you will hear from me and my lawyer."

"I wish you every success, though as the law stands, it's improbable. I'm not the enemy, as I've pointed out more than once. You should be grateful to me the Italian authorities haven't arrested you for smuggling yourself and five children into the country."

Her stomach twisted. "What do you mean?" He handed her four new passports. "Those forgeries you gave me would never have gotten through immigration."

"You knew." Katrina clutched the passports, hers, and the girls' lifeline to freedom.

"Of course, I knew and reissued you and the three girls' replacement passports before submitting them to the Italian government to arrange exit visas. Why didn't you ask for replacement passports?"

"I was afraid that I might not be able to get them for the girls since I'm not their legal guardian." She fought down a swell of terror at what might have happened with someone less tolerant. "I have much to thank you for. I'm very appreciative."

"You're welcome," he said, appearing far less formidable. "We're not as unsympathetic as you think." They exchanged smiles, and he said, "Let's get on with it."

Resigned, she led him into the room. Five expectant faces met hers. She shook her head, and the children appeared downcast. Katrina's gaze swung to Mr. Jones, pleading for understanding as she drew the two boys forward.

"This is Mr. Jones, the consul from the American embassy. He will drive you to the Italian camp, where you will be cared for until I return." She wanted to bawl but held her emotions in check and hugged the boys. Caleb's brave but pale demeanor was a wrenching sight.

The consul briefly patted the nine-year-old's shoulder and then bent to hoist Drew into his arms. "Come on, Tiger. We've lingered long enough."

Drew grinned. "Aren't you coming, Aunt Katrina?"

The corners of her mouth quivered. "No, darling, not this time. Remember to mind Caleb and the nice man."

Caleb and Drew knew better than to fight authority. The lesson had been drilled into them repeatedly throughout their brief lives.

Inherently trusting, Drew clasped her neck with his short arms. "I'll see you this afternoon, Aunt Katrina. We're going to have another adventure."

"The best adventure," Andi said, her eyes bright.

"That's right," Rachel chimed in, a tremor marking her words. "Aunt Katrina is going to take us home, so she won't return for a few weeks."

Tears streamed down Shelly's cheeks. "Drew, you have to be patient and wait."

Andi grasped Caleb's hands. "Never give up, no matter what happens. We'll all pray together, remember?"

After a final round of embraces, the boys left. Katrina and the girls stared at one another, their composure too fragile to risk words, their pain too deep to express. In unspoken agreement, they gathered their belongings, preparing for another departure.

As she readied for the flight, her thoughts wandered to home, a place Katrina had avoided thinking about, fearing their return was a dream. How would the girls handle the changes before them? Would they ever find their parents?

She phoned for a taxi. They were fortunate Pescara had an international airport with KLM flights to Houston. When the cab arrived, they got in. Abruzzo Airport was about four kilometers from their hotel. Every mile carried them farther from Lucien and the boys. Somehow, she knew Lucien and his friend had arrived home safely. Would he continue fighting the war he had grown to hate, denying the compassion that made him the man he was? So many questions. *Lord, I want to trust, but help me believe.*

Chapter 51

Fall 1993

The taxi stopped in front of the airport. Katrina paid the driver, and she and the girls climbed out. They waved goodbye to Italy and boarded the KLM 747 to Houston. One brief stopover in Amsterdam, and then they would be home. Home seemed unfamiliar and foreign. She imagined that Rachel, Shelly, and Andi must feel similarly, returning without their parents to a world of uncertainty, no matter how comfortable.

On the trek up the plane aisle, she was glad to see Rachel's dimpled smile once, despite her subdued demeanor. "I thought we'd be on an Italian plane."

Shelly tossed her head, a glint of determination in her gaze. "I never want to see Bosnia again."

Andi peered around with interest. "I kind of like Italy, especially the ice cream. Why aren't we flying on an American plane?"

"We get a discount with KLM," Katrina said.

"It's because we're missionaries, isn't it?" Shelly asked.

Katrina nodded. "Here are our seats. You three can sit together. Rachel, take the outside seat, and I'll be here across the aisle."

The sisters held each other's hands during takeoff. Afterward, they plugged in their headphones, listened to music, and leafed through magazines.

Thankfully, KLM included the entertainment in the airfare price. Katrina closed her eyes with a yawn. Guilt assailed her for having left the boys. The flight attendants passed out drinks and peanuts and then served lunch. By gradual degrees, a sense of reprieve developed, as if her inner pedometer measured the growing distance from Bosnia and the war.

She was going home to Houston, where villains didn't chase innocent civilians down with submachine guns. Katrina and her charges would be secure for the first time in years.

The sisters were too wound up to rest and opted to watch Meg Ryan and Tom Hanks in *Sleepless in Seattle*. Katrina signaled she would nap, blew them a kiss, tucked a blanket around her shoulders, and dozed.

She awoke some hours later with a groan. Immediately, her head jerked up, and she looked around to locate the children. She breathed a sigh of relief at the sight of the sleeping girls. Andi's and Rachel's heads were together. Shelly was leaning on Rachel's shoulder. How long would it be before the fear of the children going missing wouldn't be with her when she woke? She retrieved blankets from the overhead bin and covered them.

Andi said, "Mommy."

"Shush, dear. Everything's fine."

Without waking, Andi smiled and curled her palm under her cheek.

Poor darlings, Katrina mused.

When Katrina awoke next, Rachel was shaking her. "We're almost to Houston."

Katrina peered out the plane window. "I must have slept through the stopover in Amsterdam." Streaks of iridescent light marbled the shadowy horizon.

"We weren't there long," Rachel said from across the aisle. "You were asleep, and we didn't want to wake you."

A flight attendant handed her a hot towel to wipe her face and hands, the heat and moisture soothing. She enjoyed coffee and a light meal. The girls ate as well. After their trays were collected, Katrina combed her hair, excited to be seeing her aunt and uncle soon.

A thunderstorm broke as the plane's altitude decreased to prepare for landing. Lightning streaked through the turbulent jet, forcing the pilot to seek refuge at a higher altitude. The passengers grew silent. The pilot attempted to lower the aircraft but was repeatedly compelled to retreat to a greater elevation. Katrina prayed. *Not now, not after everything we've been through.*

Andi gripped her sister's hand. With a sob, Shelly buried her face in her hands. Rachel, appearing slightly green, spoke for them all in a trembling voice. "We're scared."

"Me too. But it's a thunderstorm, not war. Let's try to be brave. Can you do that?"

As the plane lowered again, it shook with the storm's fervor. Lightning bolts bleached the interior, silhouetting the passengers' frightened faces. Turbulence pitched the jet about as if it were a tin can instead of titanium, steel, and aluminum. An eerie silence followed. There was a jarring thump, and the plane was on the runway, racing at breakneck speed, then braking to a screeching halt. Applause erupted in the cabin.

Relieved and shaken, Katrina herded the girls off the plane and through customs to where Aunt Janine and Uncle York waited on the other side.

Her aunt and uncle hugged her. "Honey," Aunt Janine said, "we were so frightened we'd never see you again." She embraced the girls. "My, how you three have grown. It seems like yesterday you were babies."

"Come on," Uncle York said. "Let's go home. It's almost ten o'clock. I'm sure these youngsters are more than ready for their beds."

Katrina felt as if she were in a time warp as they strode to the exit. In her mind, she repeated Dorothy's refrain from Frank Baum's *The*

Wonderful Wizard of Oz. "There is no place like home. There is no place like home. There is no place like home."

It seemed strange to hear people speaking English and watch them hurrying from one place to the next. They rode the train to the parking garage, then the elevator to the floor where her uncle had parked. Although it was the first of September, a blanket of moist heat enveloped them, weighing Katrina down with poignant memories of her family as everyone piled into her uncle's Cadillac.

Soon, they arrived at her aunt and uncle's house. Once inside, Katrina drifted along, attributing much of her disorientation to culture shock, deepened by the war and then losing her parents and Giles. Even the girls' chatter slowed, and they grew somber. Katrina knew how hard it was for them to return to someone else's place instead of home with their mom and dad and understood the girls' feelings. Katrina wondered if they heard voices like she did and imagined family in every room.

Aunt Janine prepared her special hot cocoa, a favorite of Katrina's family. Her aunt passed it around, and the group settled in for a brief visit before dispersing to prepare for bed.

Later, settled in her aunt's best guestroom, Katrina realized she must come to terms with her memories. There would be more when they moved into her parents' home. She had no intention of burdening Aunt Janine and Uncle York with the responsibility of caring for the four of them. Yet it would be heavenly to have family near, should she need them. Katrina and the girls were home at last. If she could only hear news of Lucien and the boys and be assured of their safety.

A knock at Katrina's door interrupted her thoughts, and Rachel slipped inside. "Can I talk to you?"

"Sure." Katrina patted the edge of the mattress.

Rachel crossed to the bed and stood nervously beside it. "It's really hard to say this, but—I . . ." She stared at Katrina imploringly. "I'm so ashamed. All along, everything's been my fault." A sob tore from her. "What if my mom and dad are dead because of me? I have the Madonna."

Katrina drew in a sharp breath. "What are you saying?"

"Before the raid—one day at the mission, I was practicing piano when I noticed a loose brick." A stricken look crossed her face, as if in sudden realization. "If I hadn't touched it—your parents and mine might be alive." She wept.

Katrina hugged her. "Shh. I expect we'll hear from your folks any day. Whatever it is, it's okay."

"No, it's not! And it never will be again."

Her mind awash with conjecture, Katrina gently shook the girl. "Calm down. I can't help unless you tell me what happened."

Rachel swiped at her tears with the back of her hand. "You're going to hate me, and so is everyone else. I even hate me."

Compassion swelled within, but Katrina forced herself to be firm. "Nonsense, tell me about this brick and the Madonna."

Once Rachel began, the words tumbled out as if she sought some reprieve in the telling. "I wanted to investigate, like in a mystery book. I pulled out the brick and found a tiny picture of the Madonna set in a gold frame, sort of like the relics you see at the train station, but prettier." She glanced away defensively. "It hung on an old black ribbon, and I put it around my neck for the day. I meant to show it to Mom that night, but I forgot. Then there was the raid."

Why hadn't Rachel confided in her before? With dread, Katrina braced herself and asked, "Where is it now?"

The girl peered around the room, and her gaze landed on Katrina's tennis shoes by the bed where she'd kicked them off. Rachel stooped and scooped up the left shoe. "I hid it in here." She flipped the shoe over, opened the secret compartment in the bottom, and drew out a small oval miniature. Rachel handed it to Katrina.

Could this be the Madonna that Cosic had been willing to murder them to possess? Where had it come from? Who could have placed it behind the brick, and why? Then she remembered a Serbian officer had questioned her at the jail, claiming a Kosovo soldier had stolen it from the cathedral in Pazaric and hidden it in their home. She wondered how much of what he'd said was true. She should be angry Rachel had concealed it from her.

Katrina studied it for some clues as to its origin and value. It was scarcely bigger than a postage stamp. She was baffled and not knowledgeable enough to reach any conclusions. It drew her eye repeatedly, leaving her with the sinking feeling it might be a rare religious artifact.

"I wish you had shown me this earlier. Do you realize the danger you placed me and all of us in? You hid it in my shoe and didn't even tell me about it?"

"I had to think of my sisters first. We're all each other has. If you'd known, I don't think you could have acted natural."

"I thought you trusted me to care for you—that we were in this together, like a family."

"I do trust you. But what about when we were separated, and you were captured? You left us with Vita. She put us in jail. Those people were going to kill us!"

"I was trying to protect you. My mistake was trusting Vita. Still, what good was the Madonna to you then? Why didn't you tell Cosic where it was and save yourselves?"

Tears streamed down Rachel's cheeks. "I knew they'd never let us out—no matter what. If we escaped, I thought the Madonna might buy our way out of Bosnia. I didn't mean to hurt anyone."

"Who else knows about this?"

"No one, not even Shelly and Andi." She pointed to the icon in Katrina's hand. "This is what those men were after."

"How can you be so certain?" she asked, hoping Rachel was

wrong, because if she was right . . . Katrina shivered, not wanting to consider the possibility of an assailant tracking her across the ocean. No, such an outcome was unlikely, she told herself as she studied the miniature. It was incredible to believe the tiny picture could be so valuable. Yet it was simply too exquisite not to be.

Rachel said, "Vita searched through our things at the cave. I even caught her going through your clothes."

"You never told me Vita went through my stuff. I knew she'd gone through the children's belongings. Vita said it was to see what they needed, but she was probably rummaging for the Madonna. I'm sorry I ever trusted her."

Rachel shrugged uncertainly. "You were always taking her side. You wouldn't believe us when we said she was bad."

In the beginning, Katrina had relied on Vita and stubbornly refused to listen to any criticisms of her. She'd been wrong and now realized what that had meant to those in her care. Katrina needed to arrange counseling for them all. She hugged Rachel. "If anyone is to blame, it's me. I brought Vita to the mission." She set the icon aside. "We have to return it."

"How? We don't know who it really belongs to."

"Let me think about it. Maybe I'll get a professional evaluation."

"Wait. There's more," Rachel said. "I wanted to tell you about when Martin drove off with us in Cosic's van the day we escaped from the grave site. There was a packet of papers lying on the floorboard. I just had this feeling and grabbed them. A picture of the Madonna was in the envelope, only it was bigger."

"You've waited until today to tell me this! What did you do with the papers?"

The girl pulled a manila envelope out of the cloth bag she usually had slung across her shoulder. She handed Katrina the envelope.

Weary, jet-lagged, and saddened, it was almost too much for Katrina. She wanted to sleep and forget the horrors they'd experienced.

Her shoulders sagged. "We're both tired. Let's get some rest and talk about this in the morning."

"I love you, Aunt Katrina. I'm sorry for everything."

Katrina forced a smile. "Don't worry. We'll figure it out, sweetheart. Will you be able to sleep?"

"Like a log, since I've confessed to you about the Madonna and those papers."

They embraced again, and Rachel left. Katrina glanced at the papers in the envelope. The writing was in Serbian. They were probably provenance papers for the Madonna with a map to where it belonged. Her brain was too tired to translate tonight. She put Rachel's findings in the bedside drawer, switched off the lamp, and climbed beneath the covers. Where had the Madonna come from? Not that it mattered to her. She'd let the experts deal with it. To think Rachel had kept it hidden all these months in Katrina's shoe, and she hadn't known.

Katrina shuddered at the thought, the sheets falling to her waist. She wondered what was in the packet besides the picture. What sort of diabolical schemes might Cosic have recorded? It was as though evil tentacles stretched across nations and oceans, luring her deeper into Bosnia's nightmare. Exhausted, Katrina finally slept.

She was back in Bosnia in the middle of the fighting. Bombs exploded, and fire rocketed through the sky, the sounds deafening, the smell acrid. Katrina ran deep into the forest to escape.

The flames leaped toward a huge harvest moon and a scattering of stars above. Panicked, unsure which direction to run, she glimpsed Caleb trapped by the blaze.

Where had he sprung from? She sped forward, but the furnace-like heat shoved her back. "Caleb!" She screamed, waving her arms. "Go the other way!"

Katrina awakened from the nightmare. She stabbed a trembling hand through her hair, rose, and crossed to the window. The dawn scribbled across the horizon in a language of color. A splatter of indigo outlined in amber ambiance glowed in the east, the sky fading to blue as the sun climbed.

Chapter 52

Mostar, Bosnia-Herzegovina, Fall 1993

Croatian forces had set up temporary field quarters midway between their base and Mostar, operating on the premise the enemy would attempt to destroy them to gain access to western Mostar. At tent headquarters, Lucien stared out at the dark nimbus clouds overtaking the sky, casting the landscape in shadow. He rubbed his shoulder, which ached despite having healed some in the last week.

The commander said, "If we're lucky, the rain will hold off."

Lucien studied the worn maps spread on the rickety camp table. "If there's a downpour, the valley will be nothing more than a sea of mud."

"Keep to the high ground. Let the Serbs bring the battle to us. Are the men in place?"

Lucien pointed at the marked areas. "Our Croat forces are stationed along the upper edges, and more are in reserve in the low-lying regions for the final assault. But not nearly enough. We need time to bring in more men."

The commander grunted. "You're to lead the men out."

"It would help to know who will head the strike against us. Will it be the Serb, Bosnian Muslim, or Rogue Muslim Armies confronting us? Maybe all three."

"Tell me how you'll handle this, Captain."

Lucien drew the second map out. "Intelligence has the forward column of Bosnia's Serb Army here." He pointed to the charted area.

"We could engage the enemy there, cutting them off from the main body of their troops."

"That puts you smack between our guns and theirs, a risky place to be."

"I'm aware of that, sir, but it's imperative that we hold off the enemy until sufficient Croat units are entrenched. Our position there would buy us needed time."

The chief cursed. "At what cost? Out of all the captains in Croatia, I end up with a know-it-all Westerner." He bent forward to reexamine the maps and admitted grudgingly, "For what it's worth, you have my approval. See to your men and don't get yourself killed because they'll never pull this off alone." He waved his hand in dismissal.

Lucien saluted and stepped into the cool night beyond the canvas tent, serving as company headquarters. He tilted his head and listened to the soldiers preparing for battle—the sounds of artillery being cleaned and packed, men scribbling what might be their last letters to loved ones and family, their subdued chatter, and the controlled fear that lit into every man.

Suspicion gnawed at Lucien. Cosic had been outspoken with his men and well aware Tony and Lucien were listening. What if Lucien and his men were set up? Might not the Muslims have been duped as well? No matter how intense Serbian hatred of Croatians, their revulsion toward Bosnian Muslims went deeper.

So why would Serbia help them destroy the Croats? What if their objective wasn't to strike with conventional troops? When Lucian had overheard Cosic's plans to raze public facilities in the Croatian sector, he'd assumed Serbia intended to attack the Croat base, defeating their forces to gain access to western Mostar. The Serbs needed access to blow up the radio and TV stations, utilities, hospitals, and other facilities.

Had Lucien got it wrong? How else could the enemy get the

explosives into the area? Lucien could easily believe Cosic was a paid mercenary on the side. He peered at his men, hoping he wasn't leading the troops into a trap.

Chapter 53

Houston, Texas, Fall 1993

Katrina glanced up as Rachel came in and sat across from her at the oak table. Outside, a pair of hummingbirds sipped the nectar of Old Blush climbing roses. The faint scent of sasanqua camellias wafted in through a slightly raised window of Aunt Janine's breakfast room.

When Rachel had handed her the manilla envelope containing Cosic's papers last night, Katrina had put them in the nightstand drawer for later. This morning, she had second thoughts and dropped it in her purse for safekeeping. There was no rush. Rachel had kept it hidden all this time. A few more days wouldn't matter. Once Katrina settled her parents' affairs and found a job, she'd study the documents. She couldn't handle any more now.

Her aunt entered from the kitchen, carrying a platter of freshly baked muffins. "I hope everyone likes blueberries."

"We do," Rachel said as Shelly and Andi trailed in, looking sleepy-eyed.

Katrina bit into a muffin. "Mmm, these are good."

Her aunt said, "I've been thinking. There's no rush to move into your family home. Why not meet with the lawyer and secure a job first? Having you young folks around for a while will do your Uncle York and me a world of good."

Though the offer was tempting, Katrina declined. "That's generous, Aunt Janine, but we couldn't impose."

"Nonsense. What if you decide to sell? These girls have been through enough without another unnecessary move."

Before Katrina could respond, the telephone rang, and her aunt rose to answer it. Katrina peered around at the girls, realizing it would be hard for them to move twice. Her aunt was right. "Where do you three want to live?" Katrina asked.

"It's nice here. Can't we stay?" Shelly asked.

Rachel stared at her plate. "It doesn't matter where we live. I'm just glad we're home."

"Don't forget," Andi said, "we don't have our mom and dad back yet."

"They'll be here before we know it. Won't they, Aunt Katrina?" Shelly asked.

Three somber faces lifted to hers. "I sure hope so, honey."

Her aunt returned. "That was your uncle on the phone." She gave Katrina an excited look. "We didn't want to raise your hopes too much last night about teaching, but there's a temporary opening at the University of Houston. One of the English professors is pregnant, and her doctor has ordered bed rest. The dean, who was a close friend of your parents, knew you were returning and would be hunting for a position. She has contacted your uncle to see if you might be interested."

Katrina's thoughts darted to Caleb and Drew in the refugee camp, depending on her to get them. "Thank God for family connections."

"Your uncle arranged an interview for you this afternoon. It's an opportunity to use the English doctorate you worked so hard to get. It's already September. The fall semester started in mid-August. The dean will want to fast-track the hiring process."

Katrina felt as if she had been given a gift. "I better get moving. There's so much to do."

Her aunt laughed, and Katrina grinned. "Aunt Janine, thank you both for everything."

Katrina phoned her family's lawyer and arranged an appointment to see him the following day. Next, she called the girls' former schools about getting their records transferred and then rang the new schools about enrollment.

She drove them to the schools, filled out the required forms, and picked up and dropped off their transfer records. Afterward, she and the girls went shopping for clothes and other necessities.

Later, Katrina's interview with the dean went well, and they agreed she would start teaching in three days. The school was in a bind and would speed up the application process. Katrina was excited to begin work.

A week later, Katrina fought the morning traffic with a sense of déjà vu as the Volkswagen Golf she had purchased barreled down the freeway to the university. The tangled grass and parched flowers along the roadside seemed a carbon copy of her emotions. She'd met with her parents' lawyer and had spent a few hours each evening at her childhood home, sorting through belongings and memories. It was like saying goodbye again to the family she'd buried in Mostar.

Perhaps if their things didn't surround her, it would be easier. In Bosnia, she'd been consumed with survival. There hadn't been time to grieve. Her aunt advised her not to fight the tears. To cry was natural. Yet she was afraid to give in to the feelings that might rip her fragile self-confidence to shreds.

She tightened her grip on the steering wheel. Her parents had taught her to count her blessings daily, but neglected to warn her about how painful it could be.

Katrina took in the blue skies, willfully letting go of the bitterness and concentrating on the blessings. "Thank you, Lord, for blue skies . . . and white clouds. Why God—why?" she half-sobbed, unable to go on. "How could you allow such tragedies? First, the twins' deaths, then Giles and my parents, the orphans lost in my care, the boys thrust into a foreign refugee camp, and what about John and Ellen? Must the girls face their parents' deaths, too?"

"It's not that I'm ungrateful, Lord. We're home and safe." She clung to that thought, but the darkness seemed to overwhelm her. Every time she finally had a hold on success, disaster struck.

Katrina took the highway exit and drove to the campus. *Think about your job. Another blessing to be grateful for.* She could hardly believe she'd landed a position so quickly. The dean had learned about Katrina's experiences in Bosnia from her uncle. Fascinated, the dean had wanted to hear more when she met with Katrina. Questions were sure to come from her new colleagues, too. How could Katrina forget when well-meaning people were constantly probing?

She parked, walked to the English building, and took the stairs to her office. She worked on the following week's lesson plans. The free hour before her advanced British Literature Class passed too swiftly. She shoved the lesson plans aside and left.

Her first class was one floor down. Katrina had already started building a rapport with the students and hoped today's session would go well. She wasn't disappointed and thoroughly enjoyed the group's participation.

After a coffee break, Katrina taught a course on Keats and then headed to her office for lunch. Her last lecture would be on The Romantic Movement.

Back at her desk, her thoughts drifted. She still had nightmares about her enemies in Bosnia. They were dead, but in her mind, she hadn't stopped running. How long was she going to put off reviewing those papers Rachel had given her? What if they were vital? It was time she faced her responsibilities. With a shudder, she picked up the phone and dialed a friend who was also an expert authority on medieval Christian antiquities.

A voice on the other end of the line answered, "Doctor Hyatt's office."

"This is Katrina Winslow. Is the professor in?"

"Please hold while I check."

Bill's warm voice came across the line. "Katrina, it's been ages. Last I heard, you were in Bosnia."

Katrina greeted him and asked, "May I drop by your place this evening? I need to speak with you privately."

"Sure. I'll be home. Come about nine. Are you all right?"

She reassured him and then hung up the phone.

Katrina went to teach her last class of the day. Afterward, she returned to her office. The hours sped by. She tidied her desk and picked up her purse to leave.

Lightning streaked across the sky as she ran to her car, wishing she'd heeded the morning's weather forecast and carried an umbrella. She hurried inside the Golf and glanced at her watch. Already after six, and there were several errands she needed to run. She would have to rush to get all she wanted accomplished done and still meet Bill later with the Madonna.

Rain danced against the windshield, spinning down the hood as Katrina turned the key in the ignition and stepped on the accelerator. "What in the world?" she muttered when nothing happened. Frustrated, she tried repeatedly, then stopped lest she flood the engine.

She gazed anxiously at the gathering dusk. Her nerves were screaming. Katrina had worked late several evenings since starting back teaching, but she'd never felt uneasy before.

Well, she couldn't sit there. It was dry inside. She'd use the office phone. Katrina opened the car door and struggled out into the pouring rain. The wind whipped around her, and she recalled the weatherman's warning of a hurricane forming in the Gulf.

She sprinted across the parking lot and, once inside, walked down the hall into the office. Katrina picked up the phone by the front desk and called a taxi, then her family. After a few rings, her uncle's voice came over the recorder. Katrina left a message that she would be home late and not to worry.

The cab arrived, and she gave her parents' address and climbed in. It was nearby, and she had so much to do to settle the estate. Her appointment with Bill wasn't until nine.

On the drive there, Katrina stared out the window. Rain puddled, swelling into rising rivulets as the wind picked up speed. When the taxi stopped in the drive, Katrina paid the driver and stepped outside.

With a wave, she walked to the porch, slipped inside, and bolted the door. She scooped up the mail and crossed to the den. Her mind turned to Caleb and Drew. She imagined their innocent faces, heard their voices in her heart. "Aunt Katrina, are you coming for us soon?"

She needed this job to earn the money to start the legal process. With a secure position, an early loan might be possible. Once her parents' affairs were settled, the house could be used for collateral. She could smuggle the boys out of Italy to a country more likely to let her adopt them.

Katrina phoned Bill to see if their meeting was still on.

"You stay inside where it's dry," he said. "I'll come over to your place about nine after I finish this paperwork."

She thanked him and gave him the address, then contacted her folks' lawyer, a family friend. He'd already arranged a generous advance on her parents' estate. She'd bought the girls and herself clothes, purchased a car, and had enough extra cash to see her through until her first paycheck. Now, she wanted to ask about the feasibility of an even larger loan to sponsor the boys.

He said, "It's four months we're talking about before the estate is settled, and the property will be yours to do with as you wish."

"To Caleb and Drew, four months is an eternity."

"Those boys are in government hands and will be fine."

Their conversation left her discouraged. The boys had already experienced too much grief and terror. They were so young and alone. How must they be feeling?

Her subconscious still heard the machine gun fire, saw the explosions bursting overhead, and felt the ground rock beneath her feet. Worst of all, she heard the children's cries. Her shattered life meant little without them.

Drew's small arms wrapped around her neck, his soft lips brushing her cheek, trusting her to care for him. She thought of Rachel's smiling dimples, Shelly's sparkling humor, Andi's mischievous nature, and Caleb's crooked grin. Their precious lives meant everything. They were the future. In a moment of clarity, Katrina understood why she'd chosen to teach.

She stared across the prisms of past truths, picturing the grave site filled with the human skeletal bones of those who had once lived and loved. When she closed her eyes, Katrina saw tortured and slain men, women, and children.

And she pondered, who was to blame?

Was it some malevolent spirit which specialized in torturing humankind? Yes, that was part of it. She knew from scripture Satan walked the earth, seeking to destroy, making men his ambassadors to hell. Katrina had seen enough to believe it.

But a culture steeped in prejudice and hate too deep to uproot couldn't be passed off as solely the fault of an undefinable spirit world. Individuals had made the choices that led to Bosnia's destruction. Yet she knew Muslims, Croats, and Serbs who were generous and kind and bore no one malice, regardless of race or ethnicity. Their leaders, who had deceived the masses and manipulated them into war, were the most culpable.

Katrina shrugged half-heartedly. There was more than enough fault to share, and those with a conscience might never be free from the weight of it. Who was she to heap more condemnation upon the defeated? As for those who had no conscience—

The tension eased from her shoulders as the answer came to her. There was God and fate, politicians, and governments enough to reckon with their sins. She'd delayed long enough. It was time to face her demons and open the package.

Her phone rang, and she saw her lawyer's name on the caller ID. Her heart leaped with hope. Maybe he'd found something. "Hello?"

After greeting Katrina, he said, "It has occurred to me there is a way you can access immediate capital. Cash in your mother's CDs. She named you the sole beneficiary on her account, and you are a signatory on it as well. You are free to withdraw those funds whenever you like."

"That's wonderful news. Do you know how much the CDs are worth?"

There was the rustle of shuffling papers. "Two hundred and fifty thousand, which should be plenty. Your father left your brother the same, which will also be yours, eventually."

"Can you petition the Italian authorities about me adopting the boys?"

"Italian law might not be amenable to adoption," he cautioned. "I will look into it and contact them on your behalf if you're sure it's what you want."

"Absolutely." They discussed the boys' adoptions, and she was ecstatic to leave the matter in his capable hands. Her heart sang at the thought the boys might soon be with her. In her spirit, she believed God would make a way. There were no obstacles too big for him.

Katrina started toward her bedroom as the doorbell rang. Bill must have finished early. She pressed the intercom. "Who is it?"

Silence.

"Who is it?" she repeated, a raspy tremor revealing her disquiet.

"HPD," he said, his voice muffled through the door.

She opened the door, expecting to greet a Houston police officer. "You're not in uniform?"

He held up a badge. "No, ma'am. There have been several robberies in the neighborhood, and it's under surveillance. Call the station to verify if you like, and I'll wait out here."

She hesitated. "What's this about?"

He grimaced, a sign that what was coming would be unpleasant. "A neighbor reported a prowler in your backyard. I'd like to look around."

"Of course," she said in a soft squeak. "The side gate's unlocked."

"Wait inside, ma'am, and keep that door bolted." He left, striding across the lawn.

She secured the front door, then ran through the house to her old bedroom where she'd hidden Rachel's finds earlier in the week. Katrina needed to know what was in the manila envelope and hoped she hadn't waited too long. What if someone had stolen both it and the Madonna? Hands shaking, she dug through her bottom dresser drawer, where she'd buried it beneath a stack of rainbow-colored summer T-shirts. She grabbed the envelope and tossed the contents on the bed, revealing a packet of maps, timetables, and papers.

Among these, she found correspondence between Cosic and General Stefan Jovanovic. Though the letters were written in Serbian and somewhat challenging to interpret, Katrina translated enough text to comprehend the noxious import. She unfolded the maps, aghast to discover they centered on Mostar. Papers detailed tactical Serbian maneuvers to eradicate most of Mostar's Croats and Muslims in a premeditated multi-strike.

Katrina flipped to the timetables and nearly keeled over. Ten days left!

In the background, she heard the doorbell ringing as if from some great distance. She stuffed the papers into the envelope and put it back in the drawer. Dear Lord, Lucien was in Mostar. He would be killed. The ringing in her ears changed to pounding as she stumbled to the foyer.

Words spilled through her mind, phrases she couldn't quite grasp. *Pull yourself together. Don't just open the door.* "Who is it?" she asked, pressing the intercom.

"Ma'am, it's the police. I didn't see anyone out there. So maybe we got a false alarm."

Say something. React. Katrina swallowed, her mouth thick and cotton-like. "Thank you."

"Ma'am, are you okay? I'd be glad to check inside. Can't be too safe these days."

She recoiled at the word safe. "No. That's unnecessary," she choked out.

Several minutes later, she heard the patrol car leave. Minutes during which she came to grips with the horrible truth as her mind sifted and sorted, searching for direction. Should she contact US officials with this new information? What if they refused to take her seriously? There were always delays working through diplomatic channels. Did she dare return to Mostar? How would she find Lucien?

The storm sounded as if it was worsening. *"Lord, doesn't life ever let up?"* The doorbell pealed again. She squinted through the peephole and saw Bill, tall and athletic, brushing a shock of windswept black hair from his face. The rain beat down, and the accompanying wind almost pulled the door out of her hand.

"What a night," Bill said, stamping the wet from his shoes before entering.

Katrina gave him a brief hug. "Don't worry about the mess. Everything's topsy-turvy, anyway."

Bill's earnest expression took her back in time. They had dated some in college and remained good friends and professional colleagues in the ensuing years. She hung his jacket and umbrella on the hall tree. "If you knew how happy I am to see you," Katrina said.

"It's been too long," he agreed.

She led him down the hall into her mother's blue-on-white and saffron-painted kitchen. "Have a seat. I'll make coffee." She filled two mugs with water, added a spoonful of espresso powder in each cup, and popped them into the microwave.

He sat at the walnut-drop leaf that had belonged to her grandmother. Her gaze wandered beyond the double French doors to the overgrown herb garden lit by the patio light. She had often wondered how her mom squeezed in time from her painting and other activities to cultivate herbs like rosemary and thyme. Thank goodness they had kept a bi-monthly lawn service to tidy up enough so the neighborhood association wouldn't object in their absence.

"You sounded mysterious on the phone. Almost as if you were in danger," Bill said.

She set the coffee on the table and sank into a chair. "I'm so confused. I no longer know who to trust or what is real or imagined, and I can't afford to take any chances." She studied him. Was she expecting too much of a friend she hadn't seen in years?

Bill's eyes lit with interest. "I admit to being curious as well as concerned. Unless you tell me what this is about, there's nothing I can do. So how about it, Kat?"

Touched by his use of her old nickname, she said, "Wait here." She went to her bedroom and retrieved the Madonna and the packet of papers. She placed the icon before Bill. Now, it was her turn to rein in her impatience as she watched him examine the tiny portrait.

Awestruck, he said, "Do you realize what you have here? Some collectors would kill to own this."

She shivered, her suspicion of its worth confirmed. Katrina watched the wonder in his expressive face fade to hard questions, knowing her answers would be difficult for someone as methodical as Bill to accept. Before he could begin, she told him of her discovery of the Madonna.

Some inner sense kept her from mentioning Rachel's role in hiding it, though Katrina stuck to the story the girl had shared. "I had no idea what those people were talking about when they asked for the icon. Then, while unpacking our clothes the day after our arrival here, I noticed the secret compartment in one of my sneakers was loose and opened it to find the Madonna. Someone must have hidden it there. I can't imagine how else it came to be among our belongings."

"It sounds as if you already knew there was a hidden compartment in your shoe."

"Of course I did. The shoes were a birthday present from Giles. He'd ordered them from the States as a kind of gag gift. I had forgotten about the secret compartments with the war and everything happening." The recounting was almost too much. She suppressed a sob, swiping at the dampness on her cheeks. "I'm sorry."

"Kat, it's okay. You deserve a good cry. Come here. I have broad shoulders."

She shook her head and fought to collect herself. "What should I do?"

"If it's a Croatian or Serbian artifact, the Madonna should be returned to the proper parties there."

"That's a major problem. We may well be handing it over to war criminals. Besides, how do we determine whether it belongs to the Serbians or the Croatians? I'm assuming Bosnian Muslims wouldn't possess a Christian artifact."

"Your story suggests it must have been stolen. Let me do

some research. A painting this remarkable is bound to have a traceable history."

"Then you believe me?"

"I do," he said. "Why wouldn't I?"

The noise of the storm drew their attention outside. Torrential rain and winds slammed through the trees, scattering debris. Mesmerized, Katrina watched the sky blacken as a bicycle catapulted through the air.

The telephone shrilled. Katrina answered it and reassured her aunt she was fine. Since it was half past eleven and the storm showed no sign of abating, they decided Katrina should stay for the night. She recalled the hurricanes and tornadoes that occasionally tore through Houston and most of the Gulf Coast.

Katrina hung up the phone, and it rang again. "Hello."

"Katrina. Thank God! This is Ellen. Are our daughters with you?"

"Ellen, I can't believe it's you! It's a miracle you're alive and well. Yes, the girls are in Houston. We're staying at my Aunt Janine and Uncle York's place. I'll give you the number so you can call them."

"Praise the Lord! John, they're safe."

"John must be with you. I'm so glad. My love to both of you."

"We're at the American embassy in Vienna and will be home soon."

"The girls will be over the moon. It's such an answer to prayer." They chatted for a few minutes, then Katrina gave her the number to call the girls, and they said goodbye. She could hardly believe the fantastic news. Her heart filled with awe at the Lord's goodness. Excited, she explained the situation to Bill.

He congratulated her. "It's late, and I should be going."

"I don't think you should drive in this storm. There are plenty of extra bedrooms. Also, there's another situation I want to discuss with you. First, I need your word that what I am about to reveal will remain in the strictest confidence."

"There's no need to confide in me if you have any doubts—"

She cut in. "You're going to be tempted to seek advice on this one. The discovery of the Madonna can't compare to this."

"You have my pledge."

She set the papers before him. "Take your time and look through them. When you're finished, I'll explain."

Chapter 54

Mostar, Bosnia-Herzegovina, Fall 1993

Lucien shivered as he and his men set up camp again. Shades of crimson blazed in the sunset, reminding him of the never-ending bloodshed. Was there no end to this man-made misery? No solution to save west Mostar? His shoulders slumped beneath the weight of concern. How could his men evacuate the Croats, boxed in as they were by the Muslims and Serbs? It was impossible to protect his people without more intel. Ratko's search for Cosic's van had turned up nothing. According to Martin, the van mysteriously disappeared one night from the farm. Lucien was grateful no one had approached or harmed Martin's family. A massive attack on Croat forces hadn't materialized, but bombing incidents throughout the sector were on the rise.

Lucien fervently hoped Sara, his nephew, and Martin were okay at his parents' farm and were not in Mostar. Lucien had checked their apartment daily before leaving the city, believing they were secure at the farm. Knowing that Katrina and the children were safe in the States comforted him. He tried to imagine what her life was like. Was she teaching? Had she found the girls' family? Were the boys making new friends in Italy? He wished he could have gotten Caleb and Drew their passports so the two could have left with Katrina and the girls.

Lucien went into the tent and lit a lantern. He sat and pulled out the small packet of letters tucked into his diary. Earlier that day, a courier from the base had caught up with the Croatian troops on the move and delivered last week's mail. A letter from his Aunt Dianne caught his eye. Curiously, the postmark was from Ljubljana, a town in Slovenia about eighty-five kilometers from his family home in Austria. What was his aunt doing there? Had she left her home in Serbia? He tore open the envelope and drew out the letter.

Dear Lucien,

I pray this letter finds you well. You've sacrificed so much to help Croatia, and I wouldn't trouble you if I could find your uncles, Ivan and Feodor, or their sons. But for now, they seem to have vanished. I have no one else to turn to besides you, my nephew.

Your Uncle Stefan has cast us out. And now I have lost Mimi somewhere. I dare not contact Stefan. He was the one who had us deported. Serb authorities detained us in a Bosnian camp near Srebrenica for four weeks of interrogation. We feared for our sanity and womanhood, such was the treatment we endured.

After the first few days, they separated Mimi and me. I cannot speak of what followed, so disturbing was that period of my life.

Then, one day, the soldiers placed me in a car, drove me to the Croatian border, and left me there in the wilderness. I was frantic for news of Mimi and tried to turn back to find her but was not permitted to cross into Serbian territory. It has taken me until now to reach Slovenia. Your dear father, my brother, is deeply distressed at our plight. He is trying to arrange visas

for us to enter Austria. Yet I dare not leave without
Mimi.

My worst nightmare is that Mimi never survived the
camp or attempted to return to our home in Serbia.
She was involved in the anti-Milosevic student rebellion and was infatuated with the rebel leader. Will
you please help me find her? She is your cousin, and I
know she always looked to you. Now I am asking you
to look for her. I will wait here until I hear from you,
no matter how long it takes. My daughter is everything to me.

My dear nephew, I pray you are safe and remain so in
God's care.

With much love,
Your Aunt Dianne

Lucien was aghast that his Uncle Stefan had behaved so treacherously toward his wife and daughter. He flinched as distant machine gun
fire erupted, tightening already taut nerves. The sound of bazookas to
the north followed. Lucien reached for the small notebook he carried
in his front pocket and scribbled a message to Martin, explaining
Mimi's situation and asking him to use his contacts to help find her
with all discretion.

He then penned a letter to his aunt and urged her not to worry.
He had already begun searching for Mimi. Lucien urged his aunt to
travel to his father's house in Austria as soon as possible. "I will bring
Mimi to you there," he wrote.

His next dispatch was to the Croatian base commander, requesting that he post the enclosed correspondence and make inquiries

regarding his cousin's whereabouts. Lucien added a postscript asserting that, in his opinion, they needed to change strategies and shore up the borders. He suspected that mercenaries posing as patriots were using vehicles to smuggle explosives into the city.

Lucien put the notebook away. He'd done all he could. *God, if You're real and near enough to hear, see to Mimi for us.* He blinked hard, remembering the words of a hymn he'd sung as a child: "Savior, Savior. Hear my humble cry, while on others thou art calling, do not pass me by."

It's not for myself, I'm asking Lord, but for Mimi. She's nineteen. He bowed his head. He so desperately wanted to believe. For one moment, Lucien tasted hope mingled with fear before cynicism took over. He considered the deaths of his cousins, uncles, and comrades in arms and realized his innate belief in man's goodness and a destiny governed by a loving God had wavered.

He shook off his introspection and focused on developing a strategy. Lucien decided that half of his men would remain and stand guard. The rest of his soldiers would work with him to set up roadblocks and guard posts at entry points in the Croatian sector.

Chapter 55

Serbia, Fall 1993

As the chauffeur-driven black Mercedes streaked through Belgrade, traffic cleared its path. Stefan was late. A month had passed since President Milosevic requested his help, and Stefan had been laboring ever since to trace and untangle Peter Ražnatović's morbid deals. Now he was headed to report those findings.

He glanced at his watch, vexed. Milosevic wouldn't tolerate tardiness. Stefan leaned his head against the leather seat. It had been weeks since his final blow-out with Dianne and Mimi. Strange how the ache in his chest never disappeared. His love and intense desire to hold his wife hadn't diminished, and he found no one could replace her. It seemed he was a faithful husband, after all.

In the absence of his family, he felt the vitality sucked out of him. Too often, he awoke at three in the morning, struggling to push aside painful truths. Despite a barricade of defenses, an inner voice dared to ask, what if Mimi and Dianne were right? Did he lack humanity? Should his first loyalty have been to humankind rather than his country?

Sleep was another form of torture, in which his wife and daughter taunted him, screaming in unison, "Murderer!" He would awaken sweating and wait until the sun rose, then pour more of himself into his job, frantic to escape the haunting remorse that shadowed him.

Maybes became his consolation. Maybe when this war ended, he'd join Dianne in Vienna. Maybe they could pick up the shards of their marriage that so mirrored the sharp discord between Mimi and him. Maybe they'd somehow survive the conflict.

Chapter 56

Refugee Camp, Italy, Fall 1993

Caleb didn't feel well. He used his elbows to push himself off the cot to check on Drew, asleep on the next bed. His little friend's forehead was so hot. He must be hungry. He'd refused most of his food rations. Drew had smiled once since their arrival, and it was last night when they'd spoken to Aunt Katrina on the phone. Caleb knew she wasn't their aunt, but he liked to pretend.

When he'd first arrived at the Mostar Mission and asked if it was okay if he called her aunt, she'd smiled her pretty smile and hugged him. "I'd like that a lot," she said in a voice that sort of sounded like she wanted to cry.

He was kind of choked up, too, at the idea of having a family to belong to again. Of course, a mother and father would have been better. He blinked at the moisture in his eyes. That was impossible. Besides, an aunt was the next best thing. Aunt Katrina loved him for real. She'd promised her love for them wasn't pretend.

What troubled Caleb was he'd given his word to take care of Drew, and he wasn't doing a very good job.

Drew's eyes fluttered open. "I want Aunt Katrina and Andi."

"Well, you can't have them. They're across the ocean. It's too far to walk. You'd have to take an airplane, and the Italians won't let us."

"Will, too," Drew wailed.

Caleb helped him off the cot. "Come on. Let's use the outhouse and then get breakfast."

Drew jerked from Caleb's grasp and stamped his feet. "Don't

want food. Want Aunt Katrina." He collapsed onto the ground, crying. "Don't like it here."

In Caleb's mind, a plan was forming as he dragged Drew to the camp kitchen to pick up their food. Maybe he couldn't fly to America, but he could try to find Captain Lucien, who was almost like family. He'd know how to get Drew better.

Caleb's stomach churned at the thought of reentering Bosnia, the place where his parents had died, and he'd finally escaped. What else could he do? Bosnia was where he'd found Aunt Katrina to begin with. Something good might happen again.

He trudged with Drew to their tent and settled him on the cot. He didn't look well. Caleb handed him a slice of bread and cheese. "Here, eat this."

Obediently, Drew took a bite and started coughing. He spat it out. "Want doggie."

Caleb handed him the stuffed dog and pulled the string so it would bark.

Drew clutched it close. "Aunt Katrina gave it to me." He bowed his head. "Pray now and be with her and the girls. Say it."

Caleb bowed his head as they'd promised Aunt Katrina they would. "God, please make Drew well. Amen." When he glanced up, his little friend was sleeping.

Caleb decided if they were going to break out, he'd better check their secret pouch to see what was left. He wandered to the outhouse, secured the door, and reached under his shirt to unfasten the arm bag. Caleb sat on the wooden bench next to the hole. He found two hundred dollars in American cash and one package of cheese and crackers. He'd saved them for an emergency in case the camp got bombed, and they had to escape, even though everyone said that couldn't happen in Italy. There were lots of stamps, paper, a pen, a phone card minus one call, and three postcards left.

In the bag under the bed, they had a yo-yo, a puzzle, and three outfits each that Aunt Katrina had bought them. Caleb figured they'd need food, medicine, and a gun or knife for protection. He put their stash away, did his business, and then walked across to the first-aid station, coughing and trying to sneeze for real as he stood in line with the others.

When his turn came, the nurse stuck a stick into his mouth, then took it out and wrote on his chart. "Say, ahh . . ." She peered down his throat. "What seems to be the problem?"

He hung his head and coughed really long. "I don't feel so good."

The nurse peered inside his ears and listened to his chest. He figured something must have looked wrong because they gave him some aspirin, vitamin C, and cough medicine. Enough, he hoped, to get Drew well.

He stuffed the medicine into his pockets, then dropped by the canteen, where he filched a knife, a stash of apples, and beef jerky. Rather proud of his morning's work, he ran to their tent and hid it all inside their bag underneath Drew's cot. Caleb took out his yo-yo. He didn't think anybody saw him, since almost everyone was in line for immigration.

His next problem was how they were going to escape without getting caught. Caleb walked through the campgrounds as offhand as he could, searching for a place to sneak out. "Down, boy. Go away," he hissed as one of the guard's dogs happily leaped onto him. On any other day, Caleb would have been pleased. He'd secretly befriended the dog, feeding it part of his rations.

Caleb stood next to the tall chain-link fence in the farthest section of the camp. He got out the yo-yo he'd stuffed in his pocket earlier and played with it as he studied the area. There had to be a way out. "Hey, give it back," he yelled as the interfering dog snatched the yo-yo. The dog bounded across the grounds, with Caleb in pursuit. "Stop! Come back."

He caught the animal farther down the fence line, pawing a hole under the fence, the yo-yo already partially buried. Caleb grabbed the yo-yo and darted to their tent as fast as he could. He'd found what he needed.

Chapter 57

Houston, Texas, Fall 1993

Katrina was impatient to hear Bill's opinion on Cosic's documents and strategies. Her friend seemed too struck by the Madonna to realize the significance of the papers before him. While she waited, her thoughts shifted to Italy. More than ever, she regretted leaving the boys in the refugee camp. Why hadn't she fought harder? The two seemed dispirited last night when she'd spoken to them. Drew was sick, and Caleb was afraid to take him to the clinic, fearing whoever was in charge would keep Drew there, and Caleb would lose his one friend in the camp. She wished she could have promised they would soon be with her in America. Tomorrow, she would try to phone them again.

She shuddered, remembering the fear in Caleb's voice. "Aunt Katrina, sometimes people die here. You said I was the man now and supposed to take care of us."

She'd prayed for the right words to say. He'd fought so hard to be brave. "Honey, you're doing a great job, but if Drew's ill, he needs medicine. He must see the nurse or doctor."

Drew coughed in the background. "I want to talk to Aunt Katrina."

"Hold on," Caleb said. "Here's Drew."

His small voice was weak and raspy. "I want you to come take care of me, Aunt Katrina."

"Honey, I'll be there as fast as I can, but it may take me a while."

"Hurry," he broke off, coughing. "Your little boy sick."

"I know, dear. Caleb will take you to see the nurse, and she'll help you feel better. Be good for me and mind them." An entire twenty-four hours had passed since their talk. If only she could be sure he was better.

She refocused on the problem of the maps and letters Bill was avidly studying now. Katrina fidgeted as he continued to sort through the papers. Unable to bear the tension, she finally rose and paced. Outside, the advancing storm mirrored her inner turmoil.

He read the last page and then regarded her steadily. "How long have you had these?"

"For a while, but it wasn't until earlier this evening that I looked at them."

"How did you get them?"

"It's a long story."

Bill's gaze held hers as he sipped his coffee. "We have plenty of time."

"Time is the one commodity we don't have enough of." How could he understand what those plans meant to the people she cared about in Bosnia?

"You asked for my professional opinion, but with no background, I'm operating in a vacuum."

Katrina realized he was right and disclosed everything. It wasn't as difficult as she'd expected, sharing the horrendous events of the last two years. She finished with a shrug. "If I simply knew what to do."

Bill said sternly, "There's no question. You must contact the authorities. Think of what's at stake."

"I've thought and thought. The Defense Department would never take me seriously. I can't talk to them."

"You can't afford not to." He reached for the phone. "Trust me on this, Katrina."

"Wait." She placed a hand over his to stop him. "Dad kept a copier in his office. Let's make duplicates." She pointed to the papers spread across the table. "Then you can tell the authorities and leave me out of it."

"They'll have questions. Don't be foolhardy."

"You gave me your word. Please, Bill, meet me halfway on this."

In the end, he agreed. Despite the storm, he wanted to contact the authorities immediately. "I'll phone them from home, so they won't link the call to you."

Her instinct was to hold on to the icon. But it had already caused them too much trouble. The matter was beyond her control. Bill left with the papers and the Madonna, intending to hand them over to the authorities ASAP.

A ringing awakened Katrina. She fumbled for the bedside phone and saw it was 3 a.m. It seemed minutes since she'd said goodnight to Bill, then collapsed onto her old bed, feeling drained.

"Hello?"

The Italian consul's voice on the line startled her into frightened alertness. She knew something must be dreadfully wrong.

"Miss Winslow, I'm sorry. Caleb and Drew have run away."

"What? You said they'd be fine." The accusation in her voice was too real to be hidden. "How could two young boys who were well cared for possibly leave on their own?"

"You realize, literally thousands are there sleeping in tents. Of course, there are attendants and armed military guards, but consider how easy it is to lose sight of one or two boys."

A sob tore through her. They weren't mere statistics. They were her boys, her family. "This is the place you insisted they'd be safe. Where could they have gone?"

"We can speculate. I doubt the two could journey to you, but we have alerted the authorities to pick them up if anyone sees them. Is there someone else they might attempt to contact?"

Katrina pressed a hand against her aching forehead. If the boys couldn't reach her, they'd go to Mostar. "I'm taking the next flight out. It should get me there by tomorrow morning."

"It's better to stay where you are until we know more."

She couldn't depend on strangers to rescue the boys. Caleb and Drew needed her. Besides, she had to warn Lucien that the Serbian Army was manipulating Croatian forces into a trap that could blow up the entire city of Mostar and effectively end Tudman and Izetbegovic's negotiations for peace.

"Miss Winslow, are you there?"

"Yes."

"It has occurred to us the boys may have tried to stow away on a ship headed for Bosnia."

Her fingers tightened around the receiver as she pictured them crossing the Adriatic on a ship alone. "They're children. If only I could have brought them home with me." She tried to steady herself. "Wha . . . what are you going to do?"

He hesitated, and her spirits tumbled lower. "Miss Winslow, we've contacted the local police, who are doing everything they can. You must understand how sorry we are, but the consulate's office is not a police force, but rather . . . You know, diplomacy and all that, but we'll do what we can."

"Please keep me posted."

"Certainly. Try not to be too discouraged. These things have a way of working out for the better."

Katrina thanked him and hung up.

She logged onto her laptop and made reservations for a flight via Frankfurt to Slovenia's capitol, Ljubljana. Commercial jets weren't flying into Mostar. The city's international airport had closed at the start of the war. When Slovenia declared independence in April of '91, a ten-day war with the Yugoslav People's Army (JNA) controlled by Serbia ensued. The JNA had bombed the Ljubljana airport, shutting it down briefly, but Slovenia won that battle and their independence.

Katrina planned to rent a car at the airport and drive down through Croatia to Bosnia. If there were no cars available, hopefully, the trains would be running. It wasn't ideal, but safer than traveling across Serbia. The quickest route would be to fly to Pescara and take a boat across to Mostar. But without Lucien or Tony to arrange it, that course wasn't open to her.

At seven, she phoned the university to inform the dean of her need for an emergency absence. Thankfully, the dean understood and said she would arrange a substitute.

Katrina packed a small bag, then called her uncle and aunt to tell them about the boys and to explain why she was leaving that afternoon.

"Honey, we're so sorry," Aunt Janine said. "How can we help?" Uncle York, who was on the other line, quickly echoed her sentiments.

"You can pray the boys are okay and that I find them quickly and watch over the girls for me until their parents arrive."

"We'll do that," Uncle York said. "I'll drive you to the airport. Afterward, I can pick up your stalled car at the university and take care of whatever else you need done here."

"You two are lifesavers, and I appreciate all you've done." She hung up and called a cab to take her to the bank to withdraw cash for the trip. Mentally, she ran through the list of things needing to be done before she left.

The tornadic winds had moved on. A crisp fall breeze sifted through her hair as Katrina hugged her uncle goodbye before entering the Houston Intercontinental Airport.

She checked her luggage, passed through security, and boarded the plane. Her emotions locked her in the grip of familiar tensions, overwhelming her with facts and feelings she couldn't control.

On her flight's brief stopover at Kennedy Airport, Katrina fretted about how she would get from Ljubljana to Mostar. The irony of having to pay someone to smuggle her into the war zone was maddening after what she had endured in her efforts to escape.

The last forty-eight hours preyed on her mind like a nightmare. It began with the icon, then the discovery of Serbia's plans to destroy Mostar. None of that compared to the horror of learning that Caleb and Drew were missing and might be headed to Mostar to join Lucien in a city scheduled to be blown sky-high.

She swiped her cheeks with her palm. Tears wouldn't help. She needed to come up with a plan. The girls were safe with her aunt and uncle and thrilled after having spoken with their parents. By tomorrow evening, they would be reunited with John and Ellen. Katrina had told the girls she was flying to Italy to check on the boys. They hadn't questioned her and were too excited by the news that their parents were alive and coming home to think of much else.

She shrugged deeper into her seat. Too many lives were at stake for her to fall apart. Bill would have already contacted the State Department. She focused on the boys and Lucien. Yet her reflections on what might be happening to them made her queasy. Rather than wallow in fear, she would give thanks for—for what? The discovered maps and letters, the safety of the girls and their parents, the inheritance to pursue adopting Caleb and Drew, and all the months she'd spent with the children and Lucien. *Thank You, Lord, for everything good and bad. Help me to always give You praise and thanksgiving for all You've done.*

When beset from every corner, the prophet Job had prayed: "Oh that my grief were thoroughly weighed and my calamity laid in the balances together . . . that I might have my request and God would grant me the thing that I long for."

She prayed, reassured, as she looked beyond the narrow scope of her existence and understanding filled her. But her fears resurfaced.

She remembered when silence had sealed the gaps in her life, rustling through the crevices of time until disappointments knew no healing, and pain, no relief. In the aftermath, Katrina's love had retracted into a shell of obscurity, too scared to emerge lest fate strike again.

Iron and metal, twisted shapes, harpoons of desire never reached. What would her life become? Would her future hold meaning and fulfillment? Would she ever see Lucien and the boys again? Or had they, too, gone down the path of her parents, Giles, and the orphans lost to this war?

This cursed war! The cost, in human terms, could never be measured or weighed. Heartbreak didn't show up in statistics.

Chapter 58

Belgrade, Serbia, Fall 1993

General Stefan Jovanovic entered Slobodan Milosevic's office and stiffened at seeing his archrival and nemesis, Michael Venac, who was also a contender for Milosevic's inner circle. Stefan had assumed his meeting with the president would be private.

They shook hands all around, and Milosevic nodded to Michael. "I believe we've plowed enough ground, comrade. Keep me posted on your progress."

As Michael left, Stefan nodded in satisfaction. He didn't want or need his nemesis included in the upcoming discussion. Stefan could handle his own operations.

Milosevic resettled himself behind his desk. "What have you uncovered about Željko's nephew?" His menacing tone sent chills up Stefan's spine, and he suspected Michael was behind the attitude change.

Stefan pulled a large folder from his briefcase and set the stack of reports before the president. "The situation is as you outlined, with one minor exception. Peter Ražnatović is trading in religious artifacts, not drugs."

The president looked skeptical, his piercing brown eyes calculating. "Not an easy means to earn money. One requires the right contacts and access to collectors in the West."

"Yet they've netted millions in illegal trade and, as you suspected, are funding the Kosovo Liberation Army with the profits."

Milosevic's face reddened in anger. "After what I've done for that family in appointing Željko, the nationalist Serb military leader? His nephew, not content with staging demonstrations against me, has taken to stealing artifacts from Serbia's holy churches and selling them to arm those murdering infidel Kosovars!" He rose from his desk and paced. "Well, we've got him now. Let's see what his fellow students say when they learn he's nothing more than a thief. Stop by the TV station and brief Vico Ratomir so he can air it tonight. But first, arrest Peter Ražnatović." His scowl deepened. "This treason he's been cooking up is done."

Stefan hastened to add, "Sir, at this moment, Ražnatović is being rather painfully interrogated by my men. We will have our answers soon enough. As for his chief henchmen, they have been questioned and properly disposed of."

"Good. Good. And Željko, is he implicated?"

Stefan knew Milosevic's parents' marriage had been tragic. His father, an Eastern Orthodox priest, and his mother, a staunch communist schoolteacher, had clashed violently, their union ending in separations and suicides. He had firsthand experience of how difficult it could be to control one's family.

"Our investigation shows Željko entirely in the clear on this."

"Hmm. How do you suggest we proceed?"

Stefan was aware of his vulnerability should the president learn of Mimi's relationship with Peter Ražnatović and the anti-government demonstrations she'd helped organize. Like Željko, he was treading a thin line. With Milosevic, it was hard to tell where one stood, but Stefan was frank. "His nephew is a problem, but why blame Željko? He'd be the first to arrest Peter and put a stop to this." Stefan hoped the president understood and appreciated that Stefan had also acted swiftly to remove his troublesome family to prevent their causing harm to the Motherland.

Milosevic looked pleased. "There is some sense in what you say, comrade. Now, what's going on in Bosnia? Have you stopped the Muslims' supply of arms?"

"Mostly, yes. Operation Mostar is in place."

The president stood and shook Stefan's hand. "You've done well. I want you in Bosnia to see that nothing goes wrong."

"Yes, sir," Stefan said, covering his dismay at what he took as a warning. His career would be finished if the operation failed. No one could control events in Bosnia, with three ethnic groups seeking to annihilate one another.

But Major Cosic had scrounged up supporters from a minor rogue element bent on destroying everything and everyone who threatened them. It needed to happen while Bosnian President Izetbegovic and Croatian President Tudman were still in negotiations. Each side had been primed to believe the other was their archenemy. So when the attack began, they would seek to destroy one another while Serbia moved to gain dominance. Before Izetbegovic got wind of events, Mostar would be history, and any deals with the Croats withdrawn. That was the goal as long as the mission unfolded according to plan.

Stefan shook the president's hand and then left. His car waited outside, and he got in the back, mulling over the situation as his driver took off. Stefan returned to his office, mindful he should be on the road soon. He buzzed his chauffeur. "Swing by the house and pick up my bag. Meet me with it in about an hour and have the car ready for a long trip."

Stefan swept into his office and, seeing Ennis, decided to bring her along. He wanted a personal assistant he could trust. She'd balk because of the baby, but her parents lived nearby and could care for him.

"Good afternoon, General. Was the meeting successful?"

"It went as well as expected. We're leaving for Bosnia in about an hour on Milosevic's orders. Phone my housekeeper and have her pack my suitcase. Tell her my chauffeur will be there to pick it up and

I'll be gone about a week. Have him get your bag as well. You'll be my assistant. Call your parents to pack your case and watch the baby." Before she could object, he closed his office door and set to work.

An hour later, Ennis buzzed him. "Your chauffeur has arrived."

"I'll be right out." He picked up his briefcase. Ennis stood in the reception area, her eyes anxious. "Ready?" he asked.

"Yes, sir."

"Let's go." She trailed behind him and locked up. They stepped outside and into the car. His driver headed out of Belgrade toward Bosnia.

Chapter 59

Bosnia-Herzegovina, Fall 1993

Caleb held tight to Drew's hand as they neared Mostar. "Shh," he warned as his young friend coughed. "We have to be quiet so we can sneak into the city without anyone noticing us."

Drew plopped down on the motorway, his round face flushed with fever. Caleb dropped beside him and swiped at Drew's snot-encrusted nose. Caleb knew he should carry him but wasn't sure he could stay on his feet with the added weight. After a rest, he knelt and helped Drew climb onto his back. Caleb stood and stumbled toward the city.

By midafternoon, the highway signs marking the distance blurred before his eyes. Hungry, thirsty, and tired, he sat on the side of the road again, easing Drew onto the ground beside him. Caleb gazed across the hills, straining to see any troop movements until, at last, he was rewarded. Only he wasn't sure which army uniforms the soldiers were wearing.

He studied his little friend, asleep now. Caleb remembered Katrina and the girls' promises and prayed harder than ever before.

Chapter 60

Bosnia-Herzegovina, Fall 1993

Alex suspected he'd wandered from the coast into Bosnian enemy territory. Since he'd parachuted out of his burning plane, he'd encountered many deserted homes and abandoned animals. The mountains confused him. They wound every which way, disorienting his sense of direction. Alex was lost and had been for days.

He forced himself onward.

A fighter jet roared overhead, and as he dove for cover, he realized it was Serbian. Hope sent a rush of adrenaline charging through his body. He leaped to his feet, waving. "Down here," he shouted. "Over here!"

The pilot couldn't possibly hear him, but Alex kept yelling and jumping. He couldn't stop, as half-mad, he sprinted through the hills, following the elusive jet stream.

Then he heard a clunk, clear as a horseshoe. He stopped running and gasped for breath, listening. There it was again—clunk.

The plane slowed, then nosed into a dangerous dive, straightened, but unable to maintain altitude, continued its downward spiral.

Alex ran, tracking it, his instincts shifting into high gear. The pilot appeared to regain a measure of control as the wheels touched the ground. The jet pounded against rock and hillside, then skidded, tilting onto its side with a final sputtering cough as it groaned in the wind. Alex braced for an explosion that didn't come.

Then he was darting across hills, almost flying as he raced to rescue the pilot and lay claim to the plane. His one chance at a ride home.

In a fleeting burst of speed that tore at his gut, he confronted the truth about himself and his country. The plane, a means of escape, was as vital to him as anyone inside.

At last, he'd become one with Serbia, its army, and greed. He cried out in pain at the awful truism and rushed forward with one thought to save the pilot and salvage his soul.

Alex reached the plane as the pilot climbed out of the cockpit unharmed. The small jet appeared primarily intact. Alex saluted after seeing the major rank insignia on the older man's uniform. "Lieutenant Alexander Nikolic, at your service, sir."

"At ease, Lieutenant. How did you land out here in enemy territory?"

"I bailed out of a burning plane, missile strike."

The major shook his head. "That's tough luck. Do people call you Alexander?"

"Alex, sir."

"I'm Major Cosic." He studied the plane for a moment. "Let's see what we can do about getting this baby back in the air."

"What happened to you up there?"

"I ran into some wake turbulence that caused a computer glitch. Are you any good at electronics?"

"Good enough, I hope." Alex worked on the electronics while Major Cosic checked the plane for damage. Their luck was in, and it wasn't long before they were ready to fly, and the two men climbed aboard for takeoff.

Once they were in the sky, Alex asked, "Where are you headed?"

"I know you're eager to return to Belgrade, but Serbia is in the middle of a major operation, and I'm commandeering your help."

Though Alex was disappointed not to be going directly home, he understood that these types of situations were to be expected. "Can you tell me about the mission?"

"Operation Mostar. Its goal is to destroy Bosnia's Croats and

Muslims. Keep that under your hat. Our first stop is General Baharm's Rogue Muslim Army enclave. He's working with us to destroy the Croats."

"Now that is surprising, considering how much they hate Serbia."

The major grinned. "Pure genius and manipulation on my part."

Alex decided he didn't entirely trust the sly major.

Chapter 61

Mostar, Bosnia-Herzegovina, Fall 1993

Stefan's chauffeur slowly drove Ennis and him through Mostar to witness the Serbian operation in play. The explosions were deafening. The city had ground to a halt. On his orders, people were dead, Serb, Croatian, and Muslim alike. Rays of light glistened between cracks of the old tenements as if nature held itself aloft from human misery.

Stefan stared in horror. It couldn't have been Mimi he'd seen running down the street in torn, disheveled clothing, her cheeks smudged. Was it possible his wife and daughter were among the victims? It must have been his imagination. But what if it wasn't? He leaped from the car to find out. The girl he thought was Mimi seemed to have disappeared.

His chauffeur drove on without him, signaling he'd be back. Any minute, more explosives would ignite. Stefan ran from the screams. Why had he leapt out of the car on a mere hunch he'd seen his daughter?

She was safe in Vienna with her mother. He'd arranged their trip. The report of their arrival was buried in the dark recesses of the locked drawer of his desk, along with the pictures and other mementos of his marriage.

Mimi crept through the building on hands and knees, horrified at the destruction. Everywhere she looked, there were dead bodies amid the collapsed buildings and debris. She covered her face with trembling hands. What had she stumbled into? Was this Armageddon? Was this the end of the world? She shuddered as her foot brushed against bony fingers.

Her stomach churned, and she lowered her head to puke. She hadn't eaten for two days, and nothing but bile came up. Simultaneously cold, hot, and dizzy, she rose, clinging to the crumbling wall for support, and staggered toward the door.

For a moment, she imagined her father was there. "Dad, is that you?" No. How could she have forgotten? Her father wanted her dead. "I'm having a nightmare. This isn't happening. Is it?" She gaped at the man staring at her as though she were an apparition. He seemed so real. His hair was mussed, and dirt was on his face.

"Mimi?" He moved closer. "How in the world? What are you doing in Mostar?"

Strong arms closed around her, and she felt so safe, exactly like it used to be when . . . She stiffened, realizing this was no dream. She was no longer a little girl. This depraved man was her father, the general.

She gathered her composure and drew back. "Surprised to find me alive, Dad?"

His eyes narrowed as he stepped aside to give her space. "What's that supposed to mean? I'm stunned to find you here instead of in Vienna with your mother."

She laughed, an alarming brittle cackle bordering on hysteria. "That's a joke. No need to pretend. How I wish you'd truly sent us to Vienna instead of ordering us to the Srebrenica camp."

Mimi watched him feign surprise. Unable to bear it, she rushed past him toward the entrance.

"Wait, Mimi! Please—you don't understand. I sent you to Vienna with my driver. You have to believe me." He grasped her shoulder. "I'd never willingly hurt you."

She shook off his hand. "Then how was it that Mother and I were driven to a concentration camp? We were starved, tortured, and interrogated. Mother might be dead. And you say it was a mistake? Like Grandfather's death was a mistake, right?"

Angry tears streamed down her face as she stormed outside and rushed down the street, her feet pounding against the cobblestones until the ache in her side slowed her pace. She glanced back, ducked into an alley, and stopped, terrified that her father or his men had followed. Mimi could never forget the horror of Srebrenica, and she'd do all in her power to prevent returning there.

In agony, Stefan watched her leave and felt a funny tingling in his arms, which turned into jabbing pains in his chest when he tried to follow. He clutched at the area around his heart, his daughter's name on his lips, as he collapsed.

A ruckus near the door drew his attention. She'd come back. If only he could stand. He glanced up to see his chauffeur leaning over him, concerned.

"General, are you all right?"

Stefan's eyes closed. "Too late . . ." The city was ablaze, and explosions were scheduled throughout the day. What if Mimi was wandering out there alone?

How had his family come to this? Notch by notch, they'd chosen divergent paths—his ambition countering Mimi's rebellion and her mother's animosity. He could see no road back. No way to retrace the paths of the last few years. Everything had been in vain. He'd lost the one race in his life that mattered.

A pair of gentle, feminine hands shook him. A glimmer of hope caused him to open his eyes, but it was Ennis commanding him to take short, deep breaths. He did so, and the pain seemed to subside.

"Sir, can you sit up?" she asked.

He tried and succeeded. "Mimi . . . I've . . . got to find her." Stefan lurched to his feet.

His chauffeur and secretary exchanged glances and helped him to the car, which, incredibly, was parked in front.

"Drive slowly," Stefan breathed as the chauffeur pulled the vehicle into the street.

Then Stefan remembered. Mimi said his driver had taken her to the Srebrenica camp. Stefan glanced up. His gaze locked with his chauffeur's in the rearview mirror, silent messages transmitted.

Yes, I drove them.

"Michael?" Stefan mouthed the word. He understood the nod, confirming his chauffeur worked for his archrival.

"Why?"

A shrug.

Fear crawled up his spine. "Stop the car," Stefan said as it sped up. His command was ignored. Somehow, Michael had compromised him. And Stefan would soon find out how.

Ennis urged him to calm down. "We're driving you to the hospital."

"No!" The pain sliced through his chest. "It's set to explode. Turn around." He reached for the door and found it locked. Stefan pulled out his gun, pointing it at the back of the chauffeur's head. "Stop the car, or I'll fire."

"There are no bullets, sir. I removed them this morning as a precaution."

"You'll be court-martialed for this." Stefan was trapped. He'd played the game, but Ennis was innocent. "Run," he gasped, "before it's too late."

She looked bewildered and frightened. "Try to relax, sir. You'll feel better soon."

Sweat beaded on his forehead. Pain closed in around him until his surroundings grew hazy and black. Vaguely, he was aware that he and Ennis were dropped at the hospital. She followed as Stefan was wheeled down the corridor. He saw his life vanishing before him in a nightmare and realized how much he'd lost.

Chapter 62

Lucien's men had set up roadblocks in west Mostar, stopping and searching every car entering the city. Midmorning, they caught a break. An old black Mercedes limped toward them, its rear end sagging. Abdul was the driver's name. Lucien's Croat patrol discovered enough plastic explosives and paraphernalia in the trunk to damage an entire block.

The discovery brought Lucien no relief but intensified his fears. It gave credence to the possibility that hundreds of vehicles carrying dangerous armaments might be in the city or on the roads. He grabbed Abdul by the collar and shoved him into the guard shack. "Give me his paperwork," Lucien said.

A soldier handed him an internal green Yugoslavian passport. "This is all the identification we found, sir. We suspect it's a fake, and he's a mercenary."

He spared the soldier a chilly glance. "Stick to the facts. If I want speculation, I'll ask. Anything else?" Lucien arched an impatient brow as he riffled through the passport of one Abdul Blerim, thirty-eight years old, black hair and eyes, a Kosovar, from the capital Pristina.

The weary soldier snapped to attention. "The men found a wad of German Marks on him."

"Go on," Lucien said more congenially, sorry he'd lost his patience and struck out at a comrade. They were all on edge and pulling triple duty didn't help. The car was the second older black Mercedes containing armaments his men had stopped today, thereby saving hundreds of lives.

Croatian forces needed to preempt the bombing. The hard

expression in Abdul's black eyes meant it would take a long session with the Croat Special Interrogation Unit before he talked. By then, Lucien feared, it would be the eleventh hour for Croatia. He said to the young soldier, "Now you may speculate."

"Sir. The men and I suspect he's a hired hand. Rogue militias are desperate for money to buy guns and pay mercenaries. We uncovered enough cash on him to outfit an entire unit with Kalashnikovs."

"Okay." Lucien's attention shifted as his sergeant hung up the phone. "Did you reach the major?"

"Yes, sir. The special interrogation unit is ready. He said to tell you that Martin has been asking around town for you."

Lucien flinched. Were Martin, Sara, and the baby there in the city with it about to blow sky-high? Unable to stop himself, Lucien slugged the Kosovar in the face. "You slime." He grabbed the man, throwing him against the wall. "Talk before I kill you! Where did you get the explosives? What were you planning to demolish?"

Abdul held firm, refusing to disclose any information.

Finally, Lucien ordered him driven to the Croat base headquarters, where he could be better dealt with. Lucien followed.

During a brief early morning stopover in Frankfurt, Katrina boarded a smaller jet to Ljubljana. When the flight landed about an hour later, she gathered her carry-on, exited the plane, and passed through customs. At the airport, she rented a Lada. The drawback was it had to be returned before leaving Slovenia, as it was uninsured for the war zones in Croatia and Bosnia.

Her eyes feasting on the nearby lush green fields and mountains, she climbed into the sedan and tossed her bag onto the passenger seat. Katrina was thankful for the sunny day. Shadows from her past continually warred with fears of the not-so-distant future. She struggled to focus on the present and enjoy the drive as the Lada sped down the highway through Cellje, then Maribor, until finally, four hours later, she reached the border town of Prekmuije.

She drove to the rental bureau, collected her belongings, and went inside.

A blond clerk in his twenties asked, "Can I help you?"

"Do you speak English?" Katrina asked in halting Slovenian.

"*Ja.* What can I do for you?"

She explained about the rental return. He quickly processed it and handed her a receipt. "Would you phone for a taxi to drive me across the border to a car rental agency, please?" she asked.

"No problem. My brother would be happy to take you for a fee. He's in the back. Let me call him." He stepped away and shouted, "Leon." He moved behind the counter again.

"I appreciate this! Why don't I pay you for Leon driving me now?"

"Good idea." He accepted her credit card and rang up the payment. "Our cousin's business there can provide you with transportation."

"That's great."

Leon came out and, after introductions, led her to a utility van and drove her across the border into Croatia to the town of Međimurje and then on to his cousin's place, where she rented another sedan. After thanking both men, she left.

Katrina took the E-65 Adriatic coastal highway, munching on one of the protein bars from home and sipping on a water bought when she'd filled up the Lada earlier. The gorgeous coastal scenery enlivened the seven-hour drive to the Croatian border town of Vrgorac. She returned the car there. Bosnia was ahead, and Mostar was only an hour's drive away. She prayed Serbia's disastrous plot to destroy the city could still be prevented.

She walked across the Bosnian border near twilight and then paid handsomely to be smuggled into Mostar's Croat sector. Roadblocks had been set up at major access points, making the trip more difficult and hazardous. She gained entry and spent the night at a dilapidated hotel on the Croat side of Mostar. With the city under siege, it was impossible to tell whether the annihilation threat was even then becoming a reality.

Katrina awoke in her hotel room in the black hours before dawn. The building shook as nearby bombs shot tremors through its foundations, rattling the pictures and furniture. She pressed her palms to her ears to shut out the noise, then gave up. Terrified, Katrina listened, having nowhere to hide or run.

She didn't want to think or feel. In her weakness, she prayed. "You are our strength, and in Your power, we are made strong." Reassured, she slept.

Katrina set out early the following day in search of Croat headquarters to discover if Caleb and Drew were there and to warn Lucien of the Serbians' plot to destroy Mostar. What if Lucien hadn't seen the boys? Were they even alive? Lucien might be somewhere else or even dead.

In the commander's office at the Croat base, Lucien watched, sickened, as the major struck another blow to Abdul. If Lucien were in charge, he would have acted more humanely. Despite the harshness, the sullen-faced man refused to talk, and they were no closer to knowing where he got the explosives from and what he'd intended to blow up. He might be a mercenary, but his hatred for the Croats spewed out with every word and movement. Cigarette burns covered the man's arms and face. His broken jaw hung loose. He oozed blood and sweat, and the Croats weren't any closer to uncovering the truth.

The commander cursed. "Take him down to the chamber. Don't bring him back until he breaks." He stomped across to the corner desk and eased into a chair, then pulled a smoke from inside his jacket and lit it.

Neither Lucien nor the commander spoke. They were both too wound up, and the troops were on an all-out alert. Enemy forces had caught them by surprise, blowing up public facilities and wounding and killing many. Lucian feared the bulk of the explosives used had been smuggled in some time ago by Serbs and Muslims bent on destroying the Croat sector. Despite meager intel and limited resources, Croatian forces fought, weaving threads of intel to nullify the judgment hanging over Mostar like a black widow stretching its web to destroy them.

The commander said, "Check at the safe house for any new intel."

Lucian nodded and left. He commandeered a jeep and drove to the Mostar safe house used for in-town operations. The men there were stretched thin and hadn't been able to process all the briefs as fast as they came in. Lucien went into the back office, sat and pulled a stack forward, reading through the backup of incoming reports, hoping to find something of value.

Katrina darted through the city, alone and on foot. Mostar was in chaos. Bombs exploded intermittently, leaving wounded and dead and a haze of smoke and fires in their wake. Blessed rain poured, soaking her and impeding the spreading flames.

She'd swing by Martin and Sara's apartment first since it was nearer. Katrina clung to the absurd hope that Caleb and Drew or Lucien might be there. She scanned the faces of those walking by and stooped to peer closer at an injured child in her path who resembled Drew. She draped her jacket over him and his mother and then moved on with a prayer.

An explosion shattered a building down the street, and Katrina screamed as a flying piece of wood knocked her down. She rose, uninjured but shaken, and scurried as fast as she dared through the winding streets, picking a trail through the rubble of a city in its final stages of hate. Sick with regret, Katrina agonized about whether it was too late to warn Lucien of Cosic's Serbian plans.

Mimi paused in an open doorway, her emotions as jumbled as the city under attack. She blamed the Serbs for this nightmare. She'd wanted to believe her father. He sounded so sincere and caring. Mimi had forced herself to repulse him rather than be caught up in another of his traps.

She was counting on finding her cousin Sara at home and trusted she would help her. Sara was a Croat who had married a Muslim and should understand that despite Mimi's father's Serbian nationality, she wasn't the enemy. It was frightening how the Serbs wanted her dead while their enemies labeled her a murdering Serb.

As Mimi walked, she grappled to devise a plan to leave Mostar and reach her mother before her father had them both killed. She swung around, careening into two young boys, the smallest of whom sat down on the door stoop. Mimi backed up. "I'm so sorry."

"It's okay." He rested his chin on his hand and gazed up at his companion. "I'm hungry and tired."

The eldest tugged at his hand. "Come on, Drew. We gotta keep going. We'll get shot if we stay here."

"I don't care, not gonna move!"

"Yes, you are." The boy bent to pick up the little one, but he wouldn't let him.

"Um, excuse me." Mimi forced a smile for the two boys' sake. "Do you live near here?"

They shook their heads. The older boy squinted up at her as if trying to decide whether she was okay to speak to. Finally, he said, "We're searching for our friend, Captain Lucien."

Mimi's breath caught. Could they be looking for her cousin, too? There might be many Croatian men named Lucien. An explosion sent Drew hurtling into her arms, and she concluded the best thing for them all was to keep moving. "I'm going to my cousin's apartment. Her brother Lucien is a captain in the army. Would you like to come with me?"

He nodded, looking relieved. "He's probably the same person. There can't be that many captains with his name."

Drew gripped her hand. "I will come with you."

Warmth filled her. She'd get them to safety, then move on. It'd be nice if they were in search of the same man, though that would be almost too much of a coincidence. Mimi pulled the two boys close and hurried down the street.

Chapter 63

Bosnia-Herzegovina, Fall 1993

Alex sat in the cockpit beside Major Cosic as he navigated the jet through a bumpy landing. When they stopped, Alex opened the exit door and followed him off the plane.

"Hey," Cosic called to a nearby soldier. "Get this crate unloaded." He patted his stomach. "Let's scrounge up some food. I'm sick of army rations."

Alex studied General Baharm's Rogue Muslim Army's lean-to headquarters. It was set in the hills about ten kilometers outside Mostar. Besides ammo, barracks, and troops, it held a refrigerator, stove, and a cook.

"Chef, baby," Cosic said to the beefy man. "How about a steak and fries for two?"

The cook grumbled but waved them to a table. "It will be about fifteen minutes." He snapped out an order to an underling.

Cosic sat across from Alex and laughed in good humor, relating his last visit to this rogue base. "I taught that cook to show Serbia respect. We might have to deal with the enemy, but there's no reason to make it pleasant for them. Baharm's title is bogus and only recognized by Muslim extremists. Izetbegovic fired him, despite his supposedly being a brilliant military strategist."

Alex said, "I heard Bosnia's president objected to his ferocious bent against Croatia."

"Exactly. The move left Baharm ripe for Serbia's picking. He rushed to fit in with Serbia's plans."

After they ate, Cosic phoned for a white Mercedes loaded to kill and then bragged to Alex. "Serbia has already smuggled tons of explosives into the Croat sector. See those black Mercedes over there? They're departing for Mostar, and the trunks are loaded with more explosives. Insurance for our side."

Alex mulled over the major's comments, wondering what he'd be confronting. Obviously, the mission centered on Mostar's destruction. "What will be our role there?" he asked.

"You'll be my aide-de-camp. Serbia has a score to settle over a missing icon."

Cosic must be an ace at paying off vendettas, Alex mused.

"Whenever my shoulder and leg ache, I like to imagine myself killing the Croatian captain and his American girl who shot me. With your help, I'll do that. They are wanted enemies of Serbia."

"Wouldn't it be safer to stay out of Mostar until the operation is completed? How will you even find them?"

Cosic frowned. "We'll start looking for him at his sister's apartment. That should get the captain's attention. Those orphans, his Muslim-loving sister, and her family deserve whatever they get. They escaped the mass grave, and the icon still hasn't been found." He paused, then continued. "Afterward, we'll retreat to the hills and watch the city blow. General Jovanovic should be happy tonight when the powder settles. I will have earned us both a promotion."

"Interesting coincidence that you are under his command. My wife is Jovanovich's secretary in Belgrade." Alex's world seemed to get smaller all the time.

Soon, their car arrived, and they climbed inside the white Mercedes. Cosic drove out of Baharm's compound toward Mostar's Serb sector, their easiest place of entry. Alex pondered everything he'd heard. It was crazy dangerous to enter a city set to detonate.

Chapter 64

Mostar, Bosnia-Herzegovina, Fall 1993

Katrina gaped in horror as buildings collapsed, debris flew, and the ground seemed to sway. She clung to an old lamppost on the cobblestone street. It's happening, she thought. Katrina had to find Lucien and warn him before the Croatians retaliated and destroyed the city. Abruptly, the explosions stopped, and the shrill cries of families searching for their wounded and missing echoed in the streets. With a guilty pang, Katrina glanced about, wanting to help, but it was more important to reach Lucien with the papers she was carrying and end this.

She forced herself onward through the city, her nerves jumpy. Then, up ahead to the right, she glimpsed two boys. Could they possibly be hers? She sprinted forward, crying as their faces came into focus. "Caleb, Drew!"

Caleb released the young woman's hand he held and ran to Katrina. "You came! You didn't forget." Thin arms wrapped around her. "I was afraid you might never come."

She hugged him close. "Honey, I love you too much to forget you."

He swiped at the tears sliding down his cheeks and looked self-conscious. "Yeah, I get scared sometimes, like when Drew was so sick. What if he'd died?"

"He didn't. But even if he had died, God would have taken care of you because he loves you. Where is Drew? I saw him a moment ago."

"Right behind you. He's not sick, either. I prayed like you said, and he's lots better."

"I'm so glad he's well. You did a good job of looking after him." Katrina wanted to tell the boys she had some exciting news to share but didn't. She couldn't bear their disappointment if she told them they were flying home with her, and it didn't happen. Instead, she said, "My lawyer is working on convincing the authorities to allow me to adopt you both."

Caleb threw his arms around her. She bent down and hugged him, then whirled to see Drew standing with a pretty blonde. "Oh, thank you for keeping them safe." She swung Drew up into her arms and kissed his baby-soft cheeks.

He beamed as if her being there was expected. "Aunt Katrina, this is our new friend," he confided. "Her name is Mimi."

The two women studied each other. "How? Where?" Katrina began.

"I found them on the street alone a while ago, and it's so dangerous out here." She shrugged. "I offered to take them up."

"She's Lucien's cousin," Caleb chimed in.

Drew reached for Mimi. "She is taking us to see him."

Katrina's mouth opened in surprise. "Lucien's your cousin?"

Mimi hesitated. "If he's Captain Brezak with the Croat forces and hails from Klagenfurt, he is."

Relief whooshed through her. Their meeting was no coincidence but God's grace. How long since she'd last sensed His presence and believed in the power of spring rains and warm winds to melt the frost in her heart? Yet, hadn't she experienced a similar assurance the day her family was murdered?

Chapter 65

"Allah, we are in a heap of trouble," Martin prayed as he pushed through the city, frantic to find his brother-in-law. Martin had returned to town for work, and Sara had insisted on accompanying him.

Up the street, he recognized the stucco safe house he'd once seen Lucien leaving. He'd sworn him to secrecy, but today, Martin would have to risk entering the Croat enclave. Aware he had seconds before someone stopped him, he burst through the front door, rushing past an armed soldier. "Lucien Brezak, are you here?" Martin yelled. If his brother-in-law was there, he'd hear him.

The soldier halted him. "Stop right there, or I'll shoot."

Sweat beaded on Martin's forehead. "It's urgent I speak with Captain Brezak."

The grubby soldier jabbed his rifle into Martin's gut. "What would he want with a heathen like you? Maybe I'll end your miserable existence and save the captain the trouble."

Lucien stepped into the room. "Enough, Sergeant Ratko. You're threatening my brother-in-law."

"Nobody told me," he whined.

"For months, I've put up with that chip on your shoulder. You might have asked him what his business was and then checked with me."

Martin broke in. "Cosic has set the entire city to blow. He's working with Baharm, the rogue general that President Izetbegovic fired."

"Where did you learn this?"

"From a comrade whom Baharm tried to involve in Cosic's strategies. You've got to stop your people from retaliating. Cosic means for us to blow each other up, leaving Mostar to Serb control."

"I've been afraid of this from the start," Lucien said. "Still, I can't move on your say-so. I need proof. Like where Cosic is launching operations from or specific targets."

"You might as well ask for the Eiffel Tower."

"You're right. Where are Sara and my nephew?"

"At the apartment. There was no time to drive them to the farm. If Sara doesn't hear from me soon, she knows to leave with the children. I've got to reach Izetbegovic. Our only hope is to stop Cosic."

Lucien ran a frustrated hand through his hair. "If we knew more of his plans, we'd know how or where to fight him and would stand a chance of convincing our superiors to join forces. As it is, we're up against a moving target that could ignite any second. If you get any new intel or figure out how to contact Izetbegovic, let me know."

Martin and Lucien hugged, and then Martin left.

He fretted that if operations went as Cosic wanted, they'd both be dead by morning.

It was dark when Martin returned to Mostar's Muslim sector. An eerie silence prevailed as he walked to work at the jail. Izzy, an old school chum of his, had been promoted to manage the jail in Vita's place. Like Izetbegovic, Izzy sought to end the conflict. It was through his contacts that Martin hoped to warn Bosnia's president of Cosic's scheme to demolish Mostar.

He kicked at a loose stone on the street, venting some of his anger. Extremists like Baharm distorted the truth. Martin's people had already suffered too much. Croatia and Bosnia needed to unite to survive Serbia's attacks. Both their countries and sectors were under siege from Serbia. What was the sense of fighting with each other?

At a distant explosion, Martin broke into a run. His bitter reflections kept pace with his feet pounding against the cobblestones. For a while, Croatia had emulated Serbia, forming several Muslim prison camps. Croatia's ambitions were shackled by the strings the Americans and other Western countries tied to aid packages, or Tudman might have declared out-and-out war. Like the Serbs, President Tudman sought to carve out a part of Bosnia for Croatia. The difference was that Serbian President Milosevic and his country desired more than a piece. They wanted everything.

Chapter 66

Katrina trailed Mimi upstairs to Martin and Sara's apartment. "Come on, Drew." She lifted him into her arms so he wouldn't dawdle. His limbs wrapped around her awkwardly. He was going to be tall. She wondered if Drew had inherited his lean blond appearance from his parents. He'd been too young when they were killed to remember them.

Caleb tugged on her sleeve. "Aunt Katrina, are we truly coming to Texas with you?"

She freed a hand to ruffle his hair. "Yes. As soon as it can be arranged, dear," she said, her voice husky with emotion. Before they returned to Italy, she would check with her lawyer. If the adoption was not going forward there, she and the boys could head to Bulgaria or wherever the law was most likely to permit their adoption. At the top of the stairs, she lowered Drew to the floor as Mimi knocked.

Sara opened the door, a toddler balanced on each hip. Her dark eyes widened. "Mimi? Katrina?" Sara embraced the two women and the boys and then, as if remembering they were in a public hall, waved the group in with a furtive glance around. They stepped inside, and Sara locked the door. "Please, you are at home. Take a seat."

Katrina kissed Baby, the orphan Martin and Sara had taken in, and hugged their son. If only Sara could tell her where Lucien was. The papers hidden inside Katrina's shirt burned a reminder of how soon this town could explode and end all of their lives.

When everyone was seated on cushions scattered around a low table in the center of the small room, Sara asked, "Mimi, why aren't you with your family in Serbia? Does your mother know you're here?"

Before the girl could respond, Sara turned to Katrina. "How can this be? We thought you were in America and the boys in Italy."

Katrina explained how she came to be there, and then Mimi and the boys related their stories. Sara listened with a growing look of bewilderment.

Drew sidled over to Sara. Fascinated, he patted the tyke's feet. "Baby safe here?" His gaze flew to Katrina's, seeking confirmation, as he repeated the words like an incantation meant to reassure himself, mostly.

Despite the lump tightening her throat, Katrina choked out a response, "Yes, dear, the little ones are safe here, and so are you." She wished it were true, but frightening the children wouldn't help anyone. Katrina prayed desperately for their safety and would do everything she could to ensure it. But their future was in God's hands, and she was okay with that.

Sara's smile wobbled. "How nice to see you again, young man."

Drew scooted next to Mimi. "She's taking us to see Lucien."

Sara's face clouded. "May I offer you something to drink or eat? We haven't much, but I brought some of *Oma's Wurst* and *Brot* back from the farm."

"We're fine, thanks." Katrina knew how limited Sara and her family's goods must be. Katrina had several cheese and cracker packets in her purse that she and the boys could eat later.

Caleb licked his lips. "I'm hungry."

"I have more than enough." Sara placed her two sons by Drew. "I'll be a minute."

Katrina couldn't linger through an hour of polite niceties while the survival of thousands was at stake. She motioned for the boys to remain seated, mumbled an excuse to Mimi, and stepped into the tiny, cramped kitchen. "Sara, I've got to locate Lucien."

"I haven't seen him since that awful day at the farm when Cosic tried to kill us." Sara glanced at the porcelain-clad teapot on the stove, as if wishing it could somehow speak to her. "We all want to find Lucien. Martin's been searching for days."

The ceiling leaked where an explosion had ripped through the stucco and boards, leaving a jagged trail of wallpaper patterned with curling rings of blackened ash. Sara's hand shook as she arranged the food on an old chipped Limoges platter.

Katrina contemplated the irony of some of France's finest china ending up in Bosnia. How many wars and shattered lives had the platter survived? In yet another era and conflict, she imagined a child hiding in the corner closet alone. His wounded dog lay outside in the gutter. Hours must have passed before the scared boy retrieved the chipped platter from the floor, brushing it off with care to preserve the remnant of his past.

There weren't any keepsakes that could ever replace her father and mother. Vita had clung to a rabbit's foot, while Katrina held on to the orphans her parents had loved and lost their lives to save. She shook off her melancholy. The war wasn't finished yet. With a start, she realized the silence had grown, and she wasn't the only one dwelling on morbid thoughts. "Sara, what's wrong? Oh, I realize it's a stupid question with parts of Mostar on fire. But there's more, isn't there?"

Sara nodded uncertainly. "Martin has learned of a plot by Baharm and Cosic to destroy sections of Mostar."

Katrina drew a quick breath at the revelation, hoping Sara had been spared the knowledge that the Serbs were counting on the Croat's retaliation to wipe out what remained of the city. Katrina draped an arm around Sara. "You're frightened for Lucien and for Martin, since he's in the Croat sector now hunting for your brother."

With a soft cry, Sara pushed Katrina aside. "If it were merely that. It's so much worse. Serbia is conspiring to obliterate Mostar. Finish! Kaput! Our homes. Our people. Everything."

They glanced up in surprise as Mimi exclaimed from the doorway, "What are you saying? We're all going to be killed?" She darted across the room and grasped Sara's shoulders. "I don't believe you. If that were true, my father . . . Oh, God, he wasn't here to find me but to oversee the destruction." With a wounded whimper, she sank into a chair, her face pale with shock. "No—no," she murmured. "To crush an entire town. I no longer know him. Please. We must stop it from happening."

Katrina hesitated. For obvious reasons, she hadn't planned to confide in anyone but Lucien. Yet the three of them shared a certain kinship and purpose. Both Mimi and Sara were wondering what they could do, and possibly, she held the answer. Before she could change her mind, Katrina plunged into her story, explaining she needed to see Lucien because she had Cosic's plans. She finished, "Serbia's entire attack strategy is laid out with all its tactical maneuvers." At their disbelieving expressions, she said, "Sara, remember when you, Martin, and the children escaped from the gravesite in Cosic's van?"

"Yes." A faint light kindled in her eyes.

Katrina whirled around and reached into her blouse, pulling out the documents and maps she'd hidden, then turned to the others. "These were on the floorboard of Cosic's van."

"But you weren't with us then," Sara said, confused.

"The children were. Rachel snatched these and never said a word until we arrived in Houston."

Mimi gingerly took the papers and moved to the table to study them. Katrina and Sara joined her.

As if unable to grasp the reality, Sara continued asking questions. "Why didn't Rachel tell us?"

Katrina shrugged. "Maybe she was frightened. Perhaps she didn't realize how important the papers were with so much happening. She might have just forgotten."

Mimi, who was bent over the maps, straightened. "She was smart to take these. They lay out the whole conspiracy in vivid detail."

Katrina gathered the documents. "Now you understand why I have to find Lucien immediately."

Mimi stayed Katrina's hand. "It'll be impossible to find him. Lucien will be working across the city to stop the explosions. We have to handle this and deliver these papers ourselves."

Sara squeaked, "You may be a general's daughter, but you're mad if you think . . . Why, you're practically a child." She grabbed for the papers. "I'll take these to the jail and wait for Martin."

Mimi's eyes took on a militant glint as she pushed Sara aside. "Go on to your Muslim jail and discover how much his people care about what Martin's Croatian wife has to say without him there to protect you."

Sara paled.

Provoked, Katrina stepped in. "Since I brought the plans, I should have some say. Both of you sit down and listen." She stared them into submission. "It's possible to accomplish all we want without wasting time slinging arrows." She shot Mimi a firm look.

Before she could continue, the four boys burst into the kitchen. "We're hungry," Caleb said.

"Sorry. We didn't mean to take so long." Sara handed Caleb the food she'd prepared. "Boys, eat at the table in the other room."

"Be careful with the platter," Katrina called as they rushed off.

With the children taken care of, Katrina said to Sara, "Draw me a map so I can locate Croat headquarters. If Lucien's not at HQ, maybe they can tell me where he is. There's bound to be someone in authority who can help. Mimi, quick, get some paper and a pen. Copy down the targeted hits for the rest of today and tomorrow. Note the pertinent details."

Mimi's mouth opened, and then her lips tightened into a straight line as she bit back a reply.

Katrina said, "It'll be difficult to get anyone to believe you, but since you are the general's daughter, I'll leave it to you to work out the logistics. Sara can write out directions to the Croat border patrols nearest to each target, and you can work down the line."

"If you handed over a few of those originals, I'd have no trouble convincing anyone."

"No. They're for Lucien."

"We have to tell Martin. It's as important to reach Izetbegovic as it is Lucien. Maybe more so," Sara said.

Katrina agreed. "It'll be up to you to pen copies to take him, Sara. Or better yet, have Mimi do it while you write out directions for her. But we've got to hurry before the Croats retaliate. Thirty minutes is all I can spare you, and then I have to leave."

Sara glanced up in consternation. "What will we do about the children? Surely, we can't bring them?"

"No," Katrina said soberly. "We'll have to trust Caleb to keep them safe." She stilled herself against Sara's protests. "The roads in and out of the city are blocked. Sara, there's no way to get them out unless you know of a back route."

"No. And without a car, we wouldn't get far. You're right. They're safer in the apartment."

"I'm sorry. We don't have any choice if they're to survive."

Chapter 67

Alex and Cosic had entered Mostar's Serb sector without difficulty. Alex, however, didn't feel so sanguine about the Bosnian Muslim border patrol ahead. He disliked taking orders from Cosic, who often acted like an arrogant jerk. Besides, Alex didn't know him well enough to trust him, especially when it involved traveling into an enemy zone with a trunk full of plastic explosives.

Cosic guided the Mercedes to a stop at the temporary guard shack and flashed a forged Muslim security badge. A brief consultation followed with the chief customs officer before Cosic sped through.

"You were quite good back there, speaking like a native," Alex said. "Can you do the same in Croatian?"

"Yes, and in several other languages. The Motherland trained me well and pays me to outsmart these idiots." Cosic stopped the car, picked up the map, and traced their route with a blue ballpoint. "It's about time you pulled your weight." He threw down the pen and shoved the map into Alex's hands. "Your job is to navigate."

"I take it we're headed toward Mostar's Croat side first, and then on to find your nemesis?"

"That's right. Any objections?" Cosic asked.

Alex had a trunk load of them—carrying explosives into enemy territory sounded like a death wish. He knew better than to say what he really thought. "None. There's the obvious danger, but we are soldiers."

"Then, we agree."

"Yes," Alex said, retreating inward, determined to survive and return to his family.

The sounds of explosions were deafening as Mimi loped down the road. Her brave words at the apartment earlier now seemed boastful. The hot afternoon sun glared low in the sky as she approached the first Croat border patrol on her list.

It occurred to Mimi she was in as much danger as Sara. A lack of identification papers and being half-Serb wouldn't ingratiate her to Croatian customs officials. She quelled a growing urge to flee as each step brought her closer to her destination. But she had no place to run.

A white Mercedes stopped at the entrance checkpoint. Mimi ducked behind a grove of trees as she recognized Major Cosic at the wheel. In the early days of the war, he had visited her father often. She hadn't realized his absence meant he was posted to Bosnia. Then it clicked. He was Katrina's Cosic as well.

She rushed to the guard shack as he climbed into his car again and roared away. "Stop him! He's an enemy agent."

"Halt." The officer challenged her, hoisting his gun as Cosic drove past, oblivious to the unfolding drama.

"Halt, I said. Who are you? State your business."

She straightened her shoulders, raising her chin in defiance. "I'm Captain Lucien Brezak's cousin. Take me to your supervisor at once."

"Hey, Sergeant," the man called. "We've got a Serb accent here. You want me to lock her up until this is over?"

Mimi's heart sank. "Please. No. You don't understand." She pulled out the copy of Cosic's plans. "The man who just drove through is a Serbian major. These are copies of his plans to destroy Mostar."

"Yeah, and I'm not the son of a pig farmer, either. Give me those." He tore the papers from her hands and moved to shred them.

"Wait, please. What if I'm right?" Mimi asked. "It can't hurt to look. And you might save hundreds of lives."

"Shut up." He struck her face.

She lowered her head, pain and anger warring with overwhelming despair, because she could see no way out of her present situation.

Alex breathed a sigh of relief at having passed through the border station into the Croat sector. Then, he registered the chaos and destruction. He bent his head, and his lips tightened as he stared at the atlas and undertook to guide them through the decrepit remains of downtown. He pitied those who lived at the end of the blue line. Alex brooded about the major's designs for him after the operation ended, when Alex would no longer be of value. His attempts at subtle questioning had failed. Determined, he said, "You've been rather closemouthed about the operation you're running."

"It's classified, a need-to-know basis."

Alex felt an urge to jump out of the car and get as far away as he could, but his better sense prevailed. "Since my life is on the line, too, I have the right to know."

Cosic cursed and pointed toward several bombed-out buildings. "Any more mouth from you, and you'll be alone out there."

His threat silenced Alex. He shifted in the passenger seat. On countless missions, he'd dropped bombs on selected targets but never stayed to survey the horror of what he'd done. Misery and destruction were everywhere but most apparent in the faces of the survivors. We're in a war, he rationalized. His wife Ennis endlessly questioned and worried about the morality of Serbia's position. Alex obeyed his superiors' orders. In his defense, Serbia had left him no choice.

Was he making excuses, like the Germans who'd followed Hitler? If he kept on blindly acting on Serbian command directives, his conscience prodded, he'd become a scumbag like Cosic.

Cosic glanced at his watch, his mood apparently improved by the chaos and devastation. "Eight minutes and the TV station will blow."

Sweat beaded on Alex's forehead. "What are we doing?"

"Scared?" he jeered. "You'll be all right if you follow my instructions. With your help, I'll ensure a certain captain's family burns."

"If the city's set to incinerate, what's the point?"

"Did I ask for an analytical debate? Serbia stands to benefit from its enemies' deaths. Isn't that enough?"

"I see," Alex taunted. "The captain's too big to handle, so you're going after the wife and kids."

Cosic threw him a nasty look and retreated into a sullen silence.

Apparently, the Serbs' major offensive to destroy Mostar's Croat side was well on its way. Serbia's mania for war overwhelmed Alex. Cosic must have masterminded the operation. He had an inside track with the Muslims, Serbia's sworn enemy, landing at their bases and using their flight crew and facilities. With the city set to detonate on Cosic's schedule, Alex had to stick with him.

"We're getting close to our target," Cosic said.

Alex stared down at the marked blue circle. "A few blocks away."

Chapter 68

Mostar, Bosnia-Herzegovina, Fall 1993

Lucien hadn't slept in forty-eight hours and, before then, only in snatches. He parked the jeep in front of Sara and Martin's apartment, intent on urging her to leave the city before it decimated. Torturing Abdul had not helped. He was dead, and Lucien's unit knew too little about the enemies' plans.

He climbed from the vehicle. The stop would delay his journey to the southeastern Croat border station. But if Sara were harmed without his having tried to reach her, he wouldn't be able to bear it, much less face his parents. Lucien had a car parked nearby so that she could drive to the farm to get out of town.

He dashed into the old stucco building and jogged upstairs. As he approached his sister's door, he heard the faint sounds of a scuffle inside.

"Sara!" He tried the knob. It was locked. The flat grew quiet. He knocked. No answer, but he heard someone whispering inside. He pounded on the door. "Sara, Open up! It's Lucien. Please, let me in." He counted to ten, thrust his weight against the wooden door, and hurtled through it, landing in an empty living room. "Sara." His nerves on edge, he drew out his pistol and combed through the compact unit.

Lucien discovered the boys hiding inside a kitchen cabinet and quickly stashed the gun in the back waistband of his jeans. The four boys leaped into his arms, the two youngest crying. He gathered them close and settled on the floor.

Caleb said, "We were scared."

Drew hiccuped, wiping tears from his face with a dirty hand. "I was afraid you were the mean man coming to get us again."

Lucien released them. "I thought you two were in Italy."

Caleb straightened his shoulders and seemed to brace himself. Lucien saw the man in the boy as he brushed the hair from his face in a nervous gesture. "We ran away to find you. Drew was sick, and I didn't know anybody else who could help."

Lucien was overcome with love and pride, even as an overriding sense of panic gripped him. After everything they'd been through, the boys remained in jeopardy. He asked his nephew. "Where's your mother?"

The child grinned and made car-like sounds, then climbed into his uncle's lap.

"Caleb, do you know where my sister Sara went?"

"She's with Aunt Katrina and Mimi. They said it was important to find you and for us to wait here."

"Katrina and Mimi in Mostar?" Fear as venomous as Ursini's viper slithered through him. Lucien's image of Katrina safe in America had given him courage and kept him from losing hope. Too many of those he loved were in danger. His chest heaved, his heart splintering in despair. He would handle one situation at a time and deal with the boys first. How had they traveled from Italy to Mostar? Lucien had to move them before it was too late. He drew a shallow breath. "Boys, we've got to get you out of here."

"Don't you want us?" The hurt in Caleb's eyes pierced him.

"Of course, I want you."

"Me too?" his nephew asked.

Lucien tweaked his nose. "Very much, you too." He gazed at Caleb. "Little buddy, it's not safe to stay. I'm not saying it will happen, but this area could blow up any minute."

Caleb's shoulders slumped. "Where can we go?"

He needed to find Sara to drive the boys to the farm. Lucien glanced at the kitchen clock. Four young lives against a chance at saving thousands. Where was God in all this? Where was justice? And where were his sister, his cousin, and Katrina?

Lucien knew what he had to do and to whom to turn. Only God had the answers he sought. *Lord, I believe in you. I've been stubborn and ungrateful for far too long. I'm asking, in Jesus's name, please forgive me my sins. Come into my heart to stay.* An extraordinary peace filled Lucien, and a new purpose arose in him. *Thank you, Lord.*

Lucien knelt and called the boys to join him. "Let's pray together and ask God to lead and protect us." He bowed his head in humble thanksgiving, and they prayed.

Chapter 69

Mostar, Bosnia-Herzegovina, Fall 1993

Alex was nervous and wary as Cosic parked on the street. With a sense of foreboding, Alex followed the major's glance to an upstairs apartment window. A man and some little boys, their noses pressed against the glass, peered below.

When they disappeared from view, Cosic got out and started unloading the explosives. He handed a stack to Alex. "Take these inside and ignite them."

"There are children in there," Alex said, thinking of his son.

"So, a few more Croats will die before they grow to tote guns." At Alex's grim frown, the major said, "Get moving, soldier. That's an order. Remember, we're at war. A Croat captain is in there with those boys."

Cautiously, feeling unexpectedly old, Alex crossed himself three times in a silent plea, then bent to pick up the explosives. As he carried them, his Saint Christopher medal pressed against his chest. Never had he measured the distance between himself and God so greatly or with such regret. Alex couldn't continue to obey commands blindly, which led to the killing of innocent people. His grandmother had taught him that one day, he would have to answer to God for his actions. He didn't know if she was right, but Alex wanted to believe in a Creator, who could right wrongs and change what had been meant for evil to good.

Sure, there were wars that had to be fought, wars that had merit, but this wasn't one of those. In his heart, he'd known Serbia was in the wrong and denied the voice inside him. Alex was through hiding.

He entered the apartment building as ordered and left through the back entrance. He dropped the explosives he held into a barrel of rainwater outside. His one thought was to escape with Ennis and their son to a place of freedom. He kept walking, distancing himself from Cosic. He wandered through the city for what seemed like hours, strategizing how to stay alive and escape.

Alex rounded the corner and saw a large hospital. His gaze lit on a woman who strangely resembled his wife, standing in front of it to the side. It must be his imagination. Could he be hallucinating? He walked slowly toward her, his steps uncertain, feeling a weakness in the knees and a sudden need to sit down. His chest seemed to cave in. He wanted it to be her. Then he was running and shouting, "Ennis!"

She glanced up in surprise. "Alex!" She yelped in amazement and ran into his arms.

He hugged and kissed her. "I can't believe you're here."

With a slow, incredulous shake of her head, she touched his face. "Of all the places in Bosnia to find you. Thank God."

"How are you even in Mostar? You're supposed to be in Belgrade," he said.

"General Jovanovic was sent to oversee Major Cosic's operations in Mostar. Since I'm his assistant, Jovanovic insisted I accompany him. I left the baby with my parents."

Alex asked, concerned, "Why are you standing out here alone? Where is Jovanovic?"

"Inside. He had a heart attack and refused to calm down unless I left. He is adamant the hospital will be bombed any second. The doctor asked me to leave and return after Jovanovic had quietened and settled in somewhat."

His arm around her, they walked across the street, and he gathered her close.

"Alex, I've been so worried. They said your plane had been shot down, and you were stranded behind enemy lines."

"Now we're both stranded in enemy territory. Ennis, you've been right from the beginning. This war is evil. We can escape to Italy and start a new life, one we can be proud of."

"Darling, it's what I've wanted for so long."

Suddenly, an explosion rocked them off their feet. His ears ringing, a blast of heat hit him. Alex saw the hospital was on fire.

Ennis clung to him. "Jovanovic is inside," she shouted.

Alex tightened his hold on her. "Don't look. There's nothing we can do for him. I'm sorry."

She gasped. "Jovanovic was telling the truth, after all. I thought he was confused because of the heart attack."

"What do you mean?"

"He said his chauffeur was working against him, conspiring with his archrival, Michael Venac. Jovanovic said the hospital would be bombed. He accused his chauffeur of dropping us off there to kill us. Jovanovic saved my life by demanding I leave." Her chin trembled, and her shoulders shook with emotion.

Alex kissed her, unbelievably grateful to hold her close.

She looked at the burning hospital sadly. "If only I'd listened and not brought him here."

"How could you have known?"

"Poor man, his daughter accused him of trying to kill her and her mother, but it was his enemies, not him." Ennis gazed around at the destruction and chaos. "I'll have to find Mimi and tell her the truth. I can write to her uncle in Austria, too. Surely Mimi will contact him. She needs to know how much her father loved her and Dianne."

Alex had too much on his mind to take it in all Ennis was saying. He took her hand. "Let's go get our son."

Chapter 70

After Katrina left Sara's apartment, she hit the cobblestone pavement, soon realizing it would be next to impossible to cross the city and reach Croat headquarters. And if she succeeded, Lucien might not even be there.

She searched for hours futilely. When night came, the sounds that had echoed throughout most of the day escalated as the screams of those faced with unbearable losses grew. Run-down fire engines whined, ineffectively chugging about, as structure after structure seemed to burst into flames. Katrina struggled to weave a path through the chaos.

At some point, she'd crossed into east Mostar. Since she couldn't find Lucian, she'd search for Martin. She headed to the jail where he worked, which was nearby with great trepidation. Katrina and the children had almost died there, and the torture and abuse she'd endured still haunted her. They needed Martin's help. But what if his Muslim colleagues arrested her for spying?

Tears rolled down her cheeks. She brushed them aside, her stride never slowing. *Lord, this once, help me get it right. I'm not asking for me, but for the thousands of innocent children like Caleb and Drew. For their sake, please let me find Lucien.*

She bumped into someone and stared into Martin's surprised eyes. Thank you, Lord, she breathed, remembering the scripture, *"Before you even pray, I know your needs."* With a sob of relief, she threw her arms around him. "I've never been so glad to see anyone."

Clearly uncomfortable with her American-style welcome, he

drew back in a courteous, stiff manner. "Katrina? Lucien said you were in America. What's this?"

"It's a long story, but—"

He clasped her shoulder. "Never mind. It doesn't matter. Get out of the city as fast as you can." He shook his head somewhat helplessly. "I'm sorry. There's no time to explain." He walked off.

Katrina tried to stop him. "Martin, wait."

He motioned toward a smoking, burned-out building as he hurried away.

Katrina ran to keep up with him. "Where's Lucien?"

"He's out trying to stop the explosions. Cosic is alive and plans to destroy the entire city. Flee while you can."

"I can't," she said over the noise. "Where are you going?"

"To see President Izetbegovic."

"How were you able to contact him?"

"A friend, Izzy, who manages the jail in Vita's place, wants to help end the conflict. Through his contacts, I hope to reach Bosnia's president and relate Cosic's plot to destroy Mostar." He paused a moment. "Try to find Sara. Tell her to drive to my parents' house."

He darted up the street, and Katrina sprinted to catch him. "You've got to listen. I have Cosic's map and plans."

He scowled, accelerating his pace. "I don't believe it."

"Rachel took them from his van when you all escaped from the grave site." Katrina had Martin's attention now. They paused in an open doorway. Winded, she continued. "Rachel didn't tell me until we were at home in Texas. That's why I've come back. Please, take me to Lucien."

"If it's true, let me see them."

"Not here with people watching us."

He studied her and then seemed to reach a decision. "Come on." He grabbed her hand, leading her as they raced through the streets.

Katrina tried again to stop Martin, but he refused to listen. She tugged at his arm, panting from the pace he set. "Can we reach Croatia's President Tudman through Bosnia's President Izetbegovic?"

His steps slowed. "They've been collaborating to push back the Serbs. The two must have a direct line to each other."

An idea was forming in her mind, but it was audacious and a gamble. She asked Martin, "Can you arrange for me to meet with President Izetbegovic?"

Wariness clouded his face. "Why would such an important man want to see you? You're an American and a woman. What can you know of my people's problems?"

Indignation ripped through her. After all she'd sacrificed to Bosnia, she'd expected more.

As if to lessen the blow, he added, "Trust me to handle whatever is required."

Common sense urged her to give Martin the plans. Yet Katrina couldn't bear to think he might fail or unwittingly put Muslim interests first. Be sensible, an inner voice argued. He's more capable than you of carrying this out. Though she agreed, she still couldn't release the papers and started to explain.

But he spotted Sara across the street and, agitated at seeing his wife there, dashed to intercept her. Surprised Sara hadn't arrived at the jail sooner, Katrina surmised the delay was understandable with the city in turmoil. Sara, Mimi, and Katrina had left the apartment at about the same time. Sara had set out to give Martin her copy of Cosic's papers.

Katrina had initially hoped to find Lucien at Croatian headquarters and show him the plans, but amid all the destruction, she never got there. Mimi intended to alert Lucien through the Croat border patrol with her copy. Katrina wondered how Mimi was faring. At least if she fell into difficulty, the border patrol could contact Lucien to vouch for Mimi.

Katrina hung back a bit to allow Martin and Sara some privacy. She couldn't follow their low-voiced exchange, but at the end of it,

Martin waved her over. "Sara gave me her copy of the papers. Please take her and the children to my family's farm. Lucien has parked a car near our place. It's two streets down, a green Dasha." Martin dug into his pocket and then handed her the license number on a scrap of paper and the key.

"I've got to find Lucien," Katrina said.

Martin's eyes glinted with annoyance. "The jail is several doors down. I'll see to it these reach Izetbegovic. Surely you understand. You must tend to the children and Sara."

"Sara's old enough to drive herself." Katrina evaded his outstretched hand and hurried toward the jail. She paused at the entrance, glanced back, and saw they were still talking. Katrina hadn't forgotten the children, but the best she could do for them was to ensure Mostar didn't burn up in flames.

All at once, the ground rumbled. Katrina dove for cover inside the jail, burying her face in the circle of her arms as a series of blasts rocked the building. She raised her head and cried out as heavy metal bookcases collapsed on the officer seated behind the desk. There was nothing she could do.

When the tremors ended, her instinct was to rush to Sara and Martin. First, she attempted to free the young officer trapped beneath the bookcases. Katrina pulled and shoved at the heavy metal, but it refused to budge. She didn't have the strength to free him and feared the officer was dead. "Help, please! Is anybody there?"

An unnerving silence met her useless cries, and a strange heaviness kept her from venturing farther into the jail alone.

Katrina ran outside to find Martin and Sara. He was right. He understood this country as she never would.

She stared in shock at the spot where her friends had stood minutes before. She moaned—her universe reeling. The building they'd stood by no longer existed. Anguished sobs tore from her as ash and dust fell, mingling with her tears.

As if caught in a ghoulish nightmare, she struggled through the remains. A woman and her son trapped beneath the debris cried out. Katrina called to those nearby for help to free them. Afterward, Katrina continued wildly searching through the dead and wounded for her friends. When she found them, she felt sick. Perhaps not knowing would have been better.

She couldn't bear to look at their disfigured bodies. In that instant, when she realized Martin and Sara were dead, Katrina nearly gave up. She shook off the stupor that gripped her and forced herself to face what Martin's and Sara's deaths meant to their poor babies. And Lucien. Her soul cringed afresh at the pain their loss would bring him.

Crushed, she retraced her steps to the jail. With the Muslim sector under attack, there was the chilling possibility the Croatians had already started to retaliate. Was she too late?

Inside the jail, Katrina passed the dead officer trapped beneath the metal bookcase and sank into a chair behind the desk in despair. Wearily, she rested her head in her hands and closed her eyes. She took courage from the Psalms as the words embedded in her youth rolled over her. "The Lord is the strength of my life . . . in the time of trouble He shall hide me in His pavilion . . . set me upon a rock. . . ."

She sensed a glimmer of what David must have felt as he ended Psalm 27, "I had fainted unless I had believed to see the goodness of the Lord in the land of the living. . . . Wait on the Lord . . . and He shall strengthen thy heart."

How would she ever tell Lucien? And how would he find the words for his small nephew and Baby, waiting so trustingly for their parents' return? If only she'd stopped Mimi and Sara from leaving the apartment.

Was Mimi alive? What about the children? She couldn't let Martin's and Sara's deaths be in vain. Somehow, she would discover a way to reach Tudman and Izetbegovic and stop this horrible carnage.

Chapter 71

Bosnia-Herzegovina, Fall 1993

Katrina gradually noticed footsteps moving toward her from the rear of the Mostar jail. She braced herself but was unprepared for the dark dwarf-like figure who emerged, his Kalashnikov trained on her.

"Who are you?" she mustered the courage to ask.

"Chief Izzy, in charge of the jail." His black eyes studied her and dismissed her as unimportant. "Comrades, come on up. It's a woman." As the armed men reached him, he motioned her to the door. "Go. You are in the way here."

"I came to see Martin," she said with a break in her voice, "but he and Sara died in the last explosion. I found them outside."

The chief and his men wailed with grief until Izzy raised a hand for silence. He spoke, and the soldiers dispersed. Izzy pointed at her. "Who are you?"

"I am Katrina, an American friend of Martin's. Shortly before he died, he said you were helping him foil Serbia's plans to destroy Mostar."

"He spoke about you to me, too," Izzy said. "Mostly about when Vita, Kiro, and Cosic kidnapped his family and the rest of you."

"Please, I need your help. I must meet with President Izetbegovic." She explained what was at stake. "I have Cosic's plans."

"How is that possible?"

"We found them in the van Cosic used to kidnap us. No one knew the papers were important. I'm sorry we didn't read through them until much later." Katrina chose not to reveal how Rachel had found and hidden the papers. It was complicated, and she wanted to protect Rachel from any backlash.

"I need to verify you have Cosic's plans."

She handed him the documents.

He examined the pages and then returned them to her. "We must alert Bosnia's president about Serbia's operation at once. After Martin left to find his brother-in-law, I convinced an army pilot pal with access to a helicopter to meet us in a nearby field. He's waiting there now. Let's move." Unlike Martin, Izzy didn't question her right to accompany him. "Your presence will lend credibility to the proceedings," he said.

Within the hour, Izzy's friend fired up the chopper that would take them to Sarajevo, where Izetbegovic awaited their briefing.

The helicopter set Katrina and Izzy down in Sarajevo, and then they were driven to the meeting place. On the drive, she reflected on what she knew of the president. A former businessman, he'd spent years in prison for his writings. When he was released, the Yugoslavian nation was ending. Katrina and her family had been living in Mostar when Izetbegovic became Bosnia's president in 1992.

Though few leaders in this war could lay claim to high moral ground, Izetbegovic's refusal to attack the innocent had impressed Katrina. People often quoted him for having said, "But the only ones who are to be forgiven, regardless of everything, are the women and children. Let us not be an army that does what they are doing to us. Let us never fight against women and children. We will never win if we do."

Katrina and Izzy soon arrived at the nearby bullet-riddled presidency building. Inside, she could see that Izetbegovic and his family lived simply. His assistant Adin ushered them in to see the president and stayed at his request.

The besieged commander in chief had a long, affable face with graying, black hair, and bushy brows set above striking blue eyes. He was the first national president she had ever met. She prayed he would accept the plans as creditable and act swiftly to thwart the Serbs.

After introductions, Katrina and Izzy began to tell their stories. Filled with hope and trepidation, she prayed the president would believe them.

He listened with a grave face and interrupted periodically with questions. When they were finally finished, Izetbegovic said, "I understand you brought proof."

"Here you are, sir." Katrina handed him Cosic's plans.

He studied the documents intently. "Yes, these are quite conclusive. Thank you both for your efforts on Bosnia's behalf. You have become heroes of the revolution."

"It is our honor to serve," Izzy said.

"If I can ever assist either of you, you have only to ask."

Her pulse racing, Katrina said, "President Izetbegovic, I have cared for two orphaned boys throughout the war and grown to love them. If you could grant me a dispensation to adopt and take them home with me, the boys and I would be forever grateful."

"Send me the paperwork, and if everything is in order, I'll approve it." He motioned his assistant forward. "Meanwhile, Adin will take down the names and necessary information, so we will be prepared to move ahead." Izetbegovic bowed his head slightly. "If you will excuse me, I must contact President Tudman of Croatia immediately. Do not worry. He is also a reasonable man. Together, we will do all that is necessary to stop Serbia."

The short meeting ended, and Katrina gave Adin the details of Caleb's and Drew's lives. She told him briefly about herself and how to contact her and her lawyer. He shook Izzy's and her hands and thanked them for their service.

Izzy caught a lift in the helicopter back to the jail. Katrina turned down the invitation to join him. Adin introduced her to another official who offered to escort her to a nearby province where they housed American diplomatic personnel. She declined.

Katrina could not leave Bosnia without knowing the boys, Mimi, and Lucien were all right. For the moment, she resisted thinking of Sara and Martin, resisted the image of them in death.

At Katrina's request, they flew her to the field outside Mostar, where her trip had begun. Bone weary, barely able to walk, she trudged toward the city, hoping to spot Lucien or Mimi fleeing with the boys. A constant stream of worn and dirty refugees, who were bent on leaving and escaping the bombs, lined the outlying roads. The closer she came to Mostar, the louder the explosions grew. She prayed Izetbegovic would be successful in halting the destruction.

An eerie whistle seemed to arise from nowhere. People appeared to freeze in dread. An agony of silence pierced the approaching dawn, a contrast to the screams and cries that had punctuated the day before and most of the night. Katrina stilled herself. The threat of extinction held every man, woman, and child in suspense. People would have run or hidden, but where? The growing noise seemed to surround them, an unnamed terror.

Is this it, then? The place where I'm going to die? A certain sense of fate prevailed. An effortless acceptance on her part to meet death shook her. *Dear Lord, what will happen to us? Please let the boys and the many other orphans scattered across Bosnia survive. Lucien and Mimi, too.*

She bowed her head in prayer, not of words. Katrina was beyond those as she fell to her knees. No, this was greater than words, a communion of spirit and soul as she met destiny head-on, the unvarnished truth of her existence unveiled before God. No excuses. No ambitions. It felt so good to surrender.

She heard a familiar voice.

"Katrina, is it really you?"

"Lucien?" She was speechless at the unexpectedness of his being there right after her prayer. They gazed at one another in relief and fell into each other's arms. Her cheeks were damp, and she swiped at tears.

"Come on," he said. "The children are waiting."

She peered across the road and saw his jeep with the four boys and Mimi waving from the window. "You saved them. Thank God. I feared . . ."

"Shh." His arm came around her shoulders as he guided her toward the vehicle. "Do you imagine it was any different for me?"

Katrina gazed into his eyes and saw the depth of his heart. She slid into the front passenger seat and reached back to hug and greet the others. Tears fell as she kissed Martin and Sara's toddler and Baby. She stared across at Lucien and read the pain in his expression. "You heard."

"I went to the jail looking for you and Sara and Mimi. Izzy told me all of it, including your foolhardiness in trying to return to Mostar." His hands gripped the wheel. "You could have been killed."

She nodded, mindful of how often the children, Lucien, and she, had nearly died. "I don't know how you found me. I was headed into town to find you and the others."

"Izzy told me that, too. You weren't hard to spot. We kept an eye out for the one woman crazy enough to walk toward the city everyone else was fleeing."

Her focus reverted to the refugees jamming the road. "That whistling sound we heard?"

"It's okay. Special services are out dismantling the bombs. Sometimes, the detonators fizzle in the process. It will soon be over." Lucien turned the key in the ignition and pumped the accelerator.

A weight seemed to lift off Katrina. Still, she sighed. Yes, this battle was finished, but not the war. Who knew when or how it would end? She had no idea where they were headed or what the future held. Bosnia's rugged mountains, crowded with the endless stream of refugees, seemed to stretch infinitely before them.

She'd kept part of her promise to her mother, rescued a few of the children, and helped in some small way to preserve the city. Not because, as her father used to say, "Winslows always kept their word." But because good had ultimately triumphed. Not as she had wanted it to, or been brought up to expect it to, but slowly, just as raindrops splashing one by one into the ocean are controlled by the tide and pulled by the moon into gravity's mysterious dance. All orchestrated by God.

Her lips curved wryly, an awareness seeping through her that the pain of her loss had lessened. It was easier to accept her individuality, connected yet distinct. Whenever she'd felt invisible around her brilliant and talented family, what she'd lacked was the courage to come out from their shadows and confront life, as the war had forced her to do.

As she needed to do now with Lucien. "Izetbegovic granted me a special dispensation to adopt Caleb and Drew. They will be able to return to the States with me. I'm also teaching again."

"Aunt Katrina is going to be our new mother," Drew exclaimed from the back seat.

She smiled at the boys, pleased they were happy.

Mimi said, "Lucien's taking Sara's boys and me to his parents in Austria. My mother may already be there."

"That's wonderful news," Katrina said. "Will you return here?" she asked Lucien.

"At my commander's request, I've agreed to represent Croatia and work to further their cause in the West."

She heaved a sigh of satisfaction, knowing he would be safe.

"Katrina, I'm not sure how or when we'll meet again, but I know we will."

"I'm counting on that."

He pulled the car to a stop alongside a vantage point overlooking the Neretva River, his expression pensive. "This is where the last bridge across Mostar fell."

She stared out at the spot where Stari Most, the seventh and last bridge across Mostar, had proudly stood, a cultural crossroads for centuries before being obliterated by hate and intolerance.

So much family, so many friends gone—and for those who'd lived at this junction between East and West, Stari Most's destruction, its very absence, symbolized those losses.

Lucien started the jeep and guided it onto the rough cobblestone road.

She placed her hand on his arm. "I'm sorry about Sara. It should have been me. I sent her out there."

He hesitated. "Are you God, to decide who lives and dies? Does fate hang around your neck, asking for directions?"

She shook her head and crossed her arms over her heart in defense.

"We're human, Katrina. No more and no less. *Gott sei Dank* He's with us. Can't you accept the bad for once without feeling like you caused it? I know how much it hurts to lose those we love. We'll always miss Sara and Martin and your family."

Katrina slipped her hand into Lucien's, understanding his words were for himself as much as for her. There was a lot to be grateful for. They both carried emotional wounds that needed healing and had feelings of guilt to expunge, but they had a lifetime and the faith to do it.

And in Bosnia, that was a miracle.

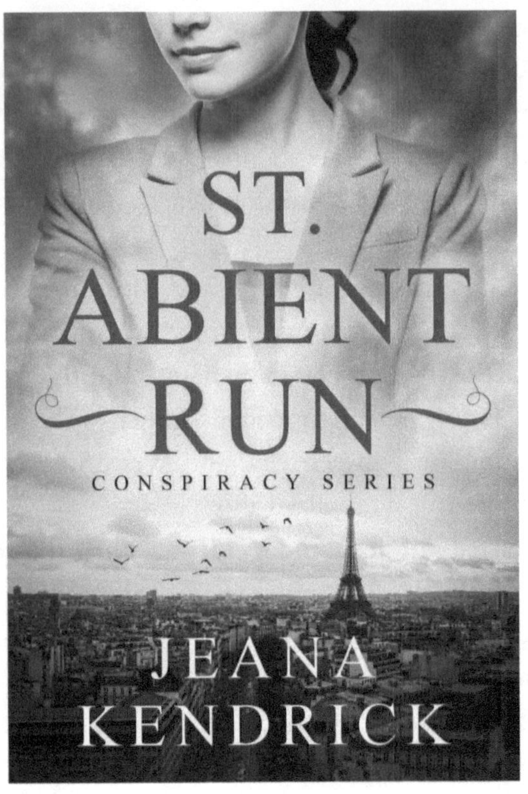

American journalist Susan Pardue's investigation of rumored tie-ins with drug and diamond trafficking at an exclusive French school soon becomes a rescue mission. Her employer's younger cousin, a student at the school, has disappeared. In a terrifying quest across East and West Europe, Susan and her boss confront a manipulative financier and his assassins.

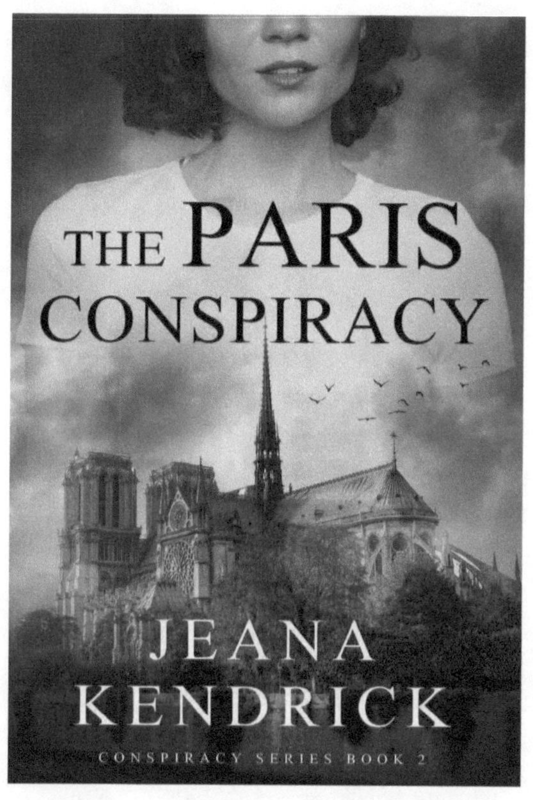

CIA agent Gayle Regan investigates alleged pension fund theft in Paris and gets dangerously close to a terrorist plot. She is mugged, left for dead, and has her identity stolen. With her apartment vacated, her bank accounts depleted, where can she go and whom can she trust—an ex-fiancé who left her at the altar, her CIA handler, or an airline executive with his own agenda? Texan Matt Carey, who is also under siege, joins her in unraveling the conspiracy threatening major cities.

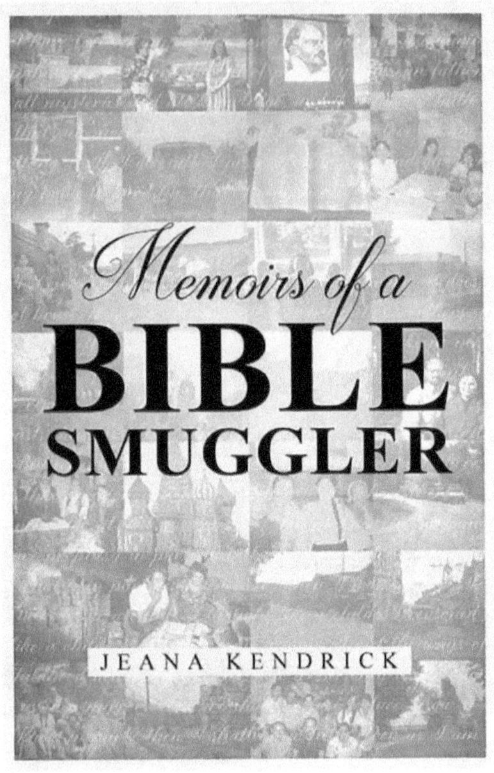

This is the story of a young Texas couple who helped smuggle thousands of Bibles to persecuted Christians behind the Iron Curtain during the Cold War.

About the Author

Jeana Kendrick is an award-winning author, editor, and publisher. Her novels and books are available most everywhere books are sold and have all won awards. Her Conspiracy Series suspense novels, *The Paris Conspiracy*, and St. *Abient Run*, will keep readers guessing until the end. *Memoirs of a Bible Smuggler* tells how she and her husband helped smuggle thousands of Bibles behind the Iron Curtain. Her latest novel, *The Last Bridge Across Mostar*, takes place during the Bosnian War.

Jeana's short stories are in *Fall From Innocence*, Page One Publications; and *Suddenly*, *Suddenly II* and *Suddenly IV*, Martin House. Her feature articles have appeared in various magazines and newspapers. She formerly served as communications director and managing editor for Door of Hope International (DOHI). Her projects include the revised bestsellers *Tortured For His Faith* and *The Fugitive*. For more than a decade, Jeana and her husband co-directed DOHI's literature distribution into Eastern Europe, traveling extensively throughout the continent. Those trips left a lasting impression.

She enjoys family, reading, walking, gardening, and baking. Jeana lives in the piney woods of East Texas. Visit her website: www.JeanaKendrick.com.

A Note from the Author

Thank you for reading my novel. If you have enjoyed it, please leave a review on Amazon or Goodreads. I love to hear from readers. You can leave me a note on my website and also sign up to receive my newsletter and a free bonus gift.